Chitra Banerjee Divakaruni is well known for her highly acclaimed novel, *The Mistress of Spices*, and her award-winning short-story collection, *Arranged Marriage*. She was born in India but now lives in California with her husband and two sons. She is a teacher of creative writing and a published poet as well as a novelist and short-story writer. Her previous collection of short stories, *The Unknown Errors of Our Lives*, is also published by Abacus.

Praise for *The Unknown Errors of Our Lives*

'An extraordinary collection ... besides elegance and delight, we can also find wisdom here'   Ha Jin, author of *Waiting*

'She defies categorization, beautifully blending the chills of reality with the rich imaginings of a fairy tale'

Wall Street Journal

'Affecting, evocative prose'   *Scotsman*

'These are wonderful examples of the short story at its best – intimate glimpses into other people's lives, unexpected insights, endings that both satisfy and intrigue ... [the] stories are told with elegance, compassion and tenderness, illuminating the beauty and mystery that exists in ordinary lives. A visit to a tiny, perfectly drawn world'   *Big Issue*

ALSO BY CHITRA BANERJEE DIVAKARUNI

CHITRA BANERJEE DIVAKARUNI

The
Vine
of
Desire

A Novel

An *Abacus* Book

First published in the United States of America in 2002 by
Doubleday, a division of Random House, Inc.
First published in Great Britain in 2002 by Abacus
This edition published in 2003 by Abacus

A CIP catalogue record for this book
is available from the British Library.

ISBN 0 349 11584 2

Printed and bound in Great Britain by Clays Ltd, St Ives plc

Abacus
An imprint of
Time Warner Books UK
Brettenham House
Lancaster Place
London WC2E 7EN

www.TimeWarnerBooks.co.uk

once more for you:
my three men

Anand

Abhay

Murthy

Acknowledgments

My heartfelt thanks to:

My agent, Sandra Dijkstra, for your ongoing championship of
  my work
My editor, Deb Futter, for your careful and clear vision
My mother, Tatini Banerjee, and my mother-in-law, Sita
  Divakaruni, for your blessings
Murthy, Abhay and Anand for making me laugh when I
  needed it most
Gurumayi Chidvilasananda and Swami Chinmayananda for
  guiding my desires

Again the day, again the night
Dawn and dusk, winter, spring.
In the play of time, life ebbs away —
Only desire remains

Again birth, again death
Again the dark journey through the womb
In this world of changes, nothing holds fast
Except the coiled vine of desire

Bhaja Govindam, Sri Shankaracharya (A.D. 788–820)

And what did you want?
To call myself beloved, to feel myself
beloved on the earth.

"Late Fragment," Raymond Carver

The
Vine
of
Desire

Book One

Subterranean

Truths

Eros is strength abandoning itself to something

elusive, something that stings.

– The Marriage of Cadmus and Harmony, Robert Calasso

Prologue

In the beginning was pain.

Or perhaps it was the end that was suffused with pain, its distinctive indigo tint. Color of old bruises, color of broken pottery, of crumpled maps in evening light. But, no, not like them, ultimately. For although men have tried for thousands of years to find the right simile—and women, too—ultimately pain is only like itself.

This, too: it is hard to tell which is the beginning, and which the end. Particularly when it is one's own story, when its segments loop around, repeating themselves randomly, like a piece of computer code gone wrong.

The woman did not think any of this, lying strapped inside the ambulance as it jolted its keening way to the hospital. She was focusing on the boy, the way he clung to the wet-silk walls of her womb. They rippled like the muscles of an angry snake, trying to shake him off. He curled himself inward, tight as a peach pit, hoping for invisibility. She hoped for him, too. But there is no fooling the flesh that formed you. The nurses were rushing them down white neon corridors to the double doors marked Emergency. They stretched her across the operating table. Hieroglyphs of blood on the paper-white sheets; she didn't know how to read them. The overhead lights were eyes, gigantic, insectile. Her womb heaved. The placid waters that had rocked the boy all these months had become a whirlpool. They spun him down toward the narrow passage that he knew to be death—yes, even the unborn know what death is. For a moment she felt his terror, became it. The crimson and black pulsing in his eyes. The taste in his mouth, sour, amniotic. Later she would think of it as the taste of failure. Hers. She heard someone scream. A metallic, spine-raking sound. Why, it was her! Inside her, she felt him scream back. Her echo, her shadow, her hope for eternity. Her golden child, in whom she had thought to bury all the errors of her past.

An immense force was tearing him from her now, past the lumped and bloody flesh in the doctor's hand, outward, upward. She followed, shaking off the ungainly body that he had shared, briefly, with her. They shot into space with such speed that it seemed she would explode. He was crying. *Keep me with you.* She was crying, too. *Don't you think I want to? More than anything else in the world? Don't you know I'd give up everything in my life, right now, if I could, for that?* But except the night clouds skimming across the moon's tattooed face, no one heard them. Except the small brown owls, birds of witness and reclamation. The clouds did not falter. Huddled into tree knots, the owls did not lift their heads to watch the bright specks hurtling upward, dual shooting stars, reversed. They had heard such wailing many times, seen many such lights disappear. Except for those to whom it is happening, death is hardly a unique occurrence.

Shimmering and gaseous, he spun into space, and she in his

wake, so light that she wondered if perhaps she no longer existed. He was looking over her shoulder, a gaze of such sorrow that she, too, turned to look. She saw the scalloped walls of the old Victorians on the hills of the city, and knew its name. *San Francisco*, she whispered, the syllables at once familiar and amazing in her mouth, and the lights in the tall triangular tower downtown flickered acknowledgment. Mist drifted, fragile as promises, over the cypresses that lined the ocean cliffs. Southward the bay gleamed like a woman's curved arm. Studded with ruby taillights, the bridges were her bracelets. Up at Point Reyes, pewter waves etched the empty shore. A cormorant rose with a black cry, a lumbering flap of its wings. Out to the west, moonlight, leaping off the backs of porpoises, flashed an enigmatic code.

It filled her with rage. That he should be given a glimpse of such beauty only to have it snatched away!

But now her eyes were caught by the cities of the south bay. San Jose, Sunnyvale, Milpitas, their smoky, stubborn sprawl. In the low apartment houses by the freeways, pinpricks of yellow lights were going out one by one as people readied themselves for bed. One of those windows had belonged to her. To her and a man—but who was he? She couldn't quite recall. Only that he'd been significant. She felt a pull as she sensed this, downward, into the tangled, unfinished life she'd left with him. Her imperfect life, her caught-in-the-body life, with its ferocious, zigzag pulse.

And with that thought she finds herself falling. Fast, faster. She tries to stop herself, to reach into the vast hushed swirling of light that hangs above her head. Where has her son gone? *Where?* No use. She plummets through space, solid as a spent bullet, rapid as rage. Galaxies blur past her. Black holes. She sinks into emptiness, that hollow metal cube in the center of her being. Clouds now, the calm, unwrinkled peaks of mountains, the lacy glimmer where ocean licks at earth. The brown glow of the city, its brave smells—gasoline and tired sweat—settling around her like arms. She wants to push them away. All of them.

I will take no pleasure in any of this. Never again.

The lights of the hospital are stark and unseeing like the whites of rolled-up eyes. They singe her as she falls through the different stories, the different wards. Surgery, Radiology, Crisis Intervention. How many ways there are to die! She is breathless by the time she reaches the room where a woman lies splayed on an operating table. A frenzy of activity around her, men and women in masks swarming like white bees. Staccato orders being barked out. A limp brown hand, a thin wrist with the pale plastic tag that offers up to strangers the woman's secrets. *Majumdar, Anju, 635-81-9900.* Why, it's her, again! There are tubes. Needles. Dark and pale liquids pumped by blinking machines. The stench of spilled membranes, hopes tattered as newspapers abandoned in alleyways. The machines whir so loudly, she cannot hear what the white-coats are saying. When she looks closer, the pores on the skin of the woman's face are enormous, black as burned-out craters. They widen like intractable mouths. She winces upward, but there is only a bumpy, spackled ceiling above her head, impenetrable. She feels herself turn thin and liquid, feels herself being sucked in.

She wakes in another room, inside the claustrophobic clutch of her flesh. A faint smell hangs around her, like rotten eggs. Pain slams into her once more, flattening her against the bed. Dazed and breathless, she is already forgetting where she has been, what she has been capable of. But the sense of emptiness.

She can't forget that. When she can move again, she pulls the hospital pillow over her head with a choking sound.

There's a ringing in her ears, someone chanting a toneless word. It takes her a moment to understand it. *Prem Prem Prem.* The name that was to have been the boy's.

The man—yes, there's a man at her bedside, suddenly, with imploring fingers, *him*—tugs at the pillow, but the woman is surprisingly strong. The tendons inside her elbows stand out like wires as she thrashes from side to side. The man is forced to call for a nurse. Two women come. One holds her down while the other shoots a chemical into her vein. They tell the man to go home. Get some rest. There's nothing you can do for her right now, one adds. Her voice is detached but not unkind. Before she leaves, she turns down the light so the room is dim and green, the color of seawater.

Alone in the sea-green light, the woman feels her muscles begin to loosen in spite of herself. She is coming apart, the way a braid does when one has been swimming a long time. Soon her eyes will flicker with furious dreams under her closed lids. Her unruly eyebrows will angle into questions to which there are only uncertain answers. *Why? Why? Where?* With the last of her strength, she pushes her body to the edge of the mattress, cups it into a shape against which a child might rest. There, that's good. With the last of her strength, she holds on to something she heard a long time ago, in another country, when she was not much more than a child herself: the dead are not irrevocably dead as long as one refuses to let them go.

One

The day Sudha stepped off the plane from India into Anju's arms, leaving a ruined marriage behind, their lives changed forever. And not just Sudha's and Anju's. Sunil's life changed, too. And baby Dayita's. Like invisible sound waves that ripple out and out, the changes reached all the way to India, to Ashok waiting on his balcony for the wind to turn. To their mothers in the neat squareness of their flat, upsetting the balance of their household, causing the mango pickles to turn too sour and the guava tree in the backyard to grow extra-large pink guavas. The changes multiplied the way vines might in a magical tale, their tendrils reaching for people whose names Sudha and Anju did not even know yet.

Were the changes good or bad?

Can we use such simple, childish terms in asking this question? Neither of the cousins were simple women, though there was much that was childlike about them when they were together alone, or with Dayita. When Sunil was away.

Sunil. Anju's husband. Sudha's cousin-in-law. A young executive with a bright future in a prestigious computer company. But no. None of this tells us who he really is. Because he wasn't a simple man either.

It is not clear when Anju first sensed this. At their double wedding, when she stood beside Sunil, their bridal garments knotted, and watched him watch Sudha's forehead being marked with the red powder of wifehood? Months back, when he told Anju that it was a bad idea to bring her cousin to America? The night before Sudha's arrival, by which time it was too late? When did she first sense that though she loved him, she didn't always trust him?

But lately Anju doesn't trust the runaway roller coaster of her own emotions either. The wild mood swings after the miscarriage that would leave her weeping or laughing hysterically. The long bouts of depression, later, that immobilized her in bed, incapable of even answering the phone.

Guilt ate at her, a slow, pernicious rust. No matter how often Sunil assured her that the miscarriage could have been caused by any number of things, she didn't believe him. When the blackness came upon her, her mind turned heavy and stubborn, like one of those cement mixing trucks you pass sometimes on the road. A sentence would catch in it and begin to rotate, *If only I'd listened to the doctor and not overworked myself,* until it broke down into a phrase, *If only I hadn't, If only I hadn't.* It ended, always, in the same anguished chant. *Prem Prem Prem.*

She would rock her body from side to side, her neglected will-o'-the-wisp hair spreading its static on the sofa, fingers digging rigidly into her arms until they left bruises shaped like tiny petals.

"I don't know how to help you when you're like this," Sunil would say.

Afterward, when the depression lifted, she would sometimes say, "You don't need to do anything."

Inside her head she added, Except love me.

Inside her head he replied, I do love you.

Inside her head she said, But not enough.

&

The night before Sudha arrives, Anju cannot sit still. Some of it is excitement, but mostly she is nervous. Why? Isn't this her dear, dear cousin, sister of her heart? They've protected, advised, cajoled, bullied, and stood up for each other all their lives. Each has been madly jealous of the other at some point. Each has enraged the other, or made her weep. Each has been willing to give up her happiness for her cousin. In short: they've loved each other the way they've never loved anyone else. Why then does Sudha's coming fill Anju with this unexpected dread?

If there are answers, she will not allow herself to think of them.

At dinner she is unable to eat. "But what if Sudha doesn't like it here?" she keeps saying.

It is the year of dangerous movements. Two weeks back, a major earthquake hit Los Angeles, causing seven billion dollars' damage and leaving more than ten thousand people homeless. Will Anju and Sunil read this as an omen? Or will they discount it in the belief that every year has its own disasters?

Anju, who is a terrible cook, has spent the day making lasagna because, she says, Sudha has never tasted any in India. The sink and their few dish towels are all dyed the same stunning orange, a color which looks fearfully permanent.

Sunil doesn't comment on this. He focuses instead on the

gluey orange mass on his plate, at which he jabs half-heartedly from time to time. He is a meticulous man, a man who detests chaos. Who takes satisfaction each evening in shining his shoes with a clean rag and a tin of Esquire Boot Polish before putting them away on the closet shelf. But he makes an effort today and says nothing—both about the lasagna and about Anju's question, which is not so much a question as a lament for something she fears has happened already. He is thinking of what she said a few weeks back, unthinkingly. *The happiest memories of my life are of growing up with Sudha.* He is thinking of what he didn't say to her.

What about me, then? What about you and me?

๛

"Let me tell you," Anju was fond of saying in the last months of her pregnancy, "who I used to be before the accident of American happened to me."

She would be lounging in bed with a cup of hot milk and honey and a novel, one of those rare days when she didn't have to go to class. She would knock on the curve of her stomach. "You, sir," she would say. "I hope you're paying attention."

She loved speaking to Prem. In an illogical way, it was more satisfying than speaking to Sunil, even though Sunil was a careful listener and made the right comments at the right times. But Prem—the way he grew still at the sound of her voice, the way he butted her ribs with his head if she paused too long in the middle of a story . . .

She told Prem about the old house, that white elephant of a mansion that had been in the Chatterjee family for generations: its crumbling marble façade, its peeling walls, the dark knots of its corridors, the brick terrace where she and Sudha went secretly at night to watch for falling stars to wish on.

"It's gone now. Demolished to make space for a high-rise apartment building. And I'm the one who kept at your grandmothers—do you know you have three grandmothers: my mom, Sudha's mom, and Pishi, who's my dad's sister?—to sell it. I used to hate that house, how ancient it was, how it stood for everything ancient. I hated being cooped up in it and not allowed to go anywhere except school. But now I miss it! I think of my room with its cool, high ceilings, and my bedsheets, which always smelled clean, like neem leaves—and which I never had to wash myself!—and the hundred-year-old peepal trees that grew outside my windows. Sometimes I wish I hadn't been in such a hurry to come to America. Sudha used to sneak into my room at night sometimes. We'd sit on the wide windowsill, telling each other stories. I'd tell her about characters in books I'd read that I liked, such as Jo in *Little Women*—and she'd tell me the folk tales she'd heard from Pishi about women who would turn into demonesses at night and the monkey who was actually a bewitched prince. She was great at doing voices! You'll see it for yourself when she gets here."

Some days, after the doctor had scolded her for not getting enough exercise, Anju went to the park. She would make a desultory round of the play area, watching the children, whispering to Prem that he'd be better than them all—more handsome, more active, and of course more intelligent. She would tell him how prettily the maples were changing color and then, choosing one to sit under, she would go back to her childhood.

"My favorite place of all was the family bookstore. For the

longest time all I wanted was to be allowed to run it when I grew up. Every weekend I'd beg Mother to take me there. I loved its smell of new paper and printing ink, its rows and rows of books all the way to the ceiling, its little ladders that the clerks would scramble up when a customer wanted something that was stored on a high shelf. There was a special corner with an armchair, just for me, so I could sit and read all I wanted. It was funny, Gouri Ma—that's my mom—was strict about a lot of things, but she never stopped me from reading anything I wanted.

"So in my teenage years, I read things like *Anna Karenina* and *Sons and Lovers* and *The Great Gatsby* and *A Room of One's Own.* I'm glad I did, but maybe Aunt Nalini—that's Sudha's mom—was right. They were no good for me. They filled me with a dissatisfaction with my own life, and a longing for distant places. I believed that, if I could only get out of Calcutta to one of those exotic countries I read about, it would transform me. But transformation isn't so easy, is it?"

What about the other places of her growing-up years? The ones she never spoke of, the ones you'd have to eavesdrop among her dreams to find? Such as: the banquet hall where she saw her new husband stoop to pick up a woman's handkerchief that was not hers? But the rest of that scene is brittle and brown and unreadable, like the edge of a paper held to a flame, another of those memories Anju keeps hostage in the darkest cells of her mind.

"The bookstore was where I met your father. He had come dressed in an old-fashioned kurta and gold-rimmed glasses—a kind of disguise so that I wouldn't guess that he was the computer whiz from America with whom Gouri Ma was trying to arrange my marriage.

"He'd come to check me out! Can you imagine! People just didn't do such things in Calcutta, at least not in traditional families like mine. When he confessed who he was, I was terribly impressed. But what made me fall in crazy love with him was that he bought a whole set of the novels of Virginia Woolf. She used to be my favorite author, you know. But he'd done it only to win me over." She sighed. "Later I couldn't get him to read even one of them!

"Still—he's going to be a wonderful father to you. I'm sure of that. He'll love you more than anyone else does—except of course me and your Sudha-aunty!"

❧

This evening, her dinner uneaten, Anju pushes back her chair and walks over to the old, discolored mirror that hangs in the small bathroom in the passage. She runs an uncertain hand through her hair and touches the dark circles under her eyes. She presses down on her jagged cheekbones—she's lost a lot of weight since the miscarriage—as though she could push them in and hide them. "God, I look like such a witch!" she groans.

Last week she opened her India suitcase and took out a framed picture of herself and Sudha at their school graduation dinner. She examined it for a long moment before setting it on her dresser with a dissatisfied thunk. Even at that heedlessly happy time in her life, she hadn't been pretty in the traditional way. She didn't have her cousin's rush of curly hair, or those wide, sooty eyes which always looked a little mysterious, a little tragic. But anyone could see (anyone except herself, that is) that she had spirit. In the photo, she stares out, a challenge in her eyes. She crooks her lean, stubborn mouth in a half-smile. There's an irrepressible intelligence to her nose. Maybe that was what made Sunil choose her from among all the girls he could have had as an eminently eligible, foreign-returned, computer-whiz groom in Calcutta.

But somewhere along the way Anju's eyes grew dull and muddy. Her mouth learned to twitch. And the expression on Sunil's face when he watches her nowadays—he does this in bed, sometimes, after she has fallen asleep—is complicated. At times it is pity. At times, regret.

༚

All through the fall of her pregnancy, while the leaves of the maple turned a crisper, brittler red until they were suddenly gone, Anju told Prem stories of Sudha. Beautiful Sudha, the dreamer, the best cook of them all, the magic-fingered girl who could embroider clothes fit for a queen. Luckless Sudha, who worked so hard at being the perfect wife to Ramesh even though she didn't love him. Until the day she walked out of the marriage.

"It was because of her witch of a mother-in-law. For years she'd been harassing Sudha because she couldn't get pregnant. You'd think she'd be delighted when she found out that Sudha was having a baby. But no. She had to have an ultrasound done, and when she discovered that her first grandchild was going to be a girl, she insisted that Sudha should have an abortion. So Sudha ran away—how else could she save her daughter— though she knew they'd make her life hell afterward.

"Oh, that old crocodile! How I wish I could have seen her when she woke up to find Sudha gone!"

For weeks afterward, Anju would describe that afternoon for Prem, over and over, in the hushed tone one saves for legends.

The entire household has fallen into a stunned sleep, even

the servants. The heavy front door, which is carved with fierce yakshas wielding swords, opens without a sound. Sudha slips out, carrying only a small handbag. She wears her cotton house sari and forces herself not to hurry so passersby will not be suspicious. The air inside her chest is viscous with fear. Her slippers slide on the gravelly road. Mango leaves hang dispiritedly in the heat, like small, tired hands. She walks carefully, she mustn't fall, she presses her hand against a belly that will start to show in a few weeks. At the crossroads she pulls the end of her sari over her head in a veil, a princess disguised as a servant maid, so no one on the street will recognize her.

"What about Ramesh?" Sunil asked when Anju told him Sudha had gone back to her mother.

"What about him?" Anju said, her voice dangerously tight.

"Didn't he try to bring her back?"

"Him! That spineless jellyfish! That mama's boy!" Anju's breath came in outraged puffs. "He did nothing—nothing he should have done, that is."

There was a doubtful look on Sunil's face. Was he wondering if there was more to Ramesh than Anju saw? If Ramesh wept for Sudha and the baby daughter he would never hold—carefully and quietly, in the shower, under cover of running water so no one would hear? At night, did his hand reach across the bed from old habit? And when he startled awake, was the taste in his mouth like iron? But Sunil knew better than to share such thoughts with Anju.

The following week, when he came back from work, she handed him an aerogram, triumphant with outrage. "Look!" It was from Aunt Nalini, informing them that Sudha had been served with divorce papers. The papers had Ramesh's signature on them and accused Sudha of desertion.

What a dastardly trick! Aunt Nalini wrote. *Now the poor girl won't get a single paisa from them. They've even refused to return the dowry I gave her at the wedding—a dowry for which I scrimped and saved and deprived myself of pleasure my entire life, as I'm sure you remember.*

"Is it really as bad as she makes it out to be?" Sunil asked.

And Anju, who would usually sigh and roll her eyes after reading one of Aunt Nalini's missives ("Missiles," she sometimes called them), snapped, "Of course it is. What makes you think otherwise?"

"Well, didn't you yourself say that she was Drama Queen Number One?"

She ignored the comment. "If I could just get my hands on Ramesh! That jerk! You remember him at the wedding, his hair all glossed down with Brylcreem? He couldn't take his eyes off Sudha. I remember thinking, He's ugly, but at least he'll be good to her. And now, just look!" She was pacing the room by now, panting a little.

"Please calm down," Sunil said, his reasonable voice giving away nothing of what he might be feeling. "It's not good for you to get so worked up at this time."

"Isn't that just like a man," Anju said, kicking furiously at the doorjamb. "To stand up for other men, no matter what they've done."

"When did I—"

"Never mind," said Anju. She didn't speak to him the rest of the evening. The next day she said, "I want to bring Sudha to America."

The words crashed into him like waves. He thought they might pull him out to sea. "And where's the money for that going to come from?" he said. Though money wasn't what he was worried about. But what he was worried about couldn't be spoken.

They had their first fight that day. Others followed in the weeks after. Thunderclouds of colliding words. Sobs. A stiff silence. A door kicked shut.

She started working secretly at the university library. She put her earnings in the bank and hid the savings book between layers of her saris. Each night her spine ached, the pain like an electric current moving up and down it, stopping wherever it wanted. "As soon as I have a thousand dollars, I'll send Sudha a ticket," she whispered to Prem as she made herself a bed on the lumpy couch. Her smile carved the dark like a thin, defiant moon. "Men! It's best not to count on them for anything important."

She rubbed her stomach gently, forcing herself to relax. "Present company excepted, of course," she added.

She didn't know that he, too, would fail her. In the worst way of all.

ॐ

Anju abandons the mirror to pace the tiny apartment. In old yellow socks, her feet make a padding, caged-animal sound on the linoleum. She ends up in the kitchen, where she takes several eggs from the refrigerator. She breaks them into a bowl and begins rummaging around for a fork. She is not a good housekeeper. In spite of the efforts she has been making to tidy up for Sudha, the kitchen counters are a shamble of dishes that haven't been put away and propped-open books and spices still in their torn plastic packets. Finally she gives up and takes a dirty fork out of the dishwasher, holds it for a perfunctory moment under the tap, and begins to beat the eggs.

"Anju! What on earth are you doing?" Irritation ripples along Sunil's voice like a sleeve of fire.

"I thought I'd bake something for Sudha," she answers uncertainly. "Maybe a devil's food cake—it'll be something new for her. . . ."

Sunil moves with an athlete's grace, stepping lightly on the balls of his feet. How fast he is! Already he has reached her. There's something frightening in the way he holds his hands, stiff and suppressed, close to his body. But she isn't afraid. There's a feverish exhilaration in her eyes. *I dare you.* But he merely pushes past her to swing the refrigerator open.

"Look!" The cords in his neck are tight with his need to shout, but he speaks softly. "Haven't you done enough?"

She looks. The refrigerator is stuffed with dishes: spaghetti and meatballs, potato salad, tuna casserole, banana bread, vanilla pudding, apple pie. All the recipes she looked up painstakingly in her *Good Housekeeping* cookbook. It is the most Indian of ways, what the women of her family had done to show love through the years of her childhood, that simple time which she longs for more and more as her adult plans seem to collapse around her. There's too much food, far more than Sudha can ever eat. Food that will spoil over the next week and have to be stuffed down the garbage disposal covertly, while Sunil is at work.

For a moment husband and wife glare at each other across the cold white spillage of refrigerator light, their faces too young, surely, to hold the tired rage stamped onto them. She grips the edge of the bowl as though she might fling it at him. Then, with a shaky laugh, she rubs her sticky knuckles across her eyes.

"I guess I did go a bit overboard," she says.

"It's only natural," he says, his voice quickly, carefully kind. "After all, it's the first time she's visiting us, and you want it to be special." There's relief in the sag of his shoulders. The last months have been hard on him, too, not knowing when she might burst into racked weeping, or retreat to bed to wrap herself in one of her relentless silences. He puts an arm around her. "Come sleep now." When she hesitates, he adds, "Don't you want to be bright and fresh tomorrow, when your cousin gets here?" And she, a faraway look on her face, allows him to take the milky-yellow mess of eggs from her and lead her to their bedroom.

⁖

Ashok. He's the one Anju never speaks of. Not to Sunil. Not even to Prem. The other man in Sudha's life, her forbidden childhood sweetheart. Is Anju secretly jealous of him? Is that why her thoughts stray to him more often than she likes? She imagines him as a teenager still, tall and gangly in a starched white shirt, his chest caving in a little. Meanly, she exaggerates his buckteeth as he waits shyly on a Calcutta pavement for Sudha to pass by. How foolishly crazy Sudha had been about him—in private, of course, such things weren't allowed in their family. Why, she'd almost eloped with him! Docile Sudha! But fortunately (that is the right word, isn't it?), at the last moment, she came to her senses.

Anju remembers with painful clarity the night on which Sudha told her that she had decided not to run away with Ashok. Anju had been sitting alone on the windowsill in her bedroom thinking of Sunil, whom she had just met. The sky was very dark—perhaps there had been a power cut in the city— and the stars seemed closer than usual. She made an arch with her hands and held it up to her eyes. She believed her life was going to be like what she saw: a safe and contained brilliance, a beauty that extended outward forever. When Sudha came up silently and put her hand on the back of her neck, she had jumped, startled. She had been that far away. Perhaps that was why she didn't question her cousin more closely, though it had surprised her when Sudha said she was afraid to take such a big risk. What if things didn't work out with Ashok? Sudha had said, looking away, her words falling from her all at once, like a bucket of water thrown out of a window. What would I do then? And Anju, intoxicated with her own thoughts, had said, quickly, You're right. It's better this way. Now, thinking of all that happened afterward, she wonders if she had said the wrong thing. She remembers Sudha's fingertips on the base of her neck, trailing feverish entreaties she'd been too much in love to hear.

Last month, Ashok asked Sudha once again to marry him. In spite of the divorce, in spite of the baby. It was something unheard-of in families like theirs.

"I'm delighted for Sudha," Anju said to Sunil when she got the news. Her face was pale and puffy, as though she'd been crying. "Truly, I am. I told her she should accept him. I told her that I'm better now, that I can manage here without her."

Sunil—wise man—said nothing.

Then Sudha wrote back to say that she had turned Ashok down. That she was coming to America.

"I feel terribly guilty," Anju told Sunil.

"You look pretty cheerful."

She gave him a wounded look. "One can be guilty and happy at the same time. I can't help thinking she gave him up because she feels she has to take care of me."

"I don't know why she needs to feel that way. Aren't I here for you?"

"Silly!" she said, smiling. She gave him a hug—something she didn't do too often since the miscarriage. "Of course you are! But Sudha—well, things between her and me are different."

At night, before she falls asleep, Anju makes a wish: that Ashok will be intelligent enough to wait for Sudha until she returns to India. At the same time she wishes that Sudha will stay on with her in America forever. Does she realize that her wishes, clashing as they attempt to rise from our sublunary plane to the ears of the gods, cancel each other out?

The beautiful Sudha. But what have we really learned about her? Only the externals, the snow that cloaks a mountain in an illusion of sleep while an entire world of actions continues below. Small creatures moving through invisible burrows, larger ones crouched, waiting, in caves. The leap, the sinking in of teeth, the outcomes that sometimes astonish but more often merely sadden. And at the center, the earth itself, rock and mud and pressed seep of glacier. Who knows if it's readying itself for another shift, one that will end, this time, in avalanche? Or in a scarlet eruption that turns the land to ash?

The subterranean truths of Sudha's life are the ones we crave.

❧

"Would you like me to comb your hair?" Sunil asks.

They are in their nightclothes, Anju sitting on the edge of the bed, staring at the photograph. She seems not to have heard him, but she does not protest when he begins moving the comb through her hair with long, gentle strokes, nor when, after a little while, he lays it down to kiss her shoulders, then her throat, and finally, tentatively—for since the miscarriage nine months ago she hasn't been able to stand him touching her in that way—her lips.

But today she kisses him back—or at least she holds still while he kisses her, while his fingers unbutton her nightdress. Then she asks him to turn off the light.

"But why? It's only the night lamp—you've always liked it."

She shudders in the lamp's deep blue shadow, pulling the bedsheet up to her neck. "I hate how my body looks. Everything slumps. The bones push out in all the wrong places—"

"Oh, Anju! You're exaggerating," he protests, but he gets out of bed to turn off the light. She watches his lean back criss-crossed with shadows, the simple arrogance of his muscles, bending. Her eyes find the photograph once again.

He kisses her eyes shut with determination. She opens her lips obediently under his. She wants them to succeed as much as he does, to be back where they were before—but where was that? She's losing her thoughts in a rainbow fog, the start of a headache at the base of her skull. Still, when he says, "Remember that afternoon at the Rabindra Sarobar when I kissed you for the first time, how shy you were," she says yes. Although in truth she can't remember it. She tries hard to pull up a detail from the crumbly quicksand of her memory: Was it sunny? Was the sky filled with clouds like puffed rice? Were children floating paper boats on the lake? Was there a Lalmohan bird, crying from a branch above? He's waiting for her to add something. (What?) She says, "The palash flowers had dropped their crimson petals all across the water," then realizes guiltily that it couldn't have been so, she had been married in winter, he would have left for America long before the first buds opened.

So she presses her face against his, and holds herself beneath him the way he likes her to. But his weight on her is cold and enormous, a giant statue, made of concrete, except that it moves. His breath is like a furnace opening onto her face with its bitter coal smell. The ache at the base of her skull has grown into a voice, calling, even though calling is of no use. *Prem Prem Prem*, until she pushes him off and feels the failure, thick as slush, settle in his bones. She opens her mouth to tell him she's sorry, she knows how hard he tried. She tried hard, too. But she just can't. And remembering how it had been once was no good, it would never be that way again, even if they were able to stitch up this chasm of a wound that runs jagged between the length of their bodies now. But she must have said something quite different because he pulls back and looks at her, asking in an angry voice, "What do you mean, you've got to make it up to Sudha for what she's sacrificing to come here to you?"

Anju doesn't answer. He knows what she means, she knows that. But always, where Sudha is concerned, he likes to act obtuse, likes to force her to explain, to drag out the emotions inside of her, unclothed, so they look sentimental, or superstitious, or plain foolish. Well, this time she isn't going to do it. She lies there mutinous, lips pressed together, thinking about Ashok. All those years he waited for Sudha when she was married to someone else. Was it out of love, or the fear of loving again? *I told him no,* Sudha had written. Anju twists a strand of hair around her finger distractedly until it snaps, wondering about that *no.* Could she have said it, in Sudha's place? If she weighed a man's devotion against a cousin's need, the security he offered against uncertainty, which is all she has to give Sudha, which way would the scales tip? She needs to think it through, and she cannot do it here, with Sunil's hand snaking from behind to cup her breast, his arm pulling her back against a chest that smells of Claiborne Sport, a tangy scent she once loved that now makes her feel slightly sick. But of course she can never tell him that. Does such consideration rise from caring, or merely habit? This, too, she needs to think about.

She can feel him now, grown hard against her. A nuclear heat radiates from his bones. *Escape, escape.* She gathers up her nightdress in alarmed handfuls. From the sudden stillness of his body, his hands falling away, she knows she has offended him. He won't try to stop her. He's too proud for that. She slips silently from the bed—what good are words now, even if she could come up with the right ones?—and gropes her way next door, where she lies down in the bed she has prepared for the cousin who's like a breathlessness inside her.

And her husband, does she love him? She turns the question, hard as a nugget of iron, around and around in her head. Ultimately she cannot imagine a life without him—and what else is that but love? She keeps her eyes averted from the crib Sunil has set up for Dayita. Ah, there's another problem, the child whom she doesn't want in her house. She's afraid she might start loving her, and that would be a betrayal of the dead. How is she to manage it, to pretend that the child does not exist? How is she to keep Dayita at arm's length without hurting Sudha? When she finally stumbles into sleep, her dreams are a chiaroscuro of uneasy strategies.

It is the year of accounting, the year of pardons, the year of uneasy alliances. Somewhere in America a man is sentenced to life imprisonment for the murder of a black activist thirty years ago. Somewhere in India a bandit queen is released after eleven years in jail. Somewhere in Russia a cosmonaut is preparing to go into space, for the first time in the history of nations, on an American rocketship.

But here is Sunil, alone in his bedroom. Is he asleep, too? No. In the blue night-light he has turned back on, his eyes are chips of stone. They glitter with a strange resignation. Under the sheet, his hand moves as he stares at Anju's graduation photograph. A rapid blur of movement until his body stiffens and arcs, then slumps down into itself, and he whispers a name into the pillow his wife has left empty. A moth-wing of a name.

Sudha.

It was her picture he'd been looking at, all this time.

But he whispered the name rather than calling it out in passion. Can we salvage a broken bit of hope from that? Out of consideration for Anju, he had whispered the name of the woman he'd been trying all this time to keep away. The woman he'd been mad for ever since he saw her in a garden tented with jasmine—too late, for by then he was already betrothed to her cousin.

But was it consideration, or was it fear? No, not fear. Not that. For there is one thing about Sunil that even Anju knows: he is not afraid of anyone—except perhaps himself.

Two

Sudha

We run barefoot on sand, impatient for water. Our hurry makes
a small wind. It is the color of our saris, which stream behind us
like the eager start of a fire. We are dressed in the same color—
one of the many childhood habits Anju and I have fallen back
into. Today we wear rebel red. It is a color that belongs to married women, one I have forfeited. I wear it with defiance.

I reach the ocean first. My first ocean. My sari is bunched up
at my knees like a heedless schoolgirl's. The spray is soap and
ice, and smells of sea horses. I imagine them somewhere deep
and green, swaying. My toes curl in exhilaration. Anju has fallen
behind, out of breath. Her panting sounds like the edge of a
blade. She clutches at her side surreptitiously. She doesn't want
me to see. Anju, who used to be so strong. My banyan tree.
Since the miscarriage, she startles at moths, echoes, the greetings of strangers. I force myself to smile. No tears, no tears now.
Once we had known everything about each other. My smile is a
bland expanse of white, dead as the shells underfoot. But loss

has made Anju incapable of detecting such things. She holds out her hand. I take it. Together we step into the sea.

He is carefully not watching us. He busies himself with amusing Dayita. Making funny faces. She gurgles at him and tries to grab his nose. He laughs and lets her, though her nails will leave sharp red moon-marks on his skin. When he looks at her, there is an odd gratitude on his face.

෯

Each evening, coming home from the office, he goes straight to her crib to pick her up. Even before he takes off his shoes. He refuses to put her down the rest of the evening. Anju says, Sunil, you're spoiling her. He acts as if he doesn't hear. Even while he eats dinner or works at the computer, he balances Dayita easily, on one knee. His arm loops lightly around her. She grabs his spoon just as he brings it to his mouth. She swats at the keyboard, deleting crucial data. He smiles. Anju tells me he's never been a patient man. He has surprised us all. Himself, too, I think. He only releases my daughter when I have to nurse her. He puts her down on the floor, so his hands won't touch mine as I pick her up.

Later he lies on the bed with Dayita on his chest. He tells her all kinds of things. All the things he doesn't talk to Anju about. The project he's working on. The accident he saw on the freeway. The places he plans to take her soon. He riffles his fingers through her curls and gives her an edited version of the daily news. He tells her the plots of movies he saw growing up in India. He changes her diapers without consulting us, though we're waiting to help.

I am jealous for Anju, who watches from the doorway.

And Dayita, who drives us crazy all day, crawling into corners, getting stuck under the bed, throwing tantrums every two minutes: she basks on his chest, listening to what happened on the stock market. Her iridescent eyes shine, the color of chameleons.

જી

"When he's with Dayita," Anju tells me later, "all the bitterness falls away from him. He used to be like that when I was pregnant. Boyish and excited and tender. He'd make a world of plans—all the things he wanted to do for—" she swallows— "Prem. He would put his mouth against my stomach to whisper them. If only I'd been more careful—"

"There's no point in torturing yourself over what's happened already," I say, as I have many times.

Useless words, falling between us like lopsided snowflakes. Melting.

"Somehow I feel I'll never get another chance to be a mother," Anju says. Her voice is toneless, it moves like a sleepwalker. "This child, he came to me too easily, and I was too casual about him. I'm going to have to pay for that. . . ."

I'm frightened by that sleepwalker voice, its thin, icy glide. "What superstition!" I say, choosing harder words, clipping them close like nails. "You never used to be this way. Listen to you—you sound like my mother! Of course you'll have more children. And isn't Dayita your own, too? Even Sunil can see that—why can't you?"

"Yes," Anju says. It is a sound like a sigh. But what is she agreeing with?

There are things she doesn't tell me about her marriage. I

see their shadows on the wall, shivery-brown and thin, like diseased branches. I try vainly to untangle silhouettes.

We do not discuss him again.

&

It began on the very first night, the night Dayita and I came into
their house. I know because I dreamed it.

So much talk and tears. So much catching up with pain. So
much still left unsaid between Anju and me, that would perhaps
never be spoken. We were afraid to touch each other's pasts, the
way one is with a cut that's just stopped bleeding. We read, in
each other's eyes, the questions that couldn't be asked, couldn't
be answered. *Why did you really bring me here? Why did you really say
no to him?* We fell to sleep exhausted on the carpet in my new
room. Lying between us, lulled by our voices, my daughter, too,
slept awhile. Then she awoke.

In the living room he was sitting at his computer. Staring at
the screen, which for once could not save him from his
thoughts. A can of Coke, gone warm and flat, stood untouched
beside him. He wanted whiskey, though he wasn't a drinker.
Whiskey to dull the points of all those thoughts whizzing at his
head like jugglers' knives. But that would have been a victory
for the women. (*The women,* that's how he thought of us.) An ad-
mission that we'd gotten under his skin.

Sleepless in front of that opal flicker, he felt thankfulness.
He could see that, with my coming, some of the sadness had
fallen from Anju. But he was annoyed, too. We made him feel
unnecessary. At dinner I had enquired about his work. Anju had
asked if he wanted more lasagna, more pudding. Still, he knew
he was an interruption to our reunion.

The last knife, the last thought. When it struck him, a tense joy spurted forth. To him I was more beautiful than before. He wanted to lick away the worry lines at the corners of my eyes. *Like a glass flower, blossomed in fire.* The words hummed like wasps inside his skull. He was light-headed with his need to take care of me, and knew he must not.

He heard the snuffling noises Dayita was making. At first he didn't know what to do. Should he let her cry until we awoke? But that might take forever. The poor child was starving—he could tell by her shrillness. He stepped gingerly into the room. He tried to keep his eyes away. There's a nakedness about sleeping people—Anju and I lay with our arms around each other, as if we were girls again. Needy, unabashed. We embarrassed him.

But here was Dayita, kicking with vigor. Screeching like an entire chorus of harpies. Her face was splotched more with rage than hunger. For the first time since we came, he was amused. *You don't like being ignored either, do you?* He leaned carefully over us to pick her up. It amazed him how light she was. And yet how solid, how real. Suddenly it was very important not to wake us. To have her to himself. She was quiet now. She stared at him, her eyes smoky with intelligence. She knew all the ways, he thought, in which he was hurting.

Shyly he laid his cheek on Dayita's head. Curly, pulsing. She smelled like every baby on earth. Like herself only. Like grass. He was thinking—he didn't allow himself to do that often—of Prem.

He fed her with the baby formula I had kept in the refrigerator. There was a rhythm to her sucking, a code he needed to decipher. He changed her and put her in the middle of his bed. He piled all the pillows he could find around her to keep her safe. Until he fell asleep he talked to her. Nonsense words at first, then adult to adult. He told her he was afraid of what might happen to us all in the next few months. He used words like craziness. Conflagration. He didn't mention my name to my daughter. (Of that I am thankful.) But he was happy she was here. He wanted her especially to know that.

That was how we found them in the morning. Sleep-entangled. Her arm flung over his eyes. His urgent hand grasping her foot as though she might fly away in the night. The way his Prem had once done.

❧

I am not the only one in this house who dreams.

"Almost every night before you came," Anju tells me, "I used to have a nightmare." She stammers a little, shamefaced, as she describes it.

A point of light travels across a swirl of ink-blue. Its arc is serene, confident. It takes her a moment to recognize it: a planet in orbit. Then, from nowhere, another light, bigger and brighter and streaming fire. It hurls itself into the planet's path. In a moment they will collide, shatter into nothingness. She moans and flails her sleeping arms, trying to avert the catastrophe. The giant meteor crashes into the planet—but there's no explosion. Instead, the planet is thrown from its orbit. It falls spinning past the edge of the dream, flat as a coin, naive as a child's cutout. The meteor takes its place, bristling with heat and life. Anju waits for someone to notice this treachery, to do something about it. All continues as before. The Milky Way shimmers, joyous chords swell in the background. She wakes with an ache in her throat, as though she's swallowed a piece of bone.

"I've finally figured it out," Anju says. "I was visualizing Dayita as the meteor and Prem as the planet. I was afraid she would take my poor boy's place, make me forget him. But it's amazing, isn't it, the way the heart expands when it needs to? I'm so glad you forced me, those first few days, to hold her, to feed her. Did you realize how scared I was? But now it's like buds opening on a branch that I'd given up for dead. Not that I don't think of Prem—I do, all the time. I think I always will. But it's different, having a baby I can hold with my hands."

Her face was hot and requesting. She wanted consolation, a hug at the very least. She deserved it. It was hard for her to talk of such things. But I couldn't.

"What time is it?" I said stiffly. "We'd better start dinner." Her eyes went shiny with hurt.

Later in the bathroom, in the middle of combing my hair, I came to a halt. Stared at the mirror a long time. I bundled all the strands into a tight, ugly knot, and took off my earrings. The dream had another meaning, though Anju didn't recognize it. Some fears are like that, slippery and deep down as mudfish.

The planet was Anju herself.

If so, was I the meteor?

≈

In the late afternoon we return laughing and wet, our legs powdered with grains of gold.

I give an exaggerated shiver. "You never told me that the American ocean was going to be so cold!"

"Whine, whine!" says Anju, giving me a little push. There's a new redness in her cheeks, something for me to hold on to. "Who was it that wouldn't leave the water? Who was it that kept saying, Oh, Anju, we've got to wait for another wave?"

I push back a tangle of strands from my face, the knot undone by wind. My hair smells like a holiday. "I was hoping to find a sea horse."

There's a sudden attentiveness in his face. He would like to know why. But he doesn't ask. Ever since I arrived, he has been cool and aloof. Never starting a conversation. Keeping out of my way—as though that's possible in a two-room apartment. Awkwardness and awkwardness. I should have stopped it right away. Should have gone up to him and said, Forget what you said about love in that garden in Calcutta. They were just words, it was a long time ago. We've been pulled through the eyes of many needles since.

But I was afraid. What if he looked at me—those lacquer-black eyes you couldn't see into? If he said, *What makes you think . . . ?*

I am a fool and a coward. Once I thought in complete sentences and acted them out. But after Ramesh . . .

Now it's too late. All I can do is avoid him also.

"Oh, you!" says Anju. When she speaks to me, her voice is indulgent, like molasses. But to Sunil, she is all polite business, not like a wife should be. Even I, newly arrived, have noted this. "Still believing in magic, like falling stars and sea horses to wish on? Next you'll be reading the lines on our foreheads and telling us our fortunes!"

The ocean is a sudden glare, the sun angled hard on waves made of metal. "I'm not sure I'd want to, even if I knew how," I say. My toes dig a hole in the sand. The air is sour with seaweed. "Sometimes the only way we can bear our lives is because we don't know what's coming up."

Anju stares unblinking at the metal-plated sea, her mouth hard with wanting to argue. She's remembering my helpless, hurried flight. The handful of rupees, the paltry trinkets stuffed into a handbag. The memory is a hot, vomity feeling in both our throats. Is it love that makes us this permeable to each other's pain?

I know what Anju wants to say. *Seeing into the future would help us prepare for it.* The possibility of arranging one's life—she's always liked to believe in it. But even she knows better. What of her miscarriage, that sense of being cracked open and scooped out? What could she have ever planned against it?

"Enough of pasts and futures!" I make my voice gay, decisive. (It is important to have a gay, decisive voice, particularly when one has nothing else.) "It's a beautiful day, the most beautiful I've seen in America. Let's enjoy it!" I spread a flowered plastic sheet on the sand, open the picnic basket. I start lifting out packets wrapped in foil, and after a moment Anju joins me.

❧

I have not exaggerated. It's the kind of day that turns the seal rocks offshore into wet gold. The Golden Gate Bridge seems close enough for us to pluck its harp string–slender wires. Impossible clarity, after so much clouding.

Ever since Dayita and I arrived, it's been raining. Two weeks of continuous chill rain. The creeks bloated with it—I saw them on TV—the hillsides beginning their black, gashed sliding. Drunken, tilted houses. Close-ups of stunned families who had to leave with nothing. I saw the others, too, the victims of the earthquake, so many people crowded onto the floors of makeshift shelters, the children crying for things they'd never see again. Freeways buckled and cracked like discarded snakeskin, entire streets gutted by fire. I felt a strange responsibility. The trains weren't running on time, so Sunil had to take the car. We were imprisoned in the apartment. The air was sticky and stale. Inescapable. Dayita fretted all day. After a week, the sound of rain takes on a relentlessness. It dredges up memories fetid as corpses. I had to press my face against the fogged-up window to keep in things it does no good to speak about. Nothing outside but concrete and a balding tree with dispirited needles for leaves.

"Do you miss India?" Anju asked disappointedly.

I couldn't lie. I said, "How do people here watch the stars?"

"From windows, I guess," said Anju, who was never much of a star-watcher.

"What's the name of that tree?"

"I'm not sure—some kind of pine, I would think." She gave my shoulder an apologetic squeeze. "Listen, how about we go camping when summer comes around?"

੭

The evenings, after Sunil returned, were the worst. Each atom of air tense, resisting inhalation. The walls loomed inward, swollen with claustrophobia. Guarded greetings all around. Only Dayita shrieked her baby-pleasure, holding up her arms to be picked up. I kept busy in the kitchen until it was time to eat. Dinner would be full of fractured words, Anju talking too much, trying to pretend everything was fine. I needed all my energies just to swallow. Dayita played by Sunil's feet. He watched her with the intense eyes of a motorist on a sleety night. The way he focuses on the shining reflectors that divide the lanes. The way he knows that to stray might mean destruction. As soon as I could, I would take Dayita into my room, prolong the nursing. I would hear them, of course, Anju and Sunil. Halted, formal sentences, mostly about Dayita. In a few minutes, silence. There's no silence like married silence, its undertow of reproach. When I brought Dayita back, they reached for her with panicked fingers, as though they'd been drowning.

ॐ

The family (can I call us that?) has finished its picnic lunch. Crisp parotas stuffed with spicy potatoes, a bowl of emerald coriander chutney. (In this one way, at least, I am helpful.) He lies back, a newspaper protecting his face. From the sun, from us. Dayita has fallen asleep, her head wedged into his armpit. His body looks relaxed, almost happy.

We speak softly, so we will not disturb them. It is a conversation I've been starting all week.

"You've got to go back to college, Anju," I say. "You're well enough now. Didn't you tell me that the new classes are starting in a few days?"

"I don't think I'm ready," Anju says. Caught in her mouth, the words are mutinous pebbles. Anju, who never stuttered as a child. I don't blame her. You drop your life and watch it roll away, growing like a monstrous ball of mud. It seems impossible that you'll ever run fast enough to catch it again.

If I show sympathy, our talk will end as it always does, in tears. So I say, "You're as ready as you'll ever be. At least while I'm here you won't have to worry about the cooking and cleaning—"

Anju cuts me off, her face furious and knotted. "I didn't invite you here to be a maid in my house. And, anyway, you're going to be here a long time."

She hates it when I speak of returning to India. But can't she see that I must? Can't she see the way we're living now—a giant hand squeezing us together, something getting ready to burst?

"Silly girl!" I say. "I love taking care of people, you know that. And don't worry about college—you'll do beautifully. You always did before."

"I'll go to college if you promise to go, too," says Anju.

The air is a black sphere around me, impossible to breathe. No, it's a vast whiteness that wants me to lose myself in it. Anju's words gleam intermittently through it. Dangerous, unthinkable spangles. "You've got to stand on your feet, take care of Dayita—"

She doesn't understand. There's too much of the past in my blood still, like a sickness I have to sweat out before I can take on the future.

Sunil sits up so suddenly, it's clear he hasn't been asleep at all. Dayita, jerked awake, begins to wail. "It's getting cold." His words are scissors. Snip, snap. "Time to head back."

❧

Some time soon, tonight or tomorrow, in bed, they're going to have a conversation. There will be frowns, tears, defiance, accusation. All very softly, because the walls are thin. Because the fictions of courtesy are still important to us.

This is how it will go.

He: She's here on a visitor's visa. She can't go to school.

She: She can change her visa—people do, all the time.

He: She's got to go back in six months. That was the deal.

She: Who made that deal? Not me.

He: She can't keep staying with us.

She: Why not?

He: *(Silence)*

She: Very well. I'll find her a room. She'll be able to get a student job, and then, once she gets her degree—

He: Let her go back to India, Anju. We've got our life, she's got hers. You can help her from here, if you like. Send her money.

She: *(Silence)*

He: Can't you understand?

She: How can you talk about money, like she's a beggar? She's my sister, my best friend. I need her here. Can't you understand?

He: *(Silence)*

She: *(Silence)*

He: *(Silence)*

She: *(Silence)*

Two turned backs, like escarpments. Anger runs from one to the other, a mouse on scrabbled feet, gnawing. In my frozen bed Dayita whimpers, rubbing her feverish eyes.

None of us will sleep this night.

❦

The sun teeters over the ocean like an overripe orange, ready to burst. The road we've taken this time curves by the rippled dunes. It seems like the edge of the world. There are long rushes, like old women's hair. But I gaze upward, always more interested in the things of the sky. Above me, bright particles, hovering. They look like kites flown by giants. I clutch Anju's arm and point.

Huge and wheeling over the bay. Every possible color. But where are the cords? It takes me a moment to see the people dangling from them.

"They must be hang gliders!" Anju leans out of the window in her excitement, shielding her eyes. "I read something about them in *California Living*—they like to take off from the cliffs around here because of the strong offshore winds."

One of the gliders is arcing back toward land. I admire the ambidextrous dip and lift of his wing spans. Their wide abandonment. Like being in love. I haven't felt this way in a long time.

I grip the seat and speak to the back of his head, forgetting to be careful. "Can we please see where they land? Can you find it?" My voice vibrates like a tuning fork. Even Anju stares, surprised. He swivels his head for a long, risky glance at me, takes the next exit. I shouldn't have asked. I shouldn't have. In the driver's mirror, a small pulse beats in his temple.

I am afraid of that erratic beating. But I will wait until later to be sorry. Right now there's a spirit wind, wild and snatching. I open my fisted hands to it, feel it fly across my palms, rearranging lines. Sunil has wrapped Dayita in his coat. We walk across the parking lot—just a dirt strip on a cliffside. A platform of sorts where one can stand. Then the gliders are all around our heads, coming in to evening. Enormous winged creatures, helmeted and goggled, something other than human. But delicate and fervent, too. Are such things possible? To be so free of gravity, so deliciously loosened from earth?

"I'd like to be up there," Anju says. She bends so far over the railing that I grow afraid and grasp her sari. There are purple shadows around her, aureoles of yearning. "It must be special, to feel the wind going right through you. All your problems slipping away—only you and the sky and the waves so far below they look painted. To maybe keep going into the light . . ." She leaves the sentence unfinished, languid with possibility.

Sunil puts out his free hand. His fingers are lean and polished as the copper the jewelers back home beat into bracelets. They encircle her elbow entirely, she's lost so much weight. "Now you've seen them, let's go home."

"Wait," said Anju, pointing. Two of the gliders are landing next to the platform. The men's legs bracing against the ground, puffs of dust, gravelly scrape of shoes. The current from their wings pulls at my hair. Someone rushes up to unharness them, but they're shrugging off their gear already, laughing, raising their arms high to clap hands with each other, pulling off helmets to let their hair—black, agile red—tumble out over their shoulders.

"Why, they're women," I cry. "Kingfisher women!"

Sunil and Anju look at me. "Kingfisher women?" asks Anju, raising her eyebrows at the bright yellow of their outfits.

I nod.

Once long ago, I'd seen them. Near a gorge. We were standing on a bridge. It was early morning, filigreed with fog. The birds were blue-backed and shining. Slim-beaked. They came out of nowhere, plunging down, soaring up, chasing each other, diving to the river for food. It seemed to me they sang. And kissed in the air. They weren't afraid of anything. Even when the train thundered by, they kept doing what they loved.

"Is this real, or is it a tale like the ones you used to make up when we were girls?" Anju asks. "Because I don't remember any such bridge—or any such birds."

I realize that I've been speaking aloud. I hadn't meant to. "You weren't there," I say reluctantly.

I don't want to say any more. But they're waiting.

"I was with Ramesh," I say. It is the first time I've spoken his name since I came to America. Heat stings my cheeks. I wait for my voice to tell me how I feel. Is it sticky with bitterness? Black with tar? No, it is cool, matter-of-fact. It tells me nothing. "It was the only time we'd gone somewhere without my mother-in-law. He'd taken me to the inauguration of a bridge he'd built. He was good at things like that. The workmen loved him because he was kind and fair and gave them all bonuses."

This part I don't say: He had stood close and put his arm around me. He asked if I were cold, would I like him to get the shawl out of the boot of the car. The birds had been flashes of blue fire. I asked him if they were kingfishers, but he wasn't sure. Maybe they were creatures from another world. I told him I longed to be like them, bright and brave. He said, We can be like them, Sudha. We can. Why not? He believed it—I saw it on his flushed, earnest mouth. I almost loved him then. But later, when his mother decided to erase our daughter from my womb as though she were a misspelled word, he didn't have the strength.

Sunil spits out an unfamiliar American invective and swings away—as though he can read my thoughts. His shoulders are high and stiff. He pulls the collar of his coat over Dayita's head, hiding her from my past.

"Forget him!" says Anju. Her hand fits tightly over mine, that old protective gesture from our childhood days. "You did the right thing. That's all that matters. A lot of women in your position would have given in. You left. You didn't care that you had to give up everything. . . ."

She doesn't know the one hundred and one faces of my cowardice. My resentment. Someday I will tell her, I did care. All the things I had to leave behind, not only clothes and jewelry but my good name. The legitimacy of wifehood that I had worked so hard to earn. But now the women fliers are walking by us. They call out cheery hellos. They are not young, I note, surprised. There's a grainy strength about them, like desert rock. Their skin is wind-rasped and bright with living. Their waists are wide and sturdy.

"What lovely saris," the redheaded one calls out.

Unexpectedly, Anju holds out her hand. It trembles a little—such overtures are hard for her nowadays—the fingers curling inward in their reluctance. Her nails are soft as wax, and very white. I see with dismay that her lifeline has acquired a new, feathery thinness. The woman takes Anju's hand in both of hers.

"You were beautiful," Anju says.

The woman smiles. There is henna in her hair, I can smell its wild, weedy fragrance. "Thank you. Would you like to try it sometimes? It's not as hard as it looks—I teach people. If you want, I can give you a lesson. We can go up together, on a tandem glider—"

"We really must go now," says Sunil. He looks at the woman with disapproval. He is suspicious of unrequired adventures. They are American in the worst possible way. Unwomanly. He gives Anju's elbow a small, proprietary tug. "Dayita's bound to catch a cold in all this wind."

"Do you have a card?" asks Anju. The woman nods and unzips a pocket, hands Anju a rainbow-colored rectangle. Her companion has joined us and drapes a casual hand around her waist. Weeks later, just before I fall asleep, it will strike me with a slight sense of shock that they are lovers.

As we walk to the car, I can feel their eyes on us, considering. Are they wondering about our little ménage, who belongs to whom? Perhaps they think all Indians live this way, the man walking in front, hunched and shivering against the wind. The child staring gravely over his shoulder. The two women stumbling a little in their wind-whipped saris.

No one speaks on the way home. Rain clouds glower through the rear window. We are tired and cranky. We've seen the amazing, the primeval human dream made real: people with wings. And it hasn't changed our lives.

Once in India I scrubbed the color of marriage from my forehead, believing I was rid of it. But it comes back. Some mornings, my pillow seems faintly powdered with red. In my lap Dayita is making puckered, sucking sounds, dreaming of milk. I try to think of objects—that's the safest. A slice of Langra mango, flame-sweet. A cool shower after a sticky Calcutta day, the separate, silver threads of water flicking my grateful skin. Currents of air which travel the earth, circling, rising, somersaulting back. Holding up cobalt wings against a cobalt sky.

Three

Sunil

Come here, kid. Let me put my arms around you and my face against your chest. Delicate bird bones, your laughter like feathers. All day I've been waiting for this.

I can hear your heart going like a runaway engine. When Anju was pregnant, I once asked the doctor, why do kids' hearts do that? He gave me a very scientific answer, but I've forgotten it.

So I'm just going to believe it's because you're happy to see me.

Sit on my lap so I can see your eyes, so much like your mother's.

Forget I said that.

Sometimes I feel I'm drowning—but not while I hold you.

They say infants' eyes look so wise because they still remember things from their past lives. If you could speak, I'd ask you what you remember. I'd ask you, Is it true, what they say about destiny being inescapable?

If you said yes, it would give me permission.

Kid, I'm so tired—and my struggle has just started.

Enough of my troubles. It's time for a story.

꿍

Imagine pigeons—flocks and flocks of them, turning the screen white—yes, this is another movie I'm telling you about. I love movies, don't you? So flat and rectangular, life simplified and contained, or at least made bearable.

Imagine an angry man whose trained pigeon is taken by another. Imagine a quarrel, insults, old incidents brought up, honor needing to be avenged. Does this sound like a different time? A different country? Or are you thinking that here, too, people are the same?

As I was saying, it was necessary to take revenge. So one of the men stole the other's daughter and took her to a city far away to sell. They locked her in a dark room. There was another girl there, also kidnapped. The two wept together. Having lost their families, they thought of each other as sisters.

Are you wondering why I'm telling you a story about two sisters?

I'm not sure myself.

Perhaps as I tell it, I'll figure it out.

The imprisoned girls—they were maybe twelve years of age—were quite docile. They ate what the woman in charge gave them. They went with her when she called. This made your Anju Aunty angry. She wanted them to slap away the hand that brought them food. She wanted them to bite and scratch. I said, But how could they? All their life they'd been trained to obey without question. Plus, they knew they'd be beaten if they fought back. Anju's chest rose and fell with emotion. She said, I can still want, can't I?

That's how she used to be, passionate about all kinds of things, even those that had nothing to do with her life.

When I watched a movie with Anju, even a movie which I'd seen before, it changed. She forced me to see things I didn't notice. Sometimes that was good, but mostly it ruined the movie, bringing in questions that no one intended you to have.

But all this is ancient history. We no longer watch movies together.

Enter a buyer. Her mistress needs a serving girl. She can't decide between the two kidnapped girls—then she chooses the other one because her mistress wants a light-skinned maid around her. And our girl, the pigeon flier's daughter, is sold to a high-class brothel.

There are a lot of brothels in movies. Anju says it's because of male fantasies.

They change her name, she becomes a famous singer, known all over Lucknow. She's desired by many men. Her name? I've forgotten it. What does a name matter, anyway? It's the concept that's important. She's the singer-girl whom everyone wants to sleep with but no one wants to marry, just as I'm the husband who lacks husbandliness and you're the child who escaped death. Though, depending on who's watching, I could be the man who's lost his voice and you the child who finds it for him.

The singer falls in love with a rich young nabab, but though he, too, loves her, he must obey his dying mother and marry the woman she chooses. Heartbroken, the singer goes away with another man, although she doesn't love him. But nothing works out and finally she finds herself back in the brothel.

Then one day she is invited to sing at a feast at someone's house and comes across the girl who was her prisonmate long ago, remember, the one who became a serving girl? She was married to her employer's son, and now she's the mistress of this household, with a handsome son. The two friends laugh and weep as they speak of their fates—how easily their positions might have been reversed. And then the husband returns from his journey—and guess what! That's right, he's the nabab the singer loved. From his eyes she can see he's still attracted to her.

Oh, these movies, Anju said when she saw this part. They're full of the wildest coincidences.

But is the real world that different? Who knows how many lovers are separated by the wills of others, or circumstance, or their own misunderstanding of duty? How many lives are ruined by chance? It's just that when it happens to you, you don't tell anyone. There's too much pain in it.

I didn't say that to Anju, though. She might have asked, How do *you* know so much about it, Mr. Experience?

Besides, my years with my father had trained me to keep my thoughts to myself, and I couldn't break that conditioning, no more than the kidnapped girls could break theirs.

(Even with you, I swallow down the things that crowd my mouth, begging to be heard. How tonight, serving spinach dal, your mother curved her fingers around the ladle. Her slim, bare wrist, at once strong and fragile. Her unpainted, glowing nails. I followed the silvery straightness of her arm up, up, until it disappeared into her blouse. Her elbow was dimpled and cool. A longing to touch it shook me so hard, I thought I wouldn't be able to stop. I had to get up and leave the table. What's wrong? Anju said. Your mother said nothing. I think she knew.)

What are we training you for, kid, without realizing it? What conditionings will stop you like those invisible electric fences suburban home-owners use to keep their dogs from running off?

The singer acts honorably. She leaves, the family stays intact, and her friend never knows that her husband had been the singer's lover.

Do you think she did the right thing? I asked Anju afterward. What would you have done?

Anju made a face. I would have made sure I didn't get into such a mess, she said.

After she went to bed, I turned on the computer. I was supposed to be testing a new software program. But instead I stared at the screen, thinking about questions of honor. How many unhappinesses they lead us into. Who can even say what honor is? Isn't it right for us to pursue happiness? Isn't that our first right?

I'd fallen into the same error as Anju, asking questions the movie never meant to answer.

The singer is back in her room, looking into a mirror, wiping dust from it. What does she see in her mirror-self? She half-turns, as though to tell us. But before she can speak, the movie ends.

I like that idea, don't you? Scary and magical, all at once. A mirror-self to show me who I really am.

But if I find one, will I have the courage to look?

Sorry, kiddo. I got carried away with the story. I've kept you up too late. Sleep now. I'll rub your back the way you like, little circles with my knuckles, as I walk up and down, carrying you on my chest.

Four

Waiting by the side of the road for the bus that is to take her to college, Anju clutches her book bag to her chest. She is dressed, as always, in blue jeans and a too-large sweatshirt, and though it is a cloudy day on the brink of spilling over into rain, she wears her dark glasses. She had gone into Wal-Mart with Sudha the day before classes began and bought the largest, most opaque pair she could find. Behind them, she feels anonymous, invisible, almost safe.

It is the year of death, the year of discovery. (Is it a rule that one must precede the other?) In Sarajevo, Johannesburg, Burundi, the ground is sludgy with blood. Christians and Muslims, Zulus and the ANC, Hutu and Tutsi. In Ethiopia scientists have unearthed the skull of humankind's earliest ancestor. In the U.S. scientists are about to capture the elusive top quark, the missing link of the atom.

School started two weeks ago, but Anju still wakes with an ache in her stomach, a tightness like a watch spring that's been wound too far. She wakes long before she needs to and lies in bed, watching the first light apply itself to the walls. It is a delicate gray, with a rhythm to it like waves on a windless day, or her own breath. She closes her eyes to learn its nature. Inhalation, exhalation, the faint antiseptic odor of Listerine mouthwash. She remembers a line she had read in childhood, she has forgotten where. *Every breath we take is another step toward our deaths.* When she opens her eyes, she sees that Sunil is watching her. He smiles and reaches over to kiss her cheek. His lips are smooth as waxed fruit. The light has grown hard, like diamonds. Each time this startles her as though it were something new.

On the bus, Anju chooses her seat carefully, counting off the rows until she is at the center of the vehicle. She prefers a seat with no other occupant. Aisles only. The window seat makes her dizzy, all that cityscape rushing past her: glassy office buildings which glint too brightly, freeways which arch their brontosaurian necks over each other. The strip malls hunker down in the middle of asphalt expanses, alien as stalled spaceships. From the corners of gas stations, signs shaped like eyeballs on stalks follow her with their unwinking stare.

There is a newspaper left on the seat next to her, sprawled open to a page that states that Steven Spielberg has won his first Oscars for *Schindler's List.* Anju considers it for a moment, reading the words and the gaps between them. She has heard her classmates (but that word is too intimate) discussing the movie. Would her rescue of Sudha, minute in scale as it is, qualify as a Schindlerism? Or is it Sudha who is saving her?

She pulls a textbook out of her bag, smooths down the red and black cover. In one of her classes they are studying letters and diaries. The instructor, an enthusiastic young woman who makes Anju feel old and slow, clasps her hands together as she explains why these genres have historically been so popular with women. She enunciates names. *Dorothy Wordsworth, Fanny Burney, Sarah Kemble Knight.* So much talent with nowhere to go except pages which only a single reader might see—or no one at all. The instructor thinks of it as a great pity.

Imagine all the letters that were lost, she said last week. *All the diaries that were thrown away unread. What a waste.* Her voice was passionate, granuled with powdered glass. Sitting in the back of the class, Anju understood what she was saying. And yet—what freedom it must have been! What exquisite loneliness. Angling words across a sheet to reach one faraway mind. Blotting a page created only for yourself, as much truth as you dared to face.

The bus brakes. The doors whoosh open. Stumbling out behind the other students into air that smells exhausted, Anju decides she, too, will write a letter. She will write a letter to her dead father.

෴

When the apartment door closes behind Anju, Sudha leans against it and shuts her eyes. Eight in the morning and she is tired already. The effort of staying out of Sunil's way until he leaves for the office, the effort of getting Anju ready after that, in the little time that is left. Most days Anju won't even get out of bed until Sudha pulls her from it. After her shower she will stand in the bathroom, a wet towel wrapped around her, until Sudha threatens to come in and dress her the way she does Dayita. She will push around cornflakes until they grow limp in her bowl. She will let the wet mop of her hair drip onto her shirt.

"Really, Anju," Sudha says in an exasperated voice as she towels it dry, as she combs out Anju's tangles. "The amount of fuss you make to go to college! It's like you're five years old. I don't know why you bother. You know I won't let you miss class and stay home."

"Yes, Mom!" says Anju as she picks up her backpack and dons her dark glasses. She tries a jokey smile, but abandons it in midformation. Nausea coils in her throat like smoke. Only when she focuses her thoughts on four o'clock does she feel better. She'll rush home as soon as she's done with classes, and Sudha will have a snack waiting, a khichuri made with rice and mung dal, a childhood favorite of them both, with a wedge of fresh lemon on the side. Afterward they'll curl up on the bed and talk, with Dayita asleep between them, until it's time for Anju to work on assignments and for Sudha to start dinner. No. Today they'll walk to the mall instead and wander around. They do this often, pretending to be aimless and extravagant, just like the other shoppers. But they have a secret agenda. "Take notes," Anju hisses at Sudha. "This is the heart of America."

"Go, Anju," says Sudha, giving her a not-ungentle push between the shoulder blades, and Anju goes.

Left alone, Sudha leans against the door, her eyes squeezed shut. She stands this way until Dayita crawls to her and tugs at her sari. Then she picks her up. Against her chest she whispers, "Oh Dayita, now we're in America—but what shall we do now?"

❧

Afternoon. Sunil finds he cannot concentrate on the report the secretary has typed up for him to review. The figures make no sense, and the words—*customer interface, product development, new virus alert*—have grown foreign, surreal. Gusts of talk and laughter flit over the cubicle wall and settle on his hair like ash. He runs his hand over the surface of his immaculately organized desk, but it gives him no pleasure. The message button on his phone blinks redly at him like a Cyclop's eye. There are consultants he must contact, programmers he must supervise, unhappy customers he must appease. His boss is waiting for an update on a project he is spearheading, an important project that could generate significant revenues and lead to a promotion, a move out of this cubicle into a real office with a solid oak door people would have to knock on if they wanted to talk to him. He turns to his computer and lays his fingers on the slight, concave coolness of the keys, familiar as a lover's dimple. But his tie feels as if it's tied too tight. He puts his hand to his throat to loosen it, then realizes he didn't wear one this morning. He walks to the window and cranks it open. There's a wind outside, a restless, rogue wind that slips in and shuffles through the report on his desk. Sheets rustle to the floor, but Sunil does not turn to look. He watches the gray sky as though for a sign. Is it at all like the sky under which he ran barefoot as a boy, yelling behind a cut-away kite? He must have done so. Don't all boys? But it is hard to find a trace of it—that sky or that boyhood—in his face.

His face which he has schooled into pleasantness, so that the secretaries—especially the older ones, touching up their lipstick or patting their hair into place in the rest room—often say, *That nice Mr. Majumdar.* But today, alone in his cubicle, his face is as uncertain as a sky over which storm clouds are passing. Will there be a hurricane? His eyes flit like evening moths that sense a flame nearby.

He takes a deep breath, pulls that maverick wind into his lungs. He moves away from the window and checks his watch. Two P.M. Is he thinking that it'll be at least a couple of hours before Anju gets back from school? Two dangerous hours that make his heart speed up when he thinks of what might be done with them. There is a recklessness in the arc of his arm as he sweeps his coat from its rack. He leaves the floor littered with pages from the unread report and stops only to tell the secretary that he has to go home.

꼰

All day Sudha works the way a deep-sea swimmer treads water, as though to stop were to drown. She cooks and vacuums and mops, she dusts the meager knickknacks in the living room. "Who would think that before I came to America I had never mopped a floor!" she says to Dayita, whom she keeps close by. "That girl's into everything!" she'll tell Anju later. "Can't let her out of my sight a minute!" Does Anju sense that Sudha is afraid of aloneness? When Dayita falls asleep, Sudha talks to herself.

She camouflages her daily cleaning by leaving a few newspapers scattered around. This is so that Anju will not scold her. ("Did I bring you here to turn you into a servant? I swear I'll stop going to college if all you do when I'm gone is clean, clean, clean.") She feeds Dayita and eats a little of the khichuri she has cooked for Anju. "It feels funny eating all by myself," she grumbles. "Civilized humans weren't meant to live like this, don't you think?" She places a clove into her mouth and chews on it abstractedly. It is an old habit that has stayed with her from girlhood.

"Oh, Sudha, don't tell me you still chew cloves like your mother made us do when we were children!" Anju exclaimed, laughing, after dinner on the first night. "Remember what she used to say—*Girls, it will give you sweeter mouths—and a husband always likes a wife with a sweet mouth!*" Then she clapped her hand over her mouth.

Sudha smiled, though a bit ruefully. "It's okay, Anju! Just because I'm divorced now doesn't mean you can't mention anything to do with marriage. Why then, we'll never be able to speak of our growing-up days—because that's what they were, a giant, nonending rehearsal for becoming married women!" Then she added, "Remember how I used to tell you that once I was married and out of Mother's control, I'd never touch another clove? But when that day came, I found I couldn't do without them."

"How we grow addicted to our tortures!" Anju said.

Sunil shot her a glance. Perhaps he wondered if there was a second meaning to her words. He should have known, by now, that Anju wasn't one to hide her meanings. She pointed her words toward people like arrows—that was the only way she knew to use them.

Now, dutifully, Sudha turns on the TV. Anju has told her she must, it will help her understand Americans. So she watches a weather report that states there's a 70 percent chance of rain; a commercial for paper towels that features a giant male, a dirty floor, and a tiny, agitated woman; and the rerun of a game show. But when a plump woman who has correctly guessed the cost of a blender shrieks with delight and jumps up and down and throws her arms around the host to kiss him, she grimaces and switches it off.

"That's disgusting!" she tells Dayita. "I'm sure that, as a self-respecting female, you'll agree with me." She plays finger games with her for a while, but she is distracted. You can see it in the way she turns her head suddenly, as though hoping to catch sight of something that lurks just outside the line of her vision. She opens the window all the way. Outside, the wind swoops and dives, scattering leaves and debris. It blows malicious grit into her eyes to make her weep. She rubs at them—a child's gesture unexpected in a woman who threw herself against the fence of marriage hard enough to knock it down—and sighs as she glances at the clock. It's only three. "Let's clean Anju Ma's bedroom, shall we?" she says.

It is a surprising decision. Though she is vigilant about keeping the rest of the apartment spotless, Sudha never enters Anju's bedroom (she thinks of it as *his bedroom*) on her own. Sometimes when Anju comes back from class, they lie on the bed in there, chatting, but that is only because Anju insists that it's ridiculous for them to scrunch themselves onto Sudha's tiny bed when her queen-sized one is sitting empty. Afterward, Sudha smooths from the bedspread every wrinkle that might betray she was there. Long before Sunil comes home, she is in the kitchen, safe behind a barricade of pots, veiled in fragrant steam.

Armed with sponges and sprays, Sudha enters the bedroom. She moves hesitantly, with trespasser footsteps. "Oh, what a mess!" she exclaims to Dayita, as though in justification—and it is. The dresser is cluttered with medicine bottles and college textbooks that have pushed Sunil's colognes into a corner. On one end is a small TV-cum-VCR in which Sunil has taken to watching, late at nights, movies that Anju would not approve of if she were awake. Blankets are balled up at the foot of the bed, and Anju's nightgown and damp towel lie in a heap on the bathroom floor. The toothpaste tube, left open, has bled blue gel onto the counter. Sudha kneels and scrubs the grime-ringed tub. There is an absorbed look on her face as she plies the cleaning brush, as she scrapes crusts of lime from the faucet. This is what she has come to America for: to set her cousin's life in order. As long as her body is contained by such necessary actions, she need not think beyond them to the blankness which is her future.

❧

For a while the child follows the movement of her mother's arm, the way it bends and straightens, the way cleanser bubbles bloom at the end of the brush's bristles. But she doesn't like the look on her mother's face, that faraway look, as though the child weren't there at all. She pulls at her arm, making sounds of protest.

"Just a minute," her mother says, "I'll feed you as soon as I'm done with the tub, okay?"

It is not okay with the child. She's more important than any stupid tub, and she knows it. She lets out a full-bodied, indignant howl.

"All right! All right! I get it!" her mother says, washing hastily and unbuttoning her blouse. The child would prefer something more exciting, those crunchy cereal balls that the man lets her have from his bowl in the morning, perhaps. But she makes do with good grace. Actually, she rather likes the familiarity of her head in the crook of her mother's elbow, the milk spraying warmth inside her mouth, its comforting smell, which is also the smell of the mother, the smell she would know at once, even in a dark room filled with strangers. She pounds on her mother's breast approvingly.

"Ouch!" her mother says. "Quit! It's time for you to go into your crib."

The child has other ideas. She clings to her mother as she tries to lower her into the crib and emits a series of shrieks, each louder than the other. She doesn't really like to do this—the sound hurts her ears, too. But what option does she have when her mother refuses to be persuaded by gentler means? This strategy has worked well in the past, especially when Aunt Anju is around.

It's successful today as well. "Oh, very well!" snaps her mother, hauling her back to Aunt Anju's bedroom and plopping her—rather ungently, the child thinks—onto the bed. "Spoilt brat!" Perspiration lines her forehead. "I should smack you." She narrows her eyes and raises her arm.

The child stops her crying. There's no longer a need for it, and she isn't one to waste her efforts. She watches her mother with some curiosity—before today, no one has threatened to hit her. But there's something else in her gaze, something steady and measuring. She knows they're engaged in some kind of battle—a staring battle maybe, and she isn't going to lose. Her mother pulls back her arm, her palm flat and swordlike. Maybe it's time to let out another wail?

But, look, she's biting her lip, backing away. She's stumbling toward the TV now, rummaging through a pile of children's videos that the man bought for the child. She slams one of them into the VCR, a last act of temper. The child considers reprimanding her with a sob or two from her considerable repertoire, but a frog puppet has appeared on the screen. It begins to sing a song she knows. She sways from side to side to the beat. *Key Largo, Montego . . . that's where we wanna go.* Everything else dwindles: small stuff, not worth sweating. In the back of her mind, she hears her mother shut the bathroom door. *Bermuda, Bahama, come on pretty mama.* The child knows that she will weep in there for a while. The knowledge makes her suddenly sad, makes her lie down, curled into herself, thumb in her mouth.

By the time the mother returns, leaving behind a gleaming bathroom that is sure to earn her Aunt Anju's wrath, the child is asleep. In sleep she senses that her mother's eyes are reddened, that the end of her blue sari is wound untidily around her slender waist. Even this way, she is beautiful, with the kind of uncared-for beauty that makes people want to be a shield between her and the world. The child knows this because the man has told her so. The mother is smiling a rainy smile at the child, who looks so much like her with her cleft chin and a small mole high on her cheekbone—except there's an added stubbornness to the child's mouth, which pouts in sleep. The mother shakes her head. In India this stubbornness would have been a disadvantage, something to be scolded—even beaten—out of a girl. But here she's not sure. All the rules are different in America, and she knows none of them yet.

She bends to pick the child up, then pauses.

"I'm scared you'll wake up," she whispers against her forehead. "And we all know what a terror you can be if your nap's disturbed, don't we!" She smiles an exhausted smile. All that kneeling and scrubbing and weeping has taken its toll. Is that why she lies down now, with a delicate, catlike yawn, curling her body around the child's? Or is she merely acquiescing to the child's wilder will? The child snuggles backward into that smell she knows so well. She is dreaming of the boy again. Cloud boy, she calls him on some days. Sandstorm boy who looks at her with such hunger. Today he flutters over them with pigeon wings. *No, no. Not here.* She wants to tell him not to be scared. What will be, will be. But she is distracted by the insistent wind, the way it presses against the windowpane, trying to find a crack so it can enter.

"Ah, mothers and daughters," she hears her mother sigh, "how we wear each other out! No matter. Anju Ma will be here in an hour to wake us up."

❧

Four P.M. Her last class over, Anju stands on a campus pavement fidgeting with her sunglasses, which she wears even to class. She is trying to decide what to do. A part of her yearns homeward, but there's the matter of the letter to her father. She knows she can't write that letter in the apartment, its charged, gunpowder air. For that she needs a space empty of history and its attendant expectations.

It is the year of passings: Ionesco and Kojak, Jackie Onassis from cancer. Anju wonders if they are expected to share the same afterlife space. She fears it might be so. But maybe it is a mistake to fear, perhaps the dead do not care about such things. She thinks of Prem for a speck second, the way one might lay a finger on the coils of a still-hot burner, then snatch it back. *Death is the great equalizer.* Is this a phrase she created just now, or had she read it somewhere before? To her dismay, she cannot remember. A dark wind tugs at her hair, brings the smell of wet earth into the space between her sunglasses and her eyes. It sends a burger wrapper, a crinkled, attention-catching silver, tumbling down a pathway toward a small concrete building onto whose wall the rain is beginning to brush stroke its transient alphabet. There's something about that tumble, a gay, I-don't-care-what-happens abandonment that Anju hasn't felt in years. She follows it—first her gaze, then her feet—and finds she is at the communications library, a building whose existence was unknown to her until today. Is this another omen? The automatic doors open all at once, like the arms of a long-lost friend. She walks until she finds a room white as the inside of an egg, circular and without windows. This pleases her. She has always thought of windows as distractions, drawing a person out of herself. And right now she needs to delve inward, to dig up the old, buried shards of her life.

In this amniotic place, Anju pushes her glasses up to her forehead, takes out a sheet of paper and a fountain pen she has carried, with a nostalgia she didn't know she possessed, all the way from India.

Dear Unknown Father, she writes.

છે

On the car radio, a voice informs Sunil that the Pentagon has dropped its eight-billion-dollar Doomsday project, that more Serb planes have been shot down in a no-fly zone, that the Germans have wrested from the French the distinction of being the world's largest consumers of alcohol.

"Bully for them," he says.

The voice goes on to warn him of a chemical spill on 101 and Montague, traffic backed up to Mathilda Avenue.

"Shit!" says Sunil. He is like an animal whose hair, ruffled the wrong way by a thoughtless hand, stands up in prickly patches. Whose skin is uneasy with exposure. Can you sense inside him the desire for speed, building like compressed steam? But the four-thirty traffic has him firmly in its embrace. Raindrops gather their fatness against the windshield and trickle lazily downward. He slashes them away with the wipers, which he operates, unnecessarily, at full speed. His handsome lips (Mel Gibson lips, a woman who knew him once said) are thin with annoyance, his fingers tap a staccato code on the steering wheel. He made himself wait in a café, drinking cappuccino after cappuccino until it was time for Anju to be home. Does he think of his act as honorable, or foolish? He hasn't had lunch and the caffeine makes him nauseous and jittery, makes him take turns too quickly, without signaling. He gives honking motorists the finger and—finally—roars into the parking lot of the apartment.

Taking the stairs two at a time, what is Sunil wishing for? He rings the bell. There is no answer. "Out at the mall again, I bet," he mutters, letting himself in with his key and dropping his briefcase on the couch. He undoes the buttons of his shirt—he's breathless today, everything tightens its coils around him—and walks into the bedroom. And sees them.

Dear Unknown Father—

It's a bit awkward, as you might imagine, writing to a person who died before I was born. A man I hated all my growing-up years because he destroyed his family. Yes, Father, you destroyed us by dying—a death you brought upon yourself by going off in search of treasure—a foolish, clichéd enterprise which should have remained where it belonged, between the pages of a children's adventure tale.

But it isn't my intention to berate you. Now that I'm mired in the middle years of my own life, I find my old hatred as useless as the adventure you went on. I need instead (the way one needs to know about the genetic defects that kill one's parents) to know what drove you. Perhaps the same desperation is beginning to drive me. I need to know what you were most afraid of in your life. Because one knows people best through their fears—the ones they overcome, and the ones they are overcome by.

These are what the people closest to me are afraid of: Sunil of earthquakes, flying insects, the sky at dusk, and the loss of control; Sudha of the silence that rises from furniture in an empty room at noon, culinary disas-

ters, and the resurrection of desires she has put to death; Prem (yes, Prem) of
dissolvement, the crying of bats and aborted babies, and my despair. Only
Dayita among us is afraid of nothing.

And me—to give you all the things I am afraid of, it would take an
aeon. So I will write only of one: love. Love which gives you a taste of itself
and makes you greedy for more. You hold it in your addicted hands, terrified
by its frailty. It makes you lie incessantly. You would kill anyone—includ-
ing yourself—to keep it from breaking. Then it breaks anyway.

All the loves I've loved, I've lost them—except one. And this one too—I
think I hear it cracking underfoot, like lake ice in a thin winter.

Father, what was it you loved so much that you had to leave us for it?
—Anju.

He stands very still in the middle of the bedroom, his unbut-
toned shirt fallen from his body. His chest does not rise and fall.
He has forgotten to breathe as he stares at the woman and the
child on his bed—which makes them, for the moment, his. He
looks like a man struck dumb by a miracle.

The frog video has ended and a static drone comes from the
TV. To this dissonant music, Sunil walks to the bed. He looks
down at Sudha, her slightly swollen lids, her hair tendriled over
his pillow, the sudden excitement of her flared hips. At the child
sleeping with her hand fisted around her mother's finger.

He kneels by the bed. He kisses her. A feather kiss on the
mole on her cheekbone, a breath kiss on her left eye, then her
right, and then he can't stop himself. His lips take hers, her face
is in his hands. He will crush her into himself, he will swallow
her if that's the only way for them to be together. This is the kiss
he has imagined over a hundred unsatisfied nights. He breathes
in the clove scent of her dreams, which will now become his.

His arms crush her to him. Her skin makes him drunk with silkiness. He strokes her shoulder blades, the curve of vertebrae, each fitted to the other like pearls on a string. His lips move to the rise of her breasts. Does her body arch up, compliant? If only he could contain himself within this perfect moment, looking neither before nor beyond.

Then she's crying out, pushing him away, he cannot read the look on her face, he would like to believe that it is an ambiguous joy, or at least desire, but her words are not ambiguous, *Let go of me, let go.* She's hitting out. To save himself from falling, he must take his hands from her, balance on his heels, kneeling by the bed. She sits up, clutching her sari to her face. Only her eyes, wide with shock, are visible above the bunched fabric. The child, too, awake now, stares—first at one, then the other, trying to decide if the situation calls for a smile. The man's breath makes a crazy, whistling sound in his windpipe. Against the lean brownness of his body, the gleam of his belt buckle. His chest hairs are dark and curly. The child laughs as she reaches out to touch them. That laugh, that touch. They bring reality crashing down around Sunil like the door to a tiger trap.

❧

In the 7:00 P.M. bus, Anju holds on to the metal armrest of the seat, her thumb caressing its smooth, bluish sheen. She feels a wondrous, party-balloon lightness, as though she might float up at any moment to the roof of the bus. The letter she wrote is safely hidden between the pages of her thickest notebook.

When she gets off, the rain hits her in immediate, wild sheets. The road has turned into a river, dull and evening-nickeled. Soaked, shivering, she hugs the bag to her chest, hoping the letter will stay dry. Rain falls on the lenses of her sunglasses, further dimming her vision. She is elated by blindness, by the mysteries of unseen puddles.

In the parking lot Sunil swings open the door of the car where he has been sitting, and calls her name. She gives a gasp, her fingers tightening on the backpack.

"You scared me!" she says. "I didn't see you in the dark!"

"You'd see a hell of a lot better if you took those blasted glasses off. How come you're so late?"

Anju is taken aback by his vehemence. She squints and bends forward to look into his face, but keeps the glasses on.

"Well?"

"I . . . something came up . . . I needed to do some work in the library. I lost track of time. Why are you so mad?"

"I was concerned, that's all," says Sunil. He steps out of the car, his shirt turning dark in the rain. Water flows over his face, obscuring his expression. "Look at you, dripping wet. What if you get sick again? Can't you carry an umbrella, at least? Here, let me take your books."

"No, no, it's quite all right—you've got your briefcase to carry."

"Anju!" says Sunil in exasperation. "Why must you always fight me when I try to do something for you?"

Anju relinquishes her backpack with reluctance and watches as he swings it cavalierly over his shoulder. To keep herself from asking him to give it back, she says, as she follows him up the stairs, "Was the traffic bad? Did you just get here, too?"

"The traffic is always bad," says Sunil, not looking back.

❧

Inside the apartment, Sudha is trying to chop onions for a curry. She cannot make up her mind as to what kind of curry it should be—some of the onion pieces are long and curved as for kurma, others chunky, as for chochori. Their edges are bruised because Sudha, usually meticulous about such things, has picked the wrong kind of knife. Large and thick, meant for cutting meat, it was the first thing that came to her hand as she felt about in the drawer. From time to time she pauses in her chopping to heft it in her fist like a weapon. But she doesn't see it—or the onions, or the dal that's on the verge of boiling over, or Dayita, who's playing in the living room with a metal paperweight she's been told not to touch. She tilts her head, the way one might when holding to a dismayed ear an expensive watch that has stopped in spite of a warranty.

Dayita bangs the paperweight on the table. She likes the sound it makes, a solid thump, followed by a pulled-out vibration that hangs in the air, and decides to make a game out of it. Bang! Bang! Bang! Until it jerks Sudha out of her trance. But where on another day she would have snatched the paperweight from Dayita and possibly given her a slap on the behind, today she merely looks. Is there something new in Dayita's face, that awareness by which children begin to separate themselves from their parents? Sudha abandons the onions and the dal, which is by now boiling over, making a yellow mess on the stove, and steps into the bathroom. She searches in the mirror for visual manifestations of the afternoon's upheaval. But there isn't always such a straight line between cause and effect. Her face remains lovely as ever, not a wrinkle added, not an iota of luminosity taken away. Only the keenest sight would detect the faint swelling of her lips, which she scrubbed over and over after Sunil, shirt in one hand, briefcase in the other, stumbled from the apartment. Anju, busy with her own dissimulations, will not be capable of such vision.

Once, when Sudha and Anju were teenagers, Pishi had told them the tale of Damayanti, a queen so beautiful that the gods grew jealous of her husband. They took away all he had and forced him to wander in the wilderness for many years. "Be careful," Pishi had ended. "A woman's beauty can be her wealth, but also her curse."

Anju had wrinkled her nose ruefully. "I guess I don't have to worry, then!" But Sudha, who would usually rush in at such moments to say that Anju was beautiful, too, and, besides, she was smart, which was more important, had been too lost in her thoughts to say anything.

Now Sudha brings her hands to her face and traces the outlines of the bones. Is it true that beauty can be a curse? She moves her fingers slowly, cautiously. The way a doctor might touch the victim of an accident, feeling for fractures. Or the way a lover might touch his beloved's face. The way Sunil touched her.

&

Dinner is preceded by a tournament of circumventions, questions shot around the table, parried, shot back in the form of other questions.

She: Goodness, Anju! How late you are! I was killing myself with worry! Why didn't you call? What were you doing all this time?

She: Please! The way the two of you are going on, it's like I disappeared for a whole month. I'm a big girl, okay? And sometimes I need to stay on campus and catch up on things I need to do. Can we talk about something else now—like what's for dinner. I'm starved.

He: Your cousin's right—next time you should let one of us know what's going on.

She: There's dal and a brinjal curry that's still cooking—sorry, I'm a bit behind today.

She: *You're* telling me to call! That's rich! How many times have you been late and not let me know? Remember the time when—

He: We're talking about now. Why do you always have to bring up ancient history?

She: Anju, can you give me a hand in the kitchen? Come on, Anju!

She: It's always like that, one rule for you, another for me. Why?

He: *(Silence)*

She: *(Silence)*

She: *(Silence)*

✣

They eat with small, jerky gestures, pushing the food around their plates, not tasting. Sudha has forgotten to add salt to the curry. But no one pays attention. The wind curls itself complacently on the windowsill. Dayita, oddly quiet, wriggles from Sunil's arms to the floor, and for once he doesn't call to her.

A tableau of silence: three people, inside their chests small black boxes, holding inside them smaller, blacker boxes. Secrets packed in secrets: velvet scraps, foam pellets, wood shavings, baby-black hair. Some of these they know, some they guess at. Others itch inside them like the start of an infection. Until, at the very center of the chest, the secret of whose existence they are totally unaware. The secret of their own self, already pollinated by time's spores, waiting to burst open when they are least prepared for it.

Five

Letters

Calcutta
April 1994

My dear Anju,

Blessings of the goddess Kali on all of you.

I miss you more than a letter can convey. The house is empty without the little one's laughter and mischief. We old women feel even older. We've taken to wandering the streets, bargaining with vendors for things we don't need, because we dread coming home to silence. Selfishly we wish we had married you to a Calcutta boy. Then our family wouldn't be scattered across the world today. But then I think, the new life you are living in a land unfettered by old customs will perhaps give you opportunities I was unable to provide. I am particularly pleased that you and Sudha have each other for companionship.

I am very glad you are taking classes again. Now I do not feel as guilty about depriving you of college in order to get you married. Perhaps I was overhasty. But I made a good choice, did I not? How many husbands would have been as supportive as Sunil about you continuing your education? And how generous he has been to take Sudha and Dayita into his home. Yes, I know what you are thinking, your nostrils flaring with annoyance (how well I remember your gestures!). It is your house, too. But if he had said no, how much trouble it would have made!

It is good that you are busy with your studies. Keeping oneself busy is the best cure for sorrow, I know that too. But do not repeat my mistake and build a wall of work between you and the people you love. Spend a little time alone with Sunil. In that land of strangers, who does he have for love and comfort except his wife?

Pishi hopes you two are telling stories from our epics to Dayita. These stories, she says, have much old wisdom embedded in them. Nalini asks if you have put up the Indian calendar she gave Sudha when she left. It is important to keep track of our holy days and celebrate them, even if in a simple fashion. How else will you pass on our heritage to Dayita, and to the other little ones who, soon, I hope, will be lighting up your home? She says you must make special note of the bad-luck hours which she had the astrologer write in for each day (though I suspect you do not believe in such things).

You will be sad to hear that Singhji, our old chauffeur, is dead. He went quietly, in his sleep. His landlord found him after a day and called us. We looked around in his rented room to see if we could find any information about a family to contact, but there was nothing. So we conducted the funeral last week ourselves. May the Goddess be with him. He served us loyally all his life, even after we could no longer pay him, and he was very fond of our Dayita.

Will you be coming to visit us soon? It is such a long time since I saw you. Our prayers are with all of you. Every month we have a puja done in Kalighat for our Prem, so that his spirit will be at peace.

Your mother

San Jose
April 1994

Dear Mother,

On receiving your letter, I couldn't stop myself from weeping, I missed you so much. How I wish you had indeed married me to a Calcutta boy, so I could take the #37 bus to your house and put my head, with all its troubles, in your lap.

Mother, I need advice. Things are going badly here, not like you imagine at all. Sunil is so tense, he's like a rubber band stretched to breaking—it's as though he's holding something in, something ominous that I need to know. But when I get up the courage to ask him, he just says, Everything's okay, you're imagining things. And Sudha—I was looking forward so much to having her here, but it isn't the same as when we were young. Remember how in childhood we always knew what the other was thinking? Well, not anymore. All I sense about her is, she's not happy living with us—and nor am I. I think I acted too impulsively in asking her to come. I wanted so much for her—that she should go to school, that she should stand on her own feet and start a business. But we don't have the money. Maybe Sunil was right in not wanting to bring her. He's so terse around her—that's another thing. I wonder if that's because he doesn't want her here, or if it's something quite different. Sometimes I look at Sudha and wonder what it is that she wants. I love her, I do, but sometimes when I look at her face, which is so much more beautiful than mine, so much more desirable—. Oh mother, I'm so afraid, I don't know what to

Dear Mother, Pishi, and Aunt Nalini,

We are all well and happy here. Dayita is a real joy and amuses us for hours. She crawls everywhere and is even trying to stand up. I think she's going to get teeth soon. Her jaws are all bumpy and she chews everything she can get her hands on. It's worse than having a puppy! Sudha is a better cook than ever—I must have put on ten pounds since she got to America, just eating her fish curries. Sunil is doing very well at work and thinks he might be up for a promotion. But with so much work pressure, it is doubtful that we can visit you soon. I find my classes challenging but like them very much. It is lovely to get all your news. Don't worry about us—as I said, we are fine. Sudha and I thank you for your blessings, Sunil sends his greetings, and Dayita gives you many wet, drooly kisses.

Anju

Calcutta
April 1994

Dear chiranjibi Sunil,

My son, I have heard nothing from you in months now, ever since Anju's unfortunate miscarriage, which as I wrote made me very sad indeed. But such is God's way. Please do write so that I know through your own words that you are well, though from your mother-in-law Gouri I get some news of you. That is how I know that your sister-in-law Sudha and her poor daughter are now with you. I am proud of your kindness in giving them a home. You have acted honorably in this. They have no man to look after them apart from you, after all.

We are well here, though your father is suffering from high blood pressure. He will not go to the doctor, however, and shouts at me if I suggest it. I do not like to complain, but since his retirement he has become more irritable and also excitable. Even reading the newspaper, about a riot somewhere, or a murder, or even something like a minister caught evading taxes, which you know happens all the time, he will shout and curse. I am having trouble holding on to any servants because he yells so many insults at them, I am sure knowing him you can imagine the words, and these days with so many factory jobs around, who except a wife will put up with such behavior? Even Nitin, our old kitchen boy, left last month, and now I am having to wash all the pots myself.

Last week your father fell down while climbing the stairs and frightened me almost to death. I asked if I could call you and he shouted at me again. His face turned red and I was afraid he would harm himself, so I dropped the matter. Do you think you could pay us a visit? Perhaps he will listen if you talk to him in person. I know you had that unfortunate fight before you left, but it has been many years, and though he is too old and stubborn to contact you, I think in his heart he regrets the quarrel. I am hoping, from your side, you have forgiven him, as a dutiful son should.

One more thing I must request—please do not send us any more money. I was shocked to discover how much you have been sending. (Your father, of course, tells me nothing, but I looked in his bureau a few days back when he forgot to lock it and saw a stack of uncashed U.S. money orders.) I hate to think how many problems this must cause you, especially now that your household has doubled in size.

I miss you, my son. Write to me soon. It is best to write to Gouri's address and she will arrange to get it to me without your father knowing. Otherwise it will cause a scene. (He waits like a hawk for the mailman, although all we get are catalogues and bills.) I am thankful I have such a good relative in Gouri. Sometimes when your father goes to play bridge at the club, I take the bus to her house. Even a brief talk with her brings me some peace.

My blessings to Anju. Tell her I remember her sweetness to me when she was here. My prayers to Lord Ganesh and to Shasthi for all your health and happiness also, and by God's will, a new baby to fill her lap soon.

Your mother

San Jose
April 1994

Dear Respected Mother,

It makes me angry to have to sneak around Father's back like this. What must Gouri Ma think of our family! But I'll do it to keep you from getting into trouble.

Don't ask me not to send money. I'm repaying Father for whatever he spent to bring me up so that he can never again say how much he's done for me. It's a way of buying back my freedom.

About his health I'm unable to feel any sympathy. He brings it on himself. I'm just sorry that you have to put up with all this hassle. Try to stand up to him a bit. Remember, he needs you more than you need him.

I'm sending you some money separately with this letter. Spend it on something you like—maybe a movie when he's out, or a new sari. Maybe you can take a trip to a holy place, if Gouri Ma is going. I wish I could do more—but the other thing you ask—to visit Father and talk to him—is not possible. I'm afraid you think too highly of me—I'm neither dutiful, nor particularly honorable. Maybe with your prayers, one of these days, I'll do better!

> *Your son*
> *Sunil*

Six

Sudha

Each afternoon I wander the pavements of the city, footstep by hard gray footstep, pushing Dayita in her baby carriage. She sucks her thumb and stares around her with eyes the color of wet licorice. The faded blue awning of a Chinese takeout. An Indian grocery where cardboard boxes of okra and bitter melon are set out on the pavement. A beauty salon that screams NAILS! ONLY $19.95! A Kmart outside which teenagers slouch, looking sulky in crew cuts and pants too big for them. She will not sleep, not until I return to the apartment. And then she will plummet into thick, exhausted dreams, refusing to wake for dinner. I am afraid she is losing weight. I am racked by guilt. Yet I find it impossible to remain in the apartment past noon. Is it fear that drives me, or desire?

I think from time to time with remorse of Singhji and the news of his death that Gouri Ma wrote of. How scared I used to be of his burned face when I was little, the disfigurement that was his disguise. All those years he worked for us—and no one had known who he was. He had loved us—me—mutely, through his service. Loved me more than I deserved. Again and again, he took risks to bring Ashok and me together. He had known—better than I—that I should have married where my heart led. I think of the letter he slipped into my bag when I left for America, explaining that he was my father, long presumed dead, begging me to keep his secret. I should have written back, telling him that I loved him, too. But I was too unsure myself, teetering on the tightrope of my new life. I felt I had to keep my eyes fixed sternly ahead. One backward glance and I'd fall, crashing, into the nothingness below. How could I risk that? And now it's too late.

Minutes fall around me in clumps, like cut hair. Keep track, keep track! I must be back on our street by the time the white-and-green bus pulls over to the side and huffs open its doors. When Anju steps out, I will be there to greet her. I will speak brightly about how nice it is to leave the apartment for a breath of fresh air. About the daffodils, eye-watering yellow by the library entrance. About the first leaves, their webbed fingers. Anju will lean down to Dayita. For a moment, her hair will enclose them in a silken fringe, faces stitched into the same tapestry. She will whisper into my daughter's ears, filling her with secrets that make her giggle as she never does with me. I will feel a twinge. A numbness at my extremities, like frostbite. Foolish jealousy! This closeness between them—isn't it the only gift I have to give Anju?

But underneath it all, I will be thinking about the kiss.

๛

I have grown disenchanted with stories, the way my life veers away from the ones I long to emulate. But once in a while, remembering Pishi's request, I tell Dayita tales from the Ramayana. I think she enjoys this—it is one of the few times when

I am not scolding. Does she understand? I don't know. Still, it makes me feel motherly and good, which is rare for me.

The story I tell her as we walk today is about how the demon Ravan stole Sita from her home.

When Sita saw the golden deer outside her forest hut, she desired it more than anything she could imagine. She said to her husband, Ram, "I gave up the palace and came to live in the forest for love of you. If you loved me as much, you would catch the deer so I could have it as a pet."

Ram suspected that the golden deer was not real but a demon trick, and he said so to Sita. But she would not listen.

"Now I know how little you care for me," she cried.

So Ram took his bow and arrow and left to find the deer. He told his brother Lakshman to remain behind at the hut to guard Sita. After a while they heard a distant voice that sounded like Ram's crying for help. Sita was distraught and asked Lakshman to go to his brother's aid.

Lakshman said, "I think this is another demon trick. Ram is a great warrior and would never need to call for help."

But Sita scolded him bitterly and said, "You are an unnatural brother. For all I know, you want Ram to die so that you can force me to become yours."

Stung, the faithful Lakshman left in search of Ram, but before he went, he drew a circle in the earth around the hut. "Do not step outside this boundary," he said to Sita. "As long as you are inside, no one can harm you."

But as soon as he went away, the demon Ravan, disguised as a sannyasi, came to the hut and begged for alms. He tricked Sita into crossing the circle, captured her and took her to his island kingdom in Lanka. It would take many years of sorrow and searching, war and death, before Ram and Sita would be united again.

This is what I do not tell Dayita: Each of our lives has a magic circle drawn around it, one we must not cross. Chaos waits on the other side of the drawn line. Perhaps in leaving Ramesh I had already stepped outside my circle. With the kiss, Sunil trampled the circle his marriage had etched around him. What is there now to keep us safe from our demons?

I am angry with Sunil, but angrier with myself. When he kissed me, it was as though a lance went through me, striking me in my most secret parts. His tongue moved in my mouth. His odor was sour and addictive, like pickled plums. My treacherous lips did not want him to stop. I pushed him away, yes. But my breasts yearned toward him. *The husband of my sister,* said my brain. But the trembling in my legs said, *I don't care.*

I fear my body. I fear his. Because bodies can pull at us, whispering.

Why not.

I deserve more.

I am young, and life is passing.

What will our bodies do, the next time they are alone?

❦

Preoccupied with storytelling, I've taken a different turn somewhere. I find myself in a park.

I have been in American parks before. But this time, looking with undistracted eyes, I see more. It is always this way. When I am alone, it is as though a scalpel has cut a cataract away.

Why then do I continue to resist loneliness?

A pretty park, clean, with new equipment. This must be a more affluent neighborhood. So neat, so bright, so much space between things. In Indian parks, people would jostle for space beneath the few banyan trees. The hot-gram and ice-cream sellers would singsong their way between families with too many children. Piebald dogs would follow them, panting endlessly. Bus fumes, spicy pakoras, the too-sweet peaks of old woman's hair candy. The odor of oleanders crushed under small, excited shoes. Anju and I always returned home exhausted, sticky with surfeit.

The slatted red cups of baby swings arc through the air. Tidy. Vivacious. On springs shaped like giant corkscrews, rocking horses bob their synchronized heads. Why should all this order make me sad? Children pour sand on each other, but it doesn't show in their blond hair. Blond mothers dressed in coordinated outfits chat animatedly. I venture a smile, they do not see me. Is it their ignorance of my world that renders me invisible, or their distrust? If I were in their place, I wouldn't have smiled either at a brown woman in a sari and windbreaker.

In the stroller Dayita scrambles and squeals. When I pick her up, she cries louder, twisting. Recently, she refuses to let me hold her. When did this start? Was it after the kiss? I am paranoid. How can a child her age understand? She stopped nursing two nights later. I'd been trying to wean her for weeks. Still, when she pushed my breast away, the condemnation in her fingertips stung my skin. All night my mouth was dry with shame.

I set Dayita down on the spongy surface of the play area that edges the sand. In America, even falls don't hurt. Entire generations of children, growing up innocent of pain . . . Something feels wrong to me about this.

Why should I think this way? I've eaten my fill of pain. What good has it done me?

Then I notice the girl. She's on the big-children's swings. She wears cutoff jeans, makes the swing go way past safety. No, it's a grown woman. Her black hair streams out, seal-sleek, as the swing sweeps forward. She wears her tight purple T-shirt with a nonchalance I envy. Kicks out with naked brown feet. Her toenails are darkly iridescent. Mynah feathers. On the ground, a boy belted into a stroller laughs and claps his hands.

Up and down and up into the sky again. The wild abandon of that movement, the first way we learn of flight. That weightless moment poised at the highest point of the arc, that total quiet before the fall. I thought I'd forgotten it, along with my childhood.

I walk up and ask, "Are you Indian?" I cannot help it, though Anju has warned me that here people do not talk to strangers this way. Not even Indian strangers. A gust following in the swing's wake blows away my words. I must shout them again. She is looking skyward, creasing her eyes, focusing on the dip and rise of the horizon. A sailor searching for a new geography. The boy looks at me, curious. His eyes are blue and brown. Her son? She does not turn to me. Her lips are the juicy red of ripe pomelos, curved in a joke she's keeping to herself.

Mortified, I begin to move away.

Then she says, "Wait."

☙

I go back to the park day after day to see her. She is so unlike any woman I've ever met. And I am so hungry.

Each time she gives me a little piece of herself.

Her name is Sara. In India it was something else. Saraswati? Sarayu? Sarojini? She doesn't tell me. It's not important, not at this time in her life. Does she believe that her name will wait for her, obedient as a brooch one has put aside because it is too old-fashioned, until she is ready to wear it again?

"I came here as an exchange student," she says. "It was only going to be for a year. I was all set to go back and get married to a guy I'd met in college in Bombay. Then, about a month before my return, it hit me that for the rest of my life I'd never have another chance to be alone. In-laws, kids, servants, you know how it is in India. Scary. So I bought myself a bus ticket to California. A last bit of adventure, I thought. Disneyland, Universal Studios, the Golden Gate Bridge—the usual tourist shit. I'd planned on being back by the end of the week, but the Greyhound broke down halfway between LA and San Francisco. Like it was fate."

She got off the bus and walked into the dunes. She hitched rides along Highway 1, learning the names of trees as she went. Scarlet gum, Madrona, ironbark. Somewhere between a grove of cypresses and a rock on which seals sunned themselves, she got addicted.

All those years of Fair and Lovely Skin Lightening Lotion and Arnica Hair Vitalizer! She let her face grow dark in the sun. She let her hair coil into dreadlocks for a while, then cut it all off. She pierced her nose, her eyebrow, but let the holes close up after a while. When her visa expired, she took all the money she had left and bought a secondhand car. Sometimes, that's where she sleeps.

She laughs at my expression. "Don't look so scandalized! It isn't hard. I love the freedom, the risk. It's like being in a play."

"What about your parents?"

She shrugs. "I send them postcards. That way they know I'm okay, but they can't get to me! When I'm ready to go back to them, I'll call, and they'll send me a ticket."

I want to dislike her selfishness, her arrogant confidence that she'll be loved, always. I want to ask, *What if they don't want you back?* But I'm caught in the net of her stories.

"You got to get out of this valley, girl," she says. "See the other Americas. There's too many men chasing after sex and money here, who think the word *no* doesn't apply to them."

Getting out. How delicious the words sound. I want the recipe for them. But she's already telling me how, in Yellowstone Park, a black bear's eye gleamed amber when the beam from her flashlight hit it. Did I know that in Yosemite, you can see rainbows forming above waterfalls on a full-moon night? In Las Vegas, there are fake Grecian palaces that spring from flat Nevada earth, white as a columned mirage in the dry desert air. She's watched extravaganzas in hotels as big as townships where a grid-metal floor can sink underwater to transform a stage into a thirty-foot-deep diving pool. But each time the Bay Area reeled her back in.

She tells me about a month she spent in the Haight with a man. They made love under a goose-down quilt in a room with no heat and ate Thai takeout. Sometimes they drove up to Napa to buy a bottle of wine, and finished it in the car on the way back. His skin was like cumin powder. His hair was dark and springy, like wool from some midnight animal. She would work her fingers into it when she was cold.

Where did this girl from India learn such recklessness? Who taught her to care so little for what people might think?

She laughs some more at the look on my face. Today she's wearing a black T-shirt and black jeans. Black ankle-high boots. She looks attractive and dangerous, a bandit lady.

"How about money?" I ask.

"When I'm broke, I come down to San Jose. I know a woman here—she finds me jobs."

My heart starts beating fast. "What kind of job?" I ask.

"Depends on what you know, and what you're prepared to do! Lupe can get you almost anything. She's a woman of connections, as they say. Sometimes I'm in a hurry to make a fast buck and leave, but this time I wanted a change. I wanted something laid back. Respectable. So I'm Joshua's nanny, at least for the moment." She unstraps the little boy in the stroller. "Go eat some sand," she says, handing him a plastic bucket and shovel, giving his diapered behind a not-ungentle smack. He toddles off equably.

"Do you think she could find me a job?" I ask. Even saying the words makes me flush. If Anju could hear me . . .

She looks at me appraisingly. "So. You want a job." I steel myself for the questions. *Why do you need to work? Don't you have a husband to take care of you?* But maybe Sara has moved away from such Indian ways of thought. She only says, "Let me check with Lupe."

I should give her something in thanks and reciprocation. But I'm not ready to speak of a life which hulks at my back like a burned house.

Behind me in the sand pit I hear screams. Dayita! She's taken hold of Joshua's bucket with both her hands and is set on wresting it from him. When he resists, she lowers her head and—before I can run to them—bites his arm. Joshua lets go of the bucket and stares at the small red indentations that mark his skin. Then he begins to wail. Dayita makes use of this opportunity to grab the bucket and scuttle away, unrepentant.

I'm aghast. From where did my daughter inherit this ferocity? Not from me, surely. Nor her father. His fault was always the opposite. Is it then his mother's legacy, passed down the indifferent channelways of blood to the granddaughter whose life she wanted to prevent?

"Hey, no big deal," says Sara. "All kids act like brats sometimes." She rocks Joshua until he calms down, then gives him his bottle. "Don't take it so hard," she adds, touching my shoulder. "Not everything your kid does is your fault. My poor mother did whatever she could to bring me up as a good Indian girl. Bharatnatyam lessons, elocution classes, a convent education, the works. And look at me! Don't scold the kid too much, okay? She's just a baby." She waits until I give a reluctant nod. "Listen, I'll call Lupe over the weekend. Why don't you give me your number—I'll let you know what she says."

I tell her Anju's number, and she writes it on the back of her palm with a red ballpoint pen. "Please call only between nine and four on weekdays," I say, and am grateful when she doesn't ask why. I watch her slim black silhouette until she is gone.

To live like Sara in the present, in adventure. To not care about the worms curled inside the apple of your future. Is that ever possible, once you have become a mother?

I shouldn't blame motherhood. From the day I was born, I had a worry in each eye.

I break my promise to Sara and scold Dayita all the way back. I can't help it. How can Sara, who's not a mother, know how frightening it is to be responsible for another life?

My words have no effect. Dayita leans back in the stroller and observes the zigzag lights in the windows of record shops. She turns her head to watch the yellow arch of a McDonald's as we pass. The first streetlamps are cat eyes, making her smile. From time to time she sings baby words to herself. How well she has learned, already, the art of ignoring mothers.

❧

Tonight, Anju asked if she could have Dayita to sleep with her, just for a bit.

"If she wakes up in the night and wants to be nursed, I'll bring her back to you," she said. "Promise!"

"She doesn't nurse anymore."

"Great!" said Anju. "Now she can sleep with Sunil and me half the time. That way, we'll be able to cuddle up with her, and you'll get some rest."

I wanted to say, That kind of rest I don't need. I wanted to tell my cousin, whom I'd once loved more than myself, Don't touch her, she's mine.

Anju held out her arms and Dayita jumped into them, not a backward glance. Anju spun her around until she screamed with excitement. They laughed all the way to Anju's bedroom.

It's past midnight. Lying here, I think I still hear them laughing. Sunil's deeper tones join theirs. But of course they're asleep. A little moonlight, pale and sickly, trickles into this room full of my daughter's absence. Her smell is pungence and wild grass. The tindery odor of stubbornness. I take a baby blanket and press my face into it. Even my teeth hurt with loneliness. My mind whips about. East and west, east and west. I want my daughter to be loved by Sunil and Anju. I want her for myself alone. I want to help Anju get back to her old, strong self. I want Lupe to find me a job so I can escape this apartment. The river of my life is speeding toward an abyss. What shall I do? I want an existence iridescent as nail polish. I want sleep. I want to bite into the apple of America. I want to swim to India, to the parrot-green smells of childhood. I want a mother's arms to weep in. I want my weathervane mind to stop its manic spinning. I want Sunil.

Seven

Beyond the mouth of the bay, past where the slender rust-red bridge sways in a rare silence, the fog rises before dawn. Here the water is deeper, colder. Things go on below the surface—the willful tug of currents which want to take you beyond everything you know, the invisible smile of water creatures coiling and uncoiling.

The fog rises like a long exhalation and begins its journey. Over the white city lit in the last of the moonlight, its buildings dulling to old silver as the fog flows over them. Down the tangled skeins of 280 and 101, where lone cars leave tracers of light as they speed from one dream to another, newer one. Southward, the rail lines, the alleys flanking the stations of Palo Alto and Menlo Park, where men and women huddle under worn jute bags just a block away from five-star restaurants with French names. The fog touches their hair with its finger, leaving swaths of white behind. It passes the dark glass rectangles of office buildings where the lights are never turned off, looks in through the windows at programmers stretched out in restive exhaustion under their desks, their heads filled with neon words: *angel, beta, IPO.* In San Jose, it moves through downtown parks strewn with newspapers and used needles, by-products of the Silicon Rush. In the underpasses, abandoned grocery carts, urine, a smell like burnt sugar. The fog circles the garishly hopeful banners of small stores in Vietnam Town; it sweeps its hem like a benediction over apartment buildings clustered like aphids along the freeway.

It is the year of random malice, the year the W4 worm will topple networks like dominoes around the globe, the year when drive-by shootings will account for 129 deaths across America.

Now the sun staggers into the sky, leaving yolky smears behind. Buses and garbage trucks groan and rattle, people blink into bathroom mirrors in disbelief of themselves. Anju and Sunil, too, Dayita and Sudha, they begin their awkward morning cotillion. KCBS announces that 237 is backed up all the way to Montague, and advises commuters to take an alternate route. Eating his cereal, Sunil swears. The alternate routes, he knows, will be just as backed up. He rinses out his bowl and wipes it with a dish towel. Leaving, he shuts the door behind him quietly. It is no use, he knows, to take out one's frustration on the necessary objects of one's life. In the bathroom, standing under a fall of warm water, Anju imagines a shower that will never end. Sudha knocks on the door, *An-ju, An-ju,* syllables drawn out in worry or impatience. Listening, Dayita slips her thumb into her mouth. Her eyes are as black as bees.

The fog witnesses all of this. It is breaking up, like the memory of an old promise you know you made but can't figure out why. The last strips of it drift into the small, slit mouths of the mailboxes that wait in the entryway. Later, when Sudha comes to check, she will find two letters there.

One is an invitation on a heavy cream parchment, addressed to Sunil Majumdar and Family. The other is a pale blue aerogram, the black Calcutta postmark blooming blotchily over a stamp that bears Indira Gandhi's haughty, surprised profile. Sudha's name, in square, male letters, a handwriting that makes her draw her breath in sharply. The name on the back says *Ashok*. She holds it as though she cannot decide whether she should press it to her chest, or fling it into the Dumpster that hulks in the parking lot. Finally, she does neither. Lately she is growing into a woman of cautious gestures, movements that give little away. She turns neatly on her heel and returns to the apartment.

☙

We want Sudha to open her letter, but she goes about her daily chores with exasperating meticulousness. Measure the rice: two cups. Leave it to soak in three and a half cups of warm water. Set out the chicken for thawing. Use the blender to grind six cloves, two teaspoons of coriander and cumin seed, a jar-lid full of peppercorns, three red chilies and a stick of cinnamon. Change Dayita's diaper. Give her a snack: apple juice in a no-spill cup, Froot Loops in a plastic bowl.

The two letters sit on the kitchen counter, side by side, calm cream, calm blue, like a husband and wife who have been married a long time.

What fibers of steel are woven into Sudha's will that she can go about her work like this, not giving in to the need to know?

Take a load of clothes down to the laundry room. Dust the furniture. Give Dayita an oil massage and then her bath. Chop the vegetables and stir-fry carefully with mustard seed—it's zucchini today, and if you leave it on the stove too long, it turns to mush. Dayita wants a bottle. Turn the stove low, warm the milk, add a pinch of sugar—an old Indian habit, a hope that the child's life will be filled with sweetness. Put her in the crib and run down to throw the clothes in the dryer. Marinate the chicken in a paste of turmeric, yogurt, and salt.

Perhaps it is not strength that keeps her from opening the letter. Maybe Ashok's letter is a painful reminder of the prospects she gave up in order to come here, into this disappointing, disturbing existence. Or is she saving it, a deferred treat, the way children hide candy in their pockets to enjoy in the sticky secrecy of their room?

The chicken simmers in the pot, filling the room with the centuries-old smell of garam masala. Sudha zips her windbreaker, smooths down her hair, the folds of her sari. In the mirror, her reflection looks dissatisfied.

"I wish I had a pair of jeans," she tells Dayita, who is trying to climb into her stroller. "I think I'll scream if one more stranger comes up and tells me how much they love my costume. Maybe I should borrow a few things from Anju." But her voice is reluctant. "No, don't climb in yet," she adds sharply. "Wait till we get downstairs. NO, Dayita! Don't you hear me?"

She turns off the chicken, checks the catches on the windows. Last week, someone broke into the apartment downstairs and trashed it. The police think it's the tenant's ex-boyfriend, but Sunil grumbles that the neighborhood's going to the dogs. She grabs a protesting Dayita in one hand, the stroller in the other. At the door she stops and comes back to pick up the letter.

≈

In the park Sudha pauses the way she does each day now and looks around. Expectation flickers over her face like a matchstick flame. She's looking for Sara of the cutoff jeans, Sara the adventurous, who has promised her entry into the real American life, and—more importantly—escape from herself. But it's as though the woman has disappeared, as though she had only been a figment of Sudha's wanting. She bites her lip and sets Dayita down near the slides. Dayita holds up a fistful of sand to show Sudha.

"Mama! Mama!"

"Yes, shona, I'm watching," says Sudha. "That's very good, shona. Just don't get any into your eyes." She nods encouragingly, but she's thinking about another place, another life. The past tugs at her with its blue aerogram fingers.

Sudha takes the letter out of her pocket and turns it over and over.

When she'd been in America for two weeks, Anju finally asked her the question she'd been expecting ever since she got here. *Why did you turn Ashok down?*

Sudha shrugged. She'd imagined the question many times, practiced the shrug, the careful answer.

"Tell me!"

"What's the point of going over what's done with, finished? We need to put the past behind us, both you and I."

Anju shook her head. "I can't put it behind me until I know. I keep thinking you did it because of me, because you'd promised to come and be with me. It makes me feel terrible, like I ruined your life all over again. Like you sacrificed yourself for me."

"I've given up sacrificing myself for others. It leaves you with the worst hangover."

"Quit joking."

"I turned him down because I didn't want him to have to

take care of me," Sudha said. "I wanted to be independent. And it seemed like America was the best place for that."

"But don't you love him?"

Sudha ignored the question. "So, as you see, it was a wholly selfish decision."

"I don't believe you," Anju said. "At least not that last part, about you being selfish."

"Dear Anju, everyone is selfish in the end!"

Anju had laughed, but uneasily. There was a new hardness in her cousin's eyes. An opaqueness, as though she wasn't telling Anju the whole truth. In order to survive, Sudha had had to learn many things. Could selfishness be one of them?

&e

Staring at Ashok's letter, Sudha thinks, *This man I loved.* But love is a code sketched in dust. You look away, the wind blows, the pattern shifts, and when you look again, you discover it says something else. She inserts a finger under the flap and pulls until the aerogram tears jaggedly along the crease.

Dearest Sudha,

For months now I have been waiting impatiently for a letter from you. At first I told myself that it was because you were settling into an unfamiliar environment. There were many pressures on you, many calls on your time. You were meeting Anju after so long, you had a lot of catching up to do, a lot of help to give. It was enough to consume anyone's attention.

But now it has been three months, and I'm beginning to worry. Sudha, why this silence? All the things I said to you, sitting by the Ganges, have you forgotten them? Is America enticing you away with its glitter? And most of all—I am afraid to ask this—is there someone else?

For me there isn't. There never will be. In spite of the obstacles that chance placed in our path these many years, I'm convinced that we're meant to be together. Who else knows you the way I do, Sudha? Who else knows how it felt to go through a decade of hopeless longing while you were married to someone else? Surely that means something to you, even in America?

Write soon. Or better, come back soon, so you and I and your little girl can finally be a family.

Love,
Ashok

Dayita is tired of sand. Her eyes fall on the slide, where the older children are playing. She crawls toward it, then tries to stand. She's on her feet, swaying precariously on the uneven sand. She takes a step, then another. She's walking—it's her first time—her face alight with the adventure of moving beyond her babyhood. Then she loses her balance and sits down with a bump.

Lost in Ashok's words, Sudha sees none of this.

Dayita will walk again soon—perhaps even this evening. They will see her then and make much of her. Still, this special moment in her life has come and gone, with no one to notice.

Small tragedies, the hairline cracks in our relationships.

She is up again already, trying to climb the iron rungs of the ladder that leads to the top of a slide that is surely far too high for her. She clings to the first rung, advances to the second. She's on the third rung, pulling herself up by the sheer force of her stubbornness. Farther, farther, until she crawls onto the little ledge on top. Then she looks down the length of the slide and lets out a scream. She screams methodically and piercingly— she doesn't waste energy in crying—until Sudha is startled out of her reverie.

"Oh, my God! How did you get up there!" she cries, rushing

to the slide. "Come down, baby. Come, Mummy will catch you." But Dayita continues her clockwork screams. A little crowd has gathered around them by now—other children want to use the slide, and their parents give Sudha eloquently accusing glances—until finally she throws off her windbreaker, tucks up her sari, climbs the ladder, puts Dayita in her lap, and slides down with her.

Let us remember her like this, no matter what happens later: a slim woman, radiant with laughter and speed, the knot of her hair loosened so that she appears younger than she is. This is the woman she would have been if the world had dealt with her more kindly. The wind sends the edge of her sari flying like a victory banner. The child in her lap claps in delight, and the woman presses her cheek to the child's head. Her burnished curls are an innocent halo around her face. Untouched by worry or need, for a moment she belongs to the world of myth. She is the beautiful princess who lived in the palace of snakes.

જ

It is a tale from the time before birth and death, when Anju sat beneath the brittle, hopeful red of a maple tree, her hands clasped over the mound of her stomach.

"Once there was a princess," Anju said to Prem. "She lived in a beautiful palace beneath a lake—a palace made of snakes. Snake pillars, snake floors, a quilt of snakes who sang her to sleep every night. As long as she never left the palace, she was told, she would be happy.

"So of course," said Anju, "one day the princess left the palace and began to make her way upward. A stairway of pearl appeared, reaching all the way to the world of men, a world she thought beautiful. As you might expect, there was, on the shore, a young man. He held out his hand to pull her out of the water, and she took it. When he kissed her, she heard a sound like thunder, and turned to see that the stairway was gone.

"The princess did not worry too much about this. She was in love. She followed the young man to his house, but his mother called her a witch and would not let her stay. The young man built the princess a cottage in the forest. They lived there happily enough, though the young man would go from time to time to visit his mother. The years passed. The princess gave birth to a baby girl. The man's visits to his mother grew longer and longer, and one day he did not return at all. When the princess went to the village to search for him, she came upon a wedding: her lover was getting married to a rich girl his mother had picked out for him.

"The princess did not confront her lover—what was the point? She took her daughter and started out for the serpent lake. She hoped the stairway would be there this time, in her need. But there was nothing. Or perhaps this was a different lake—she couldn't quite tell. Thus began her journey from lake to lake, with her daughter. Everywhere she went, men were fascinated by her and could not keep away. Some loved her, some used her badly, and some abandoned their homes to follow her. None lasted. They tired of her, or feared her. Or perhaps it was she who shrugged them off to continue on her way. But she never found the pearl stairway to the palace under the water.

"If you look up just before dawn," said Anju, "when only a couple of stars are left in the sky, you can see her pass with her daughter, still searching. The fog is the tattered end of her sari. The stars are her eyes that have learned it is of no use to weep."

There are many versions to every story. The version you choose reveals more about the storyteller than about the story.

What then did this story about the abandoned princess-turned-homebreaker say about Anju? What did it say about her feelings for her cousin—feelings she could touch only when they were wrapped in fiction's insulations?

On the way back to the apartment, Sudha stops at an overpass. Below her, cars whizz by, shimmery metallic slashes against the slateboard of the freeway. She takes the letter from her pocket and tears it into tiny pieces. She slips her hand through the wire netting put up by the city to keep people safe—as though safety could be so easily achieved—and lets the pieces fall. "The past is the past," she whispers. But perhaps we mishear, perhaps it is something quite different that she says, *everlasting,* or *hold fast.* It is the year of incomprehensible losses, of unbelievable gains. The death toll in Rwanda has crossed the half-million mark. After twenty-seven years in jail, Mandela has become South Africa's first black president. Is this the law of the world, that to go forward you must first step back? Her voice is drowned in the dizzying roar of SUVs and Harleys, BMWs and Benzes, as they vie with each other for mastery of the road. The torn bits of paper float for a moment, silver in the evening air. Fragments of phrases (but surely they weren't in the letter): *mine, happiness, why.* Then they are gone.

Eight

❧

Assignment

Write an essay examining the effects of culture and heredity upon an individual. Would you say they are more important than character traits in influencing the individual's behavior? You may support your analysis with personal as well as historical/social examples (approximately fifteen hundred words).

Loss: An Essay
by
Anju Majumdar
for
English 3353
Advanced Composition
Prof. P. Gossen

At the age of twenty-five, when she had barely stepped into her adult life, my mother became a widow. No. I'm thinking like me, not like her. She had been an adult since she turned sixteen, the year her parents married her to my father—or, more accurately, to the illustrious Chatterjee family of Calcutta.

You can weep all you want on the train to Calcutta, her mother had said as she blessed the new bride. But by the time you arrive in your new home, your eyes should be dry. My mother obeyed, as she had been taught. She wept away her girlhood on that train. By the time she arrived at her in-law's immense marble mansion in Calcutta, her eyes were dry and she was an adult. Perhaps that is why when news of my father's death came to her—she was pregnant with me at the time—she did not shed a single tear. At least not in public.

Public is all I know of my mother's life, because she never spoke of her feelings. Was this, too, what she had been taught?

Confession: this entire paper is based on hearsay and conjecture.

My father's death was the greatest loss in my mother's life. I think we can all agree on that. It turned her from a wife into a widow. In a society where property and destiny were controlled by men, it was not a good way to be.

These are the things my mother put away after my father's death:

expensive saris, jewelry, romantic thoughts. The rest of her life, she would not eat Ilish fish or read poetry, both of which my father had loved. For a Bengali woman, those were serious sacrifices.

These are the things my mother made herself forget: that she was afraid; that she was a sexual being; that she needed to weep.

This is what she made herself remember: she had made a promise to my father, and she would keep it.

Pishi, my aunt, tells us that in the weeks following my father's death, thirty-eight male relatives came to the house and offered to take on the burden of caring for my father's widow (my mother), his unborn child (me), and his property (which would turn out to be considerably less than the thirty-eight male relatives had imagined). To all of them, my mother said no—very politely, as she had been taught. She said she would take care of all three herself. She ended up taking care of a lot more than that—Pishi and Aunt Nalini and Sudha and sick employees at the family bookstore and later, for a while, Dayita. But it was not a problem.

It was not a problem because, in order to deal with her loss, my mother had turned herself into a man.

She was a very effective man, more so than my father, who, for all his goodness, was a dreamer and generous to a fault. Also, he had a tendency to trust all the wrong people. (This is why our property was considerably less.) He liked to sit in his easy-chair in the evenings and watch the stars, pointing out constellations enthusiastically but inaccurately. Sometimes he put on old Pankaj Mallik records and sang along. My mother, on the other hand, never sat in an easy chair, never listened to music, particularly the sentimental kind, and never trusted anyone except Pishi. As for stars, they were in the sky, and she was on the earth, and that was that. She also worked eighteen hours a day, seven days a week, to make sure we could keep living in the marble mansion, which by now was seriously attempting to fall to pieces, in a manner that befitted the descendants of the Chatterjees. This was the promise she had made to my father.

Because of the promise, my mother always knew what to do, even though (as with my marriage) it might turn out later to be the wrong thing.

My mother never made me promise her anything.

Growing up, I loved my mother more than anyone I knew. I admired her completely. When she embraced me, or gave me a rare word of praise, I thought, Paradise must be like this.

I learned everything I could from my mother.

But somewhere along the way, I went wrong.

How do I know this?

Because of the way I mishandle loss. The loss of my son, which

has already occurred. And the loss of my husband, which has begun

to occur, and which I cannot stanch.

Ms. Majumdar,

Interesting subject matter, though it responds to the assignment in a rather tangential way. Can you give more specific examples in the beginning to help us visualize your mother's life and times?

Your prose style is strong, but the paragraph structure is somewhat un-orthodox. Watch out for diction, e.g., "Public is all I know of my mother's life. . . ." I notice a number of fragments in the draft. I am not convinced they are necessary. You mention a number of characters without explaining who they are. This is confusing. Try to move your draft from writer-based prose to reader-based prose.

The end of the paper loses focus and becomes overly emotional. You should keep yourself out of it. Consider rewriting from "My mother never made me promise her anything." The part about paradise is a bit of a cliché.

Overall, this is a good start for an essay—but it needs to be developed in great detail. As I'm sure you remember, the assignment calls for a minimum of six pages. Please revise accordingly and turn it in by May 15.

P. Gossen

P.S. I am disturbed by the events you refer to at the end of the paper. I suggest you pay a visit to Counseling (312 Herne Hall).

Nine

Sudha

The bus comes and goes, its finger of smoke rubbing a darker gray into the evening. No Anju. Where is that girl? But nowadays she is often erratic, so I won't worry yet. Not about her.

Chilly now. The light withdraws itself. A fog descends. It surrounds me, insistent, until I must breathe it in. Tiny drops of water coat the insides of my lungs. It is like drowning, a little at a time.

In the apartment parking lot, I look for Sunil's car. If I see it, I won't go upstairs, no matter how cold it gets. I'll wrap my windbreaker around Dayita, and . . .

But, thankfully, the car is not there.

Sometimes I feel I'm being melodramatic. It's not as though he'll attack me. He's not that sort of man. But if our eyes met in an empty room, if we drew the same air, simultaneously, into our lungs, I don't know what might happen then.

Each day, weakness sings louder in me. In each fingertip, along the underside of my breasts that ache a little, through the veins lining my arms. The day after I signed my divorce papers,

Ashok kissed the vein at my wrist. Each kiss was sharp, defined, like an infusion of blood. Before that, my life had felt so unnecessary. We were sitting by the Ganges at Outram Ghat. The water was brown with silt and patience. He whispered something against my skin. I didn't hear the words. But the sound was like a remedy spoken by a medicine woman into the ears of a person whose spirit has gone roaming. I put my other hand in the water. The current pressed against my fingers, heavy with age. It reminded me that things go on.

I turned and kissed Ashok on the lips, shocking him.

Why am I thinking of this, after I tore up his letter? Why am I thinking of Sunil? What is it I want?

The apartment is so dark. Turn on the lights—one, two, three. Still, brownness hazes the bulbs. Has the fog insinuated itself into this space as well?

Seeing Ashok's letter today, my body drew itself in, tortoise-like. Tightness of shell and stone. Stiffened muscle. I should have been happy, but my body said otherwise. The body, which shows us our real desire.

I can't go back to India, to the way I was. Helpless, dependent—I can't love like that. I can't bring up my daughter to think that is how a woman needs to live.

I think there are ways of being otherwise in India, but I don't know them.

I can't stay in my cousin's home. My presence saws at the frayed rope that holds Anju and Sunil together. Maybe it would break anyway—but I can't bear to be the reason. And my dreams. Fever-crusted, bloated with—there is no way to circumvent this word—sin. The angled curve of Sunil's collarbone, a small sweat that stays on my fingertips. The dizzy salt taste of his chest, its rapid rise and fall against my tongue. I want to slough off the images stamped inside my eyelids every morning, the moistness between my legs when I wake.

Caught inside the walls of this apartment, I have no way to silence my body's clamoring.

A key rattles the lock. I am tense to my toes.

Sudha, where will you go now?

*

"Stop! Stop!" Anju says just as I'm pouring her tea. "No sugar!"

I look at her questioningly. Usually she takes a heaped spoonful. On days when she's feeling low, she indulges in a spoon and a half.

"Do you know how bad sugar is for you?" she says. "All those disease-causing empty calories that make you hyper."

I make a face. "Whence comes this sudden wisdom?" But I know. Every day she picks up snippets of self-improvement from college, some fad or other.

"I'm serious. I think you, too, should stop."

She's sitting earnest and cross-legged in jeans on the sofa, backpack thrown to the floor, the cup of tea clasped in her hands. Her face glows with zeal.

"Not me," I say in some annoyance. "I like my vices, thank you."

"Really, Sudha! It's only a habit. We form habits, we can change them into more positive ones." Then she breaks into a grin. "I know, I know, I sound like a bad copy of a Stephen Covey tape!"

I don't know who this Covey is, but I don't feel like telling her that.

She's talking about her day at school. Zora Neale Hurston, she says. Kate Chopin. More names that mean nothing to me.

She waves her arm, gathering a wideness of air to herself. On the arm, glass bangles, color of blue ice. I must have helped pack them into her wedding suitcase, but I cannot remember it. The bangles make a tinkling, water music. When did she start wearing them again?

"So that horrid Professor Gossen, who always corrects my grammar and never sees that I'm trying to do something different, is away today—some conference where she's presenting a paper, probably on comma splice—and this visiting professor is there instead. She's reading aloud from the assignments she liked because she says we learn a lot from hearing the work of other student writers. And then she starts reading my essay! I could have died! You remember that essay about my mother I was having so much trouble with, the one Gossen thought was too ambiguous and went off-topic? Her comments depressed me so much that I didn't even revise it, just turned it in, expecting a C. And this new woman thinks it's one of the best in the class! She writes on the paper that I have Originality and Voice!"

"Voice," I say, nodding as though I hear the word every day. I'm glad Anju is so happy about it, whatever it means.

"I bet Gossen's going to have a hernia when she finds out! But, wait, that's not the best part! After the class a couple of women come up to me and say that they think my writing's really strong—all this time they had no idea because of course Gossen would rather shit bricks than praise my work."

Shit bricks! I try to keep the consternation off my face. But underneath I'm thinking how little I have in common anymore with this new Anju.

"—And then they ask me to join their writers' group," she finishes in triumph.

"Writers' group," I say, trying hard to understand. But I can't. My head feels stuffy, as though I'm coming down with a cold. A writers' group? What's the use of that?

"They meet every Tuesday," Anju says, "for a couple of hours after class, and each one reads a piece and gets a response from the others—"

I want to interrupt. Does she like her unsweetened tea? Is she too tired to go for a walk? Did she answer her mother's letter? These are things I understand. I've made ghugni with chickpeas and flaked coconut, does she want some? When she talks of writing, I see once again Ramesh's signature on the divorce papers. The letters had been sharp and feral. The blue ink held a glitter in it, like something secreted by a venomous insect. I'd never seen his signature before that because he'd never written to me.

What will become of me on Tuesdays?

"You won't mind, will you, Sudha, dear?" Anju says. She's pleading, which is rare for her. "It'll be a long day alone for you—but this is so exciting! Nothing like this has happened to me, ever. I really liked this woman—she's so passionate about things. So sure. So different from anyone I know."

Different from me, she means. A wave of jealous hurt scalds my insides.

"She's from Iran," Anju says, not noticing. Does she notice anything about me nowadays? "Her family fled the country during Khomeini's rule. She's writing an essay about that time, particularly what happened to the women. I can't imagine being able to write something like that! She said I had real talent and owed it to myself to develop it."

Owed it to myself. It was not an idea we'd grown up with in Calcutta. Owed it to my parents, yes. My ancestors. My in-laws.

My children. Teachers, society, God. But *owed it to myself?* Yet how easily Anju says it today.

What is it that I owe myself?

"Do you think that's true, Sudha?" Anju leans forward and grips my wrists. "Do you think I could really be a writer?"

Her fingers are strong, still warm from the teacup. When we were girls, she'd grab me just like this, and I'd feel her excitement speeding up my heartbeat. Even when we became wives, she in San Jose and I bricked up in Bardhaman, we'd sense each other's needs without having to talk. If one of us had a secret, the other would taste it, grainy and bitter like pomegranate seeds bitten into by accident.

Today, nothing but heaviness.

I've done that which I shouldn't have, I tell her in my mind, willing her to hear. *I've kissed your husband and liked it.*

"What do you think, Sudha? Shall I join the group?"

Don't leave me alone with him.

"Sudha! Are you listening!"

"How can I tell you what to do?" I say. Disappointment sharpens my tone. "I've never been to college."

"Don't be like that!" Anju says. "You're the one closest to me, the one who understands me best. The one I trust most of all."

There's a muted hissing in my ears. I pretend to pick something up from the carpet so I can remove my hands from hers.

"Try it, then," I say. "You never know what's right for you unless you try." As soon as I've said them, the words feel ominous, loaded with a meaning I didn't intend. A meaning that applies to my life as well.

Anju leans forward and gives me a hug. "Thanks for encouraging me."

Oh, Anju! But even my grief is separate and muted. She will not guess it.

"Need any help with dinner?" she asks. "Oh, I forgot, are there any letters?"

I hand her the cream envelope.

"Sunil Majumdar and Family!" she says. "How delightfully chauvinistic!" She flips the envelope over, looks at the name embossed on the back. Shrugs. "Don't know them." She leaves it on the coffee table for Sunil to open.

Only now, in its loss, I know the value of what the two of us had. A metallic fog has wound itself around me. Is this how other people go through their lives? Hearing dimly, feeling even less? They hold out their arms, hoping to connect, but the metal glints, brutal as a mirror. All they can see is their own face. They—we—open our mouth to call out, and fog fills it like cotton candy. Loneliness candy, which melts into nothing, leaving a taste so sweet you cannot distinguish it from bitterness.

❧

"Did you hear the news?" Sunil says as he hurries into the apartment. "Nicole Brown, O. J. Simpson's wife, has been murdered!"

Another person for me to add to my list of not-knowns. But Anju asks, "You mean O. J. the athlete?"

"Yes, him," he shouts over his shoulder from the bedroom. Why is he so agitated? He carries the TV out and sets it up on the counter so that we can watch while we eat dinner.

A young newscaster in a blue suit and pale brown hair looks out at us. His face is blankly handsome. "The body of Nicole Brown has been discovered in her house on Bundy Drive in Brentwood, along with that of an unidentified male companion," he recites. "The police are trying to locate her ex-husband, football hero and actor O. J. Simpson, for questioning."

I ladle dal and brinjal curry onto our plates and bring out the fried fish, which I've kept crisp in the oven.

"Crunchy fish, yum!" Anju says. "Oh, Sudha, you're spoiling me!"

Sunil gives her a reprimanding look, then goes back to staring at the TV. His cheeks are the dusty red of burnt bricks. He hasn't touched his food, though he, too, is fond of fried fish. Pictures of a vaguely European-looking house, cordoned off with yellow police tape, flash on the screen. Then the photo of a blonde woman, beautiful in a chilly, film-star way. The camera zooms in on the dark stains on the steps. Thankfully, the bodies have been removed. "Arnelle Simpson, O. J.'s daughter, told the police that her father took a flight to Chicago some time late last night," intones the newscaster gloomily. "Brian Kaelin, a friend of O. J.'s staying at his estate on Rockingham Drive, claims . . ." The picture goes fuzzy—it's an old TV—and his words are drowned in static. Sunil jumps up to adjust the antenna, but by then the young man is describing the outbreak of yet another fire in the Oakland hills.

"Damn!"

I'm taken aback by the hard, pelleted word, the way his lips, tight as new elastic, choke it off. A murder is a terrible thing, true, but murders happen every day. Why is this one so important to him?

We eat silently. The TV gives us a reason not to talk. There's something unreal and orchestrated about news reports. Something I can't quite believe. Why is it that so many people find events which are occurring to people they don't know, in cities they'll never set foot in, more compelling than their own problems? Even Anju. Growing up, she'd fiddle for hours with the knobs of the transistor radio she'd begged Gouri Ma to get her. She'd sit on the window seat of our bedroom, entranced by the faint, crackly sounds of All India Radio, or Akashbani Kalikata. Late at night, the BBC. All those lives so far from ours, so different. Beyond understanding, beyond helping. What was the point of filling our heads with their troubles?

You can't ever really know people that way, I once said to Anju.

What fascinated me were the stories I'd hear the aunties whispering during their tea sessions. Forbidden stories about people who lived on our street. Stories of secrets that I, looking at their faces, would never have guessed at. People like Mangala, the Rai Bahadur's maidservant. Though by the time I came to know her story, she, too, was beyond our helping.

That's whose face flashed through my mind as I watched the dead Nicole's face on the screen. Mangala.

I should be more like Anju, I know that. I need to learn about this country. The TV, in spite of all its faults, can offer me images. Names. The clues of accents. But I get confused. There's a plane crash, all 262 passengers killed, for one minute on the screen. Then the story of a woman who had quintuplets, or a dog who saved a child. Also one minute. Is everything equally important in America? Or nothing important enough? I suspect codes embedded in the folds of the stories, in the curve of the anchorwoman's eyebrow. Sara would have known how to decipher them.

But why am I thinking of her in a wishful past tense, as though I won't see her again?

We eat. Nicole's murder flashes on the screen intermittently, between discussions of a rise in the stock market and chances of rain. Sunil has recovered enough to compliment me on the brinjal curry. His second sentence. Each evening he allows himself to speak three sentences to me. The first, a question about my day. The second, about food. The third, Dayita. Each requires no more than a one-word answer.

At some point in my life I will look back at these evenings and laugh. I must believe this. I must believe this.

Anju springs up from her chair. "Just remembered—this came in the mail today." She hands Sunil the envelope. "Who's it from?"

"Chopra? He's one of my clients. His company went public last year. Made a bunch of money, built a huge house up in Los Altos Hills." Sunil fingers the heavy parchment appreciatively. Or is it envy in that lingering touch? He opens the card. "It's an invitation to his twenty-fifth wedding anniversary."

"When is it?" Anju asks.

"Next weekend. We were obviously an afterthought." For a moment his expression veers toward anger.

"Then maybe we shouldn't go. Besides, we'd have to buy a gift—"

Anju breaks off. She doesn't want to talk finances in front of me. Doesn't want me to feel uncomfortable. But I know already.

I heard them once, while nursing Dayita in the back room. Furious whispers.

She: There's only a hundred and fifty dollars left in our checking account.

He: You'll have to make do with it until I get my paycheck on the fifteenth.

She: I don't know how I can. I have to get groceries, diapers, baby vitamins. Why can't you send a little less each month to your folks in India?

He: That's not possible.

She: Why not? It's not like your dad's hurting for money. Doesn't he own—what is it?—two rental properties? And here we are, living in this dump of an apartment. . . .

He: We've talked about this a hundred times. I'm not going to discuss it again. You knew money was tight. You should have thought about it before you invited your cousin to stay with us.

She: How can you compare your dad's situation to Sudha's? She really needed to get away, start over. And I needed her with me. How can you grudge us this one thing? What else have I ever asked you for? What else have you ever given me?

He: *(Silence)*

She: *(Silence)*.

&

Sunil looks down, examining the invitation. Is he thinking of his own wedding, the years it has lasted, the years it might not last?

"We'll go," he says finally, uncreasing his forehead. "We'll go and see how the rich live. Why not?" He looks at me. A rare, direct glance. A challenge glitters in them. "You, too. After all, you're part of Sunil Majumdar and Family. Aren't you?"

&

We sit on the bedroom floor among piles of clothing. Anju has pulled out our suitcases from under her bed, and we are trying to decide what to wear. We go through mine quickly—there's only a few starched cottons in there. I had to leave all my expensive saris behind when I left Ramesh's house. Anju's suitcase, though, is filled with her trousseau. Whipped clouds of chiffon and chinon. Fragile Dhakai cottons in monsoon colors. Regal Benarasis, stiff with zari thread. Touch of another lifetime on my skin, to which there is no returning.

"Look how lovely this still is," I say, picking up the sari Anju got married in. Sprays of gold flowers on royal red. So out of place in this two-room apartment, its shag-haired carpet mangy from my enthusiastic vacuuming.

"There's nothing like our Indian fabrics," Anju says. "No wonder you wanted to become a clothing designer!"

I wince. It's painful to be reminded of dreams that came to nothing. "Stop!" I tell Dayita, who is burrowing into the suit-case, tangling gauzes and satins. She rubs her face on an expensive Kanchipuram silk, undeterred by my shouts. Does she smell the presence of our young selves in the woodsy sandal powder? When I grab for her, she hides behind Anju.

"Oh, quit!" says Anju. "You're always scolding my sweet Dayu for nothing!" She turns to Dayita and drapes the edge of an embroidered veil over her head. "Don't you look pretty! Sunil, Sunil, come see our little bride!"

Tomorrow Anju will stop at the bank and take out her wed-ding jewelry to share between us. My jewelry is still in my ex-husband's family vault—or being worn by his new wife. Sometimes, because I think I should, I try to feel outrage. But her image is too far away, a tiny reflection at the bottom of a well. How can I envy it? In my imagination, she has the same cowed look as Ramesh.

"Sue them," Anju said on my first day here, talking like an American. Angry sweat on her upper lip. Her thick eyebrows drawn together. She had forgotten how things are back home. How a runaway wife has no rights.

"I paid it in exchange for my daughter's life," I told her.

Anju bit her lip to stop the tears. "The bastard." She was always more angry with Ramesh than with my mother-in-law. "Never mind. Everything I have is yours, too."

Are other people haunted by words as I am? A prickly wind on my skin, making me shiver. *Everything?*

I shouldn't go to this party. The wisest thing would be to pretend to be sick on that day. But I don't want to be wise.

I pick out a gray sari with a thin silver border, ambiguous enough for a woman whose marital status is questionable. But Anju will have none of it.

"It's a wedding anniversary, for heaven's sake, not a funeral!" she says. She chooses for me a lovely, deep silk colored like a peacock's throat, embroidered all over with tiny gold moons. "That's a great color on you." She turns to Sunil, who has come to look at Dayita. "Don't you agree?"

"Yes," says Sunil tersely. He tries to pick Dayita up, but she won't go, not until he tempts her by holding out his keys. There's a Mickey Mouse on the chain. It squeaks when he presses its stomach, making my daughter laugh and lunge for it. "Sleepytime," Sunil says, and picks her up. I stare after him in reluctant admiration. How many men would put a Mickey Mouse on their key chain just to please a little girl?

"And I have that necklace with a peacock pendant, and those earrings, you remember them, that match the sari. It'll make you look quite stunning," Anju says.

Anju, can't you smell the storm?

I choose for her a peach silk like the morning sky, the color of innocence. I tell her she must wear it with the jewelry set Gouri Ma gave her at the blessing ceremony before the wedding—tiny, twinkling diamonds set into filigreed gold.

Anju hesitates. "Don't you think it's too showy?"

"It's a wedding anniversary, for heaven's sake, not a funeral!"

We burst out laughing, filled with sudden, girlish excitement.

But later in bed I think. He had said, *You're part of Sunil Majumdar and Family. Aren't you?*

"Of course she is," Anju had replied, "and our Dayu as well. We must take her, too." She was looking at the invitation, did it say anything about not bringing children. She didn't see his eyes. Possession wound its way around me like a nylon line, impossible to break.

I should have said no right then.

I call up the necklace that Anju will wear, its sprinkle of stars clear against the dark air of my room. For a moment I'm in the wedding tent again, the humid, heavy air smelling of sweat and incense and wilting marigolds. Gouri Ma's fingers fumbling for a moment with the catch of the necklace, the way she stroked Anju's hair afterward as her lips moved inaudibly, invoking divine protection.

Pray hard, I beg her. Pray hard enough, Gouri Ma, to deflect fate.

Ten

Sunil

Today I'm not going to talk about your mother, kid. Not one word. I'm going to tell you a whole different kind of story. It's from a long time ago, when I was a boy, maybe ten, maybe eleven, going to school in Calcutta. There's a lot I've forgotten about the story, but I'll leave the gaps as they are. I don't want to make anything up, not for you. Between you and me, kid, it's always going to be the truth.

And if there's a time when I can't give you that, I'll say nothing at all.

So, picture me, kiddo: a scabby boy with pencil-thin arms and legs, khaki half-pants, white shirt—the school uniform of Deshbandhu Boys School, except my shirt's always torn or smeared with mud from the football field, and my mother's always mending and washing and ironing, tensely and in secret, so my father won't give me one of his long, deadly speeches about carelessness and inconsideration and do I think money grows on trees. I've just gotten off the school bus, I'm running to the house as fast as I can, holding up a pink notice the teacher has given me, which I hand to my mother. Her smile collapses into worry as she reads it because what that notice tells her is that the teachers of Deshbandhu Boys School are planning to take the boys to the theater next week to see a matinee show of *Puro-hit O Pradip*, which they believe will promote excellent moral values in their charges, and can the parents kindly send ten rupees fifty paise with the students by day after tomorrow for tickets and bus fare.

That's ten rupees fifty paise more than my mother has, because in our house, my father is the one who handles the cash, who gives bazaar money each morning to Manik, our servant, before leaving for the office, and takes back the change, along with detailed accounts that had better be accurate to the last paisa, from him in the evening. And who doesn't look favorably on my mother asking him for frivolities, as a trip to the theater surely is.

I'm tempted to insert a scene here about my mother begging my father for the money, about him ranting and raving and finally refusing, of my mother having to make a secret trip to her cousin in Belgachia, as she sometimes did, for a loan. She was a kind woman, the Belgachia cousin. Whenever we visited, she gave us narus made from jaggery and coconut, and cold water in tall stainless-steel glasses to which beads of condensation clung. And she always allowed my mother to pretend that she'd be able to return the money soon. At the time of my wedding, I bought her a very fancy silk sari, which annoyed my father no end. But I'm digressing.

The truth is, I don't remember how my mother managed to get hold of the theater money. Those days, I didn't pay attention to such things. In the self-absorbed way of children, I took it for granted that she would provide what I needed.

What I do remember is the theater.

I wish you could see it, kiddo. It was the most immense hall I'd ever been in, filled with maroon velvet seats so soft that when you sat, you sank into them all the way to your hips. A maroon velvet curtain hung in front of the stage, trimmed with thick gold-tasseled ropes. In the middle of the ceiling, there was a huge white-and-gold lotus, and from it hung an equally huge chandelier that threw mysterious shadows down on us, as though we were in some enchanted cave. All along the cornices, little lights flickered like flames until a flute started playing. Then they went out, leaving us in a hushed dark.

I went back to see the place once, after I was grown and in college, but it was gone and some kind of air-conditioned market had taken its place. I was sad, but in a way I was relieved. For the rest of my life now, I could continue thinking of it the way I remembered it, without my critical adult eye ruining the spell.

And the characters, when they appeared—how can I describe them to you! To me, a boy from class five who had never been taken to the movies, they were like gods. Their gestures were grand and true and touched something in me I didn't even know was there. The priest was dressed in a white dhoti and wore rings in his ears. His bald head shone with divine light, and his wooden clogs clacked across the stage with an authority that made me hold completely still. The soldiers raised their deadly swords all at once as they marched; their shields were decorated with glittery bronze studs; their commander wore a breastplate of gold and shouted orders in a terrifying voice as he directed them to capture the thief. Even the thief, dressed in tattered robes, with blacked-in circles under his crazed eyes and manacles around his ankles, was a creature out of myth.

For months afterward, I'd act out the story at home in the af-

ternoons, sometimes for my mother, but mostly for myself. I'd
take turns being each of the characters: the saintly priest who
takes in the escaped thief, who has reached his home on a
stormy night; the priest's suspicious sister, who warns him not to
trust a stranger, especially one who looks so desperate. The soldiers who spy the thief and raise an outcry as they vault over
the sofa in our living room. I improved on the dialogue as I went
along by adding long, emotional harangues. I had found my
life's vocation, I told my mother. I was going to be an actor. She
smiled unhappily. (But I was used to that.)

Most of all, I enjoyed playing the part of the thief. In the
middle of the night, when the priest and his sister were asleep, I
would rise from my mat and, on tiptoe, reach for the gold lamp
in the alcove. My face would be filled with frenzy, the face of a
man calloused by the world's cruelties. What did I care that the
lamp was the priest's one valuable possession? Fool, I sneered, as
I swept it into my sack and climbed out of the window. When
the commander caught me and brought me back to the priest
for identification, I was unrepentant. I crossed my arms over my
chest and leaned back against the wall. Do your worst, I dared
them. It was only when the priest declared that he had given me
the gold lamp as a gift that my face grew uncertain and my
hands began to tremble. My knees grew weak until I sank, sacklike, onto my mother's living room carpet. I lowered my head to
the floor in respect and said to the priest, Forgive me, I am your
servant for life. The room filled with applause from Manik and
my mother. I kept my head down as long as I could. I didn't
want to return to my life.

I thought about the play a lot over the next few years, even
after I'd exchanged my dream of being an actor for one of becoming a judge who presided over criminal cases, sentencing

men to death—or life. There was something about the play that
kept disturbing me. It was only later, after coming across
another play of a very different kind, that I realized what it was.
I really liked the guy who stole the lamp, I really wanted to believe that he changed into a good man in the end—but I
couldn't. It didn't help that our teacher told us that the story
was from a novel written by a famous French author. People
didn't change from bad to good—bam!—just like that. (Every
night when my father got home I had firsthand proof of it.)

I bet you're wondering about that other play. It was *Macbeth*.
We were reading it for class ten English—I'll tell you that story
another day. But there's a scene where Lady Macbeth is trying
to persuade Macbeth, who's very loyal to the king, that he
should kill him when he's visiting their castle. Finally, even
though he's reluctant, Macbeth agrees—and that's it for him.

Sometimes at night, I'd find myself thinking about that. Why
didn't Macbeth see what he was getting into? I'd think angrily.
He was a smart man, and pretty darn brave. Why couldn't he
stop himself then, or at least later, when he's starting to kill all
kinds of people—friends, women, babies like you?

Let me tell you, this wasn't like me—I was the kind of boy
who ran around with friends all day and fell asleep as soon as he
hit the bed. If I thought at all, it was about solid things, happy
things: football, what Ma would fix me for lunch the next day,
the girl who stood on the balcony opposite my bedroom to
comb her hair. But what happened to Macbeth, it scared me. A
few times that year, I dreamed about a man—I didn't know who
it was—stepping through a bog. Only he didn't know it was a
bog—it looked like a gorgeous tropical garden, vines loaded
with fruit, birds singing, monkeys swinging from branches—and
then, just as he's reaching out to grab a ripe mango, he slips, and

before he knows it, he's in mud up to his waist and it's sucking him in. Down, down, his chest is gone, he's shouting for help, he stretches up his neck, there's mud in his mouth and eyes, and, finally, just like in the adventure movies (by now I'd cut classes with my friends and seen several), his fingers claw the air and disappear. I'd wake up from that dream sweating, my mouth chalky with the taste of clay.

It was an important lesson. Too bad I didn't learn it.

Good people turn bad. I believed it then. I know it today. Yes, kiddo, now that you've fallen asleep—your head heavy on my collarbone, your breath tickling my chin, so much trust I don't deserve—I can say it. I know it from my own life.

I guess there are things you can do to stop yourself from falling into the bog. But most of us don't see them until we're in up to our armpits. Maybe that's what happened to O. J., too.

What I want to know, before I sink farther and my hands disappear, is there something out there that I can grab to pull myself out? Or is it true, like with Macbeth, that once you start going bad, you might as well give up, because there's no way back?

Eleven

Time passes. The hours rise and fall like the waves of the Pacific—which is only fifty miles to the west, though no one, looking at this apartment building squeezed beside a dozen others and stained by the freeway's coughs, would believe it. The hours are insidious. They wait for a chance to carry lives away, like unmoored boats swept out to sea with the tide. Already they are lapping at Anju's feet.

Anju has started staying longer on campus. I never know when I'll be back, she told Sudha. Don't wait for me at the bus stop. Sudha drew her brows together in a frown, but Anju offered neither explanation nor apology.

Some days she goes for coffee with the women from the writing group. She listens to them but says little. Most of the time she's busy trying to keep her astonishment from showing. They speak of drugs in the inner city, latchkey children, candlelight vigils for victims of domestic violence. They plan marches, work on placards for demonstrations. Who are these women? she thinks. Where were they all my life? Even their everyday talk—papers and boyfriends, vegan recipes, an art movie at Camera One, a new salon where they dye your hair with natural dyes—seems fantastic to her, a costume that her tongue would like to try on. And yet they make her feel lonelier. Large chunks of herself will always be unintelligible to them: the joint family she grew up in, her arranged marriage, the way she fell in love with her husband, the tension in her household, that ménage à trois, Indian style. Only Sudha, she thinks unhappily, can ever understand these.

On other days she sits by herself at the edge of the quad, watching. A boy in a punk haircut with a razor blade hanging from his earlobe, whizzing past on a skateboard, a young woman in slacks and a brown veil that covers her hair, an older man who carries a cat under his arm and speaks urgently and continuously to himself, an Asian couple, hands waving as they argue with energy in their language. Watching them sometimes, she forgets to breathe. That's how much she wants to glean their interiors—what they do when alone, what they wish for as they throw a penny into a fountain, where they are afraid to go in their sleep. She is convinced their lives are more interesting than her own. But perhaps all who hope to be writers must believe this? She holds them in her mind like Rubik's Cubes, turning them over to see how they are put together. She imagines their problems in jewel colors, nothing like her own fatiguing, banal troubles. In a notebook that is filling up fast, she writes to her father, *I love the problems of strangers because I am not responsible for solving them.*

In the evenings, when Anju returns, she stands at the door of her apartment for a while before she unlocks it. It is an effort to bring her eyes to focus on the door, its fake wood-grain pattern. She reels her thoughts into the confines of her body, the confines of the conversations she must pick up on the other side of that door. It is like waking—or perhaps like entering a not-so-pleasant, recurrent dream, this life that has turned out so different from what she hoped for. And yet it *is* her life—just as the woman inside is her much-beloved cousin, though of late their minds repel each other like the opposite poles of magnets. The cousin she herself called to America (but why? she cannot quite remember), and to whom her husband is (still? once again?) attracted. Ah, did they think she doesn't see? She sees it all. What she cannot ascertain is how she feels.

Her life, *her* cousin, *her* husband. *Her* son. (For even now she thinks of Prem as she glides across the bedsheets, away from Sunil's merman touch.) All these possessives, hanging from her like anchors. Anju, who feels the seductive hours lick at her feet, longs to loosen herself from them, but doesn't know how.

෴

It is the night of the anniversary party, and the women are in Anju's bedroom, getting dressed. They have handed Dayita, lacy as a confection in a white dress with satin bows, to Sunil, severe and handsome in his one expensive suit. He looks at his watch with some impatience, but not too much. In between watching the news—detectives, police statements, a car chase as exciting as any in a James Bond movie, old clips of O. J., the distraught parents of the young man whose body was found beside Nicole's—he listens curiously to the wisps of laughter that float out from the bedroom. Perhaps he, too, is excited. It's been a long time since he has been to a fancy affair like tonight's.

Inside, Sudha and Anju help each other with their saris, making sure the pleats are even, pinning the anchal to the shoulder so that the gold design on the edge is displayed to advantage. Their movements are sure and fluid, the intimate dance of their girlhood that they are enacting again, that they are delighted to find they haven't forgotten. They brush the backs of each other's necks with fragrant powder, place a sparkling bindi in the center of each other's forehead. With intense concentration each puts mascara on the other's lashes and blows on it gently. Sudha wants to bundle her hair into a bun, but Anju will not let her. She brushes it until it falls in a shining mass to Sudha's waist. When they have hooked the clasps of each other's necklaces, they look at each other in the narrow bathroom mirror and smile. It is a smile inlaid with sadness. What they have recaptured here, they know, is only an illusion. By tomorrow, it will have dissipated into dust.

"You look like a water spirit who's stepped out of a forest lake at dawn," Sudha says, touching the winking diamonds at Anju's throat.

"And you're like one of the dancing apsaras in the courts of the gods, someone they would willingly give up their godhood to win!"

They laugh at the formal extravagance of their similes. "All those romantic tales Pishi filled our heads with, they don't fit our lives anymore," Sudha says. "Not that they ever did."

"Yeah, we're more like Cinderella, to be turned to servant girls at the stroke of midnight, back to our daily lives of washing dishes and chopping cabbage for curry and writing term papers!"

"Speaking of servant girls"—Sudha hesitates, then plunges on—"do you remember Mangala?"

Anju creases her brow, taken aback by the sudden change in subject. "Mangala? Mangala who . . . ? Oh, I think I know. . . . Back in Calcutta, right? That poor woman—"

"Ladies!" calls Sunil, rapping at the bedroom door. "It's seven-thirty already. Would you perhaps like to get to the party before it ends?"

"We're done," Anju calls back. She holds out her hand for Sudha. "And when you see us, you'll be forced to admit it was worth the wait!"

"Go on," Sudha says. "I'll be with you in just a moment." She shuts the bathroom door behind Anju and stares with narrowed eyes in the mirror. What does she see?

It is the year of taking risks, of facing consequences. In Bangladesh a woman writer criticizes the Quran and must go underground to escape the fatwa. In Abidjan a twenty-year ban against big-game hunting is lifted in the hope of attracting tourist money. And here in a home not hers, Sudha, servant girl turned apsara for a night, a loveliness for the gods to squabble over, trails her finger over the spot in the mirror where Anju's reflection had been.

"Send me away, Anju," she says. "Send me away before it's too late."

&c

Chopra's house is huge and pink, like a giant, lighted cake plopped down on a bald stretch of hillside. There's a uniformed white guard at the gate, to whom Sunil has to show his invitation, then a circular driveway with an illuminated fountain and Grecian-style statuary, mostly nymphs at various stages of undress, or plump, peeing cherubs.

"I feel like I'm inside the villain's mansion in a bad Hindi movie," Anju says.

"You're right about the villain part," Sunil says.

More uniforms ahead, bustling around Benzes and Jaguars.

One of them takes the car keys from Sunil. Another opens the doors for the women. Sunil watches thoughtfully as his old Ford disappears around the bend of the drive. "C'mon, kid," he says to Dayita, swinging her up. "Let's eat them out of house and home."

The inside of the house is a dazzling assemblage of glittering surfaces—marble floors, mirrored walls, crystal chandeliers, glasswork on loud cushions that line overstuffed sofas, paintings studded with rubies and emeralds that look suspiciously real. And, everywhere, multicolored Mylar balloons announcing that it's a Happy Anniversary.

"I love it," Anju whispers. "It's in such splendidly bad taste!"

"It almost makes you want to take a vow of poverty," Sunil whispers back.

"I thought we already had," says Anju, then nudges him with her elbow. "Just kidding!"

Sudha doesn't join their conversation. She's examining one of the paintings, a miniature, the head of a princess dressed medieval-style in a diaphanous veil through which the jewels at her nose and ears shine. It's beautiful, or would be if it weren't hung next to a wincingly orange batik of a mother elephant with her calf. What's going through her mind at her first exposure to wealth in America? Admiration? Disgust? Envy? Is she wondering why Sunil, with his haunted, brilliant eyes, is still living in a two-room apartment, while Chopra wallows in wealth? Is she imagining to how much better use she would put this money if it were hers?

"Ah, I see you're looking at our Tanjore painting," says a voice at her elbow. It is a plump, diminutive woman with very pink lips and frosted eye shadow, and arms heaped with gold bangles that match the glittery furnishings. "Chopra bought a dozen of those on our last trip to India. He's crazy about art, as you can tell." She gestures around the room with a diamond-laden hand, adjusts the folds of her gold-inlaid pink chiffon sari, then looks suddenly suspicious. "We haven't met before, have we? I'm Mrs. Pinky Chopra. And who might you be?"

Sudha should be faltering at the rudeness of the question, to look around for Anju and Sunil to validate her presence. But no. "I'm Sudha Chatterjee," she says calmly. "Visiting from Calcutta. Your husband is my brother-in-law's client." Her words are as cold and distinct as silver coins falling. Her poised smile indicates that Mrs. Chopra might have all the money in the world, but she possesses something more important. She brings her hands together in the briefest of namaskars, a gesture which discourages familiarity, while Mrs. Chopra, backpedaling, gushes about how wonderful it is to meet her.

Have we underestimated Sudha? All this while our vision has been colored by Anju's, who can't help seeing her still as the girl she grew up with, always longing for the impossible, always needing to be protected from reality. But this lifted, burnished face, this steely curve of throat that says, *I won't let you put me down*—this must be how she survived her youth in a society that dismissed her as the poor cousin. She walks across the room, her back erect. Here is the woman who cut through her mother-in-law's plots to control her womb. Who stepped from the security of wifehood onto the stony path of being a mother, alone, in a country where such things meant shame. Who braved the new rules of a new continent because she wanted more in life than a man to take care of her.

Which is the real truth of Sudha? Might as well ask which is the truth of the turtle, the soft flesh its predators crave, or the shell that protects it from them?

She makes her way past crowds of guests; she accepts a glass of wine from a proffered tray; she sees Anju and Sunil and Dayita and waves to them but does not stop. They look so complete without her, the man and woman nestled close against the press of strangers, the child in his arms who sees but doesn't hold out her hands for her. Does this hurt Sudha? There is a heightened color in her cheeks, but there may be many reasons for that.

In her peacock silk, Sudha's body flickers like a blue flame. Whatever it is that burns inside her, it makes men turn to her like sleepwalkers as she passes. Women find themselves laying a vigilant hand on their partners' arms. She seems unaware of this—or is it merely that she doesn't care? She steps out through the double doors into the backyard. Beyond the lapis lazuli aureole of the swimming pool, the lights of the valley glint like a dare. She narrows her eyes; she is ready to take it on. She walks all the way to the edge of the property, to the hillside falling away from her feet. She presses the cold wineglass to her hot cheek, then shivers. When did the evening turn so cold? But she doesn't want to go back in. She takes a sip of wine, makes a slight face at the unfamiliar taste as she swallows, and stares up at the constellations, comparing them to those of her childhood—the water carrier, the crocodile, Kalpurush with his sword. She stares until, as though in response, a star detaches itself from the rest and falls. She moves her head to follow it—there it is, coming closer, its small fire only an arm's length away now, No, it's the lighted end of a cigarette.

That is how she meets Lalit.

❧

"Hi, there!"

His voice is so effortlessly Californian that Sudha is taken aback. But only for a moment.

"Hi, yourself," she says. It's what she's heard women on TV shows say when they don't want to appear too friendly. She gives his tall silhouette a cool glance, notes the dark, well-cut suit, the short, gelled haircut, very au courant. Is that flash an ear stud? She turns elaborately away to focus on the landscape.

"Lovely but cold," he says. His tone makes her turn suspiciously. "The night, I meant." He grins. "You must be freezing. Don't you have a shawl? But maybe your husband's already gone inside to get it for you . . . ?"

She grits her teeth to stop them from chattering. "I'm not cold."

"No shawl and no husband," he says, shaking his head. "Well, at least one of those problems I can help you with." He gives a short bow and disappears into the house before Sudha can say she doesn't need his help, thank you very much.

He returns with a thick black shawl, which he holds out for her to take.

She doesn't. "How did you get it so quickly? Or do you always have one ready, just in case?"

"Cruel, cruel barb. It's one of Pinky's—I know the closet where she keeps them." He pauses expectantly. "Would you like to cross-examine me on how I came upon that piece of classified information?"

"I'll save it for another time," she says and wraps the shawl around herself. She turns back to the lights, a bit bemused. She's never spoken to a man this way. She likes it, though, this thrust-

and-parry, this doubling back. When she faces him again, she says, "Here's some classified information for you. Not having a husband isn't always a problem."

"You're absolutely right! In your case, particularly, it's a wonderful asset. And now that I've conceded to you on this very important matter, my beautiful, unhusbanded stranger, may I take you in to dinner? I promise to bring you back for more view-watching and cross-examining later." He crooks his arm exactly like Rhett Butler in *Gone With the Wind*, which he watched on late-night TV last week. Sudha lays two fingers on Lalit's elegantly tailored sleeve, exactly like Vivien Leigh (she watched the movie, too) and they go in.

◆

Her mother is walking toward her, holding on to the sleeve of a young man she doesn't know. The child considers the man, considers, out of the corner of her attention, the other man (the one she sometimes calls Baba when they're alone), who is watching them as well. She feels impatience rise from him, striations of heat. The new man whispers something to make her mother smile. The child would like to know what it is that makes a smile like that ripple across the geography of her mother's face, turning it into a new, joyous country. It takes them a while to make it across the room. The new man stops a number of times to respond to greetings. When he introduces her mother to his friends, he clasps her elbow lightly and draws her forward. The child watches the other man's jaw grow tight, territorial.

"Ah, Mr. Reddy," he says, when her mother introduces them, giving the younger man's hand the barest of shakes. "And what is it you do?"

"I cut up people when they're unconscious. They even pay me for it. How about you?"

The child senses the man's dislike escalating. He does not trust people who joke so much. But Aunt Anju bursts out laughing. "That's the best description of surgery I've ever heard."

"Smart woman," says the new man. "Appreciates state-of-the-art wit, just like her sister."

"Since we're doing introductions," says the other man, pointing to the child, "this is Dayita."

"Lalit, at your service," says the new man, bowing elegantly to the child. He takes her hand. "Baby fingers, *mmmm*. My favorite food." He pretends to gobble them up. The child decides she's going to like him. She rewards him with a squirmy giggle. "Even more charming than her mother, I see," he says, smiling at Aunt Anju.

Aunt looks awkward. Satisfaction gleams like sweat on the other man's face.

"Actually, she's mine," her mother says.

Lalit's smile doesn't falter. "In that case, a slight revision—almost as charming as her mother. May I have the pleasure?" He holds out his arms and the child leans from Sunil's arms into them. She's being fickle, she knows it, and doesn't care. There's something on Lalit's earlobe, glistening. She's never seen anything like it on a man before. She tugs at his ear.

"Story of my life," sighs Lalit as he guides her mother toward the elaborately catered dinner buffet, complete with tuxedoed servers. "All they want is my body."

❧

The regular lights in the hall have been replaced with a couple of pulsing, disco-style spotlights. The DJ hired by the Chopras starts the music. "Celebration!" booms the first song, blasted from the Chopras' oversized music system. The floor is crowded with two kinds of dancers—those of the Chopras' generation, who are characterized more by enthusiasm than skill, and those of their children's, who know the fancy moves and look upon the efforts of the uncles and aunties with some amusement. A few, like Sunil and Anju, fidget at the edges of the party, watchers who know they don't quite belong. Lalit, though, seems to fit everywhere. He chats about a recent hip-hop concert with a couple of young women in black leather minis and gigantic fluttering eyelashes. He pauses to discuss hot stocks with a group of older doctors, who listen with grave attention to what he has to say. To a plump matron in a too-snug lehnga who insists on knowing who Dayita is, he stage-whispers, "Modesty prevents me from spelling it out—but I'm sure you see how closely she resembles me."

"Oh, you!" she says, shaking her head. "Never serious about anything!"

"Let's all celebrate and have a good time!" he now sings along with the CD as he rocks his way onto the dance floor, still holding Dayita. He moves with an easy, second-generation grace, beckoning to Sudha to join him. His grin is infectious, disarming. He's not a good singer, but he doesn't seem to care what people think. Perhaps it's this ability, so foreign to Sudha's upbringing, where every moment was weighted with the possibility of social censure, that makes her respond. Or is it because she feels Sunil's reproving eyes on her? For a woman who has never been to a dance before, she moves fluidly, comfortable with her body's rhythm. More songs, Hindi movie hits now, *Choli Ke Peeche* and *Jhumma Chumma De De*. She closes her eyes and sways to the beat. Sometimes she clicks her fingers and mouths the

words. When in her sequestered life in Ramesh's house did she pick them up?

Time for toasts. Chopra, a plump, balding man who looks more avuncular than villainous, tells the guests how, early in his marriage when they were living in a roach-infested one-room apartment, Mrs. Chopra pawned her jewelry to help him start his first business. "She's always been my best friend," he ends simply, putting an arm around her, and she blushes.

"You look surprised," Lalit says to Sudha.

"I'm ashamed, actually. I should have remembered how people can be other than what they seem."

Lalit raises an eyebrow—he senses a story here. But all he says is, "Bet you thought Pinky was an empty-headed social butterfly. Just like you thought I was a handsome but heartless rake. But now that you've discovered how caring and unselfish she is—did I mention that she volunteers each week at the homeless shelter in San Jose?—and how charming and intelligent I am—"

"Let's not get carried away."

"That's okay, I forgive you. After all, I thought you were one of those frosty, snobbish Indian princesses, only to find—"

She can't resist. "What?"

"Whoa! This isn't even our first date, and already you want me to expose my soul." He bats his eyelashes exaggeratedly. "What kind of a boy do you think I am?"

The music has changed to a slow number, and Mr. Chopra leads his wife in a gallant, if somewhat lumbering waltz. Most of the younger crowd have moved off the floor. Lalit, too, prepares to sit it out, but Sudha tugs at his sleeve.

"You know how to waltz?"

She laughs, pleased at having surprised him. "The nuns

taught us—with girl partners, of course. They felt it was an art all accomplished young women should know. Anju and I considered it rather ridiculous. In the kind of family we came from, waltzing wasn't exactly an accepted activity!"

"Fascinating!" says Lalit, leading her with one-armed élan, Dayita balanced between their bodies. "And what kind of family did you come from?"

"Now what was that again—about this not even being our first date?"

"Touché, Goddess!" He tries to look abashed.

The music changes again—a fast, loud song—and Sudha spins away, her smile brief and electric.

On the edge of the dance floor, Anju is trying to persuade Sunil to dance.

"Come on! Doesn't it look enjoyable?"

"Not particularly."

"Don't be so stodgy! Come on!"

"You go ahead," he says.

"I will," says Anju, lifting her chin. "Really, I don't understand you! First you make me come to a party where I don't know anyone, then you won't let me have any fun. . . ."

"Who's stopping you?"

"Fine!"

She strides angrily toward Sudha, who sees her and waves. "Join us," she calls, then turns to Lalit. "If it's okay with you . . . ?"

"Are you kidding! Dancing with three women! Is this my lucky day or what!" He must have caught the exchange between Anju and Sunil, but he gives no indication of it. When "Saturday Night Fever" comes on, he twirls first Anju, then Sudha, then swings Dayita up in the air. *"Staying alive, staying alive,"* he sings.

"He's nice," Anju says to Sudha.

"You tell her," says Lalit. "It's what I've been trying to get through to her all evening, but she won't believe me."

Someone is asking Sunil a question. He inclines his head to answer it. But his gaze, hot and pinpointed like the sun through a magnifying glass, is focused on the dance floor, on the women of his house being charmed by another man.

ॐ

Sunil stands on the marble front steps, holding his valet parking tag. He's not happy. For the last twenty minutes he'd been signaling to Anju, who was still on the dance floor with Lalit and Sudha, that it was time to leave. But she kept up an animated conversation with Lalit and wouldn't meet his eyes. Finally he walked up to them and told her he had a splitting headache, they had to go. Anju looked at him accusingly, her face full of disbelief, and Lalit asked if he would like some Excedrin.

"Wouldn't dream of imposing on you further," Sunil said. "You've done more than enough for us already."

The women have gone to change Dayita's diaper. ("Just when I was having a good time," sniffs Anju audibly on the way.) Sunil is trying to get someone to bring him his car. Two attendants who look as if they're in their early twenties are standing to the side, but they're busy ogling the red Camaro that's being driven up and don't see him.

A young couple—he in snazzy red suspenders, she in a spangly dress that barely makes it to her thigh—get into the Camaro and roar away.

One of the attendants gives a low whistle. "Did you see the legs on that broad? And that car! Man, I'd like to get some wheels like that."

His companion snorts. "Fucking Indians, showing off," he says, spitting to one side.

Sunil moves fast, grabbing the arm of the guy's jacket and spinning him around before he's figured out what's happening.

"What did you say?" His voice vibrates with rage.

"Hey, man, let go my arm!"

"I asked, what did you say?"

"Didn't say nothing to you," says the attendant sulkily, trying to pull away. The other youth has melted into the shadows of the driveway.

"Fucking Indians, huh?" says Sunil. "I'll show you exactly how fucking Indians can be." He twists the attendant's arm behind his back with one deft motion. The young man yells with pain and goes down on one knee. There are other guests on the steps now, looking on in wide-eyed horror.

"Oh my God," shouts a woman. "Quick, call Chopra-ji!"

Someone else shouts, "Get the security guard!" People are bumping into each other, trying to get back inside the house.

"Next time you want to talk about Indians, remember this," says Sunil.

Someone's pulling at Sunil's hand with both arms. It's Anju. "Have you gone crazy, let go of him! Let *go!*" She's sobbing. Behind her, Sudha's tense, shocked face, knuckles pressed to her lips. Anju yanks at his hand until he shoves the attendant away. The attendant straightens his jacket and glares at Sunil. His hands are fisted, and so are Sunil's.

But now the security guard, a plump, red-faced man in a uniform a size too small, has arrived. "Hey, hey," he pants.

"What's going on? You! Go report to your supervisor. Go on!" He gives the attendant a shove and turns to Sunil. "Let's not have any trouble here, sir, okay? Let's not ruin the nice party." He summons another valet to bring their car, and finally, thankfully, they're off.

❧

"What on earth got into you?" Anju bursts out even before they've turned the corner of the driveway.

Sunil fiddles with the radio until he finds a talk show where someone's just called in to ask the host if it's true that Nicole's blood—and Ron's—was found on O. J.'s glove.

"Turn that thing off, for God's sake!"

"I'm listening to it."

"I need you to listen to *me*. Besides, what's there to listen? He's obviously guilty."

"How can you jump to a conclusion like that?" Sunil snaps. "Here you are, always talking about people's rights, ever since you made those feminist friends at school. Isn't a person supposed to be innocent until he's found guilty? Or does that only apply to women?"

In the backseat, Sudha stares out the window at the passing dark. Does she guess the real cause for Sunil's anger? Anju presses her lips together. "Leave my friends out of this."

"Leave *me* alone, then."

"Why are you so obsessed with this stupid trial? It isn't like you—"

"What makes you think you know what I'm like?"

Anju draws in an outraged breath, ready for an all-out fight.

"Please," Sudha says in a small voice. "Dayita's sleeping."

Anju makes herself breathe out slowly. She rubs her finger-tips across her eyes, smearing makeup she isn't used to wearing.

"You should tell me what's bothering you, Sunil," she says more softly. "Tell me what that man did. Whatever it is, I'm with you, you know that." She puts her hand on his knee, though such conciliatory gestures are difficult for her. "No mat-ter how crazy you make me." She smiles. "Sorry, couldn't resist that!"

Sunil squeezes her hand briefly. "Maybe later, after I've calmed down a bit."

"You can't let people get to you like this," Anju says. She puts her hand on the back of his neck. "God! Look how tense you are." She kneads the rigid tendons. Light from a streetlamp falls on the small movements of her fingers, on the brief shine of Sudha's eyes in the backseat.

Sunil sighs. "I'm so tired of fighting, Anju."

"Oh, Sunil," Anju says. "You can't lose heart over one little incident, however bad it was."

"You're right," says Sunil unconvincingly. He turns up the radio, but the talk show is done. In its place is someone singing "Can't Help Falling in Love." Sunil listens in spite of himself. When he does speak, it is very softly, as though to himself: "It was a mistake to have come here."

Anju shakes her head. She believes he's talking about Amer-ica, his precarious position in it. But is he referring to the Chopras' dance floor, Sudha's quicksilver feet dancing away from him? Is it himself he's tired of fighting?

Twelve

Letters

Calcutta
May 1994

My dear Anju:

  Pishi and Nalini and I are making plans to go on a pilgrimage yatra, and wondered when Sudha will be returning to India. We want to make sure we are here to greet her and our little granddaughter, who must be so grown up by now.

                              Your loving mother

Dearest Sudha,

  Please let me know if you would like me to send you a copy of Thakumar Jhuli, *or* The Children's Ramayana Picture Book *to read to Dayita. I remember how they used to be your favorites.*

                              Pishi

Dear daughter Sudha,

Since last week, my legs have been swollen and now certain people who shall remain nameless have heartlessly put me on a no-salt diet because they have got it in their heads that we must go on a pilgrimage trip. Personally, I would be more than happy to remain right here in the comfort of my own home.

Your mother (Nalini)

My dear Sudha:

How are you enjoying your visit to America? I know your presence there has given my daughter a new vigor and interest in life, and for that I can never thank you enough. I hope that being with her has given you support also, and clarified what you want in your life.

Your loving aunt Gouri

My dear Anju:

You hardly mentioned Sunil in your letter, nothing except how hard he is working. Is he spending any time at home at all?

Dear daughter Sudha,

Maybe you can come back to Calcutta soon, and then I could stay with you and wouldn't have to go on that pilgrimage and stay in vermin-infested cottages and use bedding that has been urinated on by rats or worse.

Dearest Anju,

Your mother mentions that Sunil is under a lot of stress at work. I am sending some Dashmul tea for him which is very good for stress. It needs to be boiled for twenty minutes. Put in a spoon of honey.

My dear Sudha:

 You still haven't mentioned anything about when you are returning. Isn't your ticket due to expire in a month or so?

Dear daughter Sudha,

 It is at times like this a mother needs her daughter. But of course you're gaily gallivanting around in America instead of being responsibly married while here I have to hobble around half-starved. What can I say! Some people are born with ill fortune!

Dearest Anju,

 We were delighted by the recent photos of Dayita you sent. To think that she now has three teeth and can stand up holding on to things! And so much curly hair, just like when Sudha was a baby! We laughed and laughed, reading of her exploits. Sudha looks lovely as usual. Please send a recent picture of you and Sunil.

Dearest Sudha,

 In your last letter, why did you suddenly ask about Mangala and what happened to her? It was a long time ago, and it is best to forget such terrible, bad-luck things. Thinking of them calls them up into your life. Focus on the future instead.

Calcutta
June 1994

My dear Anju:

 I am disturbed to hear you have taken no recent photos of you and Sunil together. I hesitate to advise you since you are a grown woman, but please try to spend some time alone with Sunil. Can the two of you not go away somewhere for a day or two?

Dear niece Anju,

   Now that you are back in college and doing so well, don't you think it's time you folks sent Sudha back to India? As you know, Someone Very Special is waiting for her here, not to mention that it will help me, too. By the way, could you mail me two bottles of Oil of Olay (large size) and three Yardley's Lavender Soaps by return post? I am running low.

My dear Anju:

   You must know this already—Sunil's father's condition is very serious. Sunil's mother tells me she phoned him at work but he flatly refused to come to India. Please try to persuade him. His mother is very distraught and it would help her greatly to have him with her.

Dearest Sudha,

   You have not answered any of my questions. Let me know soon about the books I wanted to send you, as Book Post here takes forever. Although if you are returning soon it might not be worth the effort. Are you?

Dear daughter Sudha,

   I hope you are observing the rahukal hours listed on that calendar we sent you. Last week when I made my regular trip to my astrologer (with much agony, as my health is at an all-time low) he said that the planet Shani was ascending and it was a time for the Chatterjee women to be careful.

Dearest Sudha,

   You must not let your mother's talk of ill health make you anxious. You know how she exaggerates. The salt-free diet is working quite well, her legs are much less swollen. It would of course work better if she didn't bribe the neighbor children to sneak her pakoras from the street vendor when she is home alone. She's worse than you girls were when you were growing up.

Dear daughter Sudha,

Who told you that I've been eating pakoras? Pure slander. And what do you mean by writing that even if you were still married and in Bardhaman you couldn't have come and taken care of me anyway? I wasn't thinking of Bardhaman and that spineless Ramesh (what a mistake he was) but of our dear Ashok, waiting here so patiently (like me) for your return.

My dear Anju:

I'm surprised that Sunil had not told you about his father, but less surprised that you couldn't persuade him to visit his father. Your husband is a proud man—it's at once his strength and failing. A reconciliation would have been helpful for everyone, most of all perhaps for Sunil. But I can understand his reluctance. Mr. Majumdar is a most difficult individual. If it weren't for his poor, sweet wife, I, too, would stay away from him. Who knows what scars are hidden in Sunil's heart. Be sympathetic.

Dear daughter Sudha,

Did I remember to tell you that Ashok visits us at least once every week, and always with a thoughtful gift—a big basket of fruits from Jogu Babu's market, fresh sandesh made from a secret family recipe by his mother, or spicy fried cashews from Haldiram's (which I might add I am not allowed even to touch). And why shouldn't he! He's certainly rich enough!

My dear Sudha:

Today Ashok told me, with much hesitation, that you haven't replied to any of his letters. I was so taken aback I didn't know what to say. Is there *some problem? Please let me know what is in your mind. I will help in whatever way I can.*

Dear daughter Sudha,

    I am shocked to learn from your letter that you are selfishly thinking of changing your ticket and extending your stay. It's that headstrong Anju's doing, I'm sure. Ever since childhood, she's been a bad influence on you. Obviously, daughterly duty means nothing to you, so I won't even bring it up. But what I want to ask is, do you think Ashok will wait for you forever?

Dearest Sudha,

    I can't understand why you keep asking me about Mangala. There really isn't much to her story, though certainly it's a tragic one. She was run over by a car one night as she was crossing the road to pick up some paan from the corner shop for the old Rai Bahadur for whom she worked. Some drunk driver, I guess. They never did catch him. No, I don't remember any plot against her. I don't know where you got such a fanciful notion.

Dearest Anju,

    Your last letter sounded so sad. Don't feel guilty about not being able to persuade Sunil. Men are stubborn that way, especially with their wives. Even your dear father, the kindest of men, was no better. We are all helping Sunil's mother here. Ashok does a lot, too—picking up medicines, taking the old man to the doctor—without ever complaining. Do you have any idea why Sudha's stopped writing to him?

Daughter Sudha,

    What is this nonsense about wanting to stay in America to earn your own money! Doing what, may I ask? It's not as though you're a trained engineer or a computer scientist. You always were a foolish girl. At least think of

*Dayita's future, which will be far more stable with Ashok, who has ten times
more money than you can ever make.*

Calcutta
July 1994

My dear Anju:

*It was lovely to hear your voice on the phone yesterday when I called.
I'm sorry everyone else was still sleeping—I guess they were still tired out
from the party last night. Your description of the party was very entertaining. The vulgar rich are the same everywhere, aren't they! I'm so glad Sunil
is finally making some time to relax with you. I'm not sure what to make of
Lalit. Is he really interested in Sudha, and she in him? What does Sunil
think of this development?*

Dearest Sudha,

*I hear from your mother that you have found an admirer in America. I
can only hope that she is exaggerating as usual. If not, I must ask if you've
forgotten Ashok, who is waiting in the belief that you will return to him?
You might be in a new age and a new country, but surely there's still such a
thing as keeping trust? I'm sorry if I sound harsh, but I foresee much trouble
ahead if you give in to desire without caring for integrity.*

Dear, dear daughter Sudha!

*I'm delighted that you have finally made a debut into high society. The
party sounds wonderful. Anju has told me about the new man you met—
though not as much as I want to know. No matter. All surgeons in America,
I know, are millionaires. And all millionaires (especially dollar millionaires)
are handsome. For heaven's sake, get yourself some of that Revlon Anti-*

Wrinkle Cream with Retinol—I read about it in Femina *magazine. God knows you are no spring chicken anymore. (In case you didn't notice, I am practicing American. Who knows when it might come in handy. You'll be proud of how much I've picked up from Mrs. Jaypal, who as you know goes every year to visit her son in Poughkeepsie.) So this is why you were reluctant to hurry back to us, you sly thing! You should have confided in your mother! You know that I always want the very best for my girl. Don't worry about trouble from Certain People at this end. I will take care of Everything. A surgeon! Well, I have always wanted to visit America!*

Thirteen

Sudha

The calendar which the mothers gave me before leaving is Indian-style, printed on very thin white paper. There are no pictures—its makers did not believe in anything so frivolous. The future is, after all, a serious thing! The Indian months and days are marked in red Bengali lettering. The English ones are printed underneath in a small, innocuous blue. It indicates all our festivals, even minor ones like Jamai Shasthi, when sons-in-law are invited and served their favorite dishes. It tells us which days are auspicious, and which bad luck. Little diagrams mark full moons and no moons, and the thin sliver of the eleventh night, which is a time for women without husbands to fast and pray for purification. Handwritten notes on the bottom of each page warn us of the dangerous hours: rahukal, which shifts each day with the movement of the planets, when it is good to lie low. My mother paid an astrologer from Kanya Kumari an inordinate amount of money—or so she claimed—to calculate them for us.

I hung the calendar on the kitchen wall where Anju would

see it every time she opened the refrigerator. This way, I figured, she could keep track of festivals and holy days. But all she ever looked at were the cautionary tidbits from the margin of each page. She snickered as she read them aloud: *People who begin a journey in the month of Bhadra never come back. A wedding conducted in Aashwin ends in calamity. Books should not be read but only worshipped on Saraswati Puja, the day dedicated to the goddess of learning.* Juxtaposed against the pasteurized convictions of America, I had to admit they seemed a bit suspect. And yet our people had followed them for centuries. Could they be totally wrong?

It would be nice if I had events to jot down on the calendar, days to look ahead to. The act of recording them would have given me a semblance of control. But, so far, the few things we've scheduled and done—visits to malls and to Marine World Africa USA, a movie here and there, a poetry reading at Anju's college, where I sat like a lump of lead, ashamed because I couldn't understand—don't seem to me worth noting. My life spreads around me like spilled glue. The few important occurrences that bubble up through it—the flying women, Sara, Lalit, the kiss—are ones I didn't plan for.

There's just one thing I've marked on the calendar. I did it before I left India. I circled, with Gouri Ma's Parker fountain pen, the date on which I was supposed to return. I wrote nothing by it, but we all know. Once, when he thought no one was looking, Sunil rubbed at the ink with his thumb as though to erase it. Sometimes Anju flipped the pages to stare at the dark circle. At first she would say, Don't worry, Sudha, we can extend your visa. But now that my departure is only two months away, she says nothing. Does she want me gone, then? It hurts me. But if I had been in her place, watching my husband watch my cousin, could I have wanted anything different? I, too, long to leave. But not for India. It's been a week since the party. Lalit hasn't called. Why did I think he would? What do I think he can give me? In bed, unable to sleep, I repeat Sara's name like a mantra, willing her to reappear, holding the password that will make America swing open for me like the automatic door in a grocery.

ॐ

The phone rings on Monday morning just after Anju and Sunil have left. I rush to it, abandoning Dayita in the middle of her Cream of Rice cereal, though I know she will make use of my absence to smear it all over herself. I cross my fingers and hold my breath. *Sara?*

"You sound disappointed," says Lalit.

"No, no. It's just that I was expecting someone else."

He puts on a husky, movie-villain voice. "Who is this so-foolhardy man who dares come between us?"

This is what I like most about this man: he makes me laugh.

"It's a woman, actually—"

"Oh, Ms. Chatterjee, I'm shocked beyond belief!" Lalit makes choking sounds. "I never would have guessed that you were inclined that way. A good Indian girl like you . . ."

It takes me a moment to catch on. My face is hot with embarrassment. Then I hear myself saying, "I could be per-suaded to reform." As on the night of the party, delight ripples across my skin. What fun, what freedom, to play like this with a man.

"I live again! So how about our date?"

"What date?" My heart beats deafeningly.

"The message I left with your brother-in-law last week, ask-ing if I could take you out this Saturday. Didn't he tell you?"

I'm shocked into silence. For a moment I can't believe that Sunil would do something so deceptive. No, I take it back. It's *exactly* what I should have expected of him.

"I guess he didn't," Lalit says dryly.

I'm so furious, I can't trust my voice. How dare he!

"Sudha? You there?"

I briefly consider pretending that I forgot. No. Why should I protect Sunil? I don't owe him anything, not after this.

"Is that a silence signifying unbelievable joy, or stunned horror? Let me assure you, madam, that I am a man of honorable intentions. However, if you still don't trust me, we could take your delightful daughter along as chaperon."

From the kitchen, a crash. Dayita must have thrown down her cereal bowl. Now I'll have to clean the whole floor.

"You don't have to get that excited about it!"

"I . . . well . . ." I abandon all attempts at wit. "I'll have to check with Anju and Sunil." I hate how defensive I sound. "After all, I am their guest here—"

I'm afraid Lalit will come back with a smart comment and then I'll hate him, too. But all he says is, "That's cool. Give me a call tonight after you've spoken to them." Then he asks, "Did you ever hear the one about the surgeon and his rich patient?"

"No," I say distractedly. I must confront Sunil about what he did. Soon. But where might such a confrontation lead?

"The surgeon says, 'I think I'll give you a local anesthetic before the operation.'

" 'Oh, no, Doctor,' says the patient. 'I can afford the best. Get me something imported.' "

Against my will, a laugh breaks from me.

"And now, a riddle," he adds, sounding pleased. "What's the difference between a soldier and a lady?"

"What?" I'm feeling a little better now. Saturday, I think. A tendril of excitement unfurls inside me.

"I'll tell you when I see you."

෨෫

It's time for Dayita's bath. She wants me to fill the tub—she's seen it on some *Sesame Street* show—but our tub looks too dirty, with generations of rust stains that won't come off no matter how much I scrub. So I compromise by filling a bucket with water and putting her water toys in it. I pour in a little shampoo—we have no bubble bath—and stir it up. I put a small plastic stool in the bathtub for her to sit on. She makes her rubber duck nosedive into the foam with a terrific splash that wets my sari, but I stop myself from scolding her. So what if I have to change my clothes, and mop up the bathroom afterward. I'm tired of saying no, which seems to be the only word I'm capable of speaking to her nowadays.

When Dayita has played enough, I massage her with mustard oil. Usually she squirms away, but today she's cooperative. It's so rare, this moment of harmony between us, my hands gliding over her arms and legs. I marvel at their smoothness, their unexpected strength. "Do you know, when you were born, your whole hand was less than the length of my little finger," I tell her. She grabs my finger as I lay it on her palm. I tell her to close her eyes so I can pour water over her head. She squinches them shut obediently, and I'm struck by love for her. Sharp as shrapnel, sweet as burning tea. I wish I felt it more often.

෨෫

Anju drops her book bag on the floor with a bang, making me jump. "I've remembered! Wasn't Mangala that pretty maidservant who worked in the big white house on our street? The house owned by that rich old man, ex-king of someplace or other? Whatever made you think of her after all these years?"

She's caught me by surprise. I'd forgotten that I'd brought up the topic—when was it?—on the night of the party. Now, thinking of what Pishi wrote, I feel a moment of unease. Maybe it's true that it brings bad luck to dig into memories best left buried.

Mangala. Her slim, pretty figure comes to my eyes. Dark, glistening skin set off by a sunflower-yellow sari. A turned-up, impudent nose. She used to pass by our house on the way to the milk depot every morning. If we were at the gate, she would smile and say, Namaskar, didimonis, how are you? She wore anklets with small silver bells and lined her eyes with kajol. She swung her hips with frank exuberance. My mother said, darkly, That girl's asking for trouble.

After the accident, she said, What did I tell you? Let this be a lesson to you two.

I shiver involuntarily. "Nothing—it was nothing," I say to Anju. "Listen, we've run out of milk. How about walking down to the grocery with me?"

"Don't try to prevaricate. You're so bad at it, it's pathetic! I'm going to keep at you till you tell me, so you might as well do it now."

All through our childhood Anju's been this way. If a puzzle caught her eye, she couldn't rest until she solved it. If a situation intrigued her, she'd ask questions until the mothers, exasperated, sent her to her room. She had to get to the bottom of every mystery she came across. I'd thought marriage would have taught her more caution.

I sigh. "It was the Simpson trial. Something about the dead wife's face. Do you remember how Mangala died?"

"She got run over. It was terribly sad. She used to be so pretty, so full of life—"

"There was more to it than that. The Rai Bahadur's son fell in love with her and wanted to marry her. His father tried to stop him, but he wouldn't listen. Nor would Mangala. The old man offered her a lot of money if she left, but she refused. That was when the accident occurred."

Anju frowns. "Are you sure?"

"I'm sure," I say, though suddenly I'm not. Pishi might have pretended to forget Mangala's story, but Anju's perplexed face is guileless. "I overheard the neighborhood aunties talking about it a couple of times when they came over for tea. I'm positive I told you about it."

Anju shakes her head slowly.

"Anju! How can you forget something like that?" My voice is wobbly, disoriented. I feel as if I'm suspended in space. No, not in space. Inside a giant, suffocating ball of cotton wool. There was a book we studied in class twelve, just before Mother took me out of school. It was about a future society where they'd remove all accounts of the past that they didn't want people to know about from books, movies, songs, everything. They'd put what they wanted in its place, and after a while everyone believed that that was what actually happened. It was terrible because it was so deliberately done.

But isn't it worse when such an erasure happens unconsciously?

"Anju, try to remember! People whispered that it was a setup—the old man had sent Mangala to the corner paan shop to get some betel leaves. But there never was a trial. The old man was too powerful—he bribed all the right folks."

"Sudha," Anju says doubtfully, "are you sure you're not getting this mixed up with a movie you saw, or maybe a story from one of those mystery magazines Aunt N. used to read all the time?"

If no one recalls what you remember, is what happened real anymore?

"I'm certain!" I'm angry now, and scared. How far we've moved from each other, my cousin and I. Even our memories are marooned on separate islands. "And then, just a few months later, the old man arranged a marriage for his son with some rich factory owner's daughter. It was very grand—fireworks, a band, everything. The whole street attended the wedding feast—especially the whispering neighbors."

"Now that part I'm ready to believe!"

"It was as though poor Mangala had never existed," I say. "I can't help wondering whether, if all this had happened here, she would have found some justice."

"I don't know," says Anju. "You're too romantic about what goes on in America. There are a lot of silenced women here. The *no-money, no-rights* rule works here, too. And bribery. It's just not as blatant. The media's making all this fuss about Nicole's case only because O. J. was a celebrity, and it's the kind of scandal people love to watch. It's got very little to do with love of justice."

Sometimes when I lie sleepless, trying to comprehend the shape of my life, I imagine how the dead might spend their nights. Would they be hovering over the beds of those they had loved or hated, emanating blessings or curses? Would they haunt their dreams? I think I feel something silvery, nervelike, linking me to those who are gone, even though I knew them so slightly. Singhji, Mangala, Nicole, Prem. A breath on my forehead, sighed-out syllables I can't quite catch. A movement, shimmery with impatience, glimpsed out of the corner of an eye. A gesture which might mean, *Listen harder!*

"What are you thinking now?" asked Anju.

I say nothing. She'd just call me fanciful. In any case, how could I bear to tell her that the reason I long to connect with the dead is because she's gone from me.

❧

I wait until after I've served dinner. Then I tell them about Lalit's call. I give Sunil a hard look as I speak. He looks back at me, all innocence, then goes back to cutting his chicken into neat, unperturbed cubes.

"I knew it!" Anju clasps her hands together theatrically. "Take her to one party, and already she has suitors knocking at the door!"

"Stop it! He just wants to show me around."

"Yeah, sure!"

"I don't think she should go," Sunil tells Anju.

Speak to me directly, you coward!

"After all, we hardly know him."

I'm not exactly asking for your permission, you know. I didn't leave a marriage and travel halfway across the world so you could set yourself up as my guardian. Not that it's my welfare you're concerned with, you hypocrite.

"In that case we needn't worry!" Anju says. "Didn't we hear the other night, on one of those talk shows you seem to have grown addicted to, that women are attacked by strangers far less often than by people close to them?"

"Is that supposed to be a joke?" Sunil asks. "If it is, I must say you're developing a strange sense of humor."

"It's better than not having any humor at all, like certain people I could name."

"Excuse me," I say, before the situation deteriorates further. "I've already decided to go with Lalit. I just wanted to let you know."

Silence bristles around my announcement. Then Sunil picks Dayita up. "And what about her?" The two of them give me identical, accusing stares.

"I . . . well, I could . . ."

Anju comes to my rescue. "We'll keep Dayu!"

"I might have to go in to work," Sunil says frostily.

Anju gives him an exasperated, wifely look.

"I'll keep her, then," she says. "Don't give it another thought! You go and have a great day with your amor." She gives Sunil a wicked glance. "Oops, did I say amor? You guys will have to forgive me, this is only my first quarter of Spanish. I meant amigo, of course!"

❧

"Great!" Lalit says when I phone him. "I'll pick you up at ten A.M. and take you up to the City. We'll have the wildest, wickedest time. Maybe I'll never bring you back."

Though I know he can't hear, I shoot a quick glance at Sunil. From behind the newspaper, that refuge of so many males, he's whispering something to Anju.

"Why are you being so obsessively patriarchal?" Anju replies. "She's a grown woman—quite able to take care of herself."

I find a pen and walk to the calendar. At last I have something to write on it! But against my will my eyes are pulled to

Sunil. All I can see of him are his hands, gripping the paper. His nails are neat, careful, boyish. Why do they make me sad? When they first met, Anju was crazy about him. She would copy out entire love poems from her English textbook for him. She'd talk about him to me for hours.

No, I won't write anything. Each time Sunil passed by and saw Lalit's name, it would be like salt rubbed into a wound.

I put the pen away and start on the dishes. And so I don't see, until it's too late, that 10:00 A.M. Saturday sits squarely in the middle of the rahukal hours.

"For heaven's sake! Give her your cell phone if you're so worried," I hear Anju snap as she gathers up her books and moves to the bedroom. "Then she can call if there's a problem, and you can go get her."

Is this the way passion must end?

Only later will I be struck by my cousin's choice of pronouns. *You*, not *we*.

❧

Monday . . . Tuesday . . . Wednesday . . . Thursday. I cook and do laundry, take Dayita to the park. Out of old habit, I glance around for Sara, but am not unhappy when I don't find her. For the moment, I've given up on desperation. I play baby tag, I watch Oprah and Mr. Rogers, I learn American gestures. Impatience burns me like a heat flash, in between I'm calm as ice. I scrub the bathroom, I turn the radio up loud to dance. I eat healthy, I bathe long, I scrub my face with turmeric and besan and put fuchsia polish on my toenails. I dream terrible, guilty dreams. After dinner, Sunil plays finger games with Dayita. I wash the dishes, Anju dries. Or, rather, she flourishes the kitchen towel and recites lines from the "Clerk's Tale," which they're studying in one of her classes. The old words, half-mysterious, half-familiar, sound like bells from some foreign land.

"Talk about male fantasies!" she adds. "You won't *believe* this woman Griselda. No, actually, you will—she's a photocopy of so many of our Indian heroines. Sita, Savitri, Damayanti. It's like they all trained at the same academy, got the same M.R.S. degree."

"M.R.S.?"

"You know, short for martyrs."

I smile, but only a little part of me is listening. The rest is deep down and dancing. The strobe lights pulse. Jeweled women dart around me like hummingbirds. *That's the way, uh huh, uh huh, I like it, uh huh, uh huh.* Wild me, wicked me. The me that's given up on the M.R.S. degree. I swim through an ocean of fun, all the fun that my past denied me.

About my future I will not think.

Folly and frivolity, my mother would have said. My mother-in-law would have called it sin. Pishi would have warned me that when we desire something so much, the gods snatch it away. Even Gouri Ma would have advised caution. I turn my back on them all and ask Anju, "What's the difference between a soldier and a lady?"

She looks at me blankly. "Huh?"

My laughter carries me all the way to Saturday morning. A laughter in which anxiety is suspended like sediment in a rushing river.

❧

But first there's Friday. On Friday the phone rings, again right after Anju and Sunil leave. I'm smiling as I pick it up. Ah so, the good doctor is a creature of habit.

"Soo-dah, please," says an American-female voice.

My heart struggles like a caught animal. "That's me."

"I'm Lupe. Sara gave me your number—"

"Where *is* Sara? I haven't seen her for ages. She said she'd call me, but she never did." A thought that I hadn't considered earlier strikes me. "Is she in trouble?"

Lupe pauses. Then she says, "You still looking for a job?"

"Yes!"

"Hasn't been easy finding a job for you. It's because of the baby. No one wants a nanny with a baby. But, finally, I got something. It isn't that good a situation, though, I'll tell you up front."

"Oh," I say.

"This woman, she needs a caretaker for her father-in-law for when she goes to work. He's bedridden and has a bit of a temper. She didn't tell me that part, but I have ways. A lot of times he gets confused, loses control of his bladder, stuff like that. You've got to clean him, make him eat, give him his medicine. That kind of thing. You want it?"

My heart sinks. I'd hoped for an easygoing, sunny child to baby-sit, like Sara's Joshua. A companion to Dayita. They'd play together and take naps at the same time. They'd never fight.

"Let me think about it," I say, for politeness's sake. But I already know. As a child, I'd visited too many families where old relatives lived. Sometimes we children would peek into their rooms, which were always the small ones at the back of the house. I clearly remember the distinct, sour odor of the wasted bodies, the crazed eyes that grabbed yours and wouldn't let go, the thin, silvery drool, like snail tracks, on their chins.

I'm not that desperate.

Still, I take down Lupe's number. I'll call her each week. Surely something better will turn up.

"They're Indian, by the way. At least he is." Another strike against them. Indians are the worst employers, Sara had said. Treat you like shit, and then gossip among their friends about you.

"That's why she agreed to try you," Lupe says. "Baby and all. She thinks it'll help if you talk to him in his language."

"We have a lot of languages in India," I say. "I might not speak his."

It's a good thing I've already made up my mind not to take this job.

"Is Sara okay?" I ask one last time. "Do you have her number?"

"She'll call you when she can," says Lupe, who has obviously mastered the art of evading questions.

Fourteen

Assignment

Write a brief (approximately five hundred words) character sketch of a person you know closely. Choose a person you normally have difficulty understanding. The paper should give us a distinct sense of a personality and the motivations/obsessions that drive him/her. Clarify your relationship to this person. This assignment is to help you comprehend this character more fully and to prepare you for your next paper for the course, a full-length memoir piece about this person.

My Name is Sunil
by
Anju Majumdar
for
English 3162
Memoir
Prof. W. Lindley

The first time I dreamed of the eagle was when I was nine. My father

had just allowed me to have a pet, which I had been wanting for years. It was a gray rabbit. I named it Alexander, because we had been studying Greek history in school. My father thought it was a stupid name for a rabbit, but he didn't say too much because I had been chosen for the school football team, the youngest player in my division, and he was pleased.

We were playing against the Bakul Bagan Boys School that evening. It was a rainy day, the field was so muddy we couldn't even see the grass. I kept slipping, missing the ball. Once I fell hard and felt the pain slice through my knee. But I didn't stop because Father was out there watching, he'd come home early from work just for me. The ball was coming right at me, chased by a group of boys who all looked very large and fierce. One of them had a straggly mustache, like a hairy caterpillar that had shed most of its hair. As I was thinking this, he slammed into me. I fell with my leg twisted under me and couldn't get up until the referee blew the whistle and helped me off the field. Our team lost, bad. I was afraid to see the expression on my father's face. When I finally dared to look for him among the spectators, I couldn't find him. It took me a while to get home—the coach had to bandage up my knee, which was swollen, and when I was let off at the school bus stop, there was no one waiting for me. I didn't have enough money to hire a rickshaw, so I limped home. When I got there, Alexander was gone. No one ever told me what happened to him.

That night I dreamed of the eagle. I was in a field. It came out of the sky like a black feathered meteor. I was terrified, but then it swooped down and put me on its back. We flew up until the earth was as small as a marble, and I knew I'd never have to go back to it. I put my arms around the eagle's neck and felt the heat from her body. Her feathers were like melted bronze. The wind roared in my ears and I thought, This must be what love feels like.

For the next few years, each time something terrible happened, I dreamed of the eagle, and she kept me going. Then I went away and things got better. I did well in college, I got a job in America. I got married to a woman who was smart and funny, if not as beautiful as I'd wanted. I even liked her temper. It made life interesting. There were still some unhappy things in my life, but I didn't have to think about them. I was working hard at making a good life, I was working harder at becoming a good person, and this was important because we were about to have a baby.

But the baby died. The baby died and the field was oozy brown like chocolate sauce, no, like shit, and it was sucking me in, I breathed it, it covered my eyeballs, it seeped in through my pores. It was worse than dying. I groped to find my wife, but she was lost in her own shit field, and I didn't have the strength to care. With my last breath, I called for the eagle.

No eagle appeared, not then.

Later (there's always a later, isn't there, no matter how bad things get), when I came back to the tatters of myself, I found I was no longer the same. I no longer believed in happiness, and thus didn't believe in the need for goodness either. Still, I tried. I tried to shore up my wife; I tried to salvage my waterlogged career. I tried to cut myself loose from anger and make do with what life had seen fit to leave me. Some days, waking, I had to ask myself what my name was. But this much I knew: I wasn't ever going to want anything as desperately as I'd wanted my baby.

Then She came back into my life. Flew all the way from India with her melted bronze eyes. A dislocated gear slammed back into place in my head, and I, Sunil, kicked off morality and obligation like a pair of worn-out shoes.

Ms. Majumdar:

This is well written and powerful in its impact, but a bit of a surprise. It's more of a dramatic monologue (which we do not cover in this class) than a character sketch, which is what I'd asked for.

The character of Sunil is a strong one, though somewhat monodimensional. I am not sure this assignment has helped you understand him further. Nor am I certain of your relationship to him. The narrative intelligence in the essay is not sufficiently male (too emotional). Can you work on this?

Your comparisons are quite good (the hairy caterpillar, for example), but you tend to mix your metaphors unnecessarily (see last paragraph) and sometimes use too many, one after another, which makes all of them less effective (see last paragraph, again). Why is the eagle sometimes an "it" and sometimes a "she"? And sometimes a "She"??

What, by the way, does the last paragraph mean? It's very ambiguous.

I liked the beginning of the essay, but as the paper went along it became somewhat overwrought and abstract. I've noticed this shortcoming in other papers of yours as well.

I'm not sure how you will work this into a full-length memoir piece. Maybe you should just start over with a subject you feel less emotional about.

William Lindley

Fifteen

Anju is restless tonight. Her sleep is a cave filled with murky water, lit by the phosphorescent fins of alien fauna. She swims around it in circles, she dips her face in the water and lets the seaweed caress her features. She raises her face to snatch a breath of uncertain, brackish air. Sometimes she opens her eyes onto her bedroom and sees nothing. Sometimes she shuts them quickly as though she would rather not see what is there.

Eleven P.M. Midnight. One A.M. She leaves the bed and goes to the living room. She removes from her backpack the note-book with the letters to her father. The light from the lamp falls on them damply, as though the room were filled with fog, or tears. Anju reads with concentration, moving her lips silently. She loves the faithfulness of words. How, once you've held them in your mouth, they become yours.

She knows this also: there may come a time when theirs will be the only loyalty she can count on.

Dear Father,

Some nights, lying down to sleep, I feel I am losing my body. Where are my feet, my hands, my face? Dark erases the line of my cheek and draws in another's. Where is the shape of my life? My knees float away into the blackness of the bedroom. The hairs on my head rise into the sky in separate strands. You must not think this frightens me. I am exhilarated by the regrouping of my cells. They tell me I can be someone else—anyone I want. If only I could decide who.

Dear Father,

Today when I walked out of the classroom a sudden gust of wind tossed the smell of wild ginger at me—though of course there is no wild ginger growing anywhere on campus. Suddenly I understood why you left us. The allure of newness. It tugs at me like time tugs at the snake's skin, persuading him to shrug it off. But what if, shrugging off my old life, I find I am not a snake but an onion instead? Peel after peel after peel, and then: nothing.

Father,

Sometimes, reading a new book, I grow so excited I forget to breathe. There's so much to learn, and already I've lost so much time. Each day new worlds glimmer around me. I am like a nearsighted person wearing her first glasses. Apartheid. Midnight's Children. The Internet. Aung San Suu Kyi. Then I think, what good is all this information? What will it change in my life? In my husband's face?

Here is a fact: I am of no use to my household. If I disappeared tomorrow, Sudha would grieve, Dayita would look for me behind curtains and doors, wondering if this were some long game of hide-and-seek. Sunil would call the police. But soon they would draw together, the way flesh pulls itself close to heal a wound. Not even a scar would remain.

There is a sound at the bedroom door. Anju does not startle. She does not whisk the notebook out of sight. Does she want, then, to be discovered? Does she want Sunil to see the questions she has written for her father? Does she wish him to answer them?

"Anju! What are you doing!" says Sunil in a drowsy voice. Anju opens her mouth to speak, then realizes that he doesn't want a reply. Already he's turning away. "Come to bed," he says. "You'll be dead tired tomorrow."

Anju puts away her books. In bed, slipping into the flooded cave of sleep, she begins to make a list. It is a list of things to take with her when she disappears.

৯৯

Sudha, too, has been writing. The letter sits on her bedside table now, an oblong of ghostly white in the darkened room.

Ashok,

I apologize for not answering your letters. Writing takes a lot of strength, and I didn't—don't—have any to spare.

When I came away from India, I told you not to wait for me. I'm saying it again. I don't know when I'll return, if at all. I'm discovering that my divorce was like a surgeon's scalpel. It cut the past out of my flesh, the good with the bad. Now I must find other things to live for.

I left you twice—the first time to marry, the second time to come to America. I don't want there to be a third time.

It's best this way. Remember the old tales about the Vish Kanyas? Women bred on poison, whose kisses brought destruction wherever they went? I think I'm one of them.

When I seal this envelope, I'm going to forget you.

You must do the same. Believe me, you'll be happier for it.

꽃

"Don't tell me this is what you're going to wear!" Anju's voice rises in disbelief.

"I won't tell you, then," Sudha smiles. She's dressed in one of Anju's old jeans and a plain white T-shirt. Her hair is tied back in a no-nonsense ponytail. Her scrubbed, girl-next-door face is beautiful in a whole new way, accentuating the smoky allure of her eyes.

Anju doesn't think so. "You look like the ugly duckling," she snaps.

"We'll have to see if my frog prince recognizes me, then."

Anju refuses to be amused. "You've got your fairy tales mixed up. At least put on some makeup. A pair of earrings."

Sudha shakes her head. "I don't want—" she starts, then breaks off as Sunil enters the room. The scowl on his face gives way to a more pleasant look as he stares at the plainness of her getup. "How about I make breakfast today?" he says after a moment.

"Are my ears working right?" Anju asks. "Did I hear the man say he'll cook for us?"

"Anju!" Sudha says.

"It's just that I never knew he could," Anju says.

"She always did have a conveniently short memory."

"Stop it, you two!" Sudha says, laughing. She helps Sunil find flour and eggs, a nonstick pan. He turns out surprisingly good Indian pancakes, crisp and golden, studded with onions and green chilies and mustard seed, to be eaten with ginger pickle. For Dayita he mixes molasses into the batter and makes small sweet ones shaped like jellyfish. When she clears her plate and clamors for more, he smiles. It's the kind of smile only Dayita can pull out of him, delighted and boyish.

When Lalit rings the doorbell, Sunil swings the door open in a magnanimous arc and invites him to join them. If Lalit is taken aback by this sudden friendliness, his expression doesn't give it away. It must be part of the training they give them in med school.

Hellos all around the table. A cheery one from Lalit, a subdued one from Sudha, an exuberant one from Anju, accompanied by loud fork-banging from an excited Dayita. Lalit pulls up a chair close to Sudha.

"How's it going?" The way he cocks his head, like an intelligent bird, and waits for her answer transforms the question into something deeper. Anju clears her throat teasingly. Sudha blushes and mumbles a brief reply. At the stove Sunil's grin has turned Machiavellian. He sprinkles extra chilies onto the pancake he's making for Lalit.

"Looks great!" Lalit says, and takes an enthusiastic bite.

"Hope it isn't too spicy for you," Sunil says sweetly.

"No, no, it's fine," Lalit says. He dabs surreptitiously at his forehead, where sweat has broken out.

"Here, have some orange juice," Anju says.

"Personally, I like mine spicier," Sunil says.

Anju, who knows he has a weak stomach, gives him a look. "You don't have to eat all those chilies, Lalit. Just pick them out. Sudha, get him another glass of juice."

Lalit, who is coughing, gives her a grateful glance. But soon he's recovered enough to tell them a newlyweds joke. "So the wife's serving him his first meal. She says, This is one of the two things I cook really well, dear: chicken curry and rice pudding. And he replies, It's lovely, darling. Which one is it, by the way?"

Sunil interrupts the laughter. "Since you like jokes so much, here's one. Did you hear about the doctor whose fiancée jilted him? Not only did he take back the diamond ring he gave her, he charged her for twenty-four house calls."

There's a moment of utter silence. Then Lalit chuckles. He's amused, and not just at the joke. "I'll have to remember that one," he says and drains his glass of juice.

They're all laughing now. A sliver of sunshine falls across the dining table. Sunil holds Dayita aloft like a sign. "Say, *Have a nice day, Mother,*" he instructs. "Say, *Don't do anything I wouldn't do.*"

"Bring her back before dark," Anju says. "She turns into a pumpkin when the sun goes down."

Everyone laughs again. They are one happy family.

੭ਦ

They're eating in the gardens of the Palace of Fine Arts, festive red-and-white cartons of Chinese takeout surrounding them. Sudha confesses it's her first time with chopsticks.

"It's simple," says Lalit. "Just watch me."

He picks up a peanut from the kung pao chicken with a grand flourish of his sticks, and loses it just before it reaches his mouth.

Sudha bursts out laughing, dropping her own precariously held piece of chicken in the process. "Stop! I think I just sprained my laugh muscles!"

"Madam, you must not be exercising them regularly," Lalit says with severity. "As your doctor, I prescribe the following: ten giggles, twenty snickers, and thirty chuckles daily."

"Please! No more! You'll be the death of me! Haven't you heard what they say about too much laughter?"

"Wow, another arcane Indian maxim! Wait, let me get out my notebook. . . ."

❧

This is what Sudha doesn't know:

The day she found out that Sudha's mother-in-law was demanding she have an abortion, Anju was so upset that she did something that was rare for her: she called Sunil at work. When she told him the news, he was oddly silent. But she was too agitated to notice.

"You know how back in India people believe that each person's allotted a certain amount of good fortune when they're born?" she asked. "They say that's why people born with too much beauty have problems with other things in their lives—they've used up their luck. Do you think there's any truth to it? Sunil? Are you there?"

"I don't know," Sunil said finally. "I'm not even sure I know what's good luck and what isn't. Something happens, you think it's wonderful. A couple years later you can't stand it."

"I hate it when you make these vague philosophical statements," Anju said impatiently. "How can anyone be confused about what's good luck and what's bad? My being pregnant, for example. It's the luckiest thing that's ever happened to us."

"You're right," Sunil said. He drew in his breath as though about to ask her about something else—the possibility of Sudha's divorce, perhaps—whether it would be indicative of misfortune or its opposite. But she'd already moved on.

"It's a silly belief, anyway, about you having only so much luck in your life. When we were growing up, Aunt N. used to tell us, *Joto hasi toto kanna—How much you laugh today, that's how much you'll cry tomorrow*. I hated that saying, I still do. And I refuse to believe it."

"That's smart," Sunil said. His voice sounded tinny and small and sad, as though he envied his wife her certainty.

❦

Behind them, the fluted towers rise yellow-brown, color of roasted turmeric. Around them, groups of lovers in various combinations of race and gender are scattered on the grass, casual as dandelions. It is the year of cosmic collisions, when fragments of a comet named Shoemaker-Levy 9 will crash into Jupiter, producing gigantic fireballs. But here the grass is warm in the afternoon sun, and damp, as though it has been recently watered.

"American grass smells different," Sudha says.

"In what way?"

Sudha wrinkles her forehead, trying to find the words.

"It smells more male—you know, tough and fertilizer-fortified."

"Fascinating! I envision a whole new line of men's toiletries—*For that tough, fertilizer-fortified look, try*—"

She ignores the interruption. "If you stop taking care of it, it'll die off right away. Indian grass looks more delicate—that startling new-green color—and yet it survives, in spite of droughts and cows and all the weeds that try to choke it."

"Like women?" Lalit raises an eyebrow. "Is that what you're trying to say?"

Sudha wants to come back with something flippant, but she finds herself saying, "You wanted to know how I grew up. Well, all my life, I lived with the concept of duty—how a woman should behave toward her parents, her husband, her in-laws, her children. Don't mistake me—I didn't think of it as a burden. It gave me the boundaries I needed, a wall of moral safety behind which to live. Duty took the place of love—it *was* love. Without it, I believed, society would fall apart."

Lalit is quiet now, waiting.

"But what happens when others don't fulfill their duty toward you?" Her eyes flash. Her fingers are tightly intertwined. "Your husband, for example, who'd promised to always protect you—and, by extension, your children. That's when I walked out of my marriage. I don't think you can even imagine what that means in an orthodox family in India. My own mother kept telling me I should go back to him, go through with the abortion. The first few months, I felt so guilty and frightened and ashamed, I thought I would die. But I survived."

Lalit's eyes are on her face, intent and thoughtful. He's struggling to put together the pieces of the life she's flung at him. To understand her story, which is so different from his.

"I survived, but you know what happened? I let go of one duty, one relationship—and found that all the others were attached to it like the knotted handkerchiefs a magician pulls from his hat. I felt them rush through my fingers until I was left holding nothing. Nothing—and no one—to stop me from doing whatever I wanted, whether it was good or evil."

Lalit touches her arm lightly. Is he wondering why she's telling him this, what it means for the two of them? But maybe it doesn't mean anything. Maybe he's like the stranger on a train to whom you open your heart because you know you'll get down after a couple of stations.

On the other side of the water, where black-and-white swans glide with lazy elegance, a group of people have appeared. It's a party, festive with loud Latino music and pungent food smells: cumin, chilies, cilantro. A few teenagers begin to salsa. A young woman in a long white gauzy dress holds a lace fan and poses for a photograph with an old lady, who is perhaps her grandmother.

"It scares me," Sudha says. Two men are lying on the grass nearby, looking up at the sky. One of them holds the other's hand to his chest as he talks. A faint color stains Sudha's cheeks as she glances at them. "Especially since I came here. Everywhere I turn in America, they say, Live for yourself."

"Not everyone here is like you think." He speaks with some heat.

"Live for yourself," Sudha continues, as though she hadn't heard him. "I'm not sure what it means. I'm not sure I know how to do it and still be a good person. And I want to, you know. I still want to be a good person, even if I've failed at being a good wife. There's a terrible pull to the idea of living for myself, and a terrible emptiness. I feel like a flyaway helium balloon—all the people I know are on the ground somewhere, but so far away and small, they hardly matter. Yet I know I can't go back to the old way, living for others."

"Why do you have to choose one or the other?" He's sitting up now, his fingers tearing at the grass. "Can't you find a compromise?"

"I don't know how to," Sudha says simply. "Do you? Or do you live for yourself, too?"

"That's a tough question," Lalit says. "It'll take me some time to even begin to answer it." He throws the remains of their meal into a garbage can and holds out his hand to help Sudha up. "Remember, I promised to get you home before dark so that you don't have to live out the rest of your life in a pumpkin patch."

Sudha gives his hand a sudden yank, making him fall to his knees beside her.

"Whoa! What did they put in that kung pao—" But he breaks off at the impassioned look on her face.

"I don't care what you promised," she says, her breath coming fast. "You have to talk to me. I'm going crazy because I have no one to talk to—not even Anju, whom I loved more than I loved anyone else; even my daughter, even myself. But not anymore . . ."

Lalit looks at his hand, which she's still grasping, her nails pressing into the side of his palm.

"We'll talk as long as you want," he says quietly. "Let's get to the car, though, where we'll have more privacy."

To get to the car they have to pass by the Hispanic family, who smile and call out "Hola!" A man rises from a table to offer them a plate of pastries. "My daughter's fifteenth birthday!" he says. "Have some dulce—wish her happiness!"

Sudha and Lalit share a flaky, sugared pastry and wave at the girl, who, flushed with excitement, is leading a line dance of some kind. The low sun forms a red halo behind her head. She throws them a kiss. "Join us!" some people shout.

"They were so friendly," Sudha says as she gets into the car. She frowns a suspicious frown. "They don't even know us. Why were they so friendly?"

"Does there have to be a reason?" Lalit asks. Then he adds, "There's a lot about America that's unexpected. Don't be in too much of a hurry to make up your mind about things. Or people."

"Like you?" She's smiling a little now.

"On the contrary—I hope you've already made up your

mind that I'm the most debonair and delightful man you've ever met."

"Absolutely. Now, back to the other question I asked."

"Didn't they ever teach you that flattery will get you nowhere?" Lalit says. "Well, they were wrong."

❧

By the time he finishes talking, it's long past dusk. The swans have disappeared, and the quinceañera and her court. A wind comes up, turning the lights shining on the water into a thousand broken glimmerings. His car, a comfortably shabby Honda in which Sudha feels at home, is the only car left on the edge of the Palace of Fine Arts, to which darkness has given a surreal, ruined aspect.

"God!" he says. "It's really late."

"It doesn't matter."

"Your family will be worrying. You'd better call them."

She pushes away the cell phone he's holding out and shakes her head. "Thank you for talking to me like this," she says.

All the way back, she holds his hand. She doesn't let go even when the road swerves and he has to turn the wheel sharply with one arm. They don't speak.

In the parking lot he says, "By the way, did you figure out the answer to the riddle I asked?"

"The soldier and the lady? Not yet." She puts a finger against his lips. "No, don't tell me. Give me till next time. And, please—don't get out."

"Let me at least walk you to the elevator—"

"No, really, I prefer it this way. Thank you, once again, for everything." She opens the door.

"Wait! Is it kosher to ask for a kiss?"

"Ko—?" But already she's figured the word out. "Sure. But it's more kosher to refuse." Even in the car's shadow, her grin is pearly with mischief. Then she's gone, leaving him shaking his bemused head, the air in her wake charged with expectation.

Sixteen

Lalit

what I said

Once upon a time I used to labor under the delusion that I was unique. Special. I've learned better since. So I'll begin my story where the stories of most young men begin. With my father.

My father was a typical Indian immigrant in the following ways: he believed in his abilities, he was prepared to work hard, he was convinced America would make him rich. Oh, yes, also, he was an engineer.

In the following way he was untypical: he was an incorrigible dreamer.

All immigrants are dreamers, you're saying? Yeah, but they're practical about it. They know what's okay to dream about, and what isn't.

what I didn't say

I want to find out what you dream of. But I get the feeling your dreams are still unformed; each night they move like amoeba, reaching in a different direction. But already, inside, there's a nucleus forming. Once you learn its real shape, you'll go after it, single-minded, and God help anyone who stands in your way.

what I said

My father had a theory about money: it fell into two categories, he said, boring and exciting. His job as an engineer brought him a good amount of the first kind, enough for us to live a comfortable life, but that didn't satisfy him. He wanted to invest in ventures that would bring him millions in profits, preferably overnight. He loved the thrill of riding the roller coaster of risk. Yes, you could say he was a gambler, even though he always spoke disparagingly of casinos and such, and never bought a lottery ticket. Unfortunately, he had none of the instincts of a successful gambler, and every idea he funded—from a fish farm to a household robot that would do chores to a car that would run on wind power—went belly-up. Pretty soon we were left with very little money of any kind.

My theory? My theory is that every kind of money is exciting. You think I'm joking. You'll soon discover that I am the most mercenary of men. You're saying money can't make us happy? Maybe. But the lack of it can sure as hell make us miserable.

what I didn't say

Take yourself, for example. You're unhappy. I've been around enough people in distress to recognize the symptoms. And one reason is that you don't like living with your cousin and her husband. (I sense complications there, things you won't talk about.) You wouldn't have had to do it, would you, if you'd received a proper settlement from your divorce, which I'll bet you didn't. But if you had enough money, maybe you wouldn't have come to America. And then I wouldn't be sitting here with you in my Honda Civic, breathing in the smell of your body, which I swear is like lotus flowers, even though it's probably some synthetic American perfume you bought at the corner Walgreen's.

what I said

We were particularly miserable in our lack of money because my father had retained the Indian mentality of saving face. We couldn't afford meat more than once a week, and that, too, only whole chicken, which my mother would wrestle with for hours in her effort to create a meal because in her house in India there had always been a cook to do such things. But then someone in the community would invite us for a birthday party or a wedding, and Dad would make sure our gift was the fanciest one. On my birthday he'd throw a huge party and special-order pistachio ice-cream cake from Raja's Sweets, and have Mom put together these elaborate goody bags with imported Toblerone bars and Tonka trucks. The day after, he'd let me pick out my three favorite gifts, and return the rest to the local Toys 'R' Us for a refund.

No, my mother didn't get mad about it. She wasn't the sort. Plus, she too believed in the importance of saving face.

But I got mad enough for the two of us put together.

Yeah, I was mad with her, too. Because she'd let my father brainwash her. Only much later did I realize that she did what he wanted not because she thought it was right but only because she loved him.

You don't think that's love? Ah, but love, like Baskin-Robbins, comes in many flavors.

Here's a contemporary koan, fashioned by yours truly: In

chocolate ice cream, can you separate the chocolate from the milk? For milk, read love (alias ownership, desire, joy). For chocolate, read hate (alias burden, guilt, helpless rage).

what I didn't say
I think your cousin's husband might know a little of what I mean.

what I said
I dealt with my own rage by staying away, spending more and more time at the library, or in sports. I worked the late shift at a McDonald's and came home only to sleep. I opened a bank account and saved every penny, even though I knew it wouldn't be enough for what I wanted. I read all the joke books I could find because I wanted to be funny and popular.

No, I was never rude to my parents. That would have been a waste of energy. I just made sure I was never there.

What could they say? I was following the prescribed pathway for the children of immigrants, gathering the implements that would unlock the doors of the best colleges.

And they did, sort of. I got a partial scholarship to one of those accelerated medical programs—because of my father's income, I couldn't qualify for a full scholarship. Even with all my saved-up money, it wasn't enough. Then my mother, in one of those dramatic immigrant gestures, sold all her jewelry.

Don't worry, she told my distressed father, I picked up some high-quality costume jewelry on my last trip to India. Our friends will never know the difference.

That's how I went to medical school.

You asked me before about whether I lived for myself. Does that qualify?

I went to med school because I thought it was a sure ticket to the good life, as far away from my father's fish farm as I could get. I didn't know about student loans that would take you half your lifetime to pay off. Or HMOs. Or that Dad would cancel his medical insurance to save on the monthly payments, and then promptly develop a heart problem. That's why you're sitting in a Honda Civic right now instead of a Benz.

But along the way I discovered that I liked helping people.

Philanthropy? Are you kidding! I just love the power.

what I didn't say

I think you love it, too, by the way you incline your long throat and look at me sideways from under your lashes. The way you slip your hand into mine, the nails scraping my palm lightly. The power of the body. Whatever other power you lack, you certainly have that.

Then you look out your window into the darkness of night-eucalyptus bordering the freeway. You're biting your lip. You've forgotten me. I'm struck by a violent longing to wrench you around to face me, to force you to remember. Even if it means that we'll crash.

Do you have any inkling of this?

I bite the inside of my cheek until the longing subsides. For a moment I feel sorry for your cousin's husband, and maybe a little afraid.

what I said

No more today. What, you want all my secrets at once? I need to save some of them for next time. Yeah, like in the *Arabian Nights*. It's how we storytellers keep ourselves alive.

Seventeen

Sudha

Sunday morning drags itself heavily over us. The air rumbles like indigestion. All the sunshine that had lighted our little apartment with laughter yesterday has leached away, leaving behind walls colored like mustard stains.

Last night, when I came in, Sunil was impeccable in his courtesy. I hope you had a good time, he said, opening the door. He took my jacket from me and hung it up. There was enough fury in his fingertips to scorch the fabric.

Anju asked a hundred cheery questions. Where did you go, what did you eat, what did you talk about, was it fun, do you like him, what else did you talk about, do you think he likes you, how come you're so late, when will you see him again. From behind the newspaper, he said, "Why are *you* so excited? Anyone would think he's *your* boyfriend."

The word clattered to the floor of the living room. She narrowed her eyes the way one does when driving on a too-bright day, trying to recognize that shape up ahead, past the glare. "Why are *you* so upset?"

I could hear the unsaid words. *Anyone would think she's your girlfriend.* She went into the bedroom and slammed the door.

I excused myself, saying I was tired. But Dayita wouldn't come with me. She held on to Sunil's pant leg and screamed.

"Stop that right now!" I shouted. When I pulled at her arm, it was hot.

"She's teething," he said. "Her lower jaw is swollen on the right side."

I felt terrible. I should have noticed it right away. I got the Anbesol from the bathroom. When I tried to rub some on Dayita's gums, she bit me, hard.

Sunil rubbed her gums with the ointment. He gave her some Baby Tylenol and wiped her face with a clean, wet towel. He kissed her on the top of her head and said, "Be my good girl and go with your mom, and tomorrow I'll tell you the story of the monkey and the crocodile." He put his hands together and made snapping motions like a crocodile's jaws until she laughed.

But she was still angry with me. In bed she lay on the edge. She kicked away my arm even after I sang *Ghum Parani Mashi Pishi,* which is her favorite nighttime song. Only after she fell asleep could I pull her close. I rubbed the nubs of her shoulders, her elbows smooth as pebbles from a river. Her damp neck tasted of salt and lint.

What an end to my day with Lalit! He'd surprised me with that story. The hidden canyons under his laughter. I liked him more for it. But already, our day together, bright as the rainbow streaks on bubbles, was fading. I couldn't connect it to my real life. This flat that smelled of stale garam masala. This child who threw tantrums because I didn't give her what she needed. This I who was a bad mother, whose mere appearance caused marital battles to erupt around her. In my real life, the woman whom Lalit wanted to kiss did not exist.

ॐ

Sunday afternoon. Dayita frets and will not eat. Sunil sits in front of the TV, listening to a long discussion on Simpson's possible jury. A black woman bangs on the table and shouts something about evidence planted by the police, how they'd never do that to a white man. Anju has pulled her chair to the far corner of the room and buried herself in a book. Restlessness gnaws at me. I cannot sit. All around me, discontent, like miasma from a swamp. Our separate discontents. How can I plan my future in such a place? I try to take Dayita for a walk, but she will not come. She holds out her hands to Sunil and calls, Baba! Baba! *Father, Father.* How did she learn those words? Who taught them to her? I want to force her into the stroller, lash her down with the seat belt. But Sunil says, "Let me keep her. She doesn't look well." He picks her up and walks over to the freezer. He takes out a blue teething ring—when did he buy it?—and gives it to her to chew. She clasps his neck and watches me from the shelter of his shoulder. I'm so angry, I bang the door behind me as loudly as I can.

What is it I want?

I walk and walk, as if the exhaustion of muscles might exhaust the spiraling of thoughts inside my skull. As if the cold evening wind, smelling unaccountably of burning leaves, might blow through me, lifting before it the fog of my confusion. In school, the nuns had taught us a poem. *How do I love thee, let me count the ways.* If I were to count the ways I love Dayita, what would I say? I love you with a pained love, a nerve grown wrong, pinched between bones. Because of love for you, I left everything I knew and plunged into uncertainty. And this was

even before I saw you. When you put your arms around someone else and smile your new-toothed smile, my hair crackles
with envy. I love you so much I could die for you. But here's
where the poetry breaks down: I like you only in spurts. Sometimes I feel trapped by you. I can't stop myself from thinking, *If
I were alone, I could* . . . And so I grow angry with you. I imagine
that you blame me for Sunil's kiss. For tearing up Ashok's letter.
For dancing with Lalit. For leaving you behind to go out with
him. All my own guilts I've projected onto you, all the regrets
and rages of my snatched-away youth. I can die for you, no
problem there, but can I live for you?

My daughter, my enemy, my own wounded self.

I come home determined to be more maternal.

Dayita is asleep on Sunil's bed. He has fed her dinner already. I want to put her into the crib, but Anju says, "Let her be,
Sudha, don't disturb her. Dayu's no trouble. You know we love
having her with us."

Frustrated though I am, what can I say? This is my cousin,
whom I came here to help because her own baby died. I resort
to scrubbing the kitchen. When Anju asks if she can help, I
shake my head, not trusting words. She shrugs and goes into her
bedroom. She doesn't insist as she once would have. Sunil stays
up, reading some sort of report from his work. But I don't see
him turn a single page. A couple of times he looks up as though
to say something. He doesn't. Should I be grateful for that? Going to bed, I feel the pressure of his unspoken words squeeze
my heart like a disease.

≈

Monday morning dawns a beautiful gold, empty of clouds. The
opposite of how I'm feeling. But for Dayita's sake, I make an ef-

fort. We wave cheery good-byes to Anju. Thankfully, Sunil left before I came out of my bedroom. Dayita and I do the breakfast dishes—she stands next to me on a chair and splashes her hands in the soap water. After I've wiped the floor, I say, "Let's do something fun today that we haven't done before." I wish I could take her someplace different and exotic, beyond the dull orbit of my everyday walk.

As though in response to my wish, the key rattles in the lock. The door creaks open.

Sunil!

My heart thuds so hard, I think it's going to stop. But at the center of my startled fear is an icy lack of surprise. What else could come after this past weekend, things built up to explosion point? And yet the weekend was only a catalyst. We've been moving toward this moment, he and I—no matter how many detours we tried—ever since our eyes met at the airport in San Francisco and I knew he'd forgotten nothing of the past.

In a strange, chill manner, I'm relieved, too. For months I've been dangling from the edge of a cliff, my grip weakening. I'm exhausted from imagining my fall, over and over. The real fall—whatever I shatter in the process—can happen only once. After today, it'll pass into my past, along with the other things I thought I could not survive.

For a moment Sunil stands at the door, a look of such longing on his face that I'm almost weakened. When he starts toward me, his gait is careful and arduous, a desert traveler pushing against a windstorm. I force myself not to move back. He puts out his hand. My throat is blocked by salt and sand and dim breathlessness. I pick up Dayita and hold her between us like armor.

His hand touches Dayita's forehead, checking for fever. Perhaps that is all he had intended from the first.

Dayita scrabbles from my arms into his, chattering excited baby words that he seems to understand. He's whispering something to her, his lips moving across her forehead in little kisses. I lower my eyes, feeling stupid.

"I'm glad she's better today," he says. There's a small smile on his lips, bitter like the crushed neem leaves we take in India to clear the blood.

I know he saw the fear in my eyes.

He pulls our jackets from the closet, fills a diaper bag. "Let's go," he says and heads out the door as though this were an excursion we planned weeks ago. He doesn't check to see if I'm following. How can he be so certain? But perhaps it is only that, like that Greek hero who goes down to hell, whose name I can't remember in my agitation, he knows he must not look back.

The freeway is lined in part with factories belching smoke, in part with elegant structures of glass and metal. In between, a few dispirited palm trees. The pattern of my life, except I can't always distinguish the ugly from the beautiful.

We pull off onto a side street. Small, neat houses, freshly painted, cheerily tiled. Careful lawns set out like tea trays, not a weed in sight. I imagine, with brief envy, a life where the quality of grass can assume such importance. Dayita points at blackbirds and babbles happily. We stop in front of green. A sign says, *San Jose Rose Gardens.*

"I thought you would like this place," Sunil says. "It isn't as fancy as San Francisco, of course!" There's a challenge in his voice and, under that, a plea.

The first time we were alone, that, too, was in a garden. Arbor of jasmine and bougainvillea. Tuberoses which smelled like bridal nights, making a man forget the promises he'd made already to another woman and her family.

It's no coincidence that he has brought me here.

We walk, heading for a bench at the far end. A strange, Valium calm has replaced my agitation. Dayita rushes ahead, delighted by the colors. I call to her not to touch anything. Riot of reds. *Scarlet Knight, Rob Roy, Royal William, Don Juan.* Who would have believed that so many roses were named for men?

"I can't go on this way anymore," Sunil says. "It's killing me." He speaks softly, precisely, his eyes on the flowers. A passerby might think he was telling me the histories of roses. "I should have spoken to you earlier, but I was afraid you'd leave. All these months I thought, At least she's here in the same apartment, breathing the same air. The glass she drinks from, I drink from it, too, sometimes. Other times I insisted to myself, I'll get over her if I keep seeing her day after day. See her in the morning, face puffy with sleep, hair pulled back. See her at night, her sari stained with cooking, her eyes lined and tired." He shakes his head. "None of it was any good. And then you went out with Lalit, and I was afraid I'd lose you again."

Can one lose again what one never had? But I don't say anything. Nor do I try to stop him. It's too late for that. The moment I wrote to Anju agreeing to come to America, it started being too late. Now he must say it all.

"What's worse? To tell the truth and hurt the people close to you, or to keep it bottled inside and hurt yourself?"

Sunil, it isn't as simple as you make it out to be. Sometimes you tell the truth, and everyone's hurt. Sometimes the truth forces you into places you never intended to go when you spoke it.

"Well, here's my truth—I don't love Anju. I've failed to make myself love her. I admire her for many things. I feel responsible for her, even more so since the miscarriage. But what I felt toward you—from the day I came to the bride-viewing for Anju in the Chatterjee house—I'll be honest, I'm not sure if that's what people call love. But it's the closest thing to it that I've known. If I compare it to what I feel for Anju, it's like holding a firefly in one hand and a live coal in the other. Don't think I've enjoyed it, not for a moment. Before the wedding, I thought of you night and day. So many times I was set to tell Anju, let's call it off. But I'd see how her face lit up on seeing me, I knew the humiliation she'd undergo if the match was broken. . . ."

He twists the strap of the diaper bag so hard it breaks off in his hand. He stares at it without seeing, then lets the bag fall to the ground.

"I just couldn't do it. I thought I was being kind, but maybe it was only cowardice. Was it cowardice, Sudha, is that why I'm paying for it now?"

There's so much sorrow in his face, I could drown in it. My heart twists like the strap of the diaper bag. Perhaps it, too, will snap.

"I said to myself, love will come after marriage—that's what happened with many of my friends. When we're in America, everything will work out. I pushed you from my thoughts—and kept you out most of the time. But Anju and I grew apart anyway. Even before the . . . miscarriage. I think she sensed the coldness in me. She never spoke of it—she had too much pride—but somewhere inside, she removed herself. If our boy had been born, we would have made it somehow. Patched up our marriage because of him, like so many couples do. But his death—it towered between us like a wall of ice. We were freezing to death. And then you came."

He stops for breath. I don't think he's ever spoken like this. In an old tale Pishi told us, there was a man who tied an iron cord around his chest at all times to save himself from feeling too much. I'm hearing metal strain and snap. What I don't know is whether I'm doing him good or harm.

"I was obsessed all over again. I told myself it was wrong, but when I walked into a room where you were, the hairs on my arm stood up. I couldn't talk to you without breaking into a sweat. I wanted to kill Ramesh. At the same time, I was overjoyed that he hadn't had the sense to cherish you like I would have. Like I already did, even though I had no right to. But loving you was like breathing. How could I stop myself? All this time with Anju, I'd been only half-alive. I see that now, and I can't bear to go back into that bleakness again."

The air around me could be frozen crystal, it is so hard to draw into my lungs. Whoever could have imagined that I, Sudha, the luckless one, would be loved one day with such absoluteness? I feel Sunil's need pulse through my arteries, the most dangerous of drugs. How easy it would be to grow addicted to it.

"I've been waiting for Anju to get better. And now that she's back in college and doing so well, I'm going to sit down and talk to her. About how we're no good for each other. All we do is bring out the worst in each other. She sees it herself, I'm sure. I'm going to ask for a divorce." He swallows hard and takes my hand. "Sudha, will you marry me?"

In their simplicity, the words pierce me. I did not expect them to come at me so sudden and unadorned. Oh, Anju. A terrible hope smolders in his eyes. It fills me with pity. Pity for all three of us, and for Dayita, who must suffer the aftershock, no matter what I decide today.

"I'm rushing you, aren't I?" he says. "I don't want to do that. We'll wait as long as you like." And then, watching my face, "You're feeling guilty. Please don't. Because whatever you choose to do, I'm going through with the divorce. The break-down of our marriage began long before you came to America. It has no connection with what I feel for you."

Oh, Sunil, there's no end to what we can make ourselves be-lieve, is there?

"Everything is connected," I say sadly.

"I can't live with Anju anymore, even if it means that I'll have to live alone. But I hope it won't come to that. Please, Sudha, give me some hope." He is kissing my hand now, his face pressed into my palm. I can feel the small, warm suck of his in-breath against my lifeline. Why does it feel as though *his* palm is against *my* face, pressing? The hunger in him is a black hole into which I could so easily disappear. When you want a thing so much, does that give you a right to it? Something slashes through my body like a sword. Is it desire? It cuts me to pieces. Now there are many Sudhas, each wanting something different. To be independent. To be desired. To be true.

But what is truth, and to whom shall I be true?

"At least don't say no," he says. "At least think about it."

I want to laugh. Even if I wanted to, how could I stop think-ing about this afternoon, this hinge from which my future hangs like a door not yet opened?

Dayita comes crying. She's pricked her finger on a bush of sweetheart roses. I suck away the drop of blood, try to hush her. But she won't stop whimpering until Sunil picks her up and kisses her. *Hey, kid, hey, pumpkin, look in my shirt pocket.* She searches, tears forgotten, then holds up a lollipop in triumph.

Another man would have used Dayita in his argument. *It'll be so good for her—I love her as a father already.* I respect him for not doing that to me.

We walk back along aisles of yellow roses. *Sunsprite, Mermaid, Golden Wings.* Names free of the weight of earth, of the body's insistences. My sari palloo catches on a bush, and Sunil kneels to free it. I once read that yellow roses symbolized friendship. In his loyalty and kindness, his attempts to hold on to honor, Sunil would have made a good friend. I say a quick, silent prayer: this lifetime is lost to us, but in a future incarnation, may we be blessed by such a bond. If such a thing is possible between men and women. To guide, warn, and console each other. To love each other in that other, better way.

৯৫

In the car, we are too preoccupied to make small talk—and everything else seems to have been said already. He turns on the radio. We listen to callers giving the talk-show host their opinions as to whether O. J. is guilty or not. He bends forward as though to get closer to the radio, his nose quivers like a fine hunting dog's, picking up a scent. For all that he's told me, how little I know him.

And so I ask, "Why are you so fascinated by the Simpson case?"

He hesitates. I think he will retreat behind his usual prickliness. Then he says, "I used to play a bit of football in India—what they call soccer here. Nothing fancy, mostly just with the neighborhood boys, in a muddy field near the bus depot. But I loved it. It gave me a chance to get away from the house. My happiest memories are of being on that field, running with the ball." He looks into the distance. The years have taught him to hide his feelings, but I think I catch a glimpse of the boy he'd been, a flash of skinny brown legs across a stubbled expanse, losing himself in an exuberance of speed.

"Anyway, when I knew I was coming to America, I went to the USIS library and looked up a book on American football. That's when I came across Simpson's story, how he broke out of the ghetto and made it through college to become one of the greatest players of his time. It made an impression on me—maybe because he was brown-skinned, too. Maybe because he'd overcome so many odds, so many people telling him he was no good. I identified with that. I got a poster of him after I got to the university and put it up in my room, and when things were hard—a class not going well, a fellowship running out, an adviser giving me a hard time, I'd think it must have been even harder for him. Once I saw him on TV, talking about some kind of charity he was involved in, raising money for black kids. Maybe it was just for the publicity, but he seemed to really care. There was a poise about him that I wanted to own. And now—I guess I'm obsessed with wanting to know if I misread him, like I've done with so many people. If it was all just an act. But if it wasn't—and if he really did kill his wife—I want to know what it is that forces a good man into violence like that."

Sunil. Anju's husband. A man of many obsessions, a man who's decided to live for himself. Can he be called a good man? And I, if I follow this voice inside which says, *Take him, you'll never find a man who loves you more intensely,* will there be any goodness left in me?

We've reached the apartment parking lot. Sunil starts to get out.

"Please go back to work," I say. "I've got to be alone, to think through things."

He starts to protest, then says, "I understand."

Isn't this the greatest illusion we live by—that we understand each other?

On an impulse I ask, "What's the difference between a soldier and a lady?" Even to myself I sound foolish.

But he says, "Wait! I think I remember hearing it at school in Calcutta—what was it?—ah, yes, a soldier faces the powder and a lady powders the face. That old riddle! Who told it to you?"

The ways in which people surprise us! I am glad that we are leaving each other in laughter.

I call to Dayita, but she's fast asleep in the car seat.

"Let me carry her upstairs for you," he says.

I can't say no. What if this is the last time he'll hold her in his arms, that pink, baby-lotion smell, the compact, determined nose wedged into his neck? I follow him up the stairs, the broken straps of the diaper bag dangling from my hand.

❧

The child is sleeping, curled like a roly-bug, in her crib. The sun pulls a rain cloud over itself like a comforter. The room turns dark, so when the man speaks, the woman cannot see what he is saying. I can't see, she says. He says, Here, I'll light my hands for you, and he does. His hands are burning, they're a thousand watts each. She says, Don't touch me. He says, Only with my eyes. There is an ocean in the living room. His eyes pull her down into the foam. The waves are rocking all the words out of her. Her nipples are bare and hard under his breathing. Her body pitches like a boat in a storm.

He thinks, This is what I waited for all these years.

She thinks, *This?*

The child is sleeping, her face closed up like a bud in frost. The sun has fallen into the ocean and cannot climb out. The man's nipples are salty as sunflower seeds. The room turns into smoke, making the woman's eyes water.

Why are you crying? he asks. My sweetness, my life.

The words turn into birds and fly at her. She reaches out a hand. Wings, claws, shit. *Yes, that's what I deserve.* What nonsense are you speaking, he says. His leg between her legs, her tongue between his teeth, his hair covering her eyes, her conscience buried under his hips.

The child makes a sound like a phone ringing. The man breathes like someone who's fallen into an ocean. The woman doesn't breathe at all.

What have we done?

We haven't done anything wrong.

The ocean breaks against a phrase: My sister's husband. The birds beat out syllables with their wings: Love, love, love. The windows close their eyes so tight, there are star bursts inside. In his grasp, her wrists are as fragile as incense sticks. Wind's in the north, storm's coming up. He is asking, Shall I stay with you? The lamp shakes its shadow. *No, no.* He is saying, Tonight I'll talk to her, it'll all be settled. The words pour themselves into her ears like boiling wax. His hands are flowers embroidered in silk.

Kiss me, my heart, my queen.

Go now.

The walls are painted in the colors of ecstasy. The sofa is upholstered in regret. If you ever look at anyone else, he says as he pulls on his pants. Now you know what makes a good man crazy, the sun says from the bottom of the ocean. She's spread on the floor like a spent wave. Foam fills her eyes, her bones are coral-made. The child sleeps like a pearl in an oyster shell about to be pried open.

ॐ

How long after he leaves, when I grope around for my under-wear? My hands shake, buttoning my bra. My fingers snag on the folds of my skin. My sari is a mess of wrinkles that refuse to be smoothed out. The clock on the oven points to just after noon. Can that be right? In the space of three hours, a life, four lives—what's the verb I'm looking for—tangled, unraveled, turned upside down? There's no word that fits this disjointed feeling, this sense of everything out of place.

Everywhere I look, something of Anju's. A book left open, facedown, on the coffee table, an unwashed teacup on the kitchen counter, a kicked-off pair of sandals just outside the coat closet: silent alphabets of reproach.

I have nothing to say in my defense. If I had said no, if I had struggled, he would have stopped. I considered it, when his fin-gers were on the hooks of my blouse, fumbling, as though he hadn't undressed a woman in a long time. But a peculiar heavi-ness held down my limbs. Words swirled around in my head, their colors bleeding into each other. Morality, immorality. He desired it so much, it seemed unfair to withhold it from him. It was only a body, after all: blood and cartilage, hair and muscle and waste matter. If it gave him such pleasure, such belief in love's power, why not? I'd given it to Ramesh for far less.

Is that why you shivered in delight when his lips went travel-ing over your skin? I hear Anju say. Is that why you cried out, bucking, raking your nails across his back, raising weals that a wife may later find?

I may not know why I did what I did, but what I must do now is clear enough.

I find Lupe's number in the bottom of my purse and dial it. *Please, please.* The phone rings a long time. My heart races from hope to disappointment and back again. Of course she wouldn't be there, in the middle of the day. Clot of despair in my throat. When the answering machine tells me to leave a message at the beep, I can barely get the words out.

"This is Sudha. That job you told me about, the old man, is it still available? Please call me back, I'm interested. Please—as soon as you can. My number is—"

There's a mechanical clicking on the line. Then her voice: "This is Lupe."

"The job you told me about—"

"Yeah, I heard you. I don't pick up the phone every time it rings—a lot of people call me that I don't necessarily want to talk to. The job's still there. You want it?"

My tongue is thick with thankfulness. "Yes, yes."

"Hey, you okay? You sound kind of funny."

Even that slight concern in her voice threatens to bring on the tears I've been holding back. "I'm all right," I manage to say. "But I've got to leave here right away. Can someone come pick me up in the next couple of hours?"

I wait for her to say that isn't possible, but she only says, "I can come by in an hour and a half and drive you up to Berkeley." She doesn't ask for explanations, doesn't sound surprised. Perhaps she's used to women who need to make fast getaways. She jots down the sketchy directions I give her—I know so little beyond the few streets I walk on, it's shameful—and tells me to wait on the street for her.

I pack as quickly as I can: a bag for myself, and one for

Dayita. I leave a lot of things behind. It's becoming a pattern in my life, shedding belongings as I flee—first from Ramesh's house, then the mothers' flat in Calcutta, now from Anju's. It should make me feel lighter. But the emotions lodged in my chest like rusted anchors weigh me down.

Baby blankets, diapers, a bottle of Gripe Water. I feel a pang as I put in Dayita's favorite stuffed animal, a bear which Sunil bought her the week after she arrived here. He named it Jamba-van, after the bear in the Ramayana. They call him Jamu. What I'm doing, what I'm depriving her of—when she's old enough to understand, will she hate me for it?

Dayita, none of the choices ahead of me are good ones. This one just seems a little less bad than the others.

Now the most difficult part: the two letters. I tear up sheet after sheet, consider leaving without writing them. But that would be cowardly.

Excuse me, Dayita says in my head, sounding just like Anju. You think the rest of what you're doing is brave?

Dear Anju,

I'm sorry to leave like this. I don't know what else to do. I came here to help you put your life together—but all I've done is disrupt it. I'm leaving before I make things worse. With me gone, hopefully the tension between you and Sunil will die down.

Don't worry about me. I have a job. I'll tell you more when I can. In any case, I wanted to work and make a little money before returning to India. To experience life in this country, and not just from the shelter of your home. This will allow me to have that.

Thank you for everything you did for me. You gave me a chance to get away from the problems that were suffocating me in India. I think that's given me a better perspective on my life—at least I know what I don't want.

We haven't been too good about talking to each other recently, but I love you, Anju. I'm still your sister. That'll never change.

I'm sorry I had to take Dayita away from you. That's my biggest regret.

Don't worry, okay? I'll be in touch.

Sunil,

I can't give you what you want. For me, you'll always be my sister's hus-band. And I'll always be your wife's sister. We can't forget it, no matter what we convince ourselves of right now.

I've been no good for you, ever since the beginning. I shouldn't have come to America. There are so many things I shouldn't have done, I could fill a book with them. What's the use?

Whatever mistakes we've made, let's put them behind us. Let's not en-courage them to grow until they crush our lives.

I'm starting over. I hope you will, too, with Anju. It's best for us not to be in touch again.

There's a lot of strength in you, and goodness and intelligence. I pray you'll draw on them as you make your next decisions.

I'll always be grateful to you for all the love you gave Dayita.

I hate the letters: prim, abrupt, inadequate. Filled with clichés, they say nothing of all the things wrenching at my insides. And, yet, what can I write? What happened between Sunil and me is his secret, too. I have no right to lighten my heart by confessing it to Anju. That decision will have to be his.

I don't seal the letters. I don't mark them *private*. Maybe if they each read the other's, the letters will help them talk the way they should have talked a long time ago.

I wait nervously on the curb with my suitcases and Dayita's stroller, shifting from one foot to the other. Dayita rattles the bar of the stroller, points in the direction of our usual walk.

"Park!" she commands. "Park!" She can't understand why we have to keep standing here. Her face crumples in preparation for a robust wail—just what I need today! I search in my pockets and come up with the teething ring I picked up at the last minute. For the moment, at least, she's pacified. Another debt I owe Sunil.

I notice that I'm wearing the same pair of old jeans that I wore for my date with Lalit. The irony of it! A bitter laughter is building up inside me. Will I see Lalit again? And if I do, what can I say to him, after what happened today? But I have more immediate worries. What if Anju comes back early? Or Sunil? Every time a vehicle swerves around the corner, I cringe, willing myself to grow small and invisible. I must be emanating some type of distress signal, because passersby stare at me strangely. If this were India, at least half of them would know me. They'd ask me a thousand questions, offer to help, give advice, maybe even escort me back home. Thank God for the impersonal customs of America.

Finally—but, no, it's exactly an hour and a half—Lupe drives up. Her car is small and nondescript, perhaps intentionally so. A woman of resources, she's managed to make sense of my garbled directions, and even found a car seat for Dayita. I slide a sideways glance at her as I get into the front seat. She could be anywhere between forty and fifty, with a large, calm forehead. A slight sag to her cheeks, sharp lines running downward from the sides of her nose which deepen as she says hello. She doesn't quite smile, though she's pleasant enough. A dark blue pantsuit, with authoritative shoulders, smart but not showy. The only thing about her that surprises me is her hair, lush and black, all the way to her shoulder blades. She maneuvers the car onto the freeway between two monster trucks without blinking an eye. If she were in my situation, would she be running off like this? I don't think so. I watch her hands resting easily on the wheel and long for some of their confidence.

As we drive to Berkeley, I look around Lupe's car for a hint of where that confidence comes from, but it is totally empty. No emblems hang from the rearview mirror. No photos or notes are taped to the dashboard. Her face, too, is as impassive as tree bark. Perhaps that is the secret of success, to give nothing away? I glance at my own reflection on the side window. Restless eyes with their whites showing, patches of hectic color on the sloped cheeks, lips which look swollen even though I'm pressing them together, a tight sheen to the skin: forehead, chin, throat, so that it's hard to swallow. My hair is staticky and out of control around my face. It springs into disobedient curls no matter how often I push it back. If Lupe's the prudent quail who blends into the brush, I'm the gaudy cockatoo, easy target for any hunter.

Is that why the men are drawn to me, one after another?

Book Two

Remembrance
and Forgetting

One day a story will arrive at your town. It will come from far

away, from the southwest or the southeast—people won't agree.

The story may arrive with a stranger or perhaps with

the parrot trader. But when you hear this story,

you will know it is the signal. . . .

—Leslie Marmon Silko, **Almanac of the Dead**

One

It is raining. An unseasonable summer rain that darkens the afternoon asphalt of freeways and daubs it with oil slicks in risky rainbow colors. It causes tires to spin and unwary cars to rear-end each other until a huge snarl of traffic blocks the narrow stretch of 880 just past Milpitas. Rain pools in the low, salty flats by the freeway, studded with stunted acacia and looming billboards that announce the advent of a business park. On the other side, the land has already been overcome by the metal tentacles of factories, the huddles of concrete self-storage units to accommodate lives that are on hold. An auto mall is imminent. A shiny nexus of computer companies. It is the year of nostalgia. In a few days 350,000 people will descend upon Saugerties, New York, to celebrate a festival named Woodstock and all it had promised twenty-five years ago. But in this place where geography is reshaped overnight and recalling is less profitable than looking ahead, only the rain holds on to the past, the thick, loamy odor of miles of cabbage fields, now gone. You could pull off the road—just two lanes then—and buy vine-ripened watermelons off the backs of pickup trucks. One year, the body of a schoolgirl was found in the bushes only a hundred yards from here. They say she was killed by two of her classmates.

Lupe's car is stuck in the rain with all the others. She glances at her watch. It is hard to decipher, from her face, how deeply the delay is inconveniencing her. How many other women might be waiting for her to take them away from lives that have let them down. She rolls down her window a bit, takes a slim cell phone out of a purse that's sitting by Sudha's feet, punches in numbers, speaks to someone in quick, commanding Spanish.

Sudha, who has been sending her covert glances, hesitates. But finally she asks, "Is it costly, a phone like that?"

"Yeah," says Lupe. Her eyes crinkle in faint amusement at my aunt's attempt to figure her out, to place her economically, if nothing else. "In my line of work, I got to reach people fast—and they got to reach me. Go ahead and crack open your window if you want. I like how the rain smells—though nowadays it doesn't smell as good as it used to, what with all the chemicals."

"Did you grow up in Mexico?" Sudha's voice is eager. She's hoping for information, something that will help her understand this enigmatic woman on whom she's been forced to depend. Something to help her make a connection.

"Nope. I'm from right here," Lupe says. "Three generations in San Jose." She smiles harshly. "But people always ask if I'm Mexican."

"Sorry . . ." Sudha's voice is abashed. "I didn't mean . . ."

"I know you didn't. Don't worry about it."

"I want to thank you for helping me. For driving me up all this way. You must be really busy—"

"De nada." Lupe's voice is not unkind, but it discourages further conversation. "It's all part of the business. You'd better get some rest so that you're fresh for your interview."

&

Sunil is having lunch with Mr. Sorensen on the exclusive upper floor of the Hennessey, all dim lighting and real crystal and menus which do not list prices. It is an appointment which he'd been prepared to forgo in the crazed grip of passion, though once Sudha made him leave, he drove like a maniac to make sure he wasn't late for it. By his flushed face, you can tell he's excited to be here. Nervous, too, because Mr. Sorensen, the taciturn head of the company's marketing division, rarely invites any of the staff to have lunch with him. Sunil realizes that this is a rare opportunity, but is not sure what he should do to make the most of it. He watches Mr. Sorensen—the way he consults the menu with just the right amount of disinterest, the way he attracts the attention of the waiter, who is busy on the other side of the crowded room, by flicking a glance in his direction. The thin gold rims of Mr. Sorensen's glasses give him the benign look of a scholar-ascetic, but this is misleading. As the entire division knows, he has a killer eye for business and can be a terror if one fails to perform. He wears a pale gray suit unrelieved even by pinstripes, at once plainer and more elegant than what the other men in the room are wearing. His silk tie is the epitome of expensive understatement. Only someone like Sunil, who goes on periodic recon missions into the more exclusive stores, would recognize it as a Gucci original. Sunil takes careful mental notes. When Mr. Sorensen tells the waiter he'll have the salmon special, hold the sauce, and a mixed green salad with oil and vinegar, to be served after the meal, he says he'll have the same, although like many Indians he has a low opinion of salads, which he terms rabbit food. Like Mr. Sorensen, he orders a Perrier, no ice.

None of this escapes Mr. Sorensen, who allows a fleeting smile to rise to his lips. It brings an unexpected warmth to his thin face, as though he hasn't forgotten what it is to be a young man in search of a mentor. His eyes are the exact, glimmering gray of his tie. Sunil, who is speaking to the waiter, misses this. Mr. Sorensen, who came to America as a cabin attendant on the *Arctic Queen*, who stepped off the ship into a Miami horizon fronded with trees that should only have existed in the *Arabian Nights,* who made his renegade way across the country until he ended up in San Francisco, has stories he could tell. They hover like glowworms above his head, cautionary tales that Sunil, a renegade himself, would have profited by. But this is not the time for them. And so—like all untold stories—they must allow themselves to be sucked away through the vent into the bowels of the building's air-conditioning system, to wait there in the drafty, echoing dark, for someone to call them up again.

Over the salmon, the men discuss Sunil's clients. Sunil is surprised by how much Mr. Sorensen knows about them, until Mr. Sorensen tells him, in his slight Norwegian accent, that he's been keeping track of Sunil's progress over the last year—and is pleased with what he's seen. The company's looking for a marketing person to head their new office in Houston, someone with vision, dedication, strong nerves. Is Sunil interested?

Sunil tries to hide his delight, the way he knows a shrewd businessman should, but already it has leaped into his eyes. Here, finally, is the chance he's been waiting for—to distinguish himself, to prove that he is what the M.B.A. textbooks term executive material. Along with delight, there's another emotion.

An elated gratitude at this opportunity the gods have bestowed on him so he can start over in a new place with the woman he desires and the child he already loves more than the one he lost. A confirmation, a reward, a proof that what he has done is not wrong.

"Yes," says Sunil. He can't stop himself from adding, "Absolutely."

"Maybe you should check at home," Mr. Sorensen says dryly, "before you commit yourself. Isn't your wife enrolled in college here?"

Sunil looks absurdly young in his astonishment. How is it that Mr. Sorensen knows about his wife, when Sunil has taken care never to mention his private life at work? How does a man cultivate such impeccable sources of information? And what else might Mr. Sorensen know? He recovers himself enough to say, "You're right. I'll check at home tonight."

"Nevertheless, I applaud your enthusiasm," says Mr. Sorensen, deftly spearing a curly endive leaf onto his fork. "That's exactly the kind of attitude we're looking for." But as he instructs Sunil as to whom he should contact in Human Resources, his eyes are a trifle sad. Perhaps it is because he knows that no matter how far away you move, you cannot escape from what you carry within.

৯৹

"Have you seen the new movie at Camera Three?" one of the women in the writers' group asks Anju as they walk out of class. It's still raining a little. In the purple-gray light of early evening, the tough, thin leaves of the oleander bushes glisten like the tongues of iguanas. "It's about Indians. Want to go?"

Anju stiffens slightly. Movies about Indians, in her experience, are bad news. They force her into elaborate explanations and exhausting denials—often to people she barely knows. *No, we don't eat monkey brains. Or bugs either. Yes, we do worship Goddess Kali, but, no, not usually by sacrificing beautiful virgins.* Even movies made by Indian directors, gorgeously artistic, terrifically poignant, and atmospherically accurate, grow problematic in the contextless movie halls of America. *Yes, we do have street children. Yes, they really live hard lives. Yes, the police are brutal. Yes, famine happens, and then people starve. Yes, widows are often repressed. Wives also. But there's a lot more to India than what you're seeing here. There's . . .* The questioners nod. They pat Anju's arm with a familiarity she finds infuriating. It's as though, in seeing the movie, they've gained possession of something of hers that is intimate and shameful. *Of course there is,* they say, their voices like Hershey's syrup. *Of course there is.*

But maybe the women in the writers' group, having come from fringes and borderlands, having seen themselves pulled out of shape by the funhouse mirrors of the American imagination, would be different? Maybe with them Anju could talk about how it is when you love parts of your heritage so much that it tingles in your fingertips like pins and needles. You're ready to kill anyone who criticizes it. And then there are days when things about it make you want to drive your fist through a window.

"It's supposed to be a really good movie, entertaining and serious at the same time."

"What's it about?" Anju asks cautiously.

"It's about a group of Indian women in England, ordinary women, each with problems of her own, who decide they want to forget it all and enjoy a day at the beach."

That's what she, too, needs, Anju thinks. To forget it all and have a fun day. And the women from the writers' group, who know and like her just enough that their presence puts no pressure on her (unlike Sudha, she can't stop herself from thinking), would be perfect companions for this brief oblivion.

"There's a show today at six-thirty," says one of the group. "Shall we, then?"

"I should go home," says Anju.

"It's just for one evening," someone says. "Surely you can be late for once? Doesn't your husband ever come home late?"

"Leave a message for him," says another.

Anju is annoyed at the twinge of guilt she feels. Why shouldn't she go? Pleasure isn't illegal, is it? She deserves an evening out with her friends—it's not like she does it all the time. Sunil will probably work late and not even know that she was gone. And didn't Sudha herself go out with Lalit all day, just this past weekend? "Okay," she says. "I'll call home."

She stands inside the phone booth, whose slick plastic walls and low dome make her feel as if she's been stuffed into a capsule. The walls are covered with furious swirls of gangland graffiti, done in different colors by different hands, presumably at different times. She reads the words, cryptic as code: *DNA, Killer Luz, +KTBS+*. The calligraphies are oddly similar, as though the graffitans all went to the same school for urban mural design.

In the apartment the phone rings and rings. Half of her is relieved. She hates to apologize—and she knows that's what she'll end up doing if she talks to Sudha. But where has Sudha gone in this rain with Dayita, especially when the child was feverish over the weekend? Anju runs an anxious nail over the reptilian ridges of the metal phone cord. She must be in the basement with the laundry, even though Anju has begged her over and over to wait until she can get home from school and help her. She lets out a sigh at her cousin's stubbornness. Things with Sudha have not gone the way she hoped when she invited her to America. She had wanted something else for her cousin. What was it? Something grand, like the arch of a spread-out sky, the one they watched together months back, peopled with those winged women, soaring. But things—people (okay, *he*)—had gotten in the way. She needs to sit down with Sudha soon, talk to her about her future. (Something practical and concrete, back in India, that would be the best. Perhaps she could find out where Sudha could get a loan? There are co-ops, she's read recently, in Calcutta and Bombay, where they try to help women who want to own their own businesses.) But not today. She can only fix one life at a time. (There's an image in her mind as she thinks this; a jewelry box with a broken hinge, a woman's hand picking up a tiny golden clasp with a pair of tweezers, her steadfast brown fingers.) And she must start with her own.

❧

She hears the sound of falling water as she enters the house. She looks around. Has someone left a tap on somewhere? Then she sees it. Bas-relief on a slab of greenish slate: a mountain, a tree, fruit shaped like teardrops. Under the tree sits a meditating Buddha, an intricate halo around his head. The whole of it so tiny, she could hold it in her palm. Water flows over it all, pooling into a shallow, rocky basin, then siphoned under to begin its journey again. She puts down the car seat in which her daughter is sleeping and kneels for a closer look. She can't help it. It's too beautiful, and she's been starved of beauty for too long.

"Do you like my water sculpture?"

Sudha tilts her head to look at the speaker, a petite redhead with intense blue eyes, her potential employer. Her name, she has just told Sudha, is Myra. She is dressed in a wraparound silk batik skirt, the velvety blossoms on which match her short, crackly hair. "Trideep got it for my last birthday. He knows how much I love Eastern things. The sound of water is so soothing after a day with my clients, so filled with prana energy. Here, sit and relax for a moment while I make us some tea."

She disappears down a paneled corridor to the tinkle of silver anklet bells. Sudha sits, as instructed, on the edge of a deep leather chair, her elbows pressed to her body. The chair is so white. Has anyone ever sat in it? She touches the armrest surreptitiously, hungrily, with a single finger. It is clear that this house, all stone and wood and angled upswept ceilings and strategically lighted art objects, fills her with uneasy awe.

"I've never seen a house like this before," she whispers to Lupe. "It's so . . . dramatic. I didn't even know such things could be done." She gestures to the ceiling, where an enormous skylight allows in a drizzle of soft gray light.

"Hmmm," says Lupe, who is less impressed.

"It scares me a bit. All these beautiful art pieces. What if Dayita gets her hands on one of them and breaks it? And that water sound—I keep thinking I need to turn something off."

"Calm down. It's just a house. They're people, just like you and me. Breakable things can be put away."

"Thank God Dayita's still asleep. Otherwise she'd never let me talk properly to the lady. What should I say to her, anyway?"

"As little as possible."

"What if she doesn't like me? What if she wants someone with experience? I can't go back to—"

"We'll worry about that when it happens. I have a feeling she needs you more than you need her."

Sudha gives her a pale, unconvinced smile.

"Here we are," Myra says, coming in from the kitchen. She carries, on an elegantly hand-carved wooden tray, ceramic mugs filled with a bright red liquid that looks like no tea Sudha has ever seen.

"I do hope you like it," she says. She sets down the tray a bit hard, spilling liquid. "It's a strengthening tea, made from hibiscus and ginseng. God knows, nowadays I need all the strength I can get."

"I'll pass, thanks," says Lupe, who has long decided that politeness needs only to extend so far. Sudha takes a sip and suppresses a grimace. Fortunately, Myra has launched into a speech and does not notice.

"Oh, what a lovely baby! How old is she? Can she walk? Does she talk yet?" Her fingers make little butterfly motions in the air. Why, she's almost as nervous as Sudha. "We considered having a baby, but finally decided against it. Sometimes I feel it was a selfish decision, but my therapist tells me that that's an unproductive way of thinking. I'm probably too high-strung to be a good mother, anyway. Not like you. Indian women are so tranquil."

Sudha gives Lupe a look. Lupe shrugs. She doesn't care what delusions employers hold, as long as they treat her women right.

"Like I was telling you," Myra continues, playing with her ring, which is ornately carved in Indian gold, "ever since his mother passed away three years ago, Trideep's been asking his dad to come visit us. The old man kept putting it off. Then finally, this summer, he says okay. Tree's really excited—me, too, of course. We buy all kinds of Indian groceries, Tree rents a bunch of Bengali videos from Bombay Bazaar. He gets here, everything's going really well, he likes the neighborhood, goes for walks, even cooks for us. A bit spicy for me, but, still, it's sweet of him, and I make it a point to tell him how much I appreciate it. Weekends, Tree takes him around—that's my busiest time, as you can imagine. Did I tell you I'm a Realtor? I work for David Helm. It's a privately owned company—I couldn't stand a chain—with offices in San Francisco and Berkeley. We deal only in custom homes. But it's getting too much for me. The clients are so demanding—that's the problem with people who have too much money—by the time I get home I have the worst migraines. Tree keeps telling me I should change my field to something calmer, more sattvic and artistic."

"You were telling us about the patient," Lupe says.

"Right, right. Well, Tree takes his dad everywhere—Napa Valley, up the coast to Mendocino, Hearst Castle. They even fly down to Disneyland one weekend. The dad's a fun guy, tells us lots of Indian jokes each night at the dinner table. I don't understand all of them, but we're having a good time. Then he has a stroke—bam! just like that—which lands him in the hospital." Myra pauses to catch her breath. "It changes everything." Her face loses its animation and becomes all hollowed bone. "We bring him home from the hospital, and suddenly he hates everyone, especially me, like it's all my fault that he can't move the right side of his body. Like I—"

"What exactly do you need Sudha to do?" Lupe asks.

"Just the regular. Bathe him, give him his food and medicines, keep him cheerful. The doctor says a lot of this is mental. People can get better a lot faster if they're motivated." Myra puts a hand on Sudha's arm, appealingly. "That doesn't sound too tough, does it?"

"Not at all," Sudha begins, but Lupe interrupts.

"What happened to the woman who was here before this?"

Myra looks unhappy. "I didn't want to bring that up—you know how it is, negative thoughts create bad energy . . ."

Lupe waits, arms folded.

"She quit after a week," Myra says, speaking fast. "Said he was too difficult. Not that we can blame him. You'd be cranky, too, if you were stuck in bed all day, wouldn't you? Anyway, she wasn't Indian. He'll probably take to Sudha right away." She clasps her hands, then unclasps them. When she looks at Sudha, her eyes are wide with worry.

"About the pay . . ." says Lupe.

"Oh, right. I was thinking of a thousand dollars a month. . . ."

There's a stunned look on Sudha's face. There's a total of thirty dollars in her purse—ten of which she came with, and a twenty that Anju gave her some time back, in case she had to go to the grocery when Anju was at school. That, and a bit of cheap jewelry and her return ticket to India. This would change everything.

"Uh-uh." Lupe comes in smoothly before Sudha can speak. "Too little. Wasn't there something about the old man throwing a TV remote at her? Left a bruise big as a plum on her upper arm."

Myra flashes a startled look at Lupe, bites her thumb.

"I have my sources, you see." Lupe allows herself a quick, wolfish grin. "Nothing less than twelve hundred."

Sudha sucks in her breath at Lupe's audacity, but, amazingly, Myra agrees. They go on to other details. Sudha is to be paid in cash, Lupe stipulates. Weekly.

"She's not going to do any housecleaning, or any cooking—except for the old man. She's not going to be held responsible for anything the kid breaks. It's your job to put your valuables

away. Anything the old man needs after ten P.M. and before six
A.M., you folks have to handle. She gets every Sunday off."

Myra assents meekly to everything. They go into the other
room so she can pay Lupe her fee. Sudha continues to sit on the
edge of the leather chair, dazed at the speed with which things
have happened. She has a job, a beautiful house to live in, and an
employer who seems hearteningly malleable. Most important of
all, for the first time in her life, she has her own money. She's finally starting her new life in America. The excitement of that,
surely, must be coursing through her like a drug. Why, then, does
her back slump in a dispirited curve? What makes her grind her
knuckles into her eyes? What is it she's thinking of?

Only when Lupe comes to say good-bye does she pull herself from her thoughts to catch hold of her hands.

"You saved my life," she tells her. Her voice is hoarse, as
though after a day of shouting. "I can't thank you enough—"

"Hey, hey," says Lupe, freeing herself. "No big deal. Besides,
you shouldn't thank me yet. You haven't even started work—
you might not like it."

"Not like it!" Sudha attempts a smile. "That'd be like a
drowning person complaining about the color of the rope
thrown to her."

Lupe doesn't comment on this. She tucks in a corner of the
sleeping Dayita's blanket. "Good luck," she says, putting a hand
around Sudha's shoulders and giving her a surprising half-hug.
Then she disappears into the rain, and Sudha is truly on her
own.

Two

Sudha

It is dark, it is raining. I know this is a dream because the rain makes no sound. It merely falls, solid as uncooked spaghetti. Little pieces of it stack up outside a building. No, it's a room, a room in the night, and the spaghetti rain has reached all the way to the windowsill. The windows are open, some sticks of spaghetti have landed inside, on the carpet colored like dirty foam. They make a crisscross pattern. He sits in the dark in the recliner. He turns the TV on, then off, then on again. O. J. is on the screen, smiling with his hair, speaking with his skin, reaching out with eyes cut out of black cloth.

She left you, didn't she, says O. J. *They all do. I should know.*

There are squares of light in the room, rectangles of not-light. He unfolds one of the rectangles. It grows into a letter, my letter to him. Or is it my letter to her? He reads it again. He crumples it, he throws it down. He picks it up. She walks in through the door, her mouth makes the shape of questions, she turns on a switch, no answers flood the room. Where is she, she is asking, where is the baby. He is at the window, he holds out the rectangle which is my letter, he holds it aslant into the rain, the words slide off the page, there is blankness, she says, give me the letter, give me the letter, what did you say to her, what did you do, you bastard? She is saying, lost, she is saying, my baby.

She comes at him with her fists. Light floods the room. Spaghetti shapes whirl outside the window. In my bed I am drowning. I took the coward's way. He is holding her wrists. She is weeping. It was the only way I had. He is weeping. Words fall from the corners of their eyes. Small and black and shriveled like raisins. We read a poem in school once, *what happens to a dream deferred*. On the chair next to them is a child's book I left behind. What happens to a desire deferred? There's a scratch mark on his cheek in the shape of her nails, bleeding. Stop it, stop. Something balloons inside me, my chest is stretched to bursting. I didn't know this would happen, he says. He speaks to himself, he speaks to the rain.

Is this a good time? Is this a bad time? I have no way of knowing. I left the Indian calendar behind, too. The room I'm sleeping in is dark and unfamiliar. If I get down from this bed (too-soft, too-large) I will hit my thigh against furniture I don't know, in the morning there will be a bruise the shape and color of a half-ripe guava. It will be my fault. It was my fault. A rectangle falls over my face, white as a wedding handkerchief from long ago. The writing on it is thick and black, like spaghetti dipped in recrimination. I think of how the word *eka* in Bengali can mean both loneliness and being alone.

Where did she go, all alone?

Why didn't she tell me, one of them is saying.

One of them is saying, It hurts so much I just want to die.

In sleep my fingers search the bed. Find the small hands, the toes. In sleep my daughter moves away. When she woke from her nap, she called, Baba, Baba. She said, Anju. She would not eat, she would not stop crying. Her face was red and breathless. The woman who hired me pursed up her mouth like a raisin, as though she had made a mistake. I took my daughter into the bedroom, I begged her to be quiet. I rocked her, I sang, I told a story. She would not stop. She tried to throw herself from my arms. I slapped her. In our sleep, the rain has hard fingers.

One of them thinks, I did a terrible thing.

One of them thinks, It must have been really terrible, what you did.

The woman knocked on the door and said, Give her to me for a little bit. I am a bad mother, wherever I go. There was a purplish blotch on Dayita's cheek. When the woman took me in to see the old man, his eyes were like burning raisins. Go away, he said. He took his left hand, his right doesn't move, and pushed the dinner tray off the bed. His eyes were black and plump with hate. Get out of my sight. There was spaghetti all over the floor, red and white swirls like painted peonies. His fingers bent inward, like claws.

She shouldn't have done it, O. J. says sadly. *I shouldn't have done it.*

One of us says, I got it all wrong.

Is this my skin I'm touching now, is this my daughter's skin? Is it a handkerchief, a letter cut from black cloth? The rain shuffles like an old man's shoes. Before I lay down, I pushed the dresser against the door, then felt foolish. She said, I'm sorry, he's tired, things will be better tomorrow. She said, Let me help you clean up the spaghetti. He said, Vultures, bitches, leave me alone. He used Bengali words, too. Daini. Magi. Once in childhood, I walked into a field of sugarcane and got lost. There were leaves all around me, their sharp, sawtoothed edges. She said,

This makes it three days he hasn't eaten. Shit, what am I going to do. He said, Whores. The smell of the cane was ripe and musky, too sweet. I couldn't breathe. There was no end to the field, to the leaves whispering, *eka, eka.*

Anju, I don't even know how deep it goes, the harm I've done.

You don't know which way to turn, says O. J., *to climb out of loneliness. So you turn whichever way you can.*

I said to my daughter, I'm sorry. The woman was crying. See what I have to put up with. I'm going to have a nervous breakdown. Her face was creased with things she wanted to shout out, like a flower squeezed in a sweaty fist. My husband, he's never there when I need him. My daughter turned her face away, with a look. My daughter scooted her small body to the far end of the bed.

She says, What will happen to us now?

What will happen to us now? he replies.

Three

The earth turns, hemisphere of darkness, hemisphere of light. Winds shift, herding clouds ahead of them. In Calcutta, Ashok sits down to write another letter. In America, on a pillow dampened by fever or rage, a half-paralyzed old man dreams of flight. Their bodies flung onto separate, disparate beds, Sunil and Anju chase shadows in their sleep: silhouettes of regret, arabesques of what might have been. Stumbling to the bathroom with a tension headache, Myra counts out drops of feverfew into a tumbler of warm water. Two A.M. Three. Lalit follows a lone eighteen-wheeler on Freeway 280, on his way home from an emergency at the hospital. Over the hills at Skyline, strips of mist like torn membranes. He turns the radio from a talk show where a woman claims she was visited by Nicole's spirit to an oldies station. *Yesterday's gone, yesterday's gone.* In her sleep, Dayita's body loosens and turns toward her mother's. In her sleep, Sudha puts an arm around her and draws her close.

The sun rises like a blood orange over Grizzly Peak, supremely confident, as though the rain had never been. Dewdrops glitter in the redwood that fringes Sudha's window. The window is a huge sheet of plateglass, uncurtained. A jay preens its feathers, sassy-blue in the brilliant morning. It is the year of aggressive movements; a man named Saddam is mobilizing sixty thousand soldiers and seven hundred tanks, which will result in a reciprocal mobilization by the U.S. Army. If she were to walk to the window, Sudha would see the town of Berkeley unscrolled below her, its quirkily angled rooftops slanting down the hillside, its riotous tumbles of bougainvillea and trumpet vine and passion flower where the last of the deer feed in the evenings. Down farther, the square red-tiled buildings of the university, its narrow dorms and sprawling co-ops where students stay up nights to study and argue and get drunk and fall in and out of love, believing all the while that they are the inheritors of the world. Then the Berkeley Bowl, from which Myra buys organic oats, pesticide-free sorrel, soy cheese from Japan. The high school with its metal detectors, flanked on one side by a chain-link fence and on the other by a mural filled with faces like dark, busy rainbows. In People's Park, the homeless stir stiffly in sleeping bags lined with newspapers. A woman in Birkenstocks sweeps the sidewalk in front of the cafés of Telegraph Avenue, empty at this hour and a little sad. The roads crisscross like old shoelaces, leading us finally to the pier, that gray cement pencil pointing into the water as though it contained the solution for our landlocked lives.

But Sudha doesn't walk to the window. She lies on her side, unmoving, her knees drawn up to her chest as though she were cold. She keeps her eyes closed, though from her uneven breathing it's clear she's awake. She is contemplating interior spaces, the vistas she has left behind. Last night, brushing her teeth, she spoke to the mirror: *I will not think of the past. I will not think. Of. The past.* But now, again, she feels it: the press of a man's lips on her soul.

The room they have given her is beautiful, decorated with care and an unerring eye. Could the nervous Myra be capable of such grace? The north wall is hung with an abstract weaving in warm browns, with pieces of bleached driftwood worked in. The south wall, behind her head, holds a framed Indian minia-ture painting in jewel colors, a flute-playing Krishna positioned, unexpectedly, between two dancing lions. To the east is an al-cove with recessed lighting. In it sits a many-armed goddess with a bronze scowl and a trident. The room is sparely fur-nished: bed, dresser, leather armchair, tall brass reading lamp. This decorator—whoever she is—does not believe in clutter. The rug on the floor is Native American, its clean lines depict-ing triangular human figures, the sun and moon, animals with inquiring, coyote snouts. The quilt is a geometric design in shades of cream and henna red, silk squares over which Sudha, her eyes still closed, slides a slow, appreciative hand.

But now the alarm clock by the bed rings, and Sudha must prepare to meet her future. She pulls her jeans and a sweatshirt from the large walk-in closet where she hung her embarrass-ingly few clothes last night. In the bathroom, Grohe faucets in gleaming silver arcs, English Lavender Gel in the ceramic dis-penser, two thick Turkish towels, white as a pirate's grin. She shucks off her nightdress carelessly. *Take a shower, very hot. Wash the last traces of him from your body. Bundle the hair into a knot, don't bother to comb out tangles, there's no one here to see, thank God.* Along with gratitude, why does she feel a sense of loss so absolute it makes her dizzy? *He had cupped his hands for me, so I could pour all my loneliness into them.* On a glass shelf, bottles of lotion present their labels to her. Claiborne Sport for men guests, Victoria's

Secret Garden for women. She who is not a guest (is she more? is she less?) lifts a tube, bangs it back down with severity. *Let the skin crack and peel. That will be your penance for opening yourself to desire.*

She hesitates at the door. Should she wake Dayita? Is it a good idea to leave her in an unfamiliar room, even if she is walled in with pillows and covered with her favorite blanket? But it's getting late, she must make the old man's breakfast, he hasn't eaten in days. With a glance of misgiving, she shuts the bathroom door tight. There was a story the other night on TV about an accident, a child who drowned in a toilet. From the corridor she raises her hand toward the sleeping girl—a gesture of blessing or farewell, or a command to stay put.

෨

Sunil stands at the living room window watching the sunrise, something he has not done in years. It is a beautiful morning, clear and cloudless pink, the ubiquitous smog washed away by last night's downpour. Sunil faces it grim and bleary-eyed. Ready or not, his new life is upon him (what else can we call this day, now that his old life lies in shambles?), and he must live it.

The golden morning light has just started moving across the carpet. The same carpet where yesterday. . . . Yes-ter-day. Each syllable strikes him like a branding iron. He turns on his heel—to hell with the sunrise—to make himself a cup of tea. Before Sudha took over the tea-making duties, he used to be good at it. When Anju was pregnant, he would make her masala cha, opening the pods of cardamom carefully over the rich brown liquid as it came to a boil, carrying it to her in bed. Does he remember the dry rub of the fragrant seeds against the whorls of his fingertips? Better if he doesn't. Already I'm learning that forgetting is essential to survival.

Today he doesn't heat the water long enough. He puts in the milk too soon. He can't find the Sweet 'N Low and decides to do without. He takes a sip of the watery brew, which must taste awful, but his expression doesn't change. Is this stoicism or preoccupation? He pauses in front of the TV and hefts the remote, considering. Even this early, in this country obsessed with the ways in which violence and celebrity intersect, there are channels discussing O. J.'s chances of acquittal. But today Sunil turns away from them into the crisis of his own life. He presses his hands to his temples with a grimace. Who can acquit him? Not even himself.

"Damn," says Sunil as he pours his tea into the sink and watches the brown liquid drain away. "Damn." It's an injured sound, as though something has ripped inside him. He carries a chair from the dining area over to Sudha's room, where Anju chose to spend last night. The crib looms in a corner like the stripped carcass of some beast. He winces away from it as he sits down and waits for Anju to wake.

Last evening he had been the first to come home. He had opened the door into the dark room and taken a step backward, blinded by silence. He had known, then. Still, he read the letters, both of them, over and over. He crushed them in his fingers, smoothed them out, crushed them again. Some men would have smashed their fists into things. Some men would have wept. Sunil did neither. Was that his weakness or his strength? He opened a window, let the rain come in. His chest was wet from it by the time Anju returned.

Anju sleeps on her stomach, her face buried in Sudha's

pillow as though she were trying to inhale a memory. Her arms are spread out stiffly, gesture of embrace or crucifixion. Her fists clutch the sides of the mattress. Her hair, fallen to one side of her neck, exposes knobs of vertebrae that look intensely breakable. Although she stopped crying some time ago, her breath still comes out in ragged wisps.

Even before she read the letter last night, she said, "Where is she? What did you do to her? What did you *do?*" Her pupils were pinpricks of distrust. She went for him with everything she had—fists, knees, words. He didn't try to stop her. He let scratches bloom their trail of blood along his cheek. Did he believe this would even out things between them? "I should have known!" she said. She kicked his shin as hard as she could with the point of her shoe. She wanted him to hurt. To break apart like a tree trunk with a rotten core. *You, you, you.*

Where can a marriage travel after that?

৯৽

The kitchen in the glass house is a chiaroscuro of rectangles, light and airy shade. Sunshine pools on blond wood countertops like honey, drawing Sudha forward. Then she stops. In the foyer, voices. The female one quivers like the tip of a weapon. The man's is placating and muffled, an underwater sound.

Is this to be her role always, eavesdropper and witness to spousal strife?

She: I can't take it any longer, Tree. Last night was the worst. He hates me, I know it—he aimed that spaghetti bowl right at me.

He: But, Myra, he doesn't hate you. He's just mad at life for what it's done to him.

She: Let him throw his spaghetti bowl at life, then. It took me almost a half hour to clean up, even with the new girl's help. Some of those stains won't ever come off the carpet.

He: *(Silence)*

She: Go ahead and say it, how crass and shallow of me to worry about carpets—even though it is a horrendously expensive Persian one—when your father is bedridden and suffering. Well, I *am* crass and shallow. He's worn me down to my crass and shallow core.

He: I'm not blaming you. I understand how you must feel—

She: No, you don't. You can't. You're too busy feeling guilty because you left him behind in India and never went back. And secretly you blame me for it—the crass and shallow American who lured you into staying here.

He: You just want a big, all-out fight, don't you?

She: *(Silence)*

He: We're all going through a hard time, Myra. We have to help each other, and keep in mind that this is a temporary situation.

She: It would be easier to keep the temporariness of the situation in mind if I weren't down on my knees every evening cleaning up the mess your father makes—while you're working on your top-secret project in the lab.

He: *(Silence)*

She: I'd feel more sympathetic if he were sick and couldn't help it. But he'll purposely do something terrible and look at me with malice gleaming in his eyes. Why, even the new girl could see it.

He: Well, now that she's here, she'll take care of him—

She: If she lasts. You should have seen her face when he

threw that bowl. And the names he called us! And starving himself like this—it's just a way for him to get our attention and control us—

He: Maybe he'll get along with her once he gets to know her. From what you say, she seems nice—

She: I'm not counting on anything. Except the fact that if this one can't handle him, either he's out of here, or I am.

The door slams. A pause, then footsteps moving resignedly toward the kitchen. Sudha tries to compose her face into an appropriate expression. But what is appropriate when one has stumbled upon such a nakedness of words, no less shameful in its way than the nakedness of flesh?

❧

The stubble on Sunil's lean jawbone gives him an air of urgency, like a man on the run. But his fingers, laced in his lap, are square-tipped and patient. He's used up a lifetime of emotion in the last twenty-four hours. He's confessed and grown crazy with unexpected joy. He's closed his fist around the apple of the world, and opened his eyes to find emptiness blowing through him like a sandy sirocco. Still, he has a plan. Should we admire him for this? His lips move slightly, silently. He is practicing what he will say when Anju awakes.

Anju smiles in her sleep. She loosens her grip on the mattress, spreads out her fingers. Her only jewelry, a narrow gold band, flashes in the sunlight. The grace of her muscles, their curve and dip, surprises him as she stretches. She opens her eyes and sees him.

"Oh, Sunil," she says, "I had the most beautiful—"

"Tell me."

But remembrance has slammed Anju's face shut like an iron gate. She struggles into a sitting position, hugs her knees, looks past him at the wall.

"I don't want to talk," she says.

"We have to. That's why we're in this place today, because we didn't want to talk."

From behind the bones of her knees, Anju hardens her voice. "It's too late now. We don't know how to talk to each other anymore."

"I want to tell you something," he says.

Her eyes fly to his face. There's a sudden fear in them because—she sees it only now—no matter what she believes he has done, she loves him still. All this time she's been dreaming of departure, but now that it might be upon her, she isn't ready to go.

"What?"

"A story."

Anju stares at him. Her eyes are wide, her body still. Sometimes, she knows, you use a story like a sword, to cut through what's in your way. Wildly, she tries to find something to distract him, but he has started.

"A long time ago, just before I left India to come here," says Sunil, "I went to see a movie. It was about a man who falls in love with a dancing girl, just from seeing her on a train. She's sleeping, so he doesn't even get a chance to speak to her, but he leaves her a love letter. . . ."

Underneath the measured rise and fall of his storytelling voice are hidden phrases like small explosions. Anju feels their reverberation. *Tried my best to love you, can't control this, driving me insane.*

"I know the story already," she says quickly. "I saw that movie, too. Sudha was with me. That was when she met Ashok first, in that cinema hall. It was called Purabi. The cinema hall, I mean. I've forgotten the name of the movie." She gives a small laugh that isn't a laugh. "Funny, isn't it, what one remembers and what one forgets."

Sunil continues as though she hasn't spoken. "They can't stop thinking about each other, the woman, too, she's fallen in love with him just from reading the letter. But of course they have no hope of meeting again."

Can't forget her. In my blood like a disease. Can't live this way anymore.

Anju sees that her attempts to interrupt the story are futile. It is the story, instead, that will interrupt her life. "But they do meet," she says sadly. "There are complications—the dancing girl's jealous patron, the young man's parents who worry about family honor and want to arrange a match for him elsewhere. But love overcomes all."

Don't hold me back from. My last chance at being happy.

"I didn't pay the movie much attention. It was one of those corny Hindi-movie plots. Life wasn't like that. You did your best to find happiness, and then made do with what you got. But one day the thought struck me, why *couldn't* it happen? Isn't that how we sabotage ourselves, by not believing? If someone could imagine a happy ending, if someone could make a story out of it—"

Let me go before I start hating you.

"But in your case, the dancing girl didn't love you back. She ran off, didn't she?" Anguish makes Anju's voice cruel.

"The dancing girl in the movie ran away, too, if you remember," Sunil says, drawing on levels of calm I didn't know he possessed. "But the man found her and convinced her to come back to him."

Because I'll go anyway.

"Stories have their limits," Anju says.

"I need to test them for myself," says Sunil.

❧

In the blond kitchen, the man is short and dark, with thick hair which at the moment stands up all over his head because he's been running his hands through it. He wears a red Chinese dressing gown that is altogether too dramatic for him, that looks like a gift from his wife. Behind thick glasses, his eyes are intelligent and helpless-looking.

He ruffles his hair again, adjusts his eyeglasses and gives an embarrassed cough. "I'm Trideep," he says. "You must be Sudha. Nice to meet you." His Bengali is stilted, the vowels stiff as though cut out of cardboard, as though he hasn't used them in a long time.

She joins her hands in a brief namaskar. If she's nervous, she hides it well. Against her will, she likes the fact that he doesn't apologize for his father.

"Please!" he says. "No formalities! After what you've just overheard—no point pretending you didn't—it seems a bit useless, doesn't it?"

She runs the sponge over the black granite countertop in which little gold flecks glitter like mica, not committing herself.

"As you see—" he pauses, wrinkling his forehead, then giving up and switching to English—"we're all depending on you."

Sudha looks unconvinced, especially about that *all*. But she says, "I'll try my best. Maybe you can help by telling me what your father likes for breakfast." With a wry smile she adds, "And what he hates."

Trideep shakes his head. "I don't really know him. I hardly

ever lived at home. First it was boarding school in Dehra Dun, then IIT Kharagpur, then graduate school in America. I only went back for summer vacations, and then Mom was always there, taking care of things. I guess I never needed to notice much."

"But during this visit—?"

"He's different now. When he first got here, he wanted to try everything. Like America was a great big toy store, and he was a kid. He loved ice cream. We'd go to Baskin-Robbins every few days so he could try a new flavor. But, now, whatever I bring him—chocolate chip muffins, lemon-raspberry yogurt—he doesn't even look. All he'll say—in that painful stammer—is, *Send me home, Deepu.* But how can I?" He takes off his glasses and massages the bridge of his nose tiredly. "He's not well enough to travel, and, anyway, there's no one back there to look after him."

They stand in awkward silence, nothing left to say for the moment. Behind them the Sub-Zero refrigerator, its doors paneled with wood to match the floor, purrs contentedly.

੭੦

Sometimes, even when you know it's useless, you can't stop trying.

She says, "If you still want to hear the dream, I'll tell you."

He cannot help glancing at the clock on the dresser. He's going to be late for work. The only other time he was late was the morning after she was rushed to the hospital.

Can we forgive him that glance, the way one forgives a nervous tic?

"Tell me," he says.

"I was flying over the ocean. It took no effort, I was so light. There was a breeze. I floated on it, out and out—"

"And then?"

"Then nothing. That's why it was so special. It wasn't like life, where things have to keep happening, one new excitement after another, or else you feel like you're suffocating." She lowers her chin onto her knees, so the last words come out in a mumble.

"Anju," Sunil says. He's never spoken to her this gently. It makes her catch her breath. Strands of hair have fallen over her downturned face. He tucks them behind her ears as though she were a child, raises her chin so she must look at him. "We aren't any good for each other anymore—you see that, don't you?"

༄

Myra's note tells her to wait until the old man wakes and rings his bell. But it's 11:00 A.M. already, and he hasn't made a sound. Sudha arranges a row of chairs to form a makeshift playpen, gives Dayita a set of spoons to play with, and knocks on his door. When there's no reply, she peers in anxiously.

"Are you all right?" she asks. It's dark in here, a musty lack of light accentuated by the sun-glass-wood sheen that characterizes the other rooms. It's the only room with curtains—the old man must have asked for them. They cover the windows thickly, as anachronistic as medieval tapestries in this house. Sudha goes to open them.

"Leave it!"

The old man's voice creaks like an unoiled hinge, making her jump. He registers this. His eyes glitter with malice, the only pleasure left to him.

"Good morning! Would you like some breakfast? Shall I help you wash up?" She makes her voice professional and hearty, like the voices of nurses she's watched on TV.

"Go away."

"You know I can't do that." Sudha switches on the room light, but turns it off when he grimaces and covers his face with his good arm. In the dim glow of the night bulb, she wheels in a cart equipped with basins, towels, a pitcher of warm water. "As soon as you're clean and have fresh clothes, I'll get you breakfast," she says as she starts removing his clothes. "What would you like? Cereal? There's at least three kinds that I saw. How about whole-wheat toast? With eggs maybe, lightly scrambled? Myra picked up some really nice honey yogurt at the health food store. . . ."

She's babbling, she knows it, but she's too embarrassed to stop. Apart from her husband, she's never seen a man naked. (No—there was Sunil, but that was a kind of delirium from which no images remain.) This man—old though he is—what makes it worse is that he so obviously hates her touching him. He shuts his eyes tightly and turns his face away as far as he can. Half of his face is blank and sagging because of the stroke. On the other half, there is a look of such frustration that her fingers falter as she removes the soiled, diaperlike undergarments and runs the washcloth over his flaccid, ruined flesh.

But certain actions, once begun, must be brought to completion. She knows this. She presses her lips together and forces herself to breathe normally, though the stench sickens her. Smell of body waste and despair. A muscle jumps above the uneven crag of his left eyebrow. She wipes and powders and tugs various articles of clothing over his tense limbs. Embarrassment makes her clumsy. But apologizing would only make things worse. He is a tall man, with heavy, uncooperative bones. Push, push. Raise and bend. Finally, she heaves him into a sitting position and wedges a pillow behind his back. Sweat beads her upper lip, her breath is ragged, her hair has come undone, curls sprouting everywhere as though she's been in a wind. But she smiles, pleased at her achievement.

"There, does that feel a little better?"

He says nothing.

"How about that breakfast now?" She recites the list of foods again. He doesn't respond.

"I guess I'll just get you some cereal, then." She returns with a bed tray, which she places over his legs, and a blue ceramic bowl filled with Cocoa Krispies and milk.

"I was going to bring you Toasted Oats, but these looked like they would be more fun," she says conspiratorially. "Your son must have bought them. Somehow I can't imagine Myra crunching Cocoa Krispies, can you?"

The old man stares expressionlessly past her efforts at humor.

"Here, take the spoon." She closes his left hand over it. "Come on! After last night, I *know* nothing's wrong with that hand!"

He makes his fingers limp so the spoon falls and skitters under the bed.

"Oh, very well. I'll feed you. Though I would think you'd prefer to do it yourself." She cleans off the spoon, fills it, and brings it to his mouth. "Open, open." She butts the spoon against his lips as she does with Dayita. Perhaps it's the playfulness in her voice that makes the old man comply. Or maybe he's ravenous after all these days of holding out. He lets her pour the milky cereal into his mouth, chews for a moment, and then, just as she nods encouragingly and lifts another spoonful, he spits at her with all his strength. Half-chewed gobs, dark brown, spatter her cheek, her hair. She touches her face, looks disbelievingly at her soiled fingers. Her eyes are full of shock. He stares at her defiantly, his face twisted in a snarl that could be a grin. Her hands are shaking. She presses a knuckle against her lips. Then she snatches the tray from the bed and runs out.

≈

It is the year of temporary compromises. On a continent halfway across the world, Russia signs an accord titled "Partnership for Peace." On an island at the edge of the Atlantic, the IRA agree to cease hostilities. In the bedroom abandoned by the woman he is wild for, Sunil makes his voice toneless, the way one does when afraid of losing control. He moves his body toward Anju in cautious investigation, like someone swimming over sharp coral.

"For a long time now, we've just made each other unhappy."

She shuts her eyes and holds her breath so that a sound like airplane engines fills the space between her ears. Still, she hears him.

"I can't afford to do it anymore. Half my life is gone. I don't want to waste the rest."

She turns toward the dresser. There's dust along its top, which surprises her. Sudha is always so neat. The fake wood grain swirls like gigantic thumbprints.

"The company is transferring me to Houston very soon. I want to start the divorce proceedings as quickly as possible."

She slaps his fingers from her chin, lifts her arm as though warding off something evil. She's understood nothing, she thinks, and no one. Not her will-o'-the-wisp cousin, not her traitor husband, not herself. After she lost her baby, she thought nothing would hurt her this much, ever. What is this sensation in her chest, then, like the ribs being sawed away? She wills her mind to think of things that have nothing to do with this moment: jacarandas, saxophones, ginger tea. But everything is connected to him. She hadn't realized they'd done so many things together. Even poetry—the only line that will come to her—betrays her. *My life closed twice before its close.*

He's saying, "I know you hate me for doing this, but one day you'll see it was the right decision."

She gestures with her hand: *Please go.* She must save this last bit of herself, the dregs of her dignity. Mustn't let him see how much it hurts. She doesn't begin to cry until he has left the room.

Four

Sudha

I hold my face under the kitchen tap and scrub until the water numbs my skin. I bend my head and rub at my wet scalp roughly until all the mush is washed away. Still, I feel dirty. When I stand up, I'm light-headed with bending over for so long. Cold water dribbles into the back of my shirt and down my spine. My teeth chatter. My insides are black ice.

So many violences done to me. My mother pounding my life into the shape of her desires. My mother-in-law wanting to cut from it whatever she considered unseemly. My husband backing away, with his narrow, apologetic shoulders. Sunil plunging into the center of my body, corrosive with need. Each time, I made myself pliant. I gave a bearable name to what they did. Duty. Family honor. Filial respect. Passion. But today . . . The old man's spit on my face, so frank in its hate. I couldn't pretend it meant something else.

Why didn't I fling the cereal bowl at him?

Whore, he'd cried last night. His voice had crackled like

kindling. He'd looked straight at me, his stare flinty with recognition.

Inside the box of my chest, a rack of alphabets, rattling. When I put the letters together, they say, *This is your punishment*.

I feel a tug on my pant leg. Somehow Dayita has pushed aside one of the chairs. She holds out her arms to be picked up. When I bend down, she pats my wet face with both hands, then tries to wipe off the water. I bury my face in her chest and hold her tight. We've been running from place to place, hoping for shelter, for such a long time. And finally I thought I'd found it here. Sanctuary, if only for a few months. Enough time to lick my wounds, catch my breath.

Dayita doesn't squirm away as she usually would. She smooths my hair the way I sometimes smooth down hers. She pulls at my earlobes and sings a tuneless baby song.

Last night, while she slept, I pressed my face to her sticky fingers, fisted around a corner of her blanket. I'll take care of you, I whispered. I won't need anyone's charity.

Anju, what would you do?

An old habit. Whenever in my life I've been in trouble, I've asked this question.

I'm not thinking of the cousin I can't talk to anymore, the wife who might be cursing me right now, the woman so whittled by loss that I can hardly recognize her. My Anju is the fierce girl I grew up with, incandescent with outrage. *The old monster,* she says inside me. *The stubborn, selfish goat. Determined to make the whole world as miserable as he is. How dare he ruin things for me and my child! Who made him my judge?*

I'm not Anju. When I try to hate the old man, I can't help remembering the feel of his helpless, frozen flesh. How cold his limbs were, how stiff and reluctant. And suddenly I'm thinking of Singhji's body—how it must have felt when they found him in the morning. My father's body. A white wake of pain follows the words as they speed through me. To die alone like that!

Who knows what my future holds. And Dayita's. The futures that I have fashioned out of my carelessness. My mouth sours with fear as I think this. Still, I make myself lift Dayita high and swing her around. "If this is going to be our last day here," I say to her, "let's have some fun."

I walk over to the gleaming music system, its rows of buttons and knobs that on another day would have daunted me. I experiment until I get the tape player going. Among stacks of Tibetan chants and New Age fusion, I find a cassette of Hindi music. A song with a fast beat comes on. I remember it from the streets of India, blasted from the speakers of a hundred shops, whistled by cheerfully unemployed young men who stood on street corners, smoking and spitting. It seems appropriate, since I, too, will be unemployed soon.

Pyar Divana Hota Hai, goes the song. *Love is crazy.* The danger of clichés is that there's always a bit of truth to them. Hadn't we all believed in crazy love, waiting just around the corner of our days? Hadn't we all wanted the rush of that passion? We'd no idea how it might stalk a life, tear it to pieces.

I turn up the volume and swing my daughter around to the beat. The past is the past is the past. Dayita laughs, her new teeth gleaming. Six of them, I see with a pang. The last couple came in while I was too preoccupied to notice. Or is it that I haven't given her too many occasions to smile?

"Let's take a long bubble bath," I say, nuzzling the back of her neck. From Myra's bathroom I appropriate a bottle of aromatherapy gel that's supposed to soothe my chakras. It's the least the world owes me and my daughter. We fill the tub, climb in, splash each other. Mountains of fragrant froth rise around us. Froth on our Santa Claus eyebrows, froth mustaches on our lips. I've left the door open so our laughter mingles with the music. *Gata Rahe Mera Dil, My Heart Is Singing.* I hope the old man is listening. I hope every syllable pierces his black heart.

ॐ

In Myra's sparkling modern kitchen, I prepare an old dish. Bhaté bhat. It's a steamed dish that people ate before starting on a journey because it was quick and easy. All the years of our childhood, Anju and I never went anywhere. But sometimes, when we were sad, Pishi used to make it because we loved it so much.

I search through the kitchen: rice, yellow mung dal, potatoes. Some things I substitute for others, hoping they'll do. Isn't that the traveler's life, substitution and experimentation? For the coarse-skinned jhingay with its large seeds, I use zucchini. For sweet kumro, I use a slab of banana squash. With some misgiving, I replace the pungent mustard oil so popular in Bengal with extra-virgin olive. For some things, there is no making do: bitter melon, the small brown taro roots. Regretfully, I let them go. Tomorrow I'll tell Myra to get some from the Chinese market. Then I remember that I'm leaving.

In India we would have tied each ingredient into a piece of old cloth and steamed it with the rice, letting the flavors soak in. Here, I boil them in a pan, then mash them into balls flavored with salt and olive oil, a little pepper. I should have cooked this for Anju when I was living with her. God knows we were sad enough. She must be in her history class now, with that old professor who lisps, whose voice makes her doze off. Or is she in bed, her head burrowed under her pillow . . . ?

No, I can't afford such easy sentimentality. I removed myself from my cousin's life the way a gardener uproots a choking weed. I must not return there, even in thought.

"Half the fun of bhaté bhat was that we both ate it from the same plate," I tell Dayita. "That's what you and I'll do today." I fill a big plate, rice surrounded by a border of colorful vegetables. Then an idea comes to me. I make up another plate.

❧

I place the cart within reach of his bed, but not so close that he can snatch up something and throw it at me. Not that he looks like he's up to throwing much. The bedcover drawn up to his mouth. Only the craggy, pinched sharpness of his nose visible. The plate is so pretty, the cheerful green of zucchini, the warm yellow of the squash. The steaming rice, a small ivory hill. He must have eaten the dish many times in India. I want to taunt him with familiarity. I pour mango juice into a blue mug. He doesn't look, of course. Loose folds of skin hang from his cheekbones like Silly Putty. His breathing sounds like air forced through a too-thin pipe. I am sorry for him and angry, too.

I say, "Not eating will only make you sicker, and then you'll need to be hospitalized again. Is that what you want?"

He doesn't open his eyes. The lids are sunken, creased and purple. Is he getting dehydrated? Then I harden myself. Why should I worry? There's water on the bedside table, in plain sight, in a no-spill cup.

The air is full of the buttery smell of mashed potatoes. My stomach growls, reminding me that I haven't eaten since morning. I hear a distant crash. What has Dayita knocked over now?

I make my voice low and threatening. "If you don't let me

help you, I'll have to quit. And then what do you think is going to happen to you?"

He doesn't respond. His breathing doesn't change. I might as well be a buzzing fly. Troublesome, but not worth the effort of swatting away.

❧

We're sitting in the passage outside the old man's room because I want to make sure he can hear us. I've spread a bedsheet and put down Myra's best velvet cushions. "As though we're empresses," I tell Dayita, spooning rice into her mouth. The wall here is mostly glass. It overlooks Myra's backyard. Bearded irises. A tree filled with brilliant disk-shaped purple flowers I must ask her the name of. I imagine our conversation. *Myra, I'm quitting, I can't stand that evil old man for another minute. But before I go, what's that gorgeous purple tree in your yard called?*

Lalit would have known how to make a joke of it. But I'm not Lalit. I'm merely me. The only thing I know to do now, when all my other plans have failed, is to tell Dayita a story.

"So the old king traveled across the ocean to see the world," I say. "But he must have set out during rahukal, for when he arrived, he found that he'd lost the ability to speak. This made him sad beyond imagining, and then angry, and when in his anger he opened his mouth and screamed, a host of horrible toads fell out."

I use my sweetest voice, hoping Dayita doesn't understand the words. "This frightened his son and daughter-in-law. They didn't know how to help him, and, besides, they were getting tired of finding toads in their closet and bathtub and sometimes even their bed. They sent the man off to a castle where other old men like him were kept. There the attendants bound up his mouth so the toads would have no way of escaping, and fed him gruel through a tube attached to his nose. Every night they put him in a machine that sucked out his memories, until slowly he began to forget who he was and what he was sad about."

I pause to eat a bite of squash, grown cold by now. Lumpy and disappointing, it tastes nothing like the dish of my childhood. I maneuver some into Dayita's mouth. She promptly spits it out.

I'm not sure how to end the story, so I leave it unfinished. Isn't that the nature of today's stories, anyway? Besides, I have too much on my mind to be inventive. I must put Dayita down for her nap, call Lupe to come and get me, pack my few things. I fold away the bedsheet, replace the cushions. Dayita bangs on the glass, chattering to a squirrel that runs along a branch. My stint as Scheherazade is over.

The old man's room is very quiet. He's lying in the same position as before, his bony chin angled up to the ceiling. My heart races. *Don't die, don't die.* No, there it is, the slight fall of his chest, the long pause before it rises again. But the cart has been pulled closer to the bed! I see that he's eaten a few mouthfuls of the bhaté bhat and drunk a little juice. As I wheel the cart away, he opens his eyes and sends me a baleful glare.

I keep my smile to myself until I'm out of the room. The match continues, but this round is mine.

I cook a celebratory dinner: yogurt chicken, Basmati rice boiled extra-soft. I go easy on the spices so it won't bother the old man's stomach. When Myra comes home, I'll ask her to watch Dayita while I go for a walk. She'll be too happy to object. Hopefully there'll be a phone booth along the way.

❧

I make the easy call first.

"Where the hell *are* you?" Lalit says. "Are you okay? How's Dayita? I've been out of my mind with worry."

"We're fine. But how did you know—?"

"Sunil phoned me last night. He thought you might be with me! I've been calling everywhere since then—the police, the hospitals. Naturally no one knew anything. Just a little while back, I called Anju, hoping she'd found out something. The phone rang and rang. I was about to hang up when she answered. I asked her if they'd heard from you, and she said no. When I asked her what had happened, she hung up on me."

I swallow.

"If you're in trouble, couldn't you have called me?"

There's a riff of hurt in his voice—and something else I'm not ready for. How to explain why I couldn't ask him for help? Instead, I ask, "How did Anju sound?"

"Not good. Like she'd taken a sleeping pill or something. I'd ask something and there would be a pause, as though she were trying to get her mouth around the words. I asked where Sunil was. She said he was gone—whatever that meant. When I asked if she was feeling all right, if she needed something, she didn't answer."

All the elation I'd been feeling drains out of me. I lean against the phone booth, the metal wall sharp and chill between my shoulder blades.

"You plan on telling me what's going on?"

"When I see you," I manage to say through rubbery lips.

"I'm glad to hear that you plan on seeing me. Would it be too much to ask when?"

Don't be angry, Lalit. Not you, too. "Sunday morning, if you're free."

"If I'm free! Shit, Sudha, you know I'd rearrange—" He breaks off, then says more calmly, "Where?"

I give him Myra's address and phone number and explain about my job. I ask him not to call, except in an emergency. I tell him not to give the number to anyone.

"Want to elaborate on *anyone*?"

I don't reply.

"I won't pretend I understand," he says, sounding tired. "I just wish you'd trusted me enough to say something before you disappeared like that."

I can't bear to apologize, so I say, "Tell me a joke, a really dumb one."

"What, you think I'm a humor machine?"

"Please . . ."

He sighs. After a moment, he says, "A man goes to visit a psychiatrist. 'Doctor,' he says, 'I think I'm a frog.' 'How long has this been going on?' the psychiatrist asks. The man replies, 'Since I was a tadpole.' "

I laugh. But later I'll wonder why he chose that joke about self-delusion, if there was a message in it for me.

"I'll see you Sunday," I tell him.

"I live in anticipation," he tells me.

❧

Anju picks up on the very first ring, before I'm ready for her. Has she been waiting by the phone? I picture her sitting on the floor of the dark, dusty living room, her head bowed against the sofa, all the knots I combed out of her hair back there again.

How to begin this conversation?

"Sunil?" Anju says. "Sunil, is that you?"

"No, it's me."

Anju doesn't ask me anything—not where I am, not why I left. She doesn't even ask about Dayita.

"Anju, I'm sorry I had to leave so suddenly. I didn't want to worry you. I had no choice. Please believe me."

"You don't have to explain. It's your life."

Her tone is casual, just the slightest tremble in it, like a sitar's overtightened string. Only I, who know her from childhood, can tell how upset she is.

"Anju, listen to me. I couldn't stay there any longer. The way things were going."

"You don't have to explain," Anju repeats, her voice rough against my ear. "Sunil told me before he left."

I try to gauge from her tone what exactly he said, how much I can say now.

"You've got to hear my side of it—"

"He wants a divorce, so he can start his life over. With you."

"Anju, that's not going to happen. I told him that. He knows I don't love him. I said so again, in the letter I left for him—didn't you read it?"

Anju continues as though I hadn't spoken. "I was going to fight it every way I knew. Beg, cry, make him feel like a jerk. I was going to insist that he come with me for counseling—"

"That's a great idea! That's exactly what I was hoping for, when I left."

"But a dead love is like a dead body," Anju says, "starting to rot even while you're holding on to it, crying your eyes out."

Her words scare me, her voice, which sounds so reasonable. "Don't make any hasty decisions," I say. "You're both too emotional. Let things settle a bit."

"Can you reverse decomposition? All you're left with is the

stench on your hands. I'm going to sign the divorce papers when he sends them."

"Anju!" I cry. "Let's meet and talk first."

But she's hung up. All the way back, hunched against the cold bay wind that has come up, I hear the metallic click against my ear, the disconnection I've earned.

Five

The last rays of the sun die away, night drops over the cities of the coast like an exuberant net, the constellations play catch with each other, setting off sparks when they touch. No one down below notices this. All across the Bay Area, it is time for dinner.

Some eat it like Anju, opening the refrigerator door to peel a slice from a Saran-wrapped stack of American cheese. They stand at the kitchen counter, spooning Chinese fried rice, cold, from a too-bright red-and-white take-home container, reminder of an earlier, more festive time in their lives.

Some, like Sunil, sit at the narrow restaurant tables meant for customers eating alone, located in the back, near the door marked *Rest Rooms.* They examine a newspaper intently as they wait for their order to arrive. The NASDAQ is down again, and the Dow isn't doing much better. There's a whole column of Women Seeking Men (but where are they?). The lone customers take out pads and make notes. A few punch fervently at the numbers on their cell phone. If someone answers, their faces take on a beatific expression. *I am saved.* Sunil, who disdains such props, stares ahead as though he doesn't care that he's alone. When his food comes, he chews slowly, deliberately, not bothering to look.

At Myra's, the table is set with a silky maroon tablecloth with an Indian block print. Matching napkins, white bone china, expensively thin crystal. Brass candlesticks shaped like peacocks. Trideep opens a bottle of Beaujolais. They're celebrating.

"Don't be so hasty," Sudha says dryly. "He's only eaten twice, just a few bites each time."

"That's a hell of a lot better than our record with him," Myra says. She sweeps her hand upward, an extravagant, dancer's gesture. The wine trembles, translucent as a stained-glass window. "Here's to the magic lady!"

Sudha's smile strains like a hyphen across her face. She says nothing. From time to time she glances toward the door, as though expecting someone to enter.

"The magic lady who saved our marriage!" Trideep adds. Relief has relaxed the muscles of his face so that he seems a plumper, younger version of himself. "Delicious!" he claims, waving a forkful of curried chicken. "Who could resist this!" He bends to tickle Dayita, who has gravitated toward his deep, male laugh. "Your mom's a miracle worker, you know that, little girl?" Dayita laughs back and grabs his glasses.

"We want to give you a gift to show our appreciation," Myra says. On her way to the kitchen for another bottle, she throws her arms around Sudha and bumps cheeks with her in an air kiss. Her thin silver bracelets, twenty to each arm, jingle, exuberant.

"I don't want anything," Sudha says, though perhaps what

she means is that they can't give her what she really wants. No one can. But they insist, and over the second bottle of wine, an agreement is reached. It's to be a walker for Dayita. ("A playpen's too, too cruel," says Myra, shuddering.) They'll buy the kind with a wide, padded rim so that she can walk up to Myra's valuables but can't quite reach them.

"Think how much more relaxed I'll be," says Myra. "Why, it's really a gift for myself! We'll pick it up tonight, on our way to Sally's."

Sally is Myra's friend from college. "She owns this great boutique, right on University," Myra says. "Eastern clothing and art. Prime location, very successful. Her partner retired recently, and she's been pushing me to quit my job and join her. But what with everything that's been going on at home, I've been too stressed to even give it a thought. Maybe now I can consider it." Shyly, she adds, "She thinks I have a keen eye."

Trideep squeezes her shoulder. "You do! You chose me, didn't you!" He leaves his arm around her. Myra blushes brightly. Her hands, clasped in her lap like a madonna's, twitch once, then grow still. Her fingers are fragile and lovely in repose. They give off a sheen, like mother-of-pearl. She gives a sigh and leans into Trideep, who kisses her forehead. This is how they must have been before the old man's illness hit their life like an out-of-season hurricane.

Sudha looks away, biting her lip.

"We'll be back by ten," they assure her when they leave.

She waves them away. The wine, which has made them bubbly, has only tired her. "Take your time," she says. The evening stretches ahead of her, a desert, each minute abrasive as rock dust. "It's not like I have anything else to do."

❧

Southward, fifty miles, Freeway 880 is immobilized by an over-turned eighteen-wheeler that has jackknifed across the divider, spilling produce. Piles of tomatoes are crushed into red sludge across eight lanes, boxes of frozen spinach crunch like bones under the wheels of cars halting and starting and halting again. The drivers stare at the mess. Sirens, highway patrolmen block-ing off lanes with flares like giant sparklers. Where's the truck driver? There's a four-car pileup behind the truck, paramedics scurrying around with stretchers. A dazed young man sits on the metal divider, holding his wrist, which juts out at an unnatu-ral angle. A woman is crying, pulling at the neckline of her dress. Another woman's already been carried to the ambulance, an oxygen mask placed over her face, giving her the look of an alien. The drivers blink at the flashing lights. They swivel their heads, not wanting to let go of the wreck just yet. Are they thankful it isn't them? Are they sorry? Perhaps they're merely annoyed at the delay, the fact that they'll miss *Jeopardy*. The pa-trolman motions to them with a flare. *Move, move.* On both sides of the freeway, houses and houses, in neat, unknowing rows. People cooking dinner, checking homework, paying bills. Then sex, then finally the brief oblivion of sleep. On TV, a newscaster announces that seven million people in the world are now HIV positive. A hundred yards away, someone's speaking into a bull-horn. Someone else is screaming. The people in the houses do not hear them. Perhaps not hearing is necessary for survival. Traffic helicopters chug above, chopping at the sullen air. Spot-lights pick out the truck's name: *Lucky*. Between mouthfuls of macaroni and cheese, a boy asks his mother about perestroika.

He has to write a definition of it for school. I don't know, she says tiredly as she scrubs a pan. Ask your dad when he gets home. A hundred yards away, fumes rise from the surface of the road into the white glare, like mist off a winter river.

Off of the freeway, too, the motels, their names studded with words like Slumber and Holiday, Comfort and Discovery. Promises of rest or adventure, all at econo prices. In one of them, Sunil, in pajamas, is brushing his teeth. His pants and shirt hang neatly in the small closet, his suitcases are pushed against the walls of the narrow room. Just a bed and a small table where through the next week he'll eat his takeout meals, mostly from Meena's Chaat House ("Lowest Prices, Biggest Sizes"). At the bottom of one of the suitcases, he has two thousand dollars in traveler's checks, half the money that was in their bank account. He left the other half for Anju. Until he gets his next paycheck, he'll have to make do with it, and both the motel and the rental car (he left his car for her, too) are more expensive than he thought they would be.

He took a half-day today, though it was hard, there were so many loose ends to tie up before he left this office. But he told his secretary he had to. He drove around and around in the rental car, watching the streets for a woman pushing a baby stroller. In his mind she was wearing the same sari she'd been wearing the day of the kiss. Blue like water hyacinths, those beautiful, deadly flowers in the lakes of Bengal where mosquitoes that harbor killer diseases live. He drove to Lalit's apartment building—it was easy enough to find his address in the phone book—and parked across the street. He waited until it was dark, then darker. Until the lights came on in the apartment, and he was sure there was only one silhouette.

It's something he'll do each evening until he leaves for Houston.

He's flossing his teeth now, his hands making that careful, sawing motion. The string is too short, his fingers bump against his lips. It was the last of the floss. He'd looked at the container in annoyance, then thrown it hard into the rusted metal waste-basket.

He'd called her from work earlier today to give Anju the address of his Houston office. "I'll send you half my paycheck each month," he said. "You don't have to worry about money."

"I don't want your fucking money," she said.

The word was like a slap. She never swore like that. Inside his suit, he could feel himself starting to sweat. "Please be practical," he said. He was afraid to speak her name. He knew he'd forfeited it.

"Fuck you," she said.

In bed, he pulls up the covers to his neck, then kicks them off. The blankets smell musty, used. The sheets are abrasive with bleach. Through a crack in the curtains, beams from passing cars will travel, through the night, across his face like searchlights, startling him from slumber. Should he hire a private investigator? Perhaps he could take a loan from the credit union? But what would he say to the man? It strikes him that he doesn't even have a picture of Sudha to show him.

He rubs at the back of his neck—to be this tired, and unable to sleep. After a while, he gives up. The TV, then? No. He goes to the scuffed leather suitcase he brought from India as a student. Inside, there's a new tape player, still in its foam-padded box. He tears the cellophane cover from a tape, inserts it. Where's the electrical outlet? In the dark, he kneels to search the wall. There, there, the smooth plastic rectangle against his fingertips. The rickety table is cold under his elbows as he bends to the built-in microphone.

"Kid," he whispers, "I miss you. Where are you now?"

⁂

Eight P.M. She checks on the old man, who seems to be asleep. Eight-fifteen. She cleans the kitchen counters, but they are clean already. Dayita's bathed and in bed, tucked between pillows. Eight-twenty-five. Eight-thirty. The night is so silent, even the crickets have gone underground. Eight-thirty-five. She paces the kitchen, lies down, gets up again. Her hands feel dry—she rubs them with the aloe vera lotion she finds in the kitchen. She washes her face in cold water, makes herself a cup of chamomile tea with honey. Eight-forty. Silence packed around her body like shavings of ice. She bites her nail, an old habit. Her mother had made her dip her fingers in castor oil to get her to stop. She thought she'd been cured of it, the way she'd thought she'd been cured of other longings. Eight-forty-five.

She goes to the music console. Looks through the records. Here—how had she missed it before?—*Folk Songs of the Bengal Countryside.* In the quiet of the glass house, wood floors overlaid with carpets from Bokhara, the tinny plink of the baul's ektara is a shock, the raw tenacity of his voice. She turns off the lights. The white leather sofa gleams softly through the dark. He's singing an old song Pishi used to know, *O nodi re.*

> *River, I have just one question for you.*
> *O river, on your never-ending journey.*
> *When one of your banks breaks, you build another.*

But what of me, the banks of whose life
are all swept away?
O river.

She plays the song again, then once more. She plays it for an hour, nonstop, like a teenager. She sings along until her voice grows gravelly. The rivers of the Bengal countryside, which she saw only once or twice, from a bridge, or a passing car. Insufficiently. Nine-fifty, says the clock. To live all her life in a country and not know its rivers. Her face is hot. It hurts to swallow. Regret swells in her throat like infected tonsils. She can't let Trideep and Myra find her like this.

In the old man's room, the night-light is a keen blue. She sees that he's pulled a pillow over his face. Her breath stops. She runs to him, *Baba, what have you done?* But no, it's only his ears he'd been trying to cover. His sleeping fingers still clutch at the white edges. She loosens them slowly, not wanting to wake him.

Later she'll recall what she called him. *Baba. Father.* It's common enough in her culture to address old men this way. But still.

He knew the song, too. He thought of the rivers he would not see again. Green water. Kalmi rushes. Cranes stepping stiffly on silt. In sleep his profile is gaunt, stony. All excess fallen away. The evening has aged into ten-fifteen. Ten-thirty. Eleven. She touches the pillow cover, but it's dry. Some things are beyond tears.

༄

Anju is putting on her socks. She tugs at them with both hands. It's difficult, because she has two pairs on already. But it's so cold, the kind of cold that doesn't go away even though she's turned up the heat to the max. Her fingertips are shriveling with the cold. After she gets the socks on, she thinks, she'll put on her gloves.

One sweater, two. A brown one bought at a garage sale, a green one Sunil gave her one anniversary. She takes it off, throws it into a corner. She searches in the closet till she finds the blue-and-white shawl Pishi knitted for a forgotten birthday. On her head, a wool cap that covers her ears. She sits on the sofa and draws her knees to her chest. All the lights are turned on. The radio, too. The TV. She pushed at it until it was turned to the wall. This way she doesn't have to watch the faces watching her. She closes the curtains. The dark outside the window has faces, too. She checks the lock on the door, attaches the chain guard.

The radio describes suicide bombers in Tel Aviv, the TV talks of air raids in Bosnia. The refrigerator recites the beginning of a novel. *The scent of bitter almonds always reminded him of the fate of unrequited love.* Anju nods. Doesn't she know more about unrequited love than the rest of the world combined? How it can sit on your chest while you sleep, quiet as a cat, sucking your life-breath. That's why she must stay awake. She takes out her notebook and begins to write. The cold drags at her eyelids, pulling them down. But she mustn't. What if the phone . . . ? What if the doorbell . . . ? A cup of tea, just the thing, both to warm her and ward off drowsiness.

The kettle whistles half-heartedly. She pours, she measures, stirs. There, that wasn't so hard, was it, even with the mittens on. She lifts the cup in both hands. The lightbulb is singing a song about people who need people, how they're the luckiest people in the world. That's a good one! It almost makes her laugh. *What d'you think, Nicole?* The steam from the kettle makes a damp patch on the kitchen wall. If you stare at it long enough, you can see faces in it. Sunil's face, with that odd look of entreaty on it—when had she seen it first? When she asked him if she could bring Sudha over? His eyes said, *Don't put her so close to me. The pull between us is too strong. I won't be able to stop our lives from colliding.* All those fights they had—why, he'd been asking her for help in the only way he knew. But she'd turned away, her head too full of her own words to hear his.

And with that thought she's looking at the broken pieces on the floor, the splash of muddy liquid on her socks, the heat burning through, the splintery crash still echoing around her head. How did it happen? She takes out another cup to see. Ah, like this, the curve of china slipping through her woolly palms. Like this, the sharp star burst of fragments on the cheap, hard linoleum. She tries another, then another, jumps away from each explosion like a child from a lighted firecracker. When the shelf holding mugs is empty, she moves to the plates.

The many-colored shards around her feet are so pretty. She removes the socks from one foot and tests their sharpness with a toe. Oh, yes! The small pain anchors her to this room, this moment, keeps her safe from the vacuum that yawns beyond. In destruction lies distraction, she thinks, as she navigates the kitchen. The serving dishes hit the floor with a satisfying thunk, breaking neatly into two. Is this what people call a clean break? From the apartment below, someone yells. Someone bangs on their ceiling (or is it her floor?) with the handle of a broomstick. She barely hears. *In destruction lies distraction.* That's good! She must jot it down, use it later in an essay. But when she goes to the notebook, there's no space, the whole page filled. *Father father father father father father father.*

When even writing fails you, what else is there?

Anju moves back to the kitchen, using her arms like a swimmer to part the thickened air. Breaststroke. She'd always wanted to learn it, and now she'll never get the chance. She steps on the broken pieces as she goes: china, glass, porcelain, pottery, crystal. The crystal is from a set of wineglasses Sunil bought, was it for another anniversary? She grinds her heel into it. In the drawer, in the cutlery tray, are the knives. Each walled into its own neat compartment. The knives know the importance of not crossing borders. Once you break through a boundary, there is no way back without severe tire damage. Her foot has left bloodprints on the floor like Rorschach blots. The knives are magnets. She moves toward them unwieldily, like a block of metal.

She fits her fingertips to the drawer's ridge and pulls. The room is silver and glittery. She's listening for something she can't hear. She's closing down the compartments of her mind one by one. Click. Click. Click. A song on a tape recorder, the old one in her mother's house, with its fat spools colored a metallic gray, grainy with the static of years that cannot be re-wound: *All the lonely people* . . .

With all her strength, she slams the drawer shut. Half-runs, half-stumbles to the living area. The notebook. Her breath comes as if she's been held down underwater too long. She flips through the pages, then back again. Where the hell's that number? But when she finds it, she stares down at it. To call an almost stranger—someone she only knows through Writing Group—like this? To face the fact that this stranger is the only person she can call in the middle of a night when she's considering death?

. . . *where do they all come from?*

She was born a daughter of the Chatterjees of Bhavanipur, and grew up in a marble mansion so old and famous that passersby pointed it out to each other. *Look, that one.* On her first birthday, her mother invited a hundred Brahmins to come and perform a fire ceremony for blessing. Her marriage was written up in the social register of the Amrita Bazaar Patrika. Now, alone in a dim apartment full of broken glass, she must use the last of her willpower to lift the receiver. A sleepy voice mumbles something at the other end. Anju stiffens, all her muscles ready to apologize. To hang up.

She must grip the receiver with both hands. She has nothing else to hold on to.

"This is Anju," she says. "I'm in a lot of trouble. I need help."

They're the hardest words she's ever spoken.

Six

※

Letters

Houston
September 94

Anju,

I'm worried about you. I called the apartment several times late at night and early in the morning, and couldn't get hold of you. Are you okay? I wanted to tell you that you need not worry about money. Half of my pay-check will continue to be deposited into our joint bank account. Let me know if you need more.

I know you must be very angry with me. I feel terrible about all the pain I've caused you. Don't think I did it lightly. I'm hoping that with time you'll see this was the only solution possible for us, the only way we could move ahead with our lives. I hope, with time, we'll be able to be friends.

Please write to my Houston office address. I'm in a hotel and might move soon.

Sunil

September 1994

Sunil,

Am enclosing two letters for you that were overnighted from Calcutta some time back. The manager had signed for them and slipped them under the apartment door. I'm not living there—so I didn't get them until yesterday.

I've moved my stuff out. Inform the manager if you want to continue to keep the apartment. Or else, for a fee, she's willing to pack your things and put them in storage.

Have removed my name from the joint bank account. No point making deposits there for me. Did you really think I was going to continue taking your money?

Kindly stop writing to me. It's not my welfare you're concerned about—it's your own guilt. You'll just have to live with that. I'm not interested in being friends. I'm trying hard to "move ahead" with my life, and every time I hear from you, it sets me back. If you really want to help, leave me alone.

Mail the divorce papers to the manager. She'll inform me when she gets them.

> *Anju*

Calcutta,
August 1994

Dear chiranjibi Sunil,

Son, it is with great sorrow that I write this. Myself and various other relatives, including Gouri, have been phoning you nonstop for the last two days to inform you that your father passed away three days ago resulting from a heart attack, God grant him peace. We are very worried as to why no one picks up the phone in your flat. I could not find your office number anywhere, so finally Gouri suggested that I send this letter by overnight courier. Please call at once so I will know when you are coming. The funeral must be held within three days latest, as the body cannot be kept longer than that.

Your mother

Calcutta
August 1994

Dear Sunil,

I am writing this on behalf of your mother, who is quite overcome by all the stresses of the funeral and of course her loss. She is additionally distraught not to have heard from you, especially since the courier service insists that they delivered your mother's letter to your flat and have a signature to prove it. We have been phoning you everyday, to no avail. Finally, we heard a mechanical message that informed us that your number had been disconnected. Needless to say, this has increased our worries. Please contact us immediately so that we may know what is going on.

It was very difficult for your mother to face the funeral service alone, without your support. The hardest moment was when she had to set fire to the corpse, a duty traditionally carried out—I need not tell you this—by the son. She undertook it bravely, but broke down soon after and has been confined to bed. Now she needs you even more, for I believe your father's papers are in a confusion, and as you are well aware, she has no experience in dealing with such matters. Once again, please phone us immediately and make arrangements to come to India, no matter how inconvenient, as soon as possible.

Your mother-in-law
Gouri

San Jose,
September 1994

Dear Mother,

I was very sorry to hear from you of Sunil's father's death, though I am glad he didn't suffer long. It is too bad that it happened when we were out of town on a long-awaited vacation to Lake Tahoe. I should have left you a contact number, but I guess in my excitement I did not even think of it. However, as soon as Sunil gets a plane reservation, he will be on his way to India.

You will be glad to hear that Sudha has taken up a job in a town close by. This will enable her to earn some money, which she has been wanting to do ever since she got here. It will come in handy whether she decides to return to India or continue in this country. Money of one's own, as you have always taught us, is of great importance in a woman's life, particularly a woman who is alone.

Our dear Dayita is a joy, as always. She is so curious, and every day she learns something new. Sudha usually phones me at the end of the day and makes me laugh with her description of Dayita's antics. Both Sunil and I miss her delightful, sprightly energy and wait for Sunday, when they come and visit us. You would be so pleased with . . .

Santa Clara
September 1994

Dear Mother,

I read in your letter about Sunil's father's death. I can't pretend to be sorry. I'm too unhappy right now to be gracious, even to the dead. He was a cold and cruel man, and my only memories of him are unpleasant ones. He harmed Sunil in ways that I've been paying for ever since I became his wife.

What I'm about to write will come as a shock to you. I should have let you know earlier, but I didn't want to worry you. Now I feel that was a mistake. You're strong enough to handle the truth of anything. Had I told you, maybe you could have advised me, and matters would have turned out different. Well, it's too late now.

Sunil and I have separated. He wants a divorce. He told me he loves Sudha, has loved her a long time. (Did you suspect this? Was I the only one who refused to see?) He's gone to Houston with a new assignment, and I'm staying in a nearby city with a friend, a woman I met at the university, who took me in when I was at the end of my rope. (My new address is above.) That's why there was no one to pick up the phone when you called. Sudha has taken up a job, I think. I have not seen her, and don't wish to. She left suddenly, without explanation. I suspect it had something to do with Sunil. Maybe they're together in Houston right now. I don't know, and I don't want to know, though I do wish I could see Dayita once in a while.

My life feels like there's a gaping hole at the center of it. I tiptoe around it. One misstep, and I'll plunge in.

I can't write any more now. But mostly, I want you not to worry. I was worse before. I wanted to hurt myself. Now I've decided otherwise. I want to show them that I can survive in spite of what they've done to me.

Your daughter
Anju

Berkeley
September 1994

Dear Anju,

I don't know if this will reach you, or if you'll even read it, but I have to write it anyway. I can't concentrate on anything—I keep thinking about *you. I called the apartment and got the recording that says the number is disconnected. I asked Lalit to stop by and check on you, but he said no one's living there anymore. Where are you? I really need to talk to you. I know you blame me for Sunil's leaving, but at least you should hear my side of it. If you still want to cut me off after that, I won't bother you.*

Dayita asks for you all the time. She looks for you everywhere. Even if you want nothing to do with me, please see her, or at least talk to her on the phone. Don't punish her for what you consider my sins.

Call me at the number below. Here's my address, too, in case you prefer to write.

Sudha

Calcutta
September 1994

Daughter Sudha,

I can't believe it. You've ruined your cousin's marriage, run away from home, put Dayita in who-knows-what dangerous situation, and dashed to the ground all hopes of creating a better life for yourself with that nice surgeon. Only you could make such a complete mess of your life in such a short time.

And worst of all, to think that you've hidden it all from me with such devious cunning. Why, I'd still be knowing nothing if I hadn't come across Anju's letter quite by chance inside Gouri's bureau when I brought her a glass of barley water in bed. (Yes, I'd like you to know that after receiving Anju's letter Gouri suffered from chest pains and Dr. Mitra had to be called in the middle of the night.) Pishi, too, is quite ill with weeping and praying, and I am so mortified I can hardly hold up my head. So as you can see, you've successfully thrown two households into turmoil with your selfish-ness. This is why I advised you not to destroy your marriage with Ramesh by your foolish stubbornness. Because once a woman leaves her husband, she doesn't hesitate at anything. Even the most immoral acts come to her with ease. I shudder to think of the effect your behavior will have on your daughter's character.

But why am I taking the trouble to write all this? Most probably this letter will not get to you—for poor Anju doesn't seem to know where you've gone—and I hate to guess where that is, and with whom! And even if it does, you'll probably just throw it in the dustbin without reading and continue blithely with your life of sinful pleasure.

Your devastated and deeply ashamed mother

Houston
September 1994

Anju—

I respect your wish to be left alone. I won't trouble you with any further communication. However, you are always welcome to write to me.

I'm leaving for India to help my mother put her finances in order. I don't know when I'll return. I'm going to give up the apartment in California—I guess there's no reason in keeping it, now that you seem to have found a place that suits you better. I hope you'll let me have an address, in case of emergency.

I ask you for one last favor. Can you pack my things? I've called the manager. She'll put them in storage, but I just didn't want her snooping through them. Of course I am in no position to insist, I know that.

I'm enclosing a package for Dayita. Should you know where she is, I would be much obliged if you would forward it to her.

Sunil

P.S. You're still furious with me because I want to end our marriage. But be honest with yourself. Were you happy with the way we were, even when we were together? In our hearts, hadn't we already left each other a long time back?

Calcutta
September 1994

My dear Sudha

I'm sending this by overnight courier, in the hope that it will be forwarded to you somehow.

Your mother called me yesterday, so distraught that I failed to understand what was going on. She hinted at various calamities, and when I hurried over to the flat, neither Aunt Gouri nor Pishi would elaborate on them. I was left to conjecture about all manners of disasters that must have occurred to you, or Anju, or possibly both. When I asked when you were returning to Calcutta, your mother burst into tears. "Never!" she exclaimed, then added, "It's better if she doesn't, the shameless hussy." Knowing how she tends to dramatize, I looked to Pishi and Aunt Gouri, who are women of intellect and personality, for an explanation. But they were strangely silent.

As you may imagine, I am confused by all this, though I cannot imagine that whatever situation you have fallen into can be as bad as your mother seems to think. No matter what she implies, I cannot believe you would do anything that is truly immoral.

Sudha, all this long while I've been patient, waiting for you to make up your mind to come back to me. All your neglect, even your requests that I should forget you—as though I could ever do that—I took in my stride. I was certain that once you saw enough of the world you would realize that home, where people know you and love you in spite of it, is the best place. But it seems that my strategy was mistaken. The action I'm about to undertake now, I should have taken a long time ago.

I'm coming to America to bring you and your daughter home.

Yours always,

Ashok

Seven

Sudha

I'm sleepy all the time. Why, I don't know. The work is not hard. In fact, I wish it were harder. That way, it would tire me out so I wouldn't have the energy to worry. That way, I'd be able to sleep.

That's the other thing. I'm sleepy, but when I lie down at night, or even in the afternoon, next to Dayita as she naps, my mind won't let go. It's like the old exhaust fan we had in our school in India, in the lunchroom, covered with cobwebs. It revolved slowly and painfully as if it would stop any moment, except it never did. Round and round my mind goes, grimy with grease and soot. *I shouldn't have. I shouldn't have.* Sometimes I forget what it is I shouldn't have done and only remember the feeling.

To get myself through the nights, I'm stitching an imaginary quilt. A baby quilt, the kind one gives as a newborn gift. The kind I almost made once for a boy who was almost born. I've chosen the material already. A fine white silk, which I know is completely impractical. But this quilt, it's mine the way nothing ever was. More than Dayita. More even than my own body. I can do whatever I want with it, and what I do can cause no harm in the world outside.

Nights are when I wonder most what Anju is doing. Where she is. When we were growing up, she used to sleep with one knee drawn toward her chest. She always wanted an extra pillow, which would end up on the floor.

I pad my quilt with old cotton saris, each washed a hundred times in rainwater. I stitch it by hand. No machine shortcuts for my quilt. I use a stem stitch, which doubles up carefully on itself so it will never unravel.

Now I must plan the design. Must make it at once fabulous and real. Breathtaking in its complexity. Astonishing in its simpleness. Will there be women in my quilt? Mangala's silver anklets. Nicole's golden hair. Sara's (but why her?) iridescent nails. The lost ones, safe in a place where no one can harm them ever again.

Can I ask Lalit to go to the university? To wait outside her class, to speak to her as she leaves? No, no, that would be abusing his generosity.

I want my quilt to be like the quilts out of the tales that Pishi used to tell us. Sewn with resham thread in stitches so tiny and seamless that the images looked alive—and sometimes they were. Bulbuls flew out from these quilts on their red satin wings. Young lovers linked hands and disappeared down a shaded forest lane.

But there will be no lovers in my quilt.

೫

The old man doesn't talk to me, but sometimes he watches as I wheel in food, as I dust a little sandalwood powder over his concave chest after his daily sponge bath. Against my fingers, the white hairs on his chest are surprisingly tough, like roots. If I ask him a direct question, Shall I cook rajma beans for dinner tonight, or Shall I turn on the TV for you, what would you like to watch, he freezes like a wild animal caught in headlights. I've learned to say, Maybe the curtains should be opened a little, it's such a pretty day. I've learned to read his responses. Stiffening of the neck, eyes focused on an invisible object past my head: *no.* Eyes closed, a small, puffed-out breath: *I don't care, do what you want.*

Sometimes Dayita clatters in after me in her walker, which she loves. I'm understanding more of her baby chatter: her version of *juice* and *Froot Loops* and *blankie.* Sometimes she asks for Anju, sometimes for Sunil, whom she still calls Baba. She rolls up to the music system and wants me to turn it on, *Pay song.* Her favorite thing to do is to point to things and ask their names. *This? This?* She points to old man. This is Grandpa, I say, Dadu. Da-da, she says. She bumps against the bed. Da-da. The old man stares at her. Each time he looks astonished, as though he has never seen a child before.

Hush, I tell her. Don't bother Grandpa.

Da-da-da.

The old man exhales, a small, truncated puff of air, and closes his eyes.

"I do believe he's getting fond of us," I tell Lalit.

I wait for him to make one of his usual comments, *Uh-huh, right,* or *Dream on,* or *Hope lives forever in the human breast.* But he only says, with a new cautiousness that saddens me, "That would be very nice."

❧

Maybe I will put a river in my quilt, down which a boat travels. The boat will be shaped like a peacock, like in the fairy tales. The sails will be the color of peacock feathers. On the boat will be a woman, reading a book. Can I bear to have her resemble Anju?

&

The old man eats, but not much. Only enough, I suspect, to keep from being hospitalized. Stuffed baby eggplants, chicken baked in yogurt-almond sauce, rice pudding studded with fat raisins—nothing tempts him. He'll eat his few mouthfuls, then push the plate away. If I grumble, or try to persuade him, he covers his face with the sheet. Each morning, his profile is a little gaunter, a little more withdrawn. Each morning, the bones stick up pole-like under the tent of his bedclothes.

When Trideep and Myra come to see him, he doesn't respond to Trideep's questions. Myra's desperate small talk. He doesn't make requests anymore. He just closes his eyes.

"It was almost better when he used to yell and scream and throw things," Myra says.

"You must be joking," I reply. But I know what she means. I, too, am concerned as to where this might lead.

"Just when we thought he was getting better!" Trideep says, his face pinched with worry. "Why won't he talk to us? Is he all right?"

He isn't all right. But Trideep knows that. His father closes his eyes because he can't stand to be here. In this bed, in this house, in this country, all of which is alien to him. He tolerates me because I'm the hired help, just doing my job. But he hates them because they're his captors.

"He's sad," I say.

"How can we make him happy?" they ask.

But I, struggling under my own sadness, don't know the answer to that.

❧

This Sunday, Lalit wants to take me up to Grizzly Peak, to see the sunset across the bay.

"Go, go," Myra says. "I'll keep Dayita. She's good therapy for me. She keeps me from obsessing."

Up in the park, the cold wind stings my face, but it's clean and strong and salty. It clears my head a little. Thanks to Lalit, I'm beginning to recognize some of the trees around us—the bent black cypress, the peeled silver bark of the eucalyptus, the brittle crackly needles of ponderosa pine. Feathery yarrows, near our feet.

A small comfort, this.

"Look," Lalit says. "There's the campanile at Cal, there's the Bay bridge, backed up as usual, there's Angel Island, where at one time deer and immigrants were quarantined. That's the ferry to Sausalito, where all the decadent artists live. Did you know that Marin County is the home of the hot tub? Did you know that Coit Tower was built by San Francisco firemen in the shape of firehose nozzle? That's Alcatraz, from which no prisoners ever escaped alive."

There's such fondness in his voice. I'm racked by jealousy. To belong to a place fully, to know it so well that you believe it belongs to you. Does he even guess how lucky he is?

"Look that way," he says. "There's Mount Tam. See the Indian Maiden, sleeping? Once you get beyond the Golden Gate Bridge, you're on the Pacific Ocean. In November the whales start migrating south. The blues, the orcas. You can go out on a boat and watch them, spouting water up to fifty feet. It's like nothing else in the world. In February they come back up with babies."

"I'd like to see that," I say, though February, or November, or even next week seems distant and unreal, a fog-wrapped shore I might never reach.

"I'll take you and Dayita both," he says. "I'll take you to Point Lobos, to see the cormorants on Bird Island. And to Año Nuevo, that's where elephant seals come in December to have their babies. Did you know there's an island out there, a ruined lighthouse that's been taken over by the sea lions?" Then he says, "You never did tell me what happened."

I tried. Last Sunday, and the Sunday before, when he came to see me. But each time I'd feel dizzy, sick to my stomach. I didn't have the right phrases to make him see beyond what happened into the why. I was afraid he, too, would despise me?

"Do you believe in falling stars?" I say.

"Another brilliant prevarication, I see."

"I'm sorry, I just can't talk about it."

"Try. Don't worry about shocking me. I come across a lot of terrible things at work. Some of them so bad you can't even imagine . . ."

I fiddle with the zipper of my jacket.

"Oh, very well," he says, "what about the stars?"

I tell him about our terrace in Calcutta, the old bricks edged with moss. How Anju and I would steal away at night to look for falling stars to wish on.

"And did any of the wishes come true?"

"None of Anju's did. But she never really believed in it. She'd say things like, For my next birthday, I want my very own pet elephant. Or, I want to become the most successful female spy in the world, more famous than Mata Hari."

"What about you?"

"My wishes got all twisted around. I don't think I really knew what I wanted. My brain was so filled with old stories, and what society defined as happiness. One time, just before Anju and I got married, I was so sad to think that we'd be separated, that I wished we could love the same man, like women did in the Mahabharata, that we could all live together. . . ."

Stars are opening in the night's blackness, like startled eyes. Against them, a bird wheels across the sky, elegant and purposeful. A red-tailed hawk, perhaps, returning to his nest in some crag. Wild things always know where their home is. In India, kingfishers are bringing food to fledglings in their morning nests. In my quilt I will stitch in hawks and kingfishers.

I'd forgotten that old, foolish wish all these years. Until now, until I spoke of it. And, in speaking, saw it newly, in all its insidiousness.

"Your wish came true, didn't it?" Lalit says. The wind has died. The cypresses are icicles of dark. The clouds clap their hands over the moon's mouth. I cannot feel his eyes. I cannot read his voice. And so I cannot tell him, *It's not what you think. It's not like that at all.*

❦

It's dark when I unlock the door. In my mind I'm busy repeating the code of the burglar alarm, in case they turned it on, so I don't see him until he moves. Trideep. He's sitting on the white couch by himself, not doing anything.

"Sorry, didn't mean to startle you." His words sound slurred.

My heart gives a fearful leap. Why should he be here, waiting?

Pishi used to say, Do you know why street dogs attack certain people and not others? It's because they smell the fear. I wonder if it's the same with men, this pattern in my life repeated over. I try to edge by, intent on getting past him as quickly as possible.

"Can I talk to you?"

I massage the back of my neck with trembling fingers. I don't want to talk to him. All I want is to get to my room, shut the door, and push the dresser against it. Tomorrow I'll insist on Myra installing a lock.

Trideep slides his fingers in under his glasses and rubs his eyes. "Excuse me." He yawns, his glasses askew. I see that he'd been asleep.

A hot flash of shame hits me. The world doesn't rotate around you, Sudha. Not every man has designs on your virtue.

"Is something wrong?" I ask. "Where's Myra?"

"Myra's in bed with a terrible headache."

I know about Myra's migraines, blinding shafts of pain that make her sick to her stomach. She hasn't had one since the old man started eating. "What happened?"

"After you went out, we gave Dad his dinner—what you'd kept ready for him on his plate in the oven. He wouldn't eat while we were in the room, so we left. I'm waiting in the passage outside his room, then I hear these horrible retching sounds, and when I rush in, he's throwing up—except there's almost nothing in his stomach, so he's just heaving and shaking. I hold him as best as I can, and he doesn't even fight me, he's that exhausted. He's messed himself up, so I try to change his clothes—and he's emaciated, I didn't realize how thin he'd gotten. Then Myra comes in and sees him and gets all hysterical. She keeps saying, Oh my God, he's going to die. And I'm thinking the same thing. If only I hadn't asked him to come here. . . ." He buries his face in his hands. "If only I'd let him be."

I have no patience for his litany of guilt. "What happened then?"

"I called my friend Mihir, he's a doctor, and he came over right away and gave him some shots that stopped the retching. I ran out and bought some Pedialyte, and Dad was able to keep it down. But . . ." He shakes his head.

"What did the doctor say was wrong with him?"

"Mihir says the problem is primarily mental, compounded by malnutrition. He's suffering from severe depression, and Mihir doubts whether he can recover by himself. He prescribed an antidepressant but told us we'll have to hospitalize him within the next couple of days unless there's an improvement"—he looks up so suddenly that his glasses clatter to the floor—"and I know that'll kill him, I know it will."

❧

The old man's room is filled with the synthetic lemon smell of a deodorizer and, under that, the lingering odor of vomit and distress. I feel my way through darkness to the bed, stubbing my toe on an unexpected chair they must have brought in for the doctor. I put out my hand. Nothing but bedclothes. For a moment I think, with a strange elation, *He's disappeared.* But, no. Here's a knobby knee that twitches under my touch. I pull back—I don't want to wake him—but I'm too late. His breathing has changed, grown uneven and wary.

I'm thinking with sorrow of my father, whom I never knew. As Singhji the chauffeur, I'd always taken his devotion for granted. Tossed him the careless affection one gives to servants in India. Before my marriage, he took all his savings and mailed them to me—in an unmarked envelope so I wouldn't know who sent them. And I—I never did anything for him that a daughter should. Neither in his life nor at his lonely death.

But perhaps it isn't too late. What I couldn't do for my father, perhaps I can do for the old man. Perhaps I can prevent him from dying in an impersonal hospital bed, in a room filled with the fumes of antiseptic and dread.

"Help me to help you," I whisper.

There are shadows around the bed, jagged silhouettes like pieces broken off some larger slab of darkness. Pishi used to say, When a person is about to die, the souls of dead people that were close to him come to help him across. Maybe the old man's wife is here, maybe even his parents, come to take him home.

I yank at the curtains, slide open a window. "Leave," I whisper, "give him another chance at life." A long time ago, was there someone else dying, another room in which I performed a similar homemade exorcism? Frosty night air, fog, starlight tumbling onto the carpet. The shadows have turned into ordinary objects: TV, bedside lamp, the food trolley which Myra forgot to remove. The old man lets out a breath like a cough. On the trolley, a vase with an iris. Myra must have put it there. Does he know what I was trying to do? Does he think I shouldn't have interfered? There's an untouched bowl of something melted into a puddle. It looks like ice cream, Myra's failure to tempt him. Death is the only dish he's interested in tasting anymore.

"Don't give up," I whisper. "Help me to help you."

He gives no sign that he has heard.

In bed, I press my cheek against Dayita's back. *Calm me down, kid.* Someone I once knew had said that. The rhythm of her breath washes over me like night waves. In my quilt I must find a place for the ocean, though where I don't know yet. This is why we have children, so that in their sleep they might redeem us.

Today Lupe called to check on how things were going.

"Not too good," I said, explaining about the old man. "Do you have a number where I can reach Sara? An address?"

"Nope." Lupe sounded annoyed. "She quit the job I got her and went off somewhere. Didn't even call me. I have no idea where she is."

"I'm worried about her," I said. Though I couldn't have explained why.

"Save your worries for yourself. Maybe I should start looking for another job for you—"

"Not yet," I said. "I don't want to leave him until I absolutely have to."

"Don't get attached," Lupe said. "That's the recipe for trouble. Remember, it's just a job. They could put him in the hospital tomorrow and fire you. Then what?"

Dayita smells different, too sweet. It takes me a moment to recognize Myra's perfume, Natural Freesia. She must have held Dayita for a long time. I wait for the pang of jealousy to hit me, the way it would with Anju. Nothing. It is easy to be kind to strangers. Is Anju sleeping? When we slept together as children—a rare treat allowed us only during the holidays—she was a terrible bedmate. She kicked me all night in her sleep, stole my pillow. But we'd talk late into the night. I remember the excitement of those whispered conversations, the suppressed giggles, though I've forgotten what we spoke of. I will her to dream of me, to call me in the morning. Tomorrow I must talk to the old man. But what will I say? I slip my finger into Dayita's fist, feel the sleeping fingers tighten over mine. *Thanks, kid.*

Earlier this evening, Lalit asked, What did one psychic say to the other when they met?

The answer: You're doing great, how am I doing?

I laughed, then stopped abruptly. In all his jokes now, I look for hidden meanings.

(How am I doing? How am I doing?)

In my quilt, the waves will be the color of laughter, orange like balloons, like the sugar candy they sell on trains in India, like a parrot's beak. I will call it *The Quilt for Lost Souls.* In which company I include myself.

Tomorrow I'll tell the old man all the jokes I know.

Eight

Lalit

what I said

How about some coffee before I drop you home? Does the Café Monaco sound good to you?

what I didn't say

All right, since you won't tell me what happened, you leave me no choice but to imagine my own scenarios.

One: You guys had a fight, they (maybe he) said something related to how much they're doing for you, you left, insulted. Possibility: 35 percent.

Two: Your cousin and her husband had a fight, something to do with you, maybe related to money, maybe just the tension, too many people in too small a place. You felt you were causing a problem. You left. Possibility: 45 percent.

Three: Your cousin suspected something going on between you and her husband. She confronted you, you left in shame. Possibility: 55 percent.

Four: Your cousin's husband made a pass at you, maybe suggested an affair, you left, outraged. Possibility: 65 percent.

Five: You fell in love with him. You left so you wouldn't ruin their marriage. Possibility: 75 percent.

Six: You both fell in love with each other. You left to give him time and space to work out a divorce. Then you'll get back together. Possibility: 80 percent.

Seven: He made a pass at you. It made you realize that I was the one you really loved. You left, and are waiting for the right opportunity to tell me this. Possibility: 0 percent.

Never let it be said that I'm a romantic.

what you said
It's just where I live, it's not home.

what I said
What's home, then?

what I wanted you to say
Home is where the heart is.

(Sorry about the cliché. I can't think too creatively with you sitting in front of me with your windswept troublemaker face, the problems you won't tell me about tangled in your hair, so stubborn in your silence that I want to shake you.)

what I wanted to say
Could you make your home with me, then?

(More clichés. Thus passion doth make idiots of us all.)

what I wanted you to say next (with a demure, downcast blush)
Yes, dearest.

what you said

Could I have some hot milk with honey, instead of coffee?

(Later I took your fingers in mine. They were warm from holding the mug of milk. Your nails were like mother-of-pearl. I pretended to read your palm. I predicted that a dark and handsome stranger was about to become very important in your life. I added that he wore an ear stud. You laughed and then caught one of my hands in yours.)

what I wanted you to say

Lalit, you're already very important in my life.

what you said

Lalit, you're already very important in my life.

(I choked on the last of my coffee. You were tracing the lines on my palm with the tip of a nail. I knew what they mean when they say *an exquisite shiver went through him,* because that's exactly what went through me. I wanted to throw a twenty onto the table, take you where we could be alone and)

then you said

You're the only one I can turn to as a friend. All my life, men have wanted me. It's always been the wrong man, or the wrong time, or the wrong reason. And then I never wanted to see them again. Please don't let that happen between us. Please?

what I wanted to say

Shit shit shit shit shit

what you said

I can't be anything else to you, I'm sorry, I just don't have it in me right now. There's a lot of things I need to flush out of my system. I don't know if I'll ever manage to do it. But I really need a friend—and I'll try to be a good friend to you. That much I can promise.

what I said when I regained a bit of control

Friends don't keep secrets from each other. So are you ready to tell me why you left home?

what you said

Don't keep using that word! Haven't you realized yet that I'm homeless. That I've never had a home, only delusions of belonging which the world was quick to squish. And about secrets: they're what make friendships possible. If you knew everything about me, you wouldn't want to be my friend. But there *are* some things that friends don't do. One of them is, they don't pressure each other.

(A lamp hanging over our table threw a small shining over your face. Everything else was dim, only your face rising out of that fog of gray, the ordinary, dreary world. And your face glowed like a live coal, like a fire flower—are these clichés, too?—you glowed with your misfortune. I looked into my life and saw that it was merely a mechanical ticking. Even when I saved a life—or failed to save one—there was no meaning in it, because there was no heart. Instead, in my chest, a pendulum swung back and forth, going nowhere and so . . .)

I said

All right. (And when you slipped past my next inquiry, why you left your cousin, whom you obviously loved so much), all right. (And to whatever you asked me to do after that), all right, all right. (You raised my hand to your grateful cheek, it was cool and moist like a shell lifted from seawater, though I could not see any tears. No, the flesh of your face was soft and ripe as fruit, so sweet that it seemed to have nothing to do with sorrow, yours or mine. I thought of all the things I would never tell you now, I thought of blood, the woman they brought in last night to Emergency with a knife gash as long as her arm across her chest and stomach. I think she was Indian, but I had no way of finding out. She had no ID, only toenails painted the color of tropical birds. How the breath sounds when it's drawn into a torn lung. Sometimes in dreams I hear it. Once another woman came in with a broken jaw, she was holding it in place with her hand, when she could talk she said, I fell, I fell. I closed my eyes to hold in this one moment of brightness, my fingers on your cheek, each soft, separate downy hair, the faint, deceptive smell of lotus dust, all I would ever get [possibility: 100 percent] from you. I kept my eyes shut because your words were like a gate closing.)

and you said

Thank you.

Nine

The inside of the Los Angeles International Airport is like a speeded-up filmstrip. Seasoned travelers hurry ahead, jackets folded over their arms, pulling carry-on bags behind them like well-trained pets. They glance at their watches, adjust their dark glasses, pick up a bottle of Evian or a *USA Today*, and side-step a roadblock of eager Hare Krishnas without missing a beat. Stressed families with children strapped into strollers stutter to a stop by the flight-information monitors, matching the gate numbers on their tickets, then rush at the line snaking out of the McDonald's. Bumping into strangers, they mumble an absent-minded apology. Only the children in their strollers, thumbs in mouths, have the leisure to observe everything.

There's a certain magic in airports. Loci of arrivals and de-partures, they make the air crackle and surge. Worries circle overhead in airports like disoriented birds. Possibilities also. In airports, the horizon is always golden—but eminently reach-able. In a minute you might be pulled up into it, released of gravity. One can take on a new body here, shrug off old identities.

What of those who are left behind, who must get into their cars with only the talk-show host on the radio for company, who must pick out the parking ticket from the messy glove compartment of their lives, and pay for it?

Here's a stranger a lot of people are bumping into because he has the disconcerting habit of stopping unexpectedly in the middle of a crowded walkway. He isn't looking at anything, monitor or lighted sign or pointed arrow. He seems to know exactly where he's going, even though it's his first time at LAX. It's just that he's distracted, from time to time, by the enormity of his contemplations. It's Sunil, who left Houston this morning before daybreak, who has lost a good amount of weight. This makes him appear taller, older, more distinguished. A touch of gray at his temples gives him a new air of thoughtfulness. He's wearing his best suit, but under its elegance, his shoulders slump with disinterest, as though he's remembered that there's no one left in India to whom he has to prove his success. His eyes flick quickly through the crowd, do not rest for long on anything but the children. Correction: the girls. Older, he whispers to himself. Younger by two months. He is comparing their ages to Dayita. From time to time, he slips his hand into his coat pocket. Inside is a miniature tape recorder, complete with extra batteries. Sunil touches it lingeringly, the way an alcoholic might finger a bottle. *Not yet, not yet.* He's been speaking into it much too often recently. It's becoming a weakness, a new dependency, the last thing he needs in his life just when he's peeling off the rinds of old attachments. He must focus, instead, on what he has to do to make himself happy. But what is that? All this time he thought he knew, but nowadays certainty keeps shimmering away from him like a mirage. Dull as old coffee, his eyes indicate a betrayal. Something had been promised him, some incredible adventure, if only he left the numbing mundaneness of his days with Anju. Where did it vanish?

Passports checked, ticket stubs taken. It is the year of exiles returning home: Arafat to Gaza, Solzhenitsyn to Russia, and Sunil to a childhood he thinks of as an unhealed wound. He gives his seatmate a curt nod and leans into the window seat. He pulls a blanket over himself and instructs the stewardess that he is not to be wakened for meals. He has not taken off his jacket. The tape recorder presses against his hip, solid as a weapon. In his other pocket, earphones. Later, he will rewind the tape and listen to himself, trying to understand what he hears. *Even when I'm airborne, kid, I feel gravity's hooks in me.* Safety announcements, now. In the unlikely event of oxygen shortage, says a cheerful voice, masks will be made available. For improved safety, you must put on your own mask before assisting someone else with theirs. Sunil frowns his disbelief. Sometimes—he knows this from experience—there's only enough time to save one life.

❧

Four hundred and fifty-three miles north, Anju wakes heavily, in the old house she shares with three women, with the sense that something unpleasant looms ahead. Ah, she remembers it now, today she has to pack up Sunil's—what do they call them?—personal effects. She wanders with groggy steps into the bathroom, which is crowded with wet towels, various articles of underwear hung up to dry, an overgrown wandering Jew that trails its furry purple leaves over a wicker shelf, a stack of *Mother Jones* that is in imminent danger of toppling over, and

sundry toiletries whose labels proclaim they were never tested
on animals. She turns on the shower and washes angrily in water
that cannot seem to make up its mind to grow hot. Why hadn't
she just called the apartment manager and asked her to do it?
She doesn't owe that man one red cent. So why did she decide
to put herself through this useless, masochistic exercise? She
glowers at herself in the foggy mirror as she pulls on her oldest
pair of jeans, a fraying work shirt. She'll throw them away after
she gets back from the apartment, the way one does with con-
taminated things.

❧

Fifty-six miles to the northeast, the postman rings the bell,
hands Sudha a package too large to fit in the mailbox. When she
sees the writing, she has to sit down, her knees feel so weak.
Anju, she whispers. *Anju,* as though it is a prayer. But, inside,
there are only things from other people. She recognizes Ashok's
handwriting, her mother's dramatic slashes and loops. She
doesn't know the writing on the largest envelope. She tears it
apart, and a tape falls with a clatter to the wooden floor. *For
Dayita,* says the label. She stares at these objects, wanting to
deny their claims on her. Maybe she could just throw them into
the garbage compactor? But finally she gathers them up, her
movements rigid in their economy. For a little while she made
herself new under a new roof, among people innocent of her
history. But the past has the habit of catching up with you, even
in Berkeley. Now she must deal with it.

❧

Seven thousand eight hundred twenty-three miles to the southeast, another airport. Cacophony of coolies, blurred announce-

ments over the loudspeaker in Bengali. A man extends his passport to be stamped. The officer looks at the name.

"Going for a nice tourist visit, Ashokbabu?" he asks familiarly, leaning forward, giving the man a knowing wink. "Where do you plan to stay during your trip?" People are leaving the country all the time on visitor's visas, never coming back. Not that he cares. It's good riddance, as far as he's concerned. Let the American government deal with the illegals. Still, he likes to hassle them a bit, maybe make a few extra rupees along the way. But this man stares back at him, arms crossed.

"Yes," he says with polite self-possession. "I think it'll be a very nice visit. I'll be staying with friends. Their address is filled out on the form already." He holds the passport officer's eye until the man shifts from one foot to the other. "Watch out you don't get disappointed—or worse," he says spitefully as he stamps the passport. "I hear San Francisco is full of AIDS and earthquakes."

❧

She's pacing up and down talking to herself, as is her habit when something upsets her so much that she can't contain it inside the space of her body. Her mother's letter with its accusations, which she tore into the tiniest strips she could and threw in the backyard, it was too poisonous to keep in the house. Yet why should she expect anything different? Hasn't her mother spent her whole life putting her down, thinking the worst? The mother who couldn't bring herself to ever love her—who blamed her own bad luck on the daughter whose birth coincided with the news of her widowhood. And Ashok's kindness, his bland, infuriating goodness, like the milk-and-mashed-rice one feeds babies. What makes him think he can take her home?

What makes him think his notion of home coincides with hers? What makes him so sure that she isn't capable of immorality? She wants to do something wildly, scandalously immoral right now, just to show him. (Then it strikes her that perhaps she has done it already.) In any case, she hates them both, her mother and Ashok, though differently. For their presumption, their certainty that they know her—and what is best for her—better than she does. As though she were a callow teenager. Or a child like Dayita. And with that muttered phrase she realizes that she hasn't heard Dayita in quite a while.

"Dayita!" she calls, "Dayu!" Calmly, then louder, trying to keep the panic from her voice. She checks the bathrooms first, hounded by that old fear of drowning. (But surely the walker would keep her safe?) Now the closets, even the shut ones. (Who knows if a child might toddle in somehow and close the . . . ?) She's sweating, she clutches at the front of her T-shirt, her voice is close to tears. "Dayu, where are you? Oh God, why wasn't I watching you?" The bedroom? (Maybe she was sleepy and rolled in there and fell asleep somehow?) No. Nothing in Myra's bedroom either. She makes herself quiet before glancing through the old man's door, no sense agitating him. Then he might need something, and she isn't capable of dealing with that right now. There's the great hump of his bedclothes—he's often cold nowadays, even with the extra quilts and pillows she piles around him. She sees the back of his head, like some shriveled, fuzzy fruit. (But Dayita won't be here, she never comes here by herself.) She grips the doorframe, dizzy with terror. What to do now? Should she unlock the front door and check the driveway (but that's crazy) or the back porch, with (oh God) the narrow stone steps. Could Tree or Myra have forgotten (but they're so careful about these things) and left the sliding door open? What if someone came in while she was too preoccupied to notice and—?

Then she sees a slight movement on the other side of the bed, hidden, mostly, by the mound of blankets. Yes! She's maneuvered her walker all the way around until she's near the old man's face. She's standing there quietly, more quietly than Sudha ever thought possible for her, watching him sleep. Sudha slumps against the doorframe, then jerks upright, infuriated with relief. She's going to teach that child a lesson so she'll never scare her like that again! She's going to—. She starts toward her, then stops.

The old man isn't asleep, as she thought. (It's hard to tell, in any case. A lot of the time nowadays, he floats in an in-between state, negotiating the borders of unconsciousness.) As she watches, he shifts his hand awkwardly, his first voluntary movement in days. A few inches, slowly, along the bedsheet. It's tough to work the awkward contraption of bone and ligament that his arm has become, to force the signals of will along the crumbling paths of synapses. He's given up now. The hand limp on the edge of the bed. Dayita reaches out as far as she can, on tiptoe, it's still too far, she can't touch him, even with her stomach pressed against the walker's tray. Then she gives a hop of sorts, and her fingers close around his thumb.

At the doorway, Sudha holds still, barely allowing herself a breath. What will happen next? Dayita says something, the end of the word lifting, as in a question. Does the old man understand? Does he whisper an answer? The back of his head shows no movement; his hand, with its curled, yellowish nails, remains still. Dayita's eyes are caught by the shiny knobs of the dresser. She wanders off, intent on new explorations, the wheels of the walker rumbling softly against the wood floor.

❧

Anju is uneasy. It started when she put the key to the apartment in the lock—the key that never fit right all these years and which they never changed, though, like many things, they intended to—and it turned smoothly, allowing her in. She had the sensation that there was someone inside—or maybe something—waiting for her. Had she been writing a letter to her father, she would have said, *Not in a scary way, as in the horror movies, when the music goes high and fast and the lights turn funny and the camera moves jerkily around corners. Still, I didn't like it.* But Anju no longer writes to the dead. There was a time for that, but now it's over. Now it's the living that she must contend with.

The air inside the apartment is damp and stale. It is like being lowered into a well. She flings open the drapes, Anju who is learning all over again to be practical, to battle the amorphous world of fear and loneliness with actions that are small, precise, geometric. She up-ends the cardboard packing boxes to reinforce them. The plastic packing tape makes a tormented sound, like a prolonged crack, each time she tears off a strip. She looks around for something to cover the sound with. The TV? No, that's *his* territory. She turns on the radio, not caring which station it is. *Let music be my shroud.*

First, his books from the family room shelf, engineering and business texts from graduate school. Software manuals. She's sure they're all out of date. He should have thrown them out ages ago. It chagrins her that he should want them to go with him into his new life when he doesn't want— But she cuts off that thought. Today she's only a body. A body with two hands and two feet, here for a precise, bodily purpose. Lift. Bend. Stack. Climb on a chair. Old copies of *Business Week* and *Money*.

She throws them with vengeance into box after box. Let him pay the extra storage. Why, still, the feeling that someone's watching her? She's been to all the rooms, looked in the closets, even checked, like a foolish old spinster, under the dusty beds. She sees the calendar Sudha has forgotten on the kitchen wall, pulls it off, throws it in. She's had enough of warnings and advice. What more can happen to her? The newscaster announces another suicide bombing in Tel Aviv, a bus blown up this time, killing twenty-one and wounding forty-five. Several of the dead are children. Anju recognizes this as a tragedy far worse than what she is undergoing. She pauses in her packing to try to imagine how the parents must feel, the depth of their distress. But her capacity for compassion has shrunk, somehow. Now she cannot relate to anything beyond the distraught confines of her own skin.

The bedroom now, still smelling of his Claiborne Sport. Nonsense, she thinks, it can't be. But when she opens the bathroom cabinet, there's the frosted glass bottle, carelessly capped. She'd bought it at Macy's for some occasion, it no longer matters what. She's not going to think of why he left it behind, she's not going to let that get to her. She throws it into a box half filled with shirts. Let it reek into them. Fold, pile, close, tape. The empty hangers make a clattering, skeletal sound. The closet's just about done, only some financial papers on the top shelf. She pulls up a chair, climbs on. Bank statements. Prospectuses of old investments. In the back, *Penthouses* parading women splayed in poses that make parentheses of distaste appear at the corners of her mouth. She's not surprised, though. There's nothing he can do anymore to surprise her. She throws the last armload into the box and draws a breath of relief. There, her duty's done.

Then she sees it spiraling down, leaflike. A photograph. It must have been pushed under the stack of magazines. And though she's promised herself she won't look at anything, no more than if she were a paid packer, she can't help it. It's black-and-white, unexpectedly. Not the photo of a person, as she'd feared. (Okay, she might as well be honest, not Sudha's photograph.) Its lines and striations confound her for a moment. Then she remembers. It's the ultrasound photo from when she was pregnant. There's the lighted blip, like a cartoon star, that had been her son. Sunil had got rid of everything else before she came back from the hospital, the baby clothes, the car seat and stroller they'd bought from Babies 'R' Us, the books she'd picked up over the months, browsing through secondhand bookstores. *Mother Goose, Goodnight Moon. The Jataka Tales* she'd had her mother send from India. Why this photo, then? Was it merely an oversight? Or is this what's been waiting for her, a clue into that impossible, unfathomable man who makes her clench with rage every time she thinks of him? Except not now, she's cold now, all that wind coming in from the windows she opened. There's a commercial for a car dealership on the radio. *The best deal you can imagine and then some.* Anju holds the photo. Is it a message? But perhaps the dead do not send messages; it is only the living who imagine them. A song comes on, a woman's voice bittersweet as grenadine. *Love is a shoestring.* Why must there be so many songs about love? Though this one is more accurate than most. It's only a matter of time, Anju knows, before love comes undone, its unraveled edges dangling, causing you to trip and fall on your face.

She shivers, she's always been cold in this apartment, all these years to which she must now attach the adjective *wasted* because of his leaving. Even in her new place she's cold (is it her

karma then, coldness?), the drafty old house she shares with her
women friends. Though of course they're wonderful people and
she's thankful to them in the way one is to people who have
saved your life, a grudging, shamed thankfulness, tinted with
the desire to get away. She recognizes, suddenly, the fact that
she will never love them. Perhaps she will never love anyone
again. Her feet are cold, her backbone, even the nubs of her elbows, even her armpits. Has she been warm even once since she
left India, her childhood bedroom which, in her treacherously
selective memory, is always bathed in sunshine the color of
dahlias? Anju sits on a brown smudge of carpet in an unraveled
household and thinks of the flowers in her mother's garden. She
is still holding the black-and-white picture, the only proof that
a child was ever a part of her. *Prem? Prem, are you there?*

Alone with silence, Anju calls up the flowers of her youth,
one by one, from the depths of a lost golden world. But nothing
is fully lost, is it, as long as you can name it? Joba, Surja Mukhi,
Karabi. *He saved Prem's picture, all this time.* How is it that you can
hate and hate a person and then discover that a part of you still
loves him? Shaluk. Sarba Jaya. Damp fingerprints on the photo,
whorls like you might see, stargazing, through a telescope.
Chandra Mallika. Champa. Nayan Tara. The names drawn out
like amber taffy. Can flowers that sound so beautiful be real?
Syllables of brightness flicker inside her like a tube light with a
loose connection, which might turn steady, which might go out
at any moment.

෴

It is afternoon in the glass house. The child is lying on the bed
she shares with her mother, sucking her thumb. She's supposed
to be taking her nap. She considers sleepily whether it's worth-

while to fight this rule, stupid like so many grown-up rules. In the old man's room, she can hear her mother moving around, closing the drapes, darkening it for his rest. Her movements are elated, the child can tell this by the way her bangles clink. This is because she's managed the morning with some success, bathing and feeding both her charges without a major accident. Today she brought the child's high chair into the old man's room at lunchtime, along with his tray. She was a little nervous, the child could tell from the way she kept swallowing even though she wasn't eating anything. She spooned food alternately into their mouths as she talked to the child: Tell Da-da to drink his milk. Tell him if he eats up all his dal-and-rice, it'll make him strong. The child thought it was funny. She babbled obediently—not that any of them were smart enough to understand what she was saying. Well, maybe the old man. He gave her a conspiratorial look when the mother wasn't looking. They both ate a few extra spoonfuls to humor her.

Now, lying down, the child twists the end of her blanket around her finger and blinks with sleepy surprise at the mother, who doesn't usually come in at this time. This is because she's trying to get the child to learn a *good habit*, going to bed by herself. The child is perfectly capable of this, but doesn't always oblige—it's better, she's learned, to keep the adults off-balance at all times. The mother's wearing one of her saris today, which makes her look prettier, sleeker, like a watered plant. But what is that she's holding, that she's putting into the music machine? The child smiles. She likes bedtime songs. She starts to clap, but a voice is calling her, a man's voice she knows so well that it halts her limbs in midmotion. The mother has left in an agitation of fabric, shutting the door behind her. The child searches the room, her head jerking from side to side. She remembers the man, the warmth of his chest where she would lie for hours, listening to the stories he couldn't tell anyone else, old movies that blended backward into other, older movies, or forward into his life. She wants him, suddenly, that steady, comforting breath that she's almost made herself forget, the voice that never raised itself at her, that curve of arm, hard and soft at the same time, that held her as long as she wanted. But it's another of those cruel adult tricks, people appearing and disappearing from her life randomly, then coming back again, this time as a disembodied voice full of sorrow, *Dayita kid pumpkin I miss you so much I don't know if I can live through this when will we see each other again.* She lets the voice flow through her and out of her, carrying the pain with it. When she came to this new house, she cried for him for days, pushed away the food the mother set in front of her. Her chest hurt as if it had been caught in a slammed door. By the time she got better, it was full of silvery holes, like a sieve. She lets the voice flow through the holes upward, to where the boy waits. The dragonfly boy who darts in and out of her mind, always hungry. *Here, taste, here's what pain is like.* There's a spiderweb at the corner of the window, catching the afternoon light. A small, swaying rainbow, perfect in its symmetry. So much superior to the untidy tangles humans weave around themselves and each other. The mother has come into the room again, the mother is lying down by her, the mother has put the end of her sari over her mouth, though she makes no sound. The child lets herself wonder about this, but only for a moment. The voice on the tape calls like a thirsty bird. In the center of the web, a tiny spider, poised like a black star. She places her attention on it, lets it carry her away.

Ten

Sunil

From the airplane it looked impossibly green and forested and flat all at once, such a change to the brown hills I've been seeing for the last ten years that I thought it couldn't be. There were large irregularities of water, lakes or rivers, or even ocean. I'd heard that Houston was near the ocean, but in the gloom of this August evening, I couldn't tell.

I'm thinking of you tonight, Dayita, daughter. (Is it a presumption to call you that?) In my fancy hotel room, where the company has put me up until I find permanent accommodation, on this vast, arctic stretch of bed, speaking into a machine. I know that you might not get this tape, that I have no way of reaching you except through the goodwill of a woman who has every reason to hate me. But I must go on.

The scene from the plane reminded me of the jungle Aguirre saw on his expedition in the Amazon, a hidden violence in the vines, possibility waiting around the bend in the river, toothed like an alligator. (I grow poetic in my loneliness. Or is it melodramatic?) I must learn not to compare my life to the movies. This is America. I've left my wife, misreading invitation in another woman's eye, and ended up in a city struggling out of recession into strip malls and congested highways bordered by tenements and billboards. If you were with me, we'd laugh at them together. *To get out of Jail, Dial 713-Freedom. Fortune Cabaret, Girls Exposed. Don't Mess with Texas. Who's the Father? 1-888-DNA-TYPE.* If there are forests, they are invisible to me. The woman, a runaway, where is she now? I'm a small-time project manager beginning to lose his hair, undistinguished except by the unhappiness he has brought to everyone around him.

❧

Kid, do children know how to hate? Do you hate me?

❧

The people in the office here are surprisingly friendly. Perhaps it's because they don't know who I am. A bunch of young men invite me to go drinking with them on Friday nights. They surmise that I must be lonely for my wife. I have difficulty trusting friendliness, but one night I go with them anyway. My room is too sanitary, faceless in its luxury. The queen bed, the matching pastel bedspread and drapes, the empty writing desk and upright chair, gleaming from the maid's zealous application of Endust. The shine of the faucets in the bathroom hurts my eyes. The gilt-wrapped chocolates someone leaves each evening on my pillow make me gag. Purposely, I leave my dirty clothes on the floor, let toothpaste drip onto the bathroom counter, I who used to hate it when Anju did the same thing. My futile, animal attempt to mark my territory. This is what I've come to, kid! In the evenings when I return, the clothes are on a hanger, the counter spotless. Two golden chocolate mints sit side by side on the turned-down bed like newlyweds. I am ungrateful to complain, no, about this affluence, when all this time I'd craved it? Still, I went to the bar.

The night was blurry, even before I started drinking. There were dim lights in colored domes, the smell of sweat and expectation. Jukeboxes played sentimental country-western. Clink of glass and egos, girls in red heels that opened out in the back. Some of the guys in the group bought drinks for women they didn't know. Some of them were laughing, their hands on the bare arms of women who were trying to be beautiful. They wanted to set me up with someone. She was young, with pretty, scared-looking eyes, maybe a touch of Hispanic in her. A too-wide, too dark, lipsticked smile. I excused myself and went to the men's room. It smelled, unremarkably, of urine. A man was there, just he and I, alone. His hand was in his pocket. He pulled it out, I expected a gun. But it was pills in plastic packets. Such pretty, shiny colors. It wasn't what I wanted. The world is full of lonely people. But sometimes it feels like I'm the only one. I bought what he promised even though I don't believe in promises. Hadn't she promised, too? Your mother, the way she raised her chin at me? When I went back to the bar, everyone was laughing. No one saw me. What is worse than everyone around you laughing, and you not able to join in?

Three days later, in the hotel room, I broke the pill like the man had instructed and put it on my tongue. I said to the darkness, Since I can't have what I want.

❧

Kid, each morning I open the *Houston Chronicle,* delivered outside my door courtesy of the hotel. The headlines are thorned and black. The stories of the world have nothing to do with my life.

❧

I remember your weight on my chest. All your edges are soft and rounded, nub of elbow, tip of nose. Some nights I wake up, or maybe I have not slept at all, and bring my hand to my face. *If I touch nothing, I'll know I no longer exist.* A slight, sweet smell in my palms: aloe vera from Baby Wipes. Kid, your cheek has a dimple—but is it on the left, or the right? Memory begins to betray me, tearing along its folds like old silk. Your fingers in mine, slender like the white furl of lilies. Or is it your mother I'm thinking of? In the dark, things run together. In the dark, my body cramps with doubt. She kissed me back, I'm sure she did. Under my body, her body shook with ecstasy.

Have I made a terrible mistake? Dayita, can you hear me? Answer me, Sudha, if you're listening, too.

❧

My father is dying. No one at the company knows this. They only know that I'm the first to get to the office, the last to leave. A solid worker, tenacious as a bulldog when putting deals together. They don't know that I use work like a cough syrup, to suppress the symptoms of my disease. More work, more. It makes me loose-limbed and light-headed. But all the while, like a lump in the abdomen, the infection keeps growing.

That's the kind of thing Anju would have said. She liked talking in images. I'd laugh at them, call them fanciful. Now, having cut myself from her, I find myself taking on her ways.

Last night I woke up at 2:00 A.M., couldn't sleep again. Turned on the TV, the middle of a movie, a man and a woman

walking back in the night. I knew right away they were not husband and wife. In the same way that I knew she was married to
someone else. She was taking him to her house. There were
chimes, silvery sounds in the black night. Then he was outside
the house, she was inside. She locked the door. He picked up
a porch chair, smashed the picture window with it. Oh, the
shower of glass, falling in toward her like a waterfall, like it
would never end! The look in her eyes, shocked, as though she
hadn't led him to this. And then pleased, because she knew she
had. His face burned with wanting. I'd seen that look before, in a
mirror. I turned off the movie. I knew already how it would
end.

I think of my father in images. A clenched fist. (But that's not
accurate. He never hit me. He had other methods.) A bulge-
eyed cartoon character, yelling rage. His ears give off wavy lines
of heat. (But he rarely yelled. He didn't need to.) A diseased
root, black and misshapen, its insides eaten away with hate.
(Yes.)

What did I do—and my mother—to arouse so much hatred?

Maybe I should go to Calcutta before he dies, kid, just to
make him tell me.

❦

I left the lights off in the hotel room. Still, I could see it on my
palm. My pill. White like the September moon. It glowed all the
way down my throat. It shone like a pearl inside my stomach.
The shining took over the rest of my body. I could feel the inside of my skin, how silky it was. Pink silk, coming undone. I fell
on the floor, I felt each strand of the carpet under my cheek.
Tiny tentacles. Through the parted curtain I could see a star.
There were rays around it, as in children's pictures. Blue rays.

The rays came all the way into the room and touched my forehead. Icy. Icy. I thought my head would burst with exquisite pain. Then I was crying. I remembered the man telling me, better not do it alone. But alone is all I have. Kid, are you ashamed of my weakness? Each hair on my arm stood up, singing an anthem. The star beam was like a lance all the way from the sky to the center of the earth. Its point pierced me, there was no pain. For a moment, for a lifetime, I was a bead on a necklace, connected to all the other beads. I stretched my hand across three states and touched you, Dayita, you shivered in your sleep. She was lying on the other side of you, in a room made of glass. Her nightdress had slipped off her shoulder. There was a red mole on her collarbone. She smiled at my touch. Write my number down, I said. Here's my address. Here's my e-mail. My cell phone. The words were like underwater explosions. I thought the shaking would never stop.

Earlier today I got the letters that said he was dead. Dead. The word held a tidal wave in it. I held out my arm. In it, a million cells were dying every moment. I hated him, I did not hate him. We are all dead, only we don't know it yet. The string broke, all the beads scattered among the ashes. Call me, Sudha, do you hear me, at least send a letter. I gave up everything for you. You can't abandon me like this. The starlight withdrew itself. The pill was a cold sickness in my stomach. I crawled on all fours to the bed. I took off my clothes, I took off my legs, my right arm. I took off my head. It was hard to do, with only one arm. I gently loosened the eyes from their sockets. Pain is corkscrewing its way through me. Kid, I'm waiting for your letter, saying your mother was wrong, she was scared, she felt guilty for no reason, now she's reconsidered. For the next two days, I'll have blinding headaches. I'll throw up in the office bathroom. My coworkers will watch me out of the corners of their eyes. The bedsheet has wrapped itself around me thread by white thread, like the dhoti they must have put on him before taking him to the crematorium. If I have no forgiveness in me, can I ask to be forgiven? Dayita, are you there, can you hear me? Dayita, I'm waiting.

Eleven

Sudha

The afternoon is full of sleep and rain. Sleep like rain throughout the house, falling, and we falling into it, the old man curled on his bed like a wisp of hair, the mother and daughter lying against each other like pieces of a puzzle that don't quite fit. The rain carries flutes, mildew, the entreaties of dreams. In the dream, a male voice elongates our names with anguish, which is sometimes called love—Dayitaaa, Sudhaaa—until they sound alike. It offers us sembak jasmines, the beach at Galveston, the NASA Space Center. It offers phone numbers and a future ready for plucking like a ripe pomegranate. The old man dreams of a place named after rain, hills colored like the backs of elephants, the Tista River bounded by the years of his childhood.

In my dream, a woman is packing up an apartment and a life. She reaches into a closet, into the folds of suits belonging to a husband that no longer was. She takes a black-and-white photo, a child not yet born. She slips it into her bra. The husband that no longer was opens his arms to me: *Come, come.* I peel the pomegranate, my hands are stained with juice the color of blood. In my dream I strike out, the tape recorder falls to the ground with a sharp crack, the voice goes on calling. *Sudha, Sudhaaa.*

In my dream, I'm asking the old man riddles another man told me. *Why is a woman's mind cleaner than a man's? Why are politicians like soiled diapers? What's the difference between a soldier and a lady?* Even when I give him the answers, he doesn't smile. *Smile, damn you.* He looks at me without reproach. His eyes are full of the place named after rain.

In my dream, I tell my daughter the story of Sita's trial by fire.

After Ram had rescued her from the demon Ravan, he claimed he could not take her back because she may have slept with him.

But I didn't, Sita said.

Where's the proof? he asked.

Light me a fire then, she said. I don't want to live anymore.

He obliged. She stepped into the flames. But she didn't burn. The god of fire himself brought her back and vouched for her innocence. Ram and Sita were happily reunited.

(But, having been doubted that way, can a woman be happy again?)

In my dream, a different man this time. (This is the shape of my life, man after man, none of them right for me. Or is it I that am not right for them?) He holds out his passport to be stamped by an official in the San Francisco airport. He is taking a taxi in a country he's never visited, to an apartment he's never seen. He stares out of the window at the freeway dark with rain and oil slicks.

Sudha, Sudhaaa. In her dream, my daughter butts her head against my breasts in startled protest. When she wakes up, she will search for his voice in every room, the walker rolling over the polished wood floors like distant thunder.

I am in a vast chamber filled with incense smoke and the faces of the dead. Is it a courtroom? Is it judgment day? Am I dead, then? I see my father, I see an unborn boy. Nicole. Mangala. Sara (is she dead, too?). Their faces are dim with sadness and smoke. *Tell me,* I say, *what should I have done?*

The woman has finished packing and weeping. The taxi has reached the apartment where no one lives anymore. The unborn boy holds up his palms, white as paper on which nothing has been written. On the tape, the man's voice speaks of age and cruelty, death and home. Is death our only home? The woman walks out of the apartment, the man steps out of the taxi. They meet on the threshold, which is neither inside a house nor outside of it. The old man mumbles in his sleep, *Banglar mukh ami dekhiachi tai ami . . . I have seen the face of Bengal, so I no longer . . . . .* What comes after that? I can't remember. Once by a brown river a man spoke this same poem to a woman who was (but is no longer) me.

Tell me, I ask the dead, *what should I do?*

The dead do not give advice. They watch with sorrow as we repeat our mistakes, the same mistakes, across the world and time. I look into my father's face to see if it is still scarred or magically healed. But words like *scarred* and *healed* belong only to the living. The man from India sits on the doorstep of the apartment, listening. The woman whose husband has left her sits next to him. She is saying things to him she hasn't been able to tell anyone. Is this because he has appeared out of her childhood and mine, that time when she could say anything she wanted? He puts an arm around her.

Tell me something.

The dead do not speak. Or maybe they are speaking, but I lack the ability to hear. The rain, which had gone away, returns now with a sound like conches. The old man recites, *I wake in the dark to see, sitting under a large umbrella leaf, the doyel, bird of dawn.* The voice on the tape says, *I will not let you go unless.* I am standing in a vast chamber walled with incense smoke. The floor is clear as diamonds. The unborn boy is pointing downward with his unlined palm, the gesture of deities in temples. Once a man spoke to me of love in a temple smelling of crushed marigolds and incense. I was young, then. I look down through the diamond floor on hills the color of elephants' backs in the rain. The man and the woman sit on the doorstep, emptied of words. They lean a little into each other. They've come to a decision of sorts, though I don't know what that might be.

I've come to a decision, too. But this act I am to undertake, is it penance or gift or victory over the illegitimate needs of the body? By what name shall I call it?

In my dream, I say to the old man, I will give you what you want most in the world, but you must do as I say.

In my dream, his smile is chipped and yellow, delicate as an heirloom, as the moon.

Twelve

She sees him as she walks out of the classroom, her head so full
of people in books that at first she doesn't recognize him. Lately,
people in books seem more real to her than people in her life,
and certainly more dependable. Open to page twenty-five and
you'll find the old man and old woman, carrying bowls of rice
and soup and a leafy branch of peaches, every time. Every time
they'll invite the stranger girl to eat with them. Even when the
characters have no names, you know them by their gestures,
their tics as familiar as that of elderly relatives. In fact she's beginning to think of names as graceless conveniences, like tags
on baggage, is considering ways of shedding hers. So when the
young man detaches himself from the wall he's been leaning
against and comes forward with easy footsteps and an out-
stretched hand, *Anju,* it takes her a moment to respond.

"Anju?" he says again, his brows drawn into questioning arcs,
good-looking in such a guileless way that she finds herself smiling back, assuring him.

"Yes, I'm Anju."

And it comes back to her in a flush of memory, that party night, mirrors and strobe lights and sexy, smoky laughter, the house lit like a pink cake, all of them drunk on music and what-might-happen (how young they were then, how young and unknowing). *Tonight I'm gonna dance with someone else.*

"I'm Lalit," the young man says. "You remember . . . ?"

"Yes."

"You look different—you've cut your hair, haven't you?" He pauses, too polite to mention all the weight she's lost.

"You look different, too—didn't you used to wear a earring?"

He waves his hand dismissively, as though to suggest that he's beyond such frivolities now. There's an awkward pause, then he says, "I might as well say it—Sudha sent me to meet you."

She flinches, starts turning away.

"Please don't," Lalit says. "I'll just have to keep coming back until you talk to me, and it's hard, you know, canceling surgery and all—patients expiring like flies even as we speak—or, in this case, don't speak. . . ."

She looks at him through narrowed eyes. "Did you really cancel surgery?"

"No, my associate took over for the day. That's worse, actually. He's brand-new, and very enthusiastic. I had a gall bladder case today—for all I know by now he's removed the appendix also, and maybe a kidney as well."

"You always did like to joke."

"I guess I'm losing my touch—you're not laughing."

Anju sighs. "Ten minutes," she says. "I'll give you ten minutes. You can walk to the bus stop with me."

☙

In the glass house, Sudha is making tea. She prepares it Indian-style, the milk and water mixed together in a pan, the ground cloves and cardamom sprinkled in, lastly the tea bags—she has bullied Myra into buying a large box of Lipton's Traditional Blend—lowered dangling from their tagged strings into the bubbling liquid. ("Are you sure you want this horrible caffeinated stuff?" Myra had asked. "Absolutely," said Sudha, who is learning more every day.) She makes it strong, lets the fragrance weigh the air, stirs in sugar with a generous hand. ("Are you sure you don't want to try some of this lovely clover honey?" "Absolutely.")

The old man is lying in bed, eyes closed, but he smells the tea as Sudha wheels in the cart, and so he doesn't fuss too much when she props him into a sitting position.

"I think your stomach's settled enough for you to have some cha today," she says as she holds the cup to his mouth. "Careful, it's very hot. Do you like it?"

He doesn't reply, but he takes a tiny avid sip, and then another.

"Of course, this probably isn't as good as what you're used to in India—Trideep told me you lived near a tea estate up in the hills. . . ."

The old man stops drinking, glares at her.

"I know what you're thinking—it's cruel of me to bring up India when you miss it so much. . . ."

He's let himself fall back onto his pillow, eyes pinched shut.

"There you go again, acting like I was a bad smell. Closing your eyes won't make your problems disappear, you know. I have a better plan—if you'll give me half a chance."

He turns from her. It takes a while, his limbs are so weak, but finally he's facing the wall, breathing heavily, the quilt pulled up to his neck.

"Listen to me," Sudha says. She tugs the quilt away. "I insist. After that you can go back to being a stubborn old curmudgeon again." She pauses for emphasis. "I'm trying to help you get back home."

No sound in the room, not even a breath.

"We can do it. The doctor says that the main obstacle to your recovery is mental, and I agree. If you want to go home, you've got to start cooperating. Eat right—not just those few symbolic mouthfuls. Start doing a few simple exercises in bed, and then maybe in the wheelchair." She crosses over to the other side of the bed, kneels and puts her face near his. "I'm serious! Open your eyes! Look at me!"

He opens his eyes slowly, unwillingly. They're black with the pain he numbed himself against feeling all these weeks.

"You're thinking that Trideep won't let you go back, aren't you? Well, I have a plan. But you've got to talk to me, to say something. Something nice, mind! Or I won't tell you." She risks a grin, licks her lips lightly. Does he see how nervous she is, underneath?

He licks his lips, too. They're trembling.

"Hurry—I think I hear Dayita waking up. I'll have to go in a minute."

His voice comes out cracked and furious, so low that she has to bend closer to hear. "Stop torturing me."

"That isn't exactly what I had in mind when I said *something nice.*"

"I'll never get back home, I know it. I'm going to die here."

"You certainly will if you keep up this kind of positive

thinking," Sudha says cheerfully. "Whoa, there she goes! That kid's got a voice like a pterodactyl. See you in a bit."

She comes back with Dayita, settles her in the high chair with a cup of milk and some animal crackers, sings nursery rhymes to her until he says, grumpily, "Turn me over so I can see the child."

"Hi," Dayita says when she sees his face. "Hi, hi, hi, hi, hi." She holds out an animal cracker for him.

"It's her new word," Sudha says. "Brace yourself—you're going to hear a lot of it."

"You don't have a plan." He pauses for breath between phrases. "You're just trying to trick me."

Sudha covers her face with her hands. "I confess, I confess. It's a heinous conspiracy. I was foolish to think we could pull the wool over your eyes. I might as well tell you—the FBI is involved, too."

"Your jokes are in poor taste."

"You won't let me talk seriously, you won't let me joke, what do you want me to do?"

"Just tell me," he says in a tired voice.

"Once you're strong enough, they'll let you go back. If I go with you."

His eyes fly to her face. "What do you mean?"

"Go back with you—like a nurse, you know. Take care of you the way I'm doing here."

"Why would you want to do that?" his voice is suspicious, but she can see the rapid beat of a pulse in his emaciated throat. "Young people who come to this country never want to leave."

Sudha shrugs. "America isn't the same country for everyone, you know. Things here didn't work out the way I'd hoped. Going back with you would be a way for me to start over in a culture I understand the way I'll never understand America. In a new part of India, where no one knows me. Without the weight of old memories, the whispers that say, *We knew she'd fail*, or *Serves her right*."

"Help me sit up," the old man barks. He struggles impatiently as she places the pillows behind his back. "You're serious? You're not just saying this to fool me into getting better?" A worse possibility strikes him. "Or . . . because you feel sorry for me?"

She shakes her head. "Let's get this straight right from the first. It's got to be a good business proposition for me. They'll have to pay me well enough to bring Dayita up properly—she'll be coming with me, of course. I take it that's okay with you? I want to be able to send her to a really good school. And put away enough in savings so I never have to depend on anyone again." Does he see how her mouth hardens as she says this? "But I figured they wouldn't object. Dollars go a long way in India."

"They wouldn't have to . . . I . . ." But he doesn't complete the sentences.

"And think how much Myra will be saving once you're gone—all those stress-reducing elixirs and aromatherapy massages don't exactly come for free, you know."

He frowns.

"Just kidding. Here, Dayita wants you to have an animal cracker. It's a trifle soggy. Do you mind?"

He takes the cracker, bites into it absentmindedly.

"Attaboy!" says Sudha. "Way to go!" She's been watching reruns of *All in the Family* on afternoon TV. "I'll have only one regret when I leave."

He tightens his grip on the cracker until it crumbles onto the bedsheets.

"All the trouble I took to learn the latest American expressions—and now there'll be no one to use them on."

❧

"She misses you," Lalit says. "She wants to write to you."

"Who's stopping her?"

"She wants to make sure you'll read what she has to say. That you'll respond."

"What does she want me to write? *Dear Sudha, thank you very much for breaking up my marriage?*"

"Look—there's a lot of gaps in the story which neither of you is willing to fill in, but this much I'm sure of: she left your home as much for your sake as hers. She worries about you all the time. One of the reasons she asked me to come see you is to make sure you're okay."

"No thanks to her," Anju says. She hugs her arms, shivers a little in the evening chill. They've been sitting on the bus stop bench for half an hour. A bus pulls up to a stop with a rattle, but she doesn't even look. "She's really taking care of this old man?" she asks after a while, her tone rough. "You've been to see her?"

"I have."

"These people—they're treating her well?"

He gives her a quizzical look. "They are."

"And . . . Sunil?"

"She hasn't been in touch with him, and doesn't intend to, as far as I can tell."

"Do you—?"

"Love her? I'm not sure. People use that word too easily, anyway. I might be on the way to it. I'd certainly like a chance to find out. But she told me that what she needs right now is a friend—so that's what I'm trying to be."

"I think you do love her," Anju says. "Maybe too much." She sighs. "I don't blame you. They all do. She's very lovable, my cousin."

"Listen, you've got to put it behind you, whatever happened between her and your husband—"

"Easier said than done. But I wasn't referring to that. I was thinking about Ashok—did she tell you about him? Her childhood sweetheart?"

"Ah! A rival. Should I be concerned?"

"Well, he's here, for one thing—"

"The plot thickens. Maybe that's why Sudha ran away?"

"I hate to dash your hopes to the ground. He did send a letter—but only after she left. I didn't open it—figured it wasn't my business. Just forwarded it to her new address. A couple days back, I'm at the apartment, packing, and he shows up. It was a bit of a surprise for both of us."

"That's what I love about you, your masterly understatements."

"He's come to take her and Dayita home. He's been waiting forever to marry her—"

"I'm all for him continuing to do that."

"Ah, but he's determined this time, and that's where you come in."

He throws her a look filled with misgiving. "Oh, no, don't even think of it—"

"He needs to see her—"

"What, you think I'm the CEO of Lalit Matchmaking, Incorporated?"

"—to talk to her face-to-face. To hear her answer, whatever it is. He deserves that much—"

"Sorry. Cupid doesn't live here anymore."

"You want me to read her letter? You want that maybe I should write back?"

"Mrs. Majumdar, I'm shocked to see you stoop to such heinous blackmail."

"The name's Ms. Chatterjee, actually." She tears a sheet from a notebook, writes on it. "Here's Ashok's hotel number. Tell her to call soon—the poor man's running out of dollars."

"Good. Maybe they'll deport him."

Anju gives him a reproachful look.

"Why don't you tell Sudha yourself?" he asks. "Wouldn't that be better? I can give you her phone number—"

Anju looks up, her face suddenly harrowed. "I can't talk to her, or even write. Not yet. Not until I work out some things myself." The streetlamp, which has just come on, throws pools of blackness under her eyes. "I, too, love her too much. I think I just rediscovered that."

Lalit takes the paper. "I'm an idiot, a wimp, a pushover."

"Not at all," Anju says. "You're a better man than I am, Gunga Din." From the window of her bus, she throws him a kiss.

❧

The river is gray with age and weight. It has traveled a long way from the ice crag where it appeared out of a cave shaped like a cow's mouth to this city populated by too many people, all their histories and hopes. Their deaths. For that's what they bring to the river here, by the Kali temple. Flowers and food offered to the spirits of ancestors who hover, it is believed, on its banks until sent on with prayers. Bones and ashes and lamps to be set afloat in boats made of leaves. Elsewhere, the river is not so deified. Children pee into it, farmers bring their buffaloes for a bath, jackals drink from it at night, in the morning teenage boys kick up mud and ogle the girls bathing in the women's ghats.

"Take, take," the priest says to Sunil. "Put on your head, your shoulders. Put more water, put properly. Ask Mother Ganga to take your sins away."

Ankle-deep in sluggish mud, the two men are standing on the steps leading down from the temple area to the river. Sunil has reluctantly agreed to this ceremony to propitiate the dead, mostly to please his mother. Reluctantly, he has dressed himself in the coarse cotton dhoti which mourning sons traditionally wear and left his shoes in the car. ("Would you like to shave your head?" the priest asked earlier. "You must be kidding," Sunil said.) Now he dips a finicky finger into the liquid, which does not look too clean. The priest, who has known Sunil's family for years, shakes his head and sighs.

"Ah, you modern boys returned from America! But what to say, our boys here are no better, always talking germs and what not. There's more in this world than what you see with your physical eyes." His own eyes, magnified by thick glasses, glint as he speaks. "Don't you know the story? When Mother Ganga, river of heaven, was asked by Lord Vishnu to come to earth to save us, she wept and said, Lord, don't ask me for this, earth people will put all their dirt in me, physical things and their disgusting sins also. And the Lord said, See, I bless you with my touch, nothing can make you dirty. Never mind what-all they do, you will be most holy always."

Sunil looks unconvinced, but he chooses not to argue. He was tired even before he started from America, and the long journey has made things worse. He's still getting those headaches, is still nauseous from time to time, though his anxious mother has fixed for him, each day, the green plantain soup that they give children to settle their stomachs. He hasn't been sleeping well, either. The house is still full of guests, and so, despite his protests, he's been put in his father's bedroom, though thankfully not on his bed. (The mattress was burned along with the corpse, and there hasn't been time to get a new mattress.) He startles awake each night, roused by a shriek. Tram brakes? A night owl? But surely there are no owls left in Calcutta.

Sunil has been disoriented ever since he landed at the airport. There was a Bangla Bandh that day, processions of yelling men who shook militant placards, while policemen waited on the pavements, armed with truncheons and tear gas. Sunil, who had not been back to India since his wedding, tried vainly to read the Bengali on the placards, the uneven sticky red of letters that looked as though they had been written in a hurry, with blood. Finally, he had to ask his mother what they said. She explained that it was a march by street hawkers to protest the new law that no longer allowed them to sell their wares on pavements in Calcutta. Street hawkers? Sunil repeated, his brow wrinkled as though it were a word he had never heard before.

Many of the major streets were closed because of the bandh and the private car his mother had cajoled from a relative had to go around and around, through narrow alleys Sunil did not recall ever seeing, trying to find a way home. ("Why did you get a private car?" Sunil had asked. "Because taxis stay off the streets when there's a bandh. The crowd could beat up the driver and burn the car," his mother said tiredly. "Don't you remember anything, baba?")

Now Sunil sits by the river, where the priest has lit a small fire, and repeats mantras to bring peace to the dead. But what about peace for the living? What about the woman and the child, the lack of whom he carries like a laceration in his flesh?

The priest pours black sesame seeds in his palm, sprinkles them with river water. ("Offer, offer. Pray.") Sunil chants obediently after the priest—now they are holding up balls of cooked rice for fourteen generations of ancestors—but really he's looking at the river. The sun has come out, and the slow-flowing water shines like steel. It hypnotizes him. In his father's bureau there was a shoebox filled with uncashed money orders from America, years' worth of them. Enough to keep his mother in luxury for the rest of her life. The waves sound like a dim confusion of voices. The voices of the dead, one might think, if one didn't know better.

The priest is chanting: "Weapons cleave It not, fire burns It not. Water wets It not, wind burns It not."

Sunil repeats: "Water wets It not, wind burns It not." There's perplexity in his voice, a certain unease. He wants to dismiss the sacred verse, handed down from a time so ancient and calm that it cannot possibly have a bearing on his tortured twentieth-century life. Why then does it make him reconsider his desires, which he thought he knew so intimately?

It is time to pour the ashes into the water. He holds out the copper pot. The ash is gritty, with black lumps which might be gristle. It is studded with pieces of bone, shockingly white. An old, charred smell rises from the pot. He sways a little, as though dizzy or intoxicated.

The priest chants, "This Self is unmanifest, unthinkable, unchangeable."

"Unchangeable," Sunil says. The waves take the word from his mouth and carry it toward the sea.

"Knowing This to be such, you should not grieve."

"I should not grieve," Sunil says. He is speaking not of his father, whom he has not so much forgiven as let drop from his mind, but of himself, the addiction that he has carried on his back so eagerly all these years. Is it possible to let go of something that has cut such a deep groove into you? Ash falls from his hands. Some of it blows into his eyes and makes them water. He wipes at them. The priest nods with approval at this sign of filial piety. The gray flecks float for a moment on the gray skin of the river, then are pulled under.

Thirteen

Sudha

"Ridiculous!" Lalit says, kicking at a stone. "It's a ridiculous plan. Going back to India, to some godforsaken tea town in the boonies, to waste the rest of your life taking care of some old man that you hardly know. How can you even consider it?"

We're walking in the Botanical Gardens, up on the foothills behind the University of California. We're in the desert section, surrounded by towering cacti with thorns like witches' needles. Beyond, the acacias have burst into bloom, clustering gold coins on every branch. Is it because I'm to leave it soon that this California day looks so magical?

I smile to mask my disappointment. "Thanks for the vote of support!"

"I *do* support you. That's why I'm upset. Haven't I been doing everything you wanted? Didn't I negotiate with Anju on your behalf, convincing her with my superior use of logic? It was like pulling teeth with a pair of tweezers, in case I didn't tell you."

"You did. About twenty times."

"Well, it *is* a striking use of simile. Then I brought you your childhood beau's number—"

"I didn't exactly ask for that—"

"To provide more than the customer demands, that's my motto. And now I've brought you here to see him so he can offer you blandishments and seduce you with sweet nothings. Is that beyond the call of duty or what?"

"It is. I'm most appreciative."

"I can think of better ways of showing your appreciation than running away."

"I am *not* running away." But even as I say it, I wonder if he's right.

"There are so many opportunities here for you and Dayita"—Lalit's voice is heated—"and you're throwing them all away—stupidly, if I may say so."

"You should meet my mother sometime. The two of you would get along like French fries and ketchup."

He gives me a pleading look. "Don't ruin your life, Sudha."

Because I'm unsure, I snap at him. "What life, Lalit? What kind of life do I have here? I'm tired of this mantra that everyone chants, this cure for all ills. AmericaAmericaAmerica. For you, yes. America did help you make yourself into what you wanted. But I don't have any professional skills—"

"All you have to do is to go to school—"

"I don't have the money for it. And maybe not the patience either. My visa will run out in less than a month. I'm working illegally. Even the clothes I'm wearing aren't mine." I point to the skirt, red hibiscus on soft black cotton, Myra's, which she had insisted I wear for this meeting. ("He's come all the way from Calcutta just to see you! I can't believe it! That is *so* romantic!")

Lalit fingers the material of the sleeve. "That's why you're so high-strung this morning. It's the vibrations, as our Myra would say!"

"Quit! She's been really generous to me, and she has a good heart. I like her."

"I do, too. I never make fun of people I don't like." Then his voice grows sober. "All the things you hate about your life here, I could change them, if you'll just—"

I put my hand over his mouth. "Don't say it, whatever it is. It'll jinx things between us."

He grabs my hand, kisses it, then holds it to his face. "What things? You won't allow us to have anything."

I love the feel of his cheekbone under my fingers. The slight rasp of a day's growth of beard. He'll never know how tempted I am to give in. To let him kiss all my objections away. But sooner or later, they'd come back. I tug my hand from his. "We do have something very special. Our friendship."

"Please, sir, may I have some more?" he says in a high child's voice.

I laugh. He took me to an oldies revival to see the movie last week. Then I say, "I can't offer you any more. Everything else I have, I need it just to survive. Besides, I don't want to repeat the same mistake with you—"

"Which is?"

"I always allowed myself to be dependent on someone else's goodwill. I was the one who was always taking, the one who was taken care of."

"What's wrong with that? It would give me great pleasure to take care of you."

I shake my head. "It makes it harder to say no—"

"Personally, I don't see that as a problem. But if it's equality you want, I can think up all sorts of ways for you to take care of me, starting right now!" He leers at me unconvincingly, making me laugh again.

"It's a good thing you didn't decide to go into acting," I say.

Then I see him. Wearing a woolen Nehru jacket, on the bench next to the garden offices with his back to me. He is gazing at a bank of Niles lilies.

"Just when the conversation was getting interesting," Lalit says. "Don't tell me that's him. Man, he's ugly. Old, too. And just by looking at his back I can tell he has a mean streak as wide as the Grand Canyon. Why, he might even be a psychopath. Us doctors, we're trained to detect these things, you know. Uh-uh, he's definitely not the man for you."

In spite of my nervousness, I can't help smiling. "And you are?"

"*Mais oui! Absolument!* Maybe I should hang around, in case you need rescuing?"

"I won't need rescuing, thank you very much."

"I'm crestfallen. I'll be back in half an hour to pick you up."

❧

I stand still for a moment, reluctant to call Ashok's name. So many memories are welling up in me, sorrows I thought I was done with. Ashok in the movie theater's dark, his eyes like opals, asking my name. His white shirt blazing in the Calcutta sun as he waited for hours by the roadside to catch a glimpse of me being driven to school. The time we met in Kalighat temple, among the odors of crushed flowers, to make plans for our elopement. I should have gone with him. My first love. How could I know that the way I loved him then—I'd never be able to love anyone else like that? Not even him when he came back into my life after my marriage broke apart. How fleeting youth is, the passion that withholds nothing.

Ashok sits erect. His sleeves are rolled up, his arm muscles as well defined as ever. He must still be lifting weights. His profile is lean and thoughtful. The clean, intelligent line of his nose is so familiar that an illogical regret catches in my throat. He doesn't look any older than when I saw him last. This surprises me until I remember that I said good-bye to him just a few months ago. It's only I who have been through a century's worth of changes. There's a notebook in his lap. I step closer and see that it's an artist's pad. He's been sketching the lilies. I didn't know he drew. His style is spare, the charcoal strokes few and masterful. This, too, surprises me.

"Sudha?" he says, without turning around.

"When did you learn to draw so well?"

"I started after you left for America. I'm very much an amateur, but it helps me to stay calm." He keeps gazing at the lilies, which annoys me.

"I can't imagine you not being calm—ever," I say, an edge to my voice.

A small smile. "You think I'm calm right now?"

I step around to stand in front of him. "How can I tell when you won't look at me?"

"I was afraid—like in the story of Eurydice—that you might disappear." But he does look. And continues to look until I smooth down the thin cotton of the skirt with self-conscious fingers. Finally he says, "You've changed, Sudha. That was the other thing I was afraid of."

"Changed how?" I say, my voice belligerent. "You mean because I'm wearing Western clothes?"

He shakes his head. "That wasn't what I meant, though a sari does make you look more beautiful."

I can't help making a face. Is there anything as conservative as a conservative Indian male?

He holds up his hand. "I'm not saying it's a negative change. You're just different. I see it in the way you stand, the muscles of your shoulders, your neck. It's like you're threaded through with galvanized wire."

"You see that?" I say, taken aback. No one else has mentioned anything like that to me. But, then, who has known me for as long as Ashok has? Only Anju—and she and I have been too closely tangled to see anything but our reflected selves in each other's eyes.

He nods. "It makes me fear what you've been through—something that shook you up more than leaving your husband, even. No! I don't want to know. I'm only sorry I wasn't here to take care of you."

Again that phrase. "It's not your job to take care of me," I say heatedly. "I'm an adult."

"Even adults need to be cared for, by people who love them."

Now is the perfect time to say, *I don't love you*. But somehow I can't. Our shared history, his patient waiting, this long and expensive journey he's undertaken for me and my daughter—they stop my mouth. I cannot forget that I'm the first one he loved, too.

"Anyway, now that I'm here, you can tell the people you're working for that you're quitting. I've reserved our tickets for next week—I did that as soon as you phoned me. That should give your employers enough time to find a replacement." He adds gallantly, "Not that anyone could ever replace you."

"Whoa!" Inside me, anger is playing tug-of-war with disbelieving laughter. "I never said I'm going back with you."

"But why not? What reason do you have to remain here, now that you're not helping Anju anymore?"

I don't know how to answer him. Maybe that's why I let anger take over. "And I don't like people making high-handed decisions without consulting me."

He looks hurt. Taken aback. "I'm only trying to help, to speed things along. We've wasted so much time unnecessarily—time that we could have been together."

Guilt stings me. "You shouldn't have come, Ashok. I told you over and over to forget me. The love we felt for each other was beautiful—but it was a long time ago. We're both different people now."

"I'm not."

"Well, I am. That's what I've been trying to tell you. But you're in love with an idealized me that doesn't exist anymore—if it ever did."

"That's not true. I love the real you, the Sudha that's pure and innocent and loving, no matter what—"

"The real me! You have no idea who I am, Ashok. I don't think anyone does—except maybe Anju. Maybe that's why she won't have anything to do with me. Let me tell you. When I came to this country, I knew right away that Sunil was attracted to me. I should have left at once. Gone back. But I was greedy for something more than the life I could have had with the mothers in Calcutta. I told myself I was doing it for Anju and for my daughter, but really I was doing it for me. I was the one who wanted to be adored. I was the one who wanted to be admired. Half the time I thought of my poor daughter as an obstacle that kept me from what I longed for."

There's a pained look on Ashok's face. But he says, "That's only natural, Sudha. You never had any of those things, and so—"

"Don't make excuses for me, Ashok. That's what I convinced myself—that I deserved those things. If life wasn't going to give them to me easily, I was going to snatch them, no matter what. I went to a party. I met a young man. If you think I'm good and innocent, you should see him. He's the real thing. I knew he was attracted to me. I went out with him even though I knew it would make Sunil crazy with jealousy."

"Enough, Sudha! You don't have to say any more!"

A strange recklessness has taken me over. All those words I held back because I cared so much what Lalit might think. What freedom to finally let them go. What freedom not to care anymore. "Yes, I do! I have to say it, and you have to listen! You must!" I kneel in front of him, so that he's forced to look at me. "Sunil made me have sex with him. No, it's wrong to say it that way, putting the blame on him. Because I didn't fight it. Maybe I was even hoping for it. Why else did I lie down on his bed? And when it happened, I enjoyed it. . . ."

Ashok gazes at me—not with the shock I hoped for, but an unexpected sorrow. He leans toward me, as though to take my hand. The notepad falls to the ground, but he ignores it.

I snatch my hand back. I don't want kindness. Or pity. I want to shock him so much that he'll leave my life, never to return. Or is it my internal demons I'm trying to exorcise? "I left, but was it really because I felt guilty?" Out of the corner of my eye, I see a movement. It's Lalit, back after half an hour, as he had promised.

How much did he hear?

Almost, I stop speaking. Then I go on. Let them listen. Let

them both listen. "No. It was because Sunil frightened me. There was such a need inside him, need like a black bottomless pit. Even if I poured my entire self into it, I couldn't fill it. So I ran away."

Ashok is silent. He doesn't look at me.

I'm glad of that. It's easier to leave when they don't look at you.

I pick up the notepad and put it on the bench next to him. "I'm sorry if I hurt you, Ashok," I say as I stand up. "I'm sorry if I made you hate me. But it's best that you know the truth. Now you can forget me—the me you created, the me who wasn't real—and start over. And maybe I can, too."

"Wait."

I turn.

"I'll go back, like you want," he says. "I won't try to persuade you further. Not because I hate you—how can I? I have my own faults, too, my acts of weakness. Don't worry, I'm not planning to burden you with them. I'll go because I can see that you have, indeed, detached yourself from your past completely—I hadn't quite believed someone could do that. . . ."

If only he knew how incomplete my detachment is, how many bygones I still agonize over.

"And so I mean no more to you than a stranger you might meet at a street crossing."

I let him go on. There's pain in his voice, but I don't dare comfort him. It would undo everything I've achieved with such difficulty.

"Other people have become more important to you now. . . ."

Is he glancing toward Lalit, waiting in the shadow of the mimosas?

"I need to come to terms with all this—I don't know how

long it'll take. But that's no longer your concern." He pauses, perhaps to give me a chance to disagree. When I don't speak, he hands me the notepad. "I want you to have this."

I want to refuse, but I know I must take it. This last gift, by accepting which I accept our past together, my indebtedness. I put out my hand. In my mind, I say, *We did love each other. It's gone now, but it was good and true. I thank you for it.*

In the car, I open the pad. Page after page of sketches. Except for the lilies on the last page, they're all pictures of me. How well he's caught my expressions. How well he's remembered moods I don't even recall having felt. Here's me as a schoolgirl, looking obedient and dutiful in the sacklike uniform the nuns made us wear. Me in a salwaar kameez at the movies, a shy half-smile on my face. Me reading a book, braiding my hair, looking into a mirror with a faraway expression. Me in a sari, with a temple in the background, looking excited and scared. That must have been the last time he saw me before my wedding. Me as a wife, with a bindi on my forehead, the end of a sari covering my hair. He must have imagined that one. Me looking very pregnant, a rebellious set to my lips—that was after I left Ramesh. There are more—me in a boat on a mountain lake, laughing, the wind lifting my hair; me waking up in bed, looking sleepily surprised; me playing with a baby who isn't Dayita. With a pang I realize that I'm looking into the heart of Ashok's hopes.

The wind roars in my ears. Lalit is driving far too fast.

"Whoa," I say. "When did you get your pilot's license?"

He doesn't come back with a joke, the way I'd hoped. Instead, he says, staring straight ahead, "All those things you said about yourself, you were only saying them to force Ashok to stop loving you. Right?"

My throat hurts as though I'm coming down with the flu. "Is that what you think?" I say.

We ride the rest of the way in silence.

❧

Uncle says, "Every monsoon, the Tista used to flood. My friends and I would play hooky from school and go to see it. The water would be swollen, with brown foam from all the washed-away earth. You could hear the roar of the river from half a mile away. The best part was the whirlpools." His finger makes circle shapes on Dayita's palm, tickling her, and she laughs. "We'd throw sticks in it, watch them disappear."

They're sitting on his bed, my daughter and the old man whom I've started calling Uncle. It's been two weeks now since we made our secret plan. Already he looks stronger. He can walk to the bathroom, holding on to me, dragging his left foot. He can sit up in bed and eat by himself. He's set himself a strict regimen: breakfast is followed by a few stretches in bed; then a brief rest; then I help him into his wheelchair and take him to the living room window so he can look out on the view. After lunch, which he takes at the table with Dayita and me, he sleeps. A few easy exercises when he wakes. Then tea. After that I read to him, or we listen to music. He's surprised me with a fondness for jazz. In the evening he plays with Dayita or tells us stories. Yesterday he asked me to look in his suitcase. Inside was a wooden box that opened into a chessboard. The carved figures were dressed in British uniforms and in Mughal garb. The queens had tiny tiaras that winked with real jewels. I'll teach you next week, he said. My job is mainly to see that he doesn't overdo things and to be a listener. For after his long silence, he can't get enough of talking about the place he loves more than any other place on earth.

By the time Myra and Trideep return from work, he's back in bed, quilt drawn up to his chin, eyes closed. He'll whisper an anemic hello and pretend he's too tired to respond when they try to talk to him. He'll only eat his dinner after they've given up and gone away. "Let me have my little secret," he told me with an urchin's grin when I protested. "The day when I can walk by myself to the living room, I'll tell them!"

My own life is bleaker. No reply from Anju to the note I sent her last week. When he calls, Lalit seems distant and preoccupied. Abrupt. I guess that Ashok has returned to India, but there's no one I can ask. My sleep is knotted with complicated dreams I can't remember when I wake. They leave a faint bitterness in my mouth, as when one has had a fever. I have thrown out Sunil's tape, but sometimes I think I hear his voice, *Sudha, Sudhaaa, how can you abandon me?* The phone number he spoke is imbedded in my brain, refusing to be forgotten. My disobedient fingers yearn to dial it.

Torn strips of a story that Pishi told us years ago come back to me. Once there was a man who was addicted to thievery. One day he met a saint who convinced him to repent—yet the man found that he could not stop stealing, even though he no longer wished to. I forget the middle of the story, but it ends with the man chopping off his right hand, to save himself from himself.

To save myself, I pour my attention into preparing Uncle's meals. I nag Myra until she goes to the Chinese market for fresh catfish. I sauté it with black jeera and turmeric and make jhol, the traditional clear soup one drinks after a long illness to build strength. I curdle milk and make fresh paneer sprinkled with sugar. I soak almonds overnight in warm water until they are soft and give them to him for breakfast.

Uncle says, "There used to be elephants in the Duars forest when I was growing up, and cheetahs, too. And the trees—shal and shegun and deodar—so huge that even in the daytime you couldn't see sunlight. A lot of them have been cut down nowadays by the lumber companies, but it's still something to see."

He says, "Sometimes the bigger cheetahs would come into the Madeshia hutments and grab a goat or a calf. The tea estates were still run by the English then, and an officer would take his rifle and go into the forest, accompanied by a group of coolies with drums. Secretly, I was always on the cheetah's side!"

He says, "We'll take a boat to where the Karala River meets the Tista, to watch the sunset. There are so many rivers, each one different. We can go fishing on the Angrabhasa. On the Dudua. We'll rent a jeep and go up Assam Road to the tea gardens, to see the mist coming over the Bhutan hills. Do you think you'll like that?"

Under the excitement, a brief tremor in his voice, as though a part of him still cannot believe this will come true. I make myself nod. Smile. He's telling me that when Dayita's old enough, he'll make sure she gets into Holy Child, the best school in the area. There won't be a problem, he knows the principal well. It's close to his house, too. He can walk her there when the weather's good. Other days Bahadur will call a rickshaw from the marketplace. I try to visualize it: an old man with energetic steps and a silver-headed cane, hand in hand with a little girl in a blue-and-white uniform, her hair in a neat braid with a white bow at the end. The wrought-iron gates of the school open inward to let them in. There's a line of eucalyptus trees, a gravel drive, then the fragrant white gardenias the nuns planted half a century ago. But where am I? In this picture, where am I?

Fourteen

Assignment

Write a piece in which you reinterpret a mythic/epic character by envisioning him/her in a scene of your own creation (i.e., not from the original work). Develop the character with fictional devices such as setting, dialogue, and imagery, and use these to indicate your attitude to this character.

Draupadi's Garden
by
Anju Chatterjee
English 3353
Creative Writing
Prof. S. Liu

She was born from fire. Perhaps that is why, throughout her life, wherever she went, she left scorched footprints. The men she looked at felt a burning inside them long after she was gone, particularly when they remembered that she—unlike all good women—had five husbands. Some say she brought about the destruction of the Kurus, the greatest dynasty that ever was. Some say she corrupted her noble husbands by her insatiable longing for revenge. I think her only fault was that she wanted—and got—what was forbidden to women. For that, she would have to pay a steep price.

All this was a long time ago. Or was it?

Imagine this scene, one of the most famous from the epic Mahabharat: Draupadi's husband, King Yudhishthir, is invited to Hastinapur, to the kingdom of his envious cousin Duryodhan, to take part in a gambling tournament. The crafty Shakuni, Duryodhan's uncle, has enticed Yudhishthir to gamble away his wealth, his kingdom, his brothers, even himself—and, finally, his wife. Duryodhan sends for Draupadi—she must serve him as a maidservant now. But Draupadi refuses to come. She sends back a question, instead: what right has a man to gamble away his wife as though she were a mere piece of property?

The question is ignored by the court, and continues to be ignored down the ages. Change *gamble* to any verb of your choice, and you'll see.

Draupadi is dragged by her hair to the court by Duryodhan's younger brother, who attempts to pull off her clothes. Why not? She is now the Kurus' maidservant, their sexual plaything. They can do with her as they wish. The entire court—grandfathers, teachers, the old king, her husbands—watches in horror, held paralyzed by the conviction that if a man owns a woman, he is entitled to do whatever he wants to her.

Draupadi is saved by divine intervention, but through the next thirteen years, as she wanders through the forest with her exiled husbands, she will not forget her humiliation. She will leave her hair untied and uncombed, a shroud of knots to remind her husbands how they failed in their most important duty. She is the fire inside their lungs, blazing up each time they consider forbearance.

After the great battle of Kurukshetra, after every member of the Kuru dynasty is killed, Draupadi will finally tie her hair, gilded with the blood of Duryodhan's brother. Is she happy? Who can say. Her own sons have died in the aftermath of Kurukshetra. The land is reduced to rubble. Soon her heartsick husbands will hand over the kingdom to their last surviving grandson and, together with Draupadi, start on their fated journey up the Himalaya Mountain, where she will perish.

But I imagine Draupadi in a different, earlier scene. Here she is, in a corner of the women's courtyard in the royal palace of Hastinapur—for she is now queen here, in this palace that is too large, where the wind wraps itself around the domes at night and calls with familiar, wounded voices. She kneels on the dark, wet ground—there was an unseasonal rain last night—unmindful of her jewel-studded sari. Her nails are mud-encrusted as she places a seedling in a hole, as she gently tamps the earth into place around it.

What would Draupadi plant in her garden? Would it be the agnirekha, flame-flower, flower of virtuous courage, flower of the heroes her husbands have become? Would it be a sprig of the parijaat, the tree of fragrant bliss which their mentor Krishna wrested from Indra, the king of the gods? Is it the asha-lata, the mythical desire vine which gives you whatever you wish for? No, none of these. For she has learned that it isn't enough to be the wronged one. It isn't even enough to be the wronged one who emerges victorious. Revenge is like spiced mango chutney: delicious at first, it leaves your tongue stinging. How long can you enjoy the suffering of your enemy before you notice that you are bleeding, too? The asha-lata gives what you wanted, but it always turns out different from what you imagined it to be.

I will leave Draupadi in her garden, watering her mysterious plant. I can't give you its name, because I haven't figured it out myself, what you reach for when the consolation of righteous rage no longer consoles you. But I hope it grows into a tree so huge its roots crack the foundations of the old palace. I hope the wind blows its seeds across the land, giving birth to more trees, and more, so that long after Draupadi's bones are covered by glaciers travelers everywhere will rest under their shade, and bless that which comes after vengeance.

Ms. Chatterjee,

Though I was looking for a fiction piece rather than nonfiction, I think you have captured the spirit of the assignment very well. You have an original and powerful writing style, and though I didn't understand every reference here, it made me want to find out more. The images you use are strong and evoke emotions successfully, making us sympathize with a complexly portrayed character. I think you have quite a gift for writing, and I wish you success in developing it further.

Shana Liu

Fifteen

Letters

Berkeley
October 1994

Dearest Anju,

    I am writing one final time to let you know that I am leaving for India. I'm going to take care of Mr. Sen, the old man I was looking after here. He lives in Jalpaiguri, up in the north of Bengal. I think we'll be happy there— or at least peaceful, which is perhaps better. He is very fond of Dayita, and has offered to pay me a generous salary. Apparently he is very well off, which I did not know earlier.

    I want to see you before I leave, to say good-bye, and to tell you what happened (my truth of it). This may be our last opportunity, for I doubt very much that I'll be returning to America. But perhaps this no longer matters to you.

                         Sudha

Berkeley
October 1994

Dear Lalit,

    Imagine this scene, from last night:

    I set the table for dinner with an extra plate, and when Myra asked why, I said that Uncle would join us for dinner.

    "Uncle?" Trideep says. "Which uncle?" Myra's staring at me as though I've lost my mind, and in walks Uncle, right on cue, just as we'd planned. He walks quite well with a cane now, though he still drags his left foot. The stupefaction on their faces! Uncle and I couldn't stop laughing. Later he said it was almost worth being sick so long, just to see that look.

    Anyway, once they'd got over the shock—and the elation—they were quite positive about the idea of my taking him back to India. I suspect they're secretly relieved to be rid of us both, though I believe Myra when she says she will miss Dayita. She's been spending much of her evenings playing with her, and speaks intermittently of adoption. However, knowing Myra, I doubt that will happen!

    Uncle tells us more stories of Jalpaiguri each day. No place can be as beautiful as he makes it out to be, and Trideep has warned me that it's actually a sleepy little hill town where very little happens. Still, I'm excited. Myra has bought us piles of woolens—we'll get there right at the start of the cold season, and she's convinced that without central heating, we'll freeze to death. They plan to come and visit us soon—perhaps in the spring. Myra has asked me to keep an eye out for things she might want to buy for the boutique, where she's become a partner.

    Trideep's bought our tickets. We leave two weeks from today. Hard to believe that my ill-fated stay in America (ill-fated except for you, that is— you've been such a good friend) is coming to an end.

    The other night I asked Uncle that riddle you'd once asked me— What's the difference between a soldier and a lady? *I thought for sure he wouldn't know the answer. I was getting ready to tell him when he said, "There's no difference at all, my dear. You of all people should know that." From time to time, he startles me like that.*

When are you coming to see Dayita and me? Since our last meeting—when you took me to talk to Ashok—you've been awfully quiet. I'm afraid to ask why.

Sudha

Berkeley,
October 1994

Dear Pishi,

I am sorry I haven't written to any of you for so long—but whatever I could have written would have only made you sad.

Maybe Anju has told you what has happened, the four people that made up her household scattered like chaff in the wind. I cannot claim to be innocent. But at least I was the first to leave. And though I could have done it, I didn't go with Sunil.

I was so scared the day I left Anju's flat with an empty purse and a child to take care of, going to work in a stranger's house as a maid. Yes, that's what I was, though they were nice enough never to behave toward me in that fashion. It was more frightening than when I left Ramesh. Then at least I had you to run to, and Anju, though she was physically far, was always with me in my heart. Now she is only an hour's drive away, but we might as well be on two different planets.

I'm coming back to India, Pishi, but not to Calcutta. I must start over—without the memories, the whispers. And this job I have, taking care of old Mr. Sen, who is recovering from a stroke, will allow me to do so. He is a kind man, and old enough that I need not fear him in that way. Dayita likes him, too.

I was going to say that must mean he is a good person. Then I remember how attached she was to Sunil.

But I cannot say Sunil is a bad person. He just wanted what he was not supposed to want.

Do you think I'm making a mistake by coming back?

But think of this: for the first time in my life, I'll have my own bank account. It makes me feel—finally—like a grown-up!

Please tell Gouri Ma and my mother. I will write to you again from Jalpaiguri.

> With love and pranams,
> Sudha

Berkeley
October 1994

Sunil

I write this letter the way one performs an exorcism, so that I can start on my new life. I do not ask to forget you. There is a fear of repeating that which is forgotten, and I pray that neither of us repeats the mistakes we made, the words we left unspoken until too late, the things we should have held inside that exploded out of us.

We were both to blame—but blame isn't the right word. We both wanted too much, wanted the things life had decided we shouldn't have. You longed for the perfect romance, and looked to me to fulfill that longing. And I—I came to America in search of freedom but was swept away by the longing to be desired. How mistaken we were to think that such things could make us happy.

I will not think of you in anger—if you will not think of me with hate.

> Sudha

Calcutta
October 1994

Dearest Sudha

I am so thankful finally to receive a letter from you. The scenes one creates inside one's head, worrying, are usually worse than what is real.

No, my child. I don't think you are making a mistake by returning. It is a fine thing for a woman to have her own, self-earned bank balance! If the times had allowed me, I would have liked to have one, too! How things will turn out no one can guess. Your motives are good—as they were when you left Anju's home. God and the world will decide the rest.

It is a pity that your American plans did not work out. You went there with such high hopes of being reunited with your sister, of making a fortune—or, if not a fortune, at least a decent living. We Chatterjee women are not lucky that way, I guess. But we always pick ourselves up and go on.

Sunil came to see us before he returned to America. That was a brave and decent thing for him to do—it must have been difficult for him to face us. He was very quiet. I think his father's death has changed him in ways that have surprised him. He spoke alone with Gouri for a while. She says he intends to meet with Anju when he returns, if she will agree to it. He wants there to be no ill feeling between them. But whether that is possible, I cannot guess.

Gouri Ma sends you love and blessings, as do I. Your mother, as you might imagine, is quite distraught, going on and on over thrown-away chances, impractical foolishness, and "that nice surgeon boy." She imagines the worst of old Mr. Sen. But as always, she will get over it.

Don't worry about Anju's anger. Whether she wants to or not, she can't hate you. You are too much a part of each other. Can the left hand hate the right?

Yours
Pishi

Palo Alto
October 1994

   Notice is served herewith to all concerned that Sudha Chatterjee is to be whisked away at 5:00 P.M. this coming Friday for several hours of dangerous fun.

                                        Lalit

Santa Clara
October 1994

Sudha,
   If you really want to see me before you go, take the 4:00 P.M. BART train to Daly City this Saturday. I'll wait for you in the parking lot. Come alone.

                                        Anju

Berkeley
October 1994

Dear Sara,
   I've written many letters to you, over and over, in my mind, though this is the first actual one. Yesterday I called Lupe to tell her I was leaving America, and she gave me this post box number. But she warned me that it's an old one, and that she hasn't heard from you in quite a while.
   I feel a great need to connect with you before I leave, to close the loop that began with my seeing you in the park, high up in the swing, the way I never would have dared to, because in my world a grown woman didn't do such things. You made me realize that even when everyone around you is saying no, you can say yes.

Not that I think you'll get this letter. Or that you'll reply. Sometimes I dream that you've returned to your family. Or that you're dead.

Still, writing it is enough, like releasing seeds into the wind.

I've made a lot of mistakes in the last year, Sara, and might be leaping into another. I'm returning to the country I'd been in such a desperate hurry to quit. I'm leaving behind in America a charming man, one who is determined to make me happy in spite of myself. (Only, no one can do that for another person, can they?) So many people are convinced I'm doing the wrong thing, tying my life to the caring of an old man. But Mr. Sen's son would never have allowed him to go on his own. So perhaps finally I'm being of use to someone. It won't make up for destroying my cousin's marriage, but it is a small reparation.

And my one chance to be free.

Wish me well, Sara. Tomorrow I must meet Anju. For the first time since I made love to her husband. I'm so afraid.

                    Sudha

Sixteen

Lalit

what I said
Did you change your mind yet about going to India?

what you said
Where are you taking me?

what I said
Depends on whether you've changed your mind or not.

what you said
Are you going to act like this all evening? On our last date?

what I said
Our last date? Excuse me?

what you said
Well, unless you plan on coming out to Jalpaiguri—

what I said

I just might do that. (And was surprised to find that I was actually considering the possibility.)

what you said

Come to think of it, even that wouldn't work. Dating isn't allowed over there.

what I said

Another reason for you to not go.

what you said

So how come you didn't call me all these days? How come you wouldn't even return my calls?

what you didn't say

Was it what you heard me tell Ashok? Did it shock you?

what I didn't say

Yes, partly it was that. I was shocked at how shocked I was. I hadn't realized I'd been nursing one of those purer-than-pure-Indian-woman fantasies about you. That one of the reasons I was attracted to you was that you seemed so different from the desi girls brought up here, with their free-and-easy ways. And I was jealous. I was burning up with jealousy just thinking of—

what I said

I was playing hard to get. Learned it from you.

what you said

Hmmm. So what's this dangerous fun you promised me?

what I said

What, being with me isn't fun enough? And dangerous enough? In that case— (And I swung the car south and headed toward Great America. And after we'd strapped ourselves in and shot up to the highest height and been plunged down deeper than despair and you'd screamed louder than you thought you could ever scream and I'd held you longer than I'd ever held you and you'd slapped away my hands and said, Quit, and I'd said, Why d'you think they designed these scary rides—and all the while I was thinking of you going so far away, all the things that might happen, what if the old man didn't treat you right once he was on home turf . . .)

I said

I'm serious about it, you know. Coming to India. To see you and Dayita. (You went very silent.)

so I added

Did you think you'd get rid of me so easily? I'm planning on corrupting your daughter with Hershey's Kisses and the latest Barney videos, and then there'll be two of us working on you to come back here. (You leaned your head lightly against mine.)

I said to myself

Careful! Don't read too much into it. Maybe she's just dizzy from the ride.

and you gave an enigmatic smile and said

You can go ahead and try.

Seventeen

She turns the key but the car will not start, not even when she pumps the accelerator, not even when she pounds the dashboard. She leans her forehead on the steering wheel and tries to remember what the man who used to be her husband did on such occasions. She checks her watch. Her hands are trembling. She feels the prickle of sweat in her underarms. *Mustn't panic. Mustn't.* She'd given herself a bit of extra time to reach Daly City because she's a nervous driver, and the Bay Area traffic is so bad, even on the roundabout scenic highway she plans on taking. She can feel the minutes falling through the gaps between her fingers. *As though time were water in a cupped palm in a desert.* She whispers the words, feels the vowels begin to calm her. To distance her from crisis. Language does this for her, even now. She removes the key, rubs it on her jeans, tries again. The engine gives a reluctant cough and turns over, and Anju is on her way to meet her cousin.

Sudha stands on a platform of the North Berkeley station, shivering a little—more from nervousness than from the cold. She looks up at the sky, which is the color of faded jeans today. There's a hint of mist in the air, and through it the softest of lights brushes the tops of the yellow poplars. Sudha, chewing on her lip, sees and doesn't see. She had to leave Dayita with the old man because there was no one else. "Are you sure you can manage?" she'd asked over and over. He had nodded, rolling his eyes in mock exasperation, waving his hands in dismissal. "Go on, go!" He had even demonstrated his ability to change a diaper. "Now are you satisfied?"

The platform vibrates ever so slightly under her feet, the earth getting ready for upheaval. No. It's merely the train approaching. She counts on her fingers. She has kept their lunches ready on the kitchen table. The diapers and wipes are by his bed. Dayita's blanket. She's made a little bed for her on the floor of his room in case he can persuade her to nap, and lifted her out of her walker because the old man won't be able to do it by himself. She has kissed Dayita on her forehead and told her, in a fierce whisper, to be good. She has left Lalit's cell phone number in case of emergency.

The train's automatic doors swoosh shut behind her. A scattering of leisurely midmorning people on the benches. She finds a seat by the window, across from an oldish woman wearing several sweaters, an enormous, scruffy backpack and a gap-toothed smile. Is she homeless? Sudha smiles back warily. When she was a child, her mother used to tell her, "Stay away from bad-luck people. Misfortune is contagious." Outside, patches of yerba buena, a clump of waving Queen Anne's lace blurring into seashell silver. Once she said to the old man, "No matter where fate saw fit to throw me down, it always gave me someone from whom to learn the names of plants." He nodded. "When you know the names of the green things around you, you're no longer a stranger." Already he has begun telling her of the trees she will find in his garden in Jalpaiguri: mango, jackfruit, shiuli, the champak with its gold and velvet fragrance.

The train is entering a tunnel. She blinks in the sudden dark. Small red emergency lights stud the tunnel like jewels in some underworld cave. In the window, her face is as pale and lovely as Persephone's. She lifts a hand to the perfectly formed cheekbones, the beauty she both loves and hates. There are no wrinkles to show what she has been through, no circles of suffering under the eyes. How then will she convince Anju of her regret?

෴

"Come here," he says. "Come on now. Don't be naughty. Let me check that diaper." He reaches for her but the child toddles away, laughing. This is a new game, and she likes it. She's glad to be out of that confining walker, the horrid cacophony of its wheels that echoed inside her head even after she stopped moving. She resolves to scream very loudly if her mother even thinks of putting her back in it. She flings her arms out in a burst of ecstasy, loses her balance and lands on her behind. She considers the situation for a moment, then decides to cry.

"My poor baby!" the old man says. He can't bend very well, so he lowers himself to the floor stiff-hipped, one limb at a time, holding on to the bed. "Bad floor!" He strikes it with his cane.

The child likes this, too. "Bad floor!" she says, hitting the wood with her palm, though the words come out sounding different, as if her mouth were full of Froot Loops. And with that thought she's hungry. No, she's starving. She pulls at the old man, but the fine, wrinkled skin on the back of his hand distracts her. She picks up a soft fold and lets it drop. Does it again. She straightens out his finger, then curls it inward into his palm. Straighten, curl up. Straighten, curl up. Why, he's more fun than a whole boxful of toys! Then she's starving again. "Eat," she says emphatically, pointing to the kitchen. But she waits for him to get to his feet, creaking like an ancient tree. She lets him hold her hand.

ॐ

The parking lot looks very large to Anju as she pulls in—larger than it really is. And very full. It seems to her that there are no spaces, that she will have to circle it forever. The tracks glitter faintly. A train is pulling in. Anju shades her eyes and looks. Is that her? Suddenly she cannot remember what Sudha looks like. Even the Passenger-Loading-Only-Driver-Must-Remain-with-Vehicle-at-All-Times spots are full. Anju parks illegally at a bus stop and watches her rearview mirror with some anxiety for the meter maid to whir up, avenging-angel-like, in her blue cart. From experience, she knows her parking karma is poor.

And so she doesn't see Sudha until she reaches the car, until she taps, tentatively, on the window. As she leans over to unlock the door, the thought comes to Anju that her cousin's hand, with its slender, ringless fingers and unpainted nails, resembles a white lotus.

They sit in silence for a while. Anju stares at the windshield, clasps the steering wheel, then puts her hands in her lap. She tries to regulate her breath, four counts in, pause, eight counts out, pause, as the instructor in the yoga class she has started taking advised, but she is having trouble drawing in air. She gropes near Sudha's foot for her water bottle, but it's rolled to the other side of Sudha's legs and she can't reach it.

"Here," Sudha says. Their hands touch as Anju fumbles for the bottle. Sudha's palms are damp with nervousness.

"Your palms are sweating," Anju says.

"Yours, too, I notice."

They wipe their palms on their jeans, and one of them—it's not clear—begins to laugh, a thin sound like an ice floe cracking. The other joins in.

"Don't tell me you were afraid of meeting me," Anju says.

"Not afraid," Sudha says. "Terrified."

"Me, too."

They laugh again. Then comes the pause they feared, taut as a rubber band stretched to breaking. Sudha clears her throat, coughs.

"Want some water?" Anju asks.

Sudha nods, takes the bottle from Anju, drinks. When she hands it back, Anju drinks from it, too. Her lips touch the mouth of the bottle where Sudha's mouth had been just a moment earlier.

"Anju," Sudha is examining her nails, "are you still mad at me?"

Anju looks out the window at two blackbirds fighting over an abandoned container of French fries. She wonders if the fries will make them ill, if she should get out of the car and shoo them away. But the birds look tough and feisty, with impudent sequin eyes. They've probably been living on French fries and onion rings their entire lives. She hears herself saying, "No," and is startled to find that it's the truth.

"I want to tell you what really—"

Anju shakes her head. "I don't want to hear it."

"But—"

"No," Anju says, her voice firm. "It took me a long time to close that door. Don't start opening it again."

"But unless you know, you'll always blame me—"

"Whatever happened," says Anju, her whole being focused on trying to find the right words for what she's feeling, "I tell myself that it's like the dream I had last night. What does it matter if it was a good dream or a bad one? Neither kind is going to help me live my life today, is it?"

Sudha frowns. She isn't comfortable with this line of reasoning. She isn't sure she understands where it leads. "How about me? How do I fit into that life? Or don't I?"

"I'm not sure. I'm not even sure how *I* fit into my life."

"Oh, Anju!" Sudha says. She takes Anju's hand in both of hers and strokes it as one might an injured child's. "I wanted so much to help you, but I've done just the opposite, haven't I?"

Anju shrugs. "I could say the same thing." But she leaves her hand in her cousin's.

There's a rap at the window. Sure enough, it's the meter maid—or man, to be exact. He twirls his pen and gestures at them to lower the window. "This is all very touching, ladies," he drawls, "but unless you want a ticket, you'd better move the car."

"As soon as you step back, Officer," Anju says in syrupy tones, revving the engine. "You wouldn't want me to run over your foot, would you?"

இ

In the glass house, luncheon has been successfully concluded, with only minor damages—a plate that slipped from the old man's hands, a few ketchupy handprints on the fridge door.

"Nothing a bowl of good hot soapy water won't take care of," he says as Dayita wriggles down from her chair. "Hold still, Miss Naughtiness." Amazingly, she does. He wipes her hands and mouth with a damp towel. His fingers shake a little. "Due to the excitement of being with you," he explains. "Your mother will have to do the rest when she returns. Shall we change diapers now?"

Twenty minutes later, he steps back from the bed, eyeing the lopsided diaper he's managed to get onto her. "A fine job, if I do say so myself! I think your mother will be proud of us, won't she?" The child smiles and pulls strings of half-words out of her mouth.

"Exactly," says the old man, wiping his forehead. "Just what I was thinking. Siesta time. There's your little bed and blanket, on the floor, and here's mine." He lowers himself slowly onto his mattress, maneuvers his legs up under his quilt. He's exhausted, though he'd never admit it to Sudha, not in a thousand years. He feels himself drifting off. He's half-asleep when he feels the child pushing against his back with determined palms. He turns to make space for her under his quilt. She presses her back against his breastbone. She wiggles her head onto his pillow. It is slightly damp and smells, he thinks, of wild mustard greens. He takes a big breath and runs his fingers through the tangly curls. Under the softness of hair, the small, solid curvature of skull. When was the last time he held a child so close? He thinks, suddenly, of his wife, wrinkled and spectacled, in her red-bordered handloom sari, cutting brinjals in the kitchen for their lunch. In his memory, she looks up with a half-smile. She has a missing front tooth which she never cared to have replaced. Sunlight glints on the wire rims of her glasses. *Our grandchild?* He is not sure whether he hears the words inside his head, or whether he speaks them. How disappointed she had been when Trideep informed them they weren't going to have any children. He starts telling Dayita the story of how he met his wife on their wedding day. It was an old-fashioned marriage, even for those times. She was only fourteen, and he'd barely started college. Later, he'd climb the guava tree in the yard, pick her the best fruits from the top branches, just beginning to ripen. She liked to eat them with salt and chili powder. If they fought, she'd cry and say, I want to go back to my mother's house. But then they fell in love. He's trying to remember how it happened, but it was so long ago. She used to believe that the person you married in this life had been your spouse in earlier lifetimes, too. Just before she died, she beckoned him close and said, with that same half-smile, Wherever I'm going, I'll wait for you. In the middle of telling this to the child, he falls asleep.

&

Sunil is walking in a forest. (It's really the Houston Arboretum, but he likes to think of it as something wilder, more adventure-some.) Green ash, water oak, maple, pecan. He sees a hedge with tiny red berries. He must look up its name. The pine trees startled him the first time. He hadn't known any would grow so far south. Every time he comes here, he writes in his diary—he's started that habit recently—*I went for a walk in the woods.* The path leads past a lily pond with frogs, a stretch of swamp-land, a wooden lookout platform. Then he's in his favorite spot, a small lake with an island in the middle where migrating birds nest. He sits on the pier and listens to them calling to their mates. On the far bank, turtles are sunning themselves. One lifts its head to look, and he notices the thin red stripes by its ears, the greenish sheen of its neck. Sunil likes turtles, *their* (he writes) *wise patience.* Sometimes he smuggles in chopped green apples to feed them. The fields behind him are full of weeds. In spring, someone told him, the bluebonnets will bloom. I like weeds, too, Sunil said. He puts his chin on his knees and gazes at the water. Daddy longlegs skitter across, a small ripple widens and widens. The sun is warm on his shoulders. In his diary, he has written, *In winter, the Houston sun is very sweet. Can this be the same killing sun of summertime? But why should this surprise me? Are people not the same way, in the different seasons of their lives?* Sometimes he writes other things in his diary, aphorisms, jokes he made up himself. *To her lover, a beautiful woman is a blessing beyond belief, to a monk, she is a distraction, to a mosquito, a good meal.* And *How does one learn patience? Very slowly.*

There's a train line that runs beyond the arboretum. Sunil hears a whistle, the ground beginning to rumble a bit. He did not reply to the note Sudha mailed him, although he cannot bear to throw it away. Sometimes he takes it out late at night and reads it again in the alien blue light from his computer. He feels an old pain flare in him, the way, soldiers say, they feel the ache of a cut-off limb. In his diary he has written, *Old desires run deep.* He has written, *I am determined to overcome myself.* In his last letter he asked Anju if he could see her the next time he went to San Francisco. He does not hope for anything except forgiveness. But, then, forgiveness itself is a large thing to hope for.

A turtle swims close to the pier, beneath the surface of the water. It is larger than the others and murky brown all over. A snapper, Sunil guesses. The sun dips behind the lookout platform. He stretches and gets to his feet. It is a long way home to the one-room apartment he rents, though he could afford a bigger place, especially now that he no longer has to send money back to India. But he doesn't see the need for such extravagance. *Jasmines grow here all year,* he has written to Anju. *In the Hindu temple, I've heard, there's a peacock sanctuary.* She does not reply to his letters, but she no longer asks him not to write. On the way back to the car, he will watch for armadillos. They like to come out at this time of day. Tonight in his diary he will put, *I am amazed by armadillos in all their seeming ugliness, their ability to be intimate in spite of their plated hides.* Tomorrow he will write to Anju, ask if she would get him a photo of Dayita.

❧

Anju has turned off 280 and takes a highway that winds through a sleepy town. Scattered signal lights, a small roadside store advertising tree-ripened avocados. She looks upward. Good, the fog has cleared. Sudha is telling her about the new things Dayita can do, about the old man's stories, the Bhutan ranges which he wants to take them to see. How Myra is threatening to visit them soon. Anju responds with tales about her professors. A movie she saw some time back about Indian women, very funny but strong also, called *Bhaji on the Beach.* How she's done well enough in all her classes to make the dean's list. She asks how Lalit is taking the news of Sudha's departure. He, too, is threatening a visit to India, Sudha informs her with a smile she cannot quite hold back. He's given her a calendar of *Peanuts* cartoons so she can mark off the days until he gets there.

Beneath the spoken words, a whole different conversation is going on. Emotions crash against the windows of the car like birds intent on escape.

What shall we do about the love that's lost, the love that can never be recovered all the way?

I'm so tired of being angry, of being lonely.

This good-bye is so unlike the previous ones, so sadly tinged with relief.

What shall we do with our thwarted desires, which is also our grief?
I don't know, I don't know.

On the radio, someone is singing "Achy Breaky Heart."

"They should ban all songs that have hearts in them," Anju says.

To the east, planes are taking off from San Francisco International Airport, light gleaming on their dragonfly wings. Anju has agreed to come and see Sudha and Dayita off next week. She plans to take pictures, if she can remember where she's packed her camera.

Sudha asks, "Did Ashok talk to you before he left?"

"Yes."

"Was he really upset?"

"What do you think?"

Sudha bites her lip. Some actions always make us feel guilty, no matter how impossible the alternative. "I felt really bad turning him back, but I *had* to—"

"He said to me, There's no point to it anymore. We've become ghosts to each other. I advised him to get married—to a solid, older woman, perhaps a widow, who'd be suitably grateful."

Sudha bends her head, accepting the rebuke. Freedom doesn't come cheap. She knows this. "I hope he agreed," she says after a moment.

But Anju has lost interest in the subject. "Close your eyes," she orders her cousin.

Sudha frowns. (Even this, Anju thinks, makes her look charming.) "Why?"

"Questions, questions! Just do it."

Sudha shuts her eyes, but warily. "You sound like you're up to something."

Anju is going very fast now, up a rattly hillside road. Sudha bites her lip and puts out a hand to brace herself against the dashboard. A line of sweat breaks out on her lip.

"Don't worry," Anju says with a dry laugh. "I'm not going to kill us. Though I must confess there were days when I fantasized about it, the two of us in this car, going off the hillside together—"

"Slow down, for heaven's sake," Sudha says, her face pale, her eyes squinched shut.

Anju applies the brake. The tires skid on gravel, the car comes to a stop. "Okay," she says, "you can look now." They are in a makeshift parking lot on the side of a bluff. She swings open her door, and Sudha smells the brine in the air. She looks around, her brows wrinkled, trying to recall why the place looks familiar. When she looks up, the sky is full of colorful shapes wheeling about like giant kites.

"It's that same place!" she says, her voice slowing with remembrance. Her first outing in America, the picnic on the beach, the Pacific blue as a flame, opening out and out the way she thought her life was going to. The hang gliders swooping down to flirt with waves. The man who is not with them today.

"How many things have changed," she whispers.

"They sure have," Anju says. "That's what I brought you up here to see." She takes Sudha's hand and pulls. "Come on! Hurry!" The two of them break into a run, heading for the landing area at the edge of the cliff.

"What is it, Anju?" Sudha gasps.

A grin breaks over Anju's face. "You won't believe it, Sudha," she says. "I've learned to fly."

Epilogue

Her first attempt is a failure, her second one also. She feels her hands shaking violently. A muscle near her mouth starts jumping. The wind is freezing cold and uncooperative. The harness cuts into her shoulders, the Velcro straps rasp her ribs. Strapped to her back, the glider is bulky, inflexible as concrete. How could she have believed it would ever hold her up against gravity? Most of all, she feels Sudha's eyes on her. Even though she doesn't turn to look, the apprehension in them weighs her down. *Another of Anju's harebrained schemes. Isn't she ever going to learn!* The boy is there, too, suspended somewhere above, watching just as anxiously. She is sure of this, but not in an anguished way. A haiku comes to her mind:

> *Summer evening, parched insects,*
> *I seem to hear your voice*
> *In the song of the hototogisu.*

Here's her instructor now, her red hair streaked dashingly with silver, deep laugh lines bracketing her mouth. She's gesturing with her hands: *Hold yourself like this, lightly. Walk into the wind. Angle the keel. Just like the times when we did it in tandem.* The woman can't hear the words against the roar in her ears. *Trust your body.* Still, their shape on the instructor's lips urges her forward to the edge. *You can do it.* She's running. This time she feels the air current catch the sail, the yanking lift of it on her backbone. Cold swirls inside her clothes, a sudden, intimate shock. Then she's airborne.

The woman thinks she'll never get used to the sensation of flight, no matter how many times she does it. She pulls the control bar close to her and feels the kite gain speed. All those dreams, since childhood, of gliding and soaring. (But always, finally, her wings melting, that Icarian downward plummet, the black razor edges of rock rushing up and up until she'd startle herself awake with a cry.) This is better, infinitely. She'd never thought that real life could be an improvement on what the imagination constructed. It gives her a certain faith.

Up, down, the wind carries her. Turn the nose to the left, move out farther over the ocean. She empties her mind of cautionary commands. *Your initial flight should always be in a straight line. Flights over water are definitely unsafe.* To think of them would be to doubt, and doubt is the greatest killer. Beneath her the waves are igniting, the whole ocean is diamond fire, it makes her eyes water, she starts to wipe them and realizes she cannot because she's wearing flight goggles. Blind now, she's flying by feel, unafraid. *It would be a fine end, to keep going like this, into the light.* She remembers someone saying the words long ago. It was herself. Such a young, fledgling self. She does not want that anymore, not now. Her life is just beginning.

Then she remembers the other thing. She takes one hand, stiff in its glove, off the bar and works in into her breast pocket. She feels around, but there's nothing. For a moment she panics, and the glider rocks dangerously. Below, she can feel her instructor's indrawn breath, her cousin holding her fingers crossed, *pleasepleaseplease*. Then it's there, its stiff, reassuring edge nudging her forefinger. She draws it out and looks at it blurrily, the photograph taken in some doctor's office in some other world, the ultrasound pulse a small lighted blip against the gray grainy background of her insides, and along the border, the smudged ink of her handwriting, *Baby Prem, due March 16, 1993.* She opens her fingers.

The photograph is falling, turning lazily in the wind which has traveled up all the way from the Farallons. Salt and the cry of bay gulls, the ammoniac odor of developer fluid. But there are so many smells suddenly, all at once. The astringence of antiseptics in an emergency room in Redwood City, Lalit bending over a slashed arm he must repair. In a Calcutta bus, sweat and exhaust and people joking about how rib-cracking crowded it is. ("Don't worry, Dada, you might faint but you won't fall down—there isn't enough space for that.") Anju's old apartment, where old whiffs of methi and coriander now mingle with green onion and kim chee from the family that has moved in. The glass house is filled with pollen from the ginger flowers that grow on the Assam hills, the old man in his wheezy voice singing monsoon songs for the child. *Come, rain, come soon, I'll give you a full measure of shalidhan grain.* On his veranda, Ashok sets up an easel and begins to mix colors. He's starting on a landscape today, oil and acrylic—something new for him. Maybe it will turn out to be a California scene? In his Houston office Sunil explains to a

client how a configuration problem can be fixed, but underneath he's thinking of the trip he's planning to the Bay Area
next month. What might come of it.

The woman leans her body into the wind, into this moment
that is sparking blue and silver, the same colors as Sunil's computer screen. This moment that is dissolving. She laughs. Smell
of herbal shampoo in her hair. The instructor is waving a large
orange banner. YOU DID IT! The woman makes a last lazy
turn, dipping a wing downward. Sudha is waving with all her
might, her curls blowing every which way. In the glass house
Dayita bangs a spoon in time to the beat. This is what you do
with grief, you lean into it and open your fingers. You let it support you like the frail beauty of the turning, luminous earth. On
Año Nuevo beach, a weaner seal turns its face toward Alaska,
considering its first ocean journey. In the Sundarbans, the last of
the cheetahs balance on mangrove branches. Somewhere machines are cutting down thousand-year-old trees. Somewhere a
leaking pipeline spews crude oil into the sea. Somewhere juries
are beginning to decide they don't have enough evidence to de-
clare a man guilty of murdering his wife. An old man stretches
his legs to catch a buttery slab of sunlight. A surgeon cuts open
an abdomen and finds it so filled with cancer cells there's nothing he can do but stitch it up again. It is the year of stubbornness, Bosnia rejecting a call for cease-fire, India test-firing a
missile powerful enough to reach China. On the radio, the an-
nouncer informs us that a sixty-two-year-old Italian woman—
the oldest on record—has successfully given birth. That
democracy in Haiti has been restored without firing a single
shot. Which is more important? Which is less? The dead clap
solemnly to the old man's song. The hang glider bumps down
on the landing strip, comes to a skittery, triumphant halt. The

woman on the ground opens her arms for the woman who was in the sky. This is what we do with grief. The dead are droplets of seawater and ash, riding the air. Are they rising? Are they falling? Look, there's no difference. The earth's curvature is like a smile. The old man sings, *O rain, come, I've been waiting for you so long.*

If you enjoyed *The Vine of Desire*, here is the title story from
Chitra Banerjee Divakaruni's collection of short stories:

The Unknown Errors

of Our Lives

Abacus
0 349 11394 7

Ruchira is packing when she discovers the notebook in a dusty alcove of her apartment. It is sandwiched between a high school group photo in which she smiles tensely at the camera, her hair hacked short around her ears in a style that was popular that year, and a box of brittle letters, the sheets tinged with blue and smelling faintly of sweet betel nut, from her grandmother, who is now dead. For a moment she fingers the book's limp purple cover, its squished spiral binding, and wonders what's inside, it's been that long since she wrote in it. Then she remembers. Of course! It's her book of errors, from her midteens, a time she thinks back on now as her Earnest Period.

She imagines telling Biren about it. "I was a gawky girl with a mouth full of braces and a head full of ideas for self-improvement."

"And then?" he would ask.

"Then I turned twenty-six, and decided I was perfect just the way I was."

In response, Biren would laugh his silent laugh, which began at the upturned outer edges of his eyes and rippled through him like wind on water. He was the only person she knew who laughed like that, soundlessly, offering his whole body to the act. It made her heart feel like a popcorn popper where all the kernels have burst into neon yellow. She'd respond with a small smile, the kind she hoped made her appear alluring and secretive, but inside she'd be weak with gratitude that he found her so funny.

That, and the way he looked at her paintings. Because otherwise she doesn't think she could have agreed to marry him.

To think that none of this would have happened, that she wouldn't be sitting here this beautiful rainy morning, pale blue like jacarandas, packing, getting ready to move out of her Berkeley apartment into their newlywed condo in San Francisco in two weeks, if she hadn't mumbled an ungracious agreement when her mother said, "Why don't you meet him, Ru? Kamala Mashi writes so highly of him. Meet him once and see how you like each other." Ruchira shudders when she realizes how close she had come to saying No, she wasn't interested, she'd rather use the time to go to Lashay's and get her hair done. Just because Aunt Kamala had written, *Not only is the boy just two years older than our Ruchira and handsome looking, 173 centimeters tall and holds a fast-rising job in the renowned Charles Schwab financial company, he is also a nephew of the Boses of*

Tullygunge—you recall them, a fine, upright family—and to top it all he has intelligently decided to follow our time-tested traditions in his search for a bride. It would have been the worst error of her life, and she wouldn't even have known it. It saddens her to think of all the errors people make (she has been musing over such things lately)—the unknown errors of their lives, the ones they can never put down in a book and are therefore doomed to repeat.

But she had shown up at the Café Trieste, sullen in old blue jeans and a severe ponytail that yanked her eyebrows into a skeptic arch, and met Biren, and been charmed.

"It's because you were so wary, even more than me," she told him later. "You'd been reading—wasn't it one of those depressingly high-minded Russians?"

"Dostoyevsky. Brought along for the precise purpose of impressing you."

"And for the first fifteen minutes of our conversation, you kept your finger in the book, marking your place, as though you couldn't wait to get back to it."

"You mean it wasn't my suave Johnny Depp looks that got you? I'm disappointed."

"Dream on," she said, and gave him a little push. Actually, she'd been rather taken by the stud he wore in his ear. Its small, beckoning glint in the smoke-fogged café had made him seem foreign and dangerous, set him apart from the Indian men she knew, at least the ones who would have agreed to meet a daughter-of-a-friend-of-a-distant-relative for late-afternoon coffee with matrimony in mind. But most of all she liked that he admitted up front to feeling sheepish, sitting like this in a café after having declared, for all those arrogant years (just as she had), that *he'd* never have anything to do with an arranged marriage.

"But the alternative—it doesn't seem to work that well, does it?" he would say later, shrugging, and she'd agree, thinking back on all the boys she had dated in college, Indian boys and white boys and black boys and even, once, a young man from Bolivia with green eyes. At a certain point they had all wanted something from her, she didn't know what it was exactly, only that she hadn't been willing—or able—to give it. It wasn't just the sex, though that too she'd shied away from. What throwback gene was it that stopped her, a girl born in America? What cautionary spore released by her grandmother over her cradle when Ruchira's parents took her to India? Sooner or later, the boyfriends fell away. She saw them as though through the wrong end of a telescope, their faces urgent or surly, mouthing words she could no longer hear.

Thumbing through her book of errors, Ruchira thinks this must be one of life's most Machiavellian revenges: one day you look back at your teenage self and realize exactly how excruciatingly clueless you were, more so even than you had thought your parents to be. And pompous to boot. Here, for

380

example, is the quotation she'd copied out in her tight, painstaking handwriting: *An unexamined life is not worth living.* As if a fourteen-year-old had any idea of what an examined life was. The notion of tracking errors possesses some merit, except that *her* errors were so puerile, so everygirl. The time she told Marta that she thought Kevin was cute, only to have that information relayed back to her, with crude anatomical elaborations, from the walls of the girls' bathroom. The time she drank too many rum-and-cokes at Susie's party and threw up on the living room carpet. The time she believed Dr. Vikram, who wore maroon suspenders and gave her a summer job in his dental office, to be so cool—and then he made a groping pass at her.

She tosses the purple notebook onto the growing pile of things to be recycled. (Recycling mistakes, now that's a thought!) She's come to terms with misjudgments and slippages, she's resigned to the fact that they'll always be a part of her life. If there are errorless people in the world, she doesn't want to know them. She's certain they'll be eminently disagreeable. That's something else she likes about Biren—all the mistakes he has already admitted to. How he dropped out of college for a semester during his freshman year to play electric guitar with a band aptly named The Disasters. How late one night, coming back to the city from Sausalito, he gave a ride to a hitchhiker of indeterminate sex only to have him/her try to throw him/herself from the car and off the Golden

Gate bridge. How, for a short time last year, he got involved with a woman who had a knife tattooed on her chest, even though he knew she did drugs.

Ruchira was shocked and enthralled. She wasn't sure why he was telling her all this. To impress her? To start clean? To gain her (or was it his own) forgiveness? Small disquiets nipped at the edge of her mind like minnows; she let them slip away. Questions filled her mouth. What had he lost by jilting Tina Turner for Standard and Poor? What had he said to the hitch-hiker to stop her—Ruchira was sure it was a woman—from jumping? (He *had* tried to stop her, hadn't he?) What made him break up, finally, with the knife-woman?

She pushed the questions into a corner of her cheek like hard candy, saving them for later. Meanwhile, he was the most exciting man she knew. His was a geography of suicide bridges and tattoo parlors, night concert alleys and skyscrapers rising into the sky like blocks of black ice. A galaxy far, far away from the blandness of auto-malls and AMC cinemas which she'd never really escaped, not even by moving from her parents' suburban house to Berkeley. But now conjugality would confer that same excitement on her.

He saw the paintings when he came to pick her up for a concert. They'd discovered a common interest in classical Indian music, and Chaurasia was playing at the Zellerbach. She had not intended for him to come up to the apartment—she felt

382

she didn't know him well enough. She was going to meet him downstairs when he rang the buzzer. But one of the other tenants must have let him in because here he was, knocking on her door. For a panicked moment she thought of not opening it, pretending she wasn't there, calling him later with a fabricated disaster.

He was severely suave in a jacket with a European cut and, although the sun had set already, dark glasses in which she could see herself, convex and bulbous-headed. She felt mortified. Behind her, she knew, paint rags were strewn across the floor. A cereal bowl left by the armchair, swollen flecks of bran drowning in bluish milk. A half-eaten packet of Cheetos on the counter. Jelly jars of turpentine with brushes soaking in them on the coffee table. The canvas she'd been working on (and which was totally wrong, she knew it already) was the only thing she'd managed to put away.

'Very nice," he said, lightly touching the sleeve of her short black cocktail dress. But already he was looking beyond her at the canvases hanging on the wall.

"You didn't tell me you paint," he said accusingly.

This was true. She had told him a lot of things about herself, but they were all carefully chosen to be shielding and secondary. Her work as events coordinator in an art gallery, which she liked because the people she met had such intense opinions, mostly about other people's art. Her favorite college class, "Myth and Literature" in junior year, which she had picked quite by chance because "Interpersonal Communication" was full. The trip she took two winters back to New Zealand to stay for a few nights in a Maori village—only to discover that it had water beds in the more expensive rooms and a Jacuzzi strategically positioned among the lava rocks. She felt bad now about her duplicity, her reluctance to give of herself, that old spiral with her boyfriends starting again.

He'd moved close to the wall and was standing very still. It took her a moment to figure out that he was examining her brushstrokes. (But only artists did that. Was he a closet artist, too?) Finally he moved back and let out a long, incredulous breath, and it struck her that she had been holding hers as well. "Tell me about your work," he said.

This was hard. She had started painting two years ago, and had never talked to anyone about it. Even her parents didn't know. When they came for dinner, she removed the canvases from the wall and hid them in her closet. She sprayed the room with Eucalyptus Mist and lit incense sticks so they wouldn't smell the turpentine. The act of painting was the first really risky thing she had done in her life. Being at the gallery, she knew how different her work was from everything in there, or in the glossy art journals. Her technique was crude—she hadn't taken classes and didn't intend to. She would probably never amount to much. Still, she came back from work every evening and painted furiously. She worked late into the night, light-headed with the effort to remember. She stopped inviting

384

people over. She made excuses when her friends wanted her to go out. She had to force herself to return their calls, and often she didn't. She ruined canvas after canvas, slashed them in frustration and threw them into the Dumpster behind the building. She wept till she saw a blurry brightness, like sunspots, wherever she looked. Then, miraculously, she got better. Sometimes now, at 2.00 A.M., or 3:00, her back muscles tight and burning, a stillness would rise around her, warm and vaporous. Held within it, she would hear, word for word, the stories her grandmother used to tell.

Ruchira has seen her grandmother no more than a dozen times in her life, once every two or three years during summer vacation, when her parents visited India. She loves her more than she loves anyone else, more than her parents. She knows this to be unfair; they are good parents and have always done the best they can for her in their earnest, Quaker Oatmeal way. She had struggled through the Bengali alphabet, submitting to years of classes at that horrible weekend school run by bulge-eyed Mrs. Duttagupta, just so she would be able to read her grandmother's letters and reply to them without asking her parents to intervene. When a letter arrived from India, she slept with it for nights, a faint crackling under her pillow. When she had trouble making up her mind about something, she asked herself, What would Thakuma do? Ah, the flawed logic of loving! Surprisingly, it helped her, although she was continents and generations apart, in a world whose values must have been unimaginable to a woman who had been married at sixteen and widowed at twenty-four, and who had only left Calcutta once in her entire life for a pilgrimage to Badrinath with the members of her Geeta group.

Someday she plans to tell Biren all this.

When her grandmother died two summers back of a heart attack, Ruchira spent an entire week in bed. She refused to go to India for the funeral, though maybe she should have, because she dreamed over and over what she had thought she couldn't bear to look at. The hard orange thrust of the flames of the cremation pyre, the hair going first, in a short, manic burst of light, the skin warping like wood, the eyeballs melting, her grandmother's face blackening and collapsing in on itself with terrible finality. It didn't help that her parents told her that the event, which occurred in a modern crematorium rather than the traditional burning ghats, was quick and sanitary and invisible.

She started the paintings soon after that.

"It's a series." Ruchira stammered now, speaking too fast. "Mythic images from Indian legends. I've only managed to complete three so far. The first is Hanuman, the monkey god, carrying the magic herb that can bring you back to life—you know the story? When Lakshman was hurt in battle, and Hanuman plucked up an entire mountain because he wasn't sure which herb he was supposed to bring back ...?" She'd painted Hanuman in purples and blues and looped his tail in an elegant, gentlemanly manner over an arm. In his right hand he held a miniature mountain the way one might hold a box of chocolates when paying a visit. She had given him a human face, her father's (unexpectedly, she'd turned out to be good at portraits), his expression of puzzled kindness. She remembered the ecstatic day when the idea had first swooped down on her like a taloned angel. Now the painting looked fanciful, garish. It made her blush.

"But it's brilliant. They're all brilliant," Biren said. "An amazing concept. I've never seen anything like it. This next one, isn't that the magic cow, what's her name, who possesses all the riches of the world—"

"Kama dhenu," she supplied shyly, delighted by his recognition. The cow in the painting reclined on a cloud, her chin resting on demure, folded forelegs. A shower of gold coins fanned out from her hooves, carpeting the earth below. Her white wings were as tidily pleated as a widow's sari. Around her head, words from old stories arched in a rainbow. *Long long ago. Beyond the fields of Tepantar. Once there was a poor brahmin who had a clever wife. And the snake carried a jewel on its head.* Her stubborn, alert face was that of Ruchira's grandmother.

By the time they got to the third painting, it was too late to go to the concert and Ruchira no longer stammered. With precise gestures she explained to Biren that the huge eagle creature was Jatayu, who died trying to save Sita from the evil ten-headed Ravana as he was abducting her. In Ruchira's

387

painting Jatayu's feathers were saffron and white and green, the colors of the Indian flag. His face was that of her grandfather, whom she only knew from sepia photographs because he died long before she was born—in the Andaman prisons, where the British used to send freedom fighters. Her grandmother had told her the story. They had caught him making bombs, he'd been part of a conspiracy to assassinate Lord Minto, the hated governor-general. In Ruchira's painting, Ravana, pasty-faced and with a prominent overbite, was clearly British, and Jatayu had knocked off all his bowler hats with one giant swipe of his claw.

"I love it!" said Biren. "I just love it!"

They kissed their first kiss soon after that. He tasted of salted sunflower seeds (his secret weakness, she would learn later). His tongue was thin and pointy and intelligent. She doesn't remember leading him to the bedroom, only that they were there already, lying on the crumpled blue bedcover, his fingers, her fingers, the small hollow inside his elbow and the vein pulsing in it. She thought she could see a faint radiation of heat where their skins touched. Did his hair smell of lemons? In her hurry she tore a loose button off his shirt. (Later they would laugh about that.) The back of his ear stud rasped her hand, raising a weal. He brought it to his mouth and licked it. The small mirrors embroidered into the bedcover pressed their cool disks against her bare back, then against his. His nipples were brown and hard as apple seeds in her mouth.

Then his hands were on hers, tight, stopping her as she tugged on his zipper.

"Don't. It isn't safe. I didn't expect this. I don't have anything with me. And I take it you don't either ..."

The blood rocked so hard in the hollows of her body, she feared she'd break open. He had to repeat himself before she could understand the words. She shook her head vaguely, not caring. She wouldn't let go. Her body, thwarted so long, had seized on wildness like a birthright. A part of her cried, *You're insane, girl.* She pushed her face against him, his chest hairs wiry against her tongue, until finally his hands were gone. She could feel fingers, their drowning grip on her hair. She heard him say something. The words were too close, out of focus. Later she would think they had started with *God.* As in *God I hope you know what you're doing.*

Just three days left before her wedding, and Ruchira thinks, Does anyone ever know what they're really doing? What the tightening of certain muscles and the letting go of others, the aspiration of certain vowels and the holding back of others, will lead to? What terrifying wonder, what injured joy? But she *had* known one thing that night, even before he asked her to marry him and she said yes. She'd known what this, the next and final painting in her Mythic Images series, would be.

She adds a last stroke of burnt sienna to the painting and stands back to examine it. It's her best one so far, and it's ready now, at least this phase of it. Just in time, because it's to be her surprise wedding gift to Biren. She thinks how she'll do it—steal into their new condo the evening before the wedding—she has the key already—and hang it in the foyer so that he will see it first thing when they enter together as husband and wife. Or maybe she'll hang it opposite their bed, so they can look at it after lovemaking, or in the morning, waking each other up. The tree with its multicolored jewel leaves, its branches filled with silky birds. It's the kalpa taru, the wish-fulfilling tree, and the birds are shalikhs, those bold, brown creatures she would find everywhere when she visited Calcutta, with their clever pin eyes and their strident cry. Her grandmother used to call them birds of memory. Ruchira had meant to ask her why but never got around to it. Now she doesn't want to ask anyone else. She has given the birds the faces of the people she loves most dearly. And Biren too—she borrowed one of his photo albums, secretly, for this purpose. She has put him and herself, feathers touching, at the very center of the tree. (Why not? It's her right as artist to be egoistic if she wants.) Below them she has left empty branches, lots of them, for the birds she will paint in. New friends, children. Is it sentimental to be thinking about grandchildren already? She'll fill every space, and more. Maybe she'll never be done.

Then Biren's knocking, and she lifts the easel into the closet and rushes to the door and opens it. But it's not him, of course not, it's the middle of the afternoon, he's at work. She really should be more careful and keep the chain on while she checks who's outside, though this person doesn't look particularly dangerous. It's a young woman—well, maybe not so young, once you take in the cracked lines at the corners of her eyes— very thin and very pregnant, with spiky blond hair and a pierced eyebrow, wearing a shapeless pink smock that looks borrowed and a studded black leather jacket that she can no longer button over her belly. There's a look on her face— determined? resigned? exhilarated? Ruchira gets ready to tell her that she has come to the wrong address. Then she sees it, above the smock's meandering neckline, against the too-pale freckled skin. Red and blue. A bruise, or a half-healed wound. No. It's the hilt of a tattooed knife.

Ruchira sits awkwardly at her kitchen table, knees pressed together, as though she were the visitor here, and stares at the knife-woman. She had realized, right away, that she shouldn't let her in. But she couldn't just shut the door in the face of a pregnant woman who looked like she was starving, could she? It was not, however, a totally altruistic act. Ruchira knows this, though she is unable to articulate what it is that she hopes to gain from Biren's ex-lover. Now she stares at the woman, who is sitting in a chair opposite her and crumbling, with self-possession, the muffin that Ruchira has given her into a small anthill. Ruchira tries to be angry with her for being here. But she feels like someone who drowned a long time ago. In the underwater world she inhabits, there are no emotions, only a slow, seaweedy drifting. She asks, "Why did you come?"

The woman looks up, and the light slip-slides over her hungry cheekbones. What is she hungry for? She's finished demolishing the muffin, but her fingers continue to twitch. Ruchira suspects scars under the leather, puckered fang marks in the dip inside the woman's elbow, the same place she loves to kiss on Biren's arm. Where she has chewed away the lip-stick, the woman's lips are papery, like palest cherry blossom. Then she speaks, an unexpected dimple appears in her cheek, and Ruchira is shocked to discover she's beautiful. "My name's Arlene," she says.

Ruchira wants to ask how she knew about her and Biren, about this apartment. Did she see them on Telegraph Avenue, perhaps, late one night, returning from a movie at the Pacific Film Archives? Did she follow them back? Did she watch from the shadows as they kissed under a streetlamp, their hands inside each other's coats? Ruchira wants to ask if she loved him, too.

But she knows enough to wait—it's a game of silences they are playing—and after a while Arlene says, "It'll be born in a month, in February." She narrows her eyes and stares as though Ruchira were a minor fact she's memorizing for a future test, one she'd rather not take.

This time Ruchira loses the game because she can't bear not to know.

"Does he know about the baby?"

"Yes."

Ruchira holds this new, trembling knowledge like a too-heavy blob of paint at the end of a brush, threatening to ruin the entire painting unless she finds the right spot to apply it.

"He gave me the money for an abortion. But I didn't."

Ruchira closes her eyes. The insides of her eyelids are like torn brown silk, like hundreds of birds taking flight at a killing sound. When she opens them, Arlene lifts her shoulders in a shrug. The knife hilt moves up and down over the bumpy bones of her thin chest. The blade is curved in the shape of a Nepali kukri. Ruchira wonders how much it hurt to get the tattoo done, and how the tattooer knew about Nepali knives, and if Arlene ever looked in the mirror and thought of it as a mistake.

"He doesn't know I kept it," Arlene says. She grins suddenly, for the first time, with gamine charm, a kid who's just won at kickball. There's a small, neat gap between her front teeth. A famous poet—who was it?—had proclaimed gap-toothed women to be sexy. Why is it that Ruchira can never remember crucial information when she needs to?

Arlene stands up with a decisive scrape of her chair.

"Wait," Ruchira cries. "Where do you live? Do you have health insurance? Do you need money?" She reaches for her purse and digs frantically in it, coming up with all the bills she can find, ones and fives and a twenty, and extends them to Arlene.

"I'm going to Arizona," says Arlene. She doesn't offer further details. She doesn't stretch out her hand for the money. She does a little pirouette (was she a dancer, before?) and from the door she calls out, "Think of me in February, in Arizona."

The first thing Ruchira does after she is sure Arlene is gone is to run down the stairs to the garbage area. There it is, next to the Dumpster: the blue recycling bin with its triangle of arrows. In her mind she's seeing the garbage bag, white, with a red tie, that she upended over it—was it just two days back?—freeing a tumble of papers and books. In her mind she's already dug past the discards of other people's lives—term papers and love letters and overdue bills—to grab it. She's opened its purple cover and has started writing, she isn't done writing even when her hand begins to cramp up, she fills her book of errors all the way to the back cover and has more to put down, that's how much she's learned in this one hour.

But the bin is empty.

Ruchira leans into the wall, pressing her forehead against the fake stucco. It smells of sour milk and diapers, and its bumps leave indentations on her skin. Behind her she hears footsteps approach.

"Arlene," she calls, turning wildly, as though hoping for instructions. But it is a different woman, one of Ruchira's neighbors, who looks vaguely alarmed. She carries a Hefty bag in one hand and holds on to a little boy with the other.

"Mommy," the boy asks, "what's wrong with the lady?"

It's very late now, and Ruchira has packed everything, even the bedsheets, even the pillow. She lies down on the bare mattress and watches the shadows on the wall. She's chilled, but inside her brain it feels hot and spongy. *What would you do, Thakuma?* Inside her brain, her grandmother says, Why do you ask me? Can you live your life the way I lived mine? She speaks with some asperity. Or maybe it's sorrow she feels for the confused world her granddaughter has inherited. Ruchira recalls a prayer her grandmother used to chant in the mornings after her bath, in her raspy, sugarcane voice, as she waved a stick of incense in front of the brightly colored pictures on her altar. *Forgive us, O Lord Shiva, all our errors, both the known and the unknown.* It had seemed impossible to Ruchira that her grandmother could commit any errors. Now she knows better, but she is still unsure what those errors might have been. *Errors that took your life between their thumb and forefinger, Thakuma, and crumbled it like a muffin until you were alone, separated by oceans and deserts and a million skyscrapers from the people you loved, and then you were dead.* Ruchira wants to say the old prayer, but she has forgotten most of it. Does a fragmented prayer merit a fragmented forgiveness? On the wall the shadows move like sleepy birds. If there really were a kalpa taru, what would she wish for?

She had called Biren at home and got his answering machine. But how could you tell a machine, You lousy jerk, you son of a bitch, forget about the wedding? How could you explain to metal and plastic why you needed to grasp the promises a man had made to you and break them across the middle, snap-snap, like incense sticks?

At his work, his secretary informed her he was at a lunch meeting. Could she call back in an hour?

No, she could not. She rummaged through her phone book. Here it was, his cell phone number, written in his expansive, looped hand.

On this machine, his voice sounded huskier, sexy in a businesslike way. Against her will, she found herself listening as he asked people to leave a message at the tone. But the tone didn't come on just yet. Instead, the voice said, "And in case this is Ruchira, I want you to know I'm crazy about you."

There were three short, impatient beeps. She held the phone pressed to her ear until the machine disconnected her. He hadn't informed her about that voice mail greeting, which was a kind of public avowal of his love. He trusted that one day, at the right time, she would find out.

Was that trust enough to outweigh a lifetime of imagining, each time she kissed Biren, that Arlene's papery lips had bloomed there already? He had never pretended Ruchira was his first. How could she blame him for a past he had admitted to right at the start, just because it had come to her door wearing a pierced eyebrow, an implosive, elfish smile? And the baby, smooth and oval in its ivory sheath, its head pushing up against the echo of a knife. The error its father had paid to erase. She couldn't blame Biren for that either. Could she?

She won't tell Biren about Arlene and the baby. Ruchira knows this as she watches the shadows detach themselves from her walls to flap their way across the ceiling. And she won't be sad for him. The baby, she means. A boy. She knows this inside herself as surely as though she were his mother. A boy—she whispers this to herself—named Arizona. There are many ways in the world to love. With luck he'll find one. And with luck Ruchira will, too. But what is she thinking? She already loves Biren. Isn't that why all evening she has been folding and stuffing and tearing strips of tape and printing words on brown cartons in aggressive black ink? *Books: living room. China: dining alcove.* Their lives are already mixed, like past and future, promise and disappointment, linseed oil and turpentine. Like the small exhalations of birds on a wish-fulfilling tree. Maybe they can be separated, but she doesn't have the expertise for it, even if she wanted to. Marriage is a long, hobbled race, learning the other's gait as you go, and thanks to Arlene she has a head start.

The wind has dropped. On Ruchira's window sill the shadows lie stunned, as though they've been shot. She wonders if Biren and Arlene did drugs together. It wouldn't have been a needle, he was too fastidious for that. Maybe pills. Ecstasy? Dexedrine? It annoys her suddenly that she doesn't know enough about these things. *Clothes: master bedroom. Medicines: bathroom cabinet. Paints: studio.* Because Biren wants her to have a studio in their new condo, on the airy top floor with its view of Coit Tower, next to the balcony where they're planning to sit in the evenings and drink jasmine tea and talk. (But what will they talk about?) Until one day in February the wind will be like cherry blossoms, and she'll take down the painting she hung in the foyer and go into the studio and add in a bird with a boy-face and spiky gold hair, with Biren's square chin and an unsuspected dimple. And if Biren asks about him ...? This is what Ruchira wants from the kalpa taru: that when Biren asks, she'll know how to ask him back.

THE UNKNOWN ERRORS
OF OUR LIVES

Chitra Banerjee Divakaruni

Whilst packing up her flat in preparation for forthcoming marriage, Ruchira discovers her childhood 'book of errors', a teenage notebook in which she wrote down ways to improve her life. But as she contemplates her future, what worries her are the unknown errors of our lives – the mistakes that people don't realise they are making . . .

Chitra Banerjee Divakaruni's astonishing collection of short stories depicts life in East and West with touching perception and colour. From the widow who discovers her old-fashioned ways are an embarrassment to her daughter-in-law to a young American woman's pilgrimage in Kashmir, Divakaruni tells her stories of love, expectation and betrayal with passion, poignancy and a delicate sense of humour.

Praise for *The Mistress of Spices*

'A dazzling tale of misbegotten dreams and desires, hopes and expectations, woven poetry and storyteller magic'
Amy Tan

'Divakaruni's magic [is] her ability to craft such a complex tale written so exquisitely without overwhelming her reader'
Los Angeles Times

'Fascinating stuff . . . appealingly flavoured and colourful'
Mail on Sunday

Abacus
ISBN 0 349 11394 7

BREATH, EYES, MEMORY

Edwidge Danticat

I come from a place where breath, eyes and memory are one, a place from which you carry your past like the hair on your head.

'A first novel of precocious maturity which mingles past and present, the horrors and delights of Haiti, in a quiet and dignified prose'
Independent

'Through the eyes of Sophie Caco, caught between a traumatised mother far away in the United States and a beloved aunt enduring the poverty of Haiti, Edwidge Danticat's *Breath, Eyes, Memory* tells the story of four generations of Haitian women, trying to survive in a world made strange and violent by men'
Vogue

'Extraordinary . . . Danticat is a young and genuinely fresh voice. The story she tells is worth a whole shelf of feminist theory'
Time Out

'Stuffed with folk wisdom and seasoned with a sprinkling of urban angst, *Breath, Eyes, Memory* offers a brief thumbnail sketch of life in the Haitian diaspora, as well as a vivid portrayal of rural Haiti . . . It offers hope through its vision of a female solidarity which transcends place and time'
Sunday Times

'A haunting novel giving a luminous picture of the ways and traditions in Haiti'
Daily Mirror

'Edwidge Danticat delicately tiptoes through bougainvillaea and butterflies into minefields of rape, mayhem, insanity, suicide, terror'
Fay Weldon, *Mail on Sunday*

Abacus
ISBN 0 349 10682 7

THE FARMING OF BONES

Edwidge Danticat

One of the *New Yorker's* '20 Writers for the 21st Century'

One of *Granta's* 'Best Young American Novelists'

'Confirms that Danticat is a writer of great force with still more potential'
Independent on Sunday

It is 1937, the Dominican side of the Haiti border. Amabelle, orphaned at the age of eight when her parents drowned, is maid to the young wife of an army colonel. She has grown up in this household, a faithful servant, but is still a Haitian in a foreign land – useful to the Dominicans but not really welcome.

Amabelle loves Sebastien, an itinerant farm labourer who works in the sugarcane fields, 'farming the bones'. Handsome despite the scars on his face from the lashing cane, Amabelle longs to become his wife. But with rumours that Haitians are being persecuted, even killed, their future is far from settled . . .

'Unforgettable . . . It is a testament to her talent that the novel, while almost unbearably sad, is still a joy to read'
Newsweek

'Her greatest strength is to resist sensationalism and sentimentality. Her portrait of lives in the aftermath of massacre is haunting . . . but most of all Danticat captures the terrible uncertainties. She uses fiction to portray a world in which there is no resolution'
The Times

Abacus
ISBN 0 349 11163 4

EAST INTO UPPER EAST

Plain Tales from New York and New Delhi

Ruth Prawer Jhabvala

'These stories are funny, tragic and very beguiling but, most
original of all, they really, truly belong together'
Julie Myerson, *Mail on Sunday*

This brilliant collection spans two worlds – the restless, aspiring
society of New York's Upper East Side and the world of India's
capital city, New Delhi, where the old India symbolised by
Gandhi's spinning wheel is giving way to one powered by industry
and property development. A rich cast of characters inhabits
these stories – Indian businessmen and holy women, society
hostesses and ambitious young politicians, New Yorkers
preoccupied with money yet also in search of meaning – their
hopes and struggles depicted with warmth, sensitivity and
compassion.

'Dense and satisfying, poignant and wise'
Anne Chisholm, *Literary Review*

'Extraordinarily deft'
Philip Glazebrook, *Spectator*

Abacus
ISBN 0 349 11249 5